All The
Reasons
I NEED

Praise for Jaime Clevenger

Three Reasons to Say Yes

This is without a doubt my new favourite Jaime Clevenger novel. Honestly I couldn't put it down from the first chapter. *Three Reasons to Say Yes* is written solely from Julia's point of view and what a view on her life she has. Many of my blog readers know I am not a massive fan of one protagonist point of views but in this instance it worked perfectly...the secondary characters of Mo and Kate (Julia's best friends) left me wanting more. I mean these two had clear underlying feelings but Jaime Clevenger leaves every moment with them open and I just craved more from them. The hurrah part of the book was when I heard there is to be a sequel and these characters will get their day...not sure if it will be happy ever after but I'm already dying to get my hands on it. All in all this book has the potential to be my book of the year. Truly, books like this don't come around often that suit my reading tastes to a tee.

- *Les Rêveur*

...this one was totally my cup of tea with its charming relationship and family dynamics, great chemistry between two likable protagonists, a very convincing romance, some angst, drama and tension to the right extent and in all the right moments, and some very nice secondary characters. On top of that, the writing is technically very good, with all elements done properly. Sincerely recommended.

- Pin's Reviews, *goodreads*

This is different than a traditional lesfic romance. It almost was a romantic family drama. I guess it's more on the border between the two. The main premise is about two women wanting to have no-strings sex. But what happens when feelings get involved? We have all read this premise before, but this take on it felt different. There was more involved and it just absolutely worked for me. I have to give a nod to really well done secondary characters. The secondary characters had such strong and real personalities that I almost cared about them as much as the two mains. This was better writing of secondaries than we normally get to read. There are actually a few unanswered questions about the secondary characters. I don't know if this is intentional because a sequel starring them might be planned. I sure hope so as I would absolutely read that book.

I definitely recommend this to people looking for something different than the traditional romance books. This was way better than I thought and I have high hopes others will enjoy this as much as I did.

- Lex Kent's Reviews, *goodreads*

This was a really easy story to get into. I sank right in and wanted to stay there, because reading about other people on vacation is kind of like taking a mini vacation from the world! It's sweet and lovely, and while it has some angst, it's not going to hurt you. Instead, it's going to take you away from it all so you can come back with a smile on your face.

- *The Lesbian Review*

Party Favors

This book has one of the best characters ever. Me. Or rather you. It's quite a strange and startling experience at first to be in a book, especially one with as many hot, sexy, beautiful women in it, who incidentally all seem to want you. But believe me, you'll soon get used to it. This may be the first book in a very long time that I've read that used a second person point of view. That's when the narrator tells you, the reader, what you're doing in the story. It's exactly like those old choose-your-own-adventure novels, but I have to tell you, this journey is a lot more fun than I ever remember those books being. By the end of the first chapter, I was used to the point of view, and was entertained and amused by what I was doing.

In a word, this book was FUN. It made me smile, and laugh, and tease my wife. I definitely recommend it to everyone, with the caveat that if you don't like erotica you should probably give it a pass. But not only read it, enjoy it, experience it, also find a friend, or a spouse, or even a book buddy online to talk to about it. Because you'll want to, it's that great.

- The Lesbian Review

I've read this book a few times and each time changed my decisions to find new and inviting destinations each time. This is a book you can read time and time again with a different journey. If you're looking for a fun Saturday night read that's sexy and hot as hell then this book is 100% for you! Go buy it now. 5 Stars.

- Les Rêveur

The story is told in the second person, present tense, which is ambitious in itself–it takes great skill to make that work and for the reader, who is now the narrator, to really connect to the thoughts and actions that are being attributed to them. Not all of the scenes will turn everyone on, as we all have different tastes, but I am pretty sure there is something for everyone in here. And if you do as you're told and follow the structure the author uses, you can dip into this book as much or as little as you wish. An interesting read with some pretty hot interactions.

- Rainbow Book Reviews

About the Author

Jaime Clevenger lives in Colorado with her family. She spends her days working as a veterinarian, but also enjoys swimming, teaching karate, playing with her kids, and snuggling the foster kittens and puppies that often fill her home. She loves to hear a good story and hopes that if you ever meet her, you'll tell her your favorite. Feel free to embellish the details.

Other Books by Jaime Clevenger

Bella Books
Call Shotgun
A Fugitive's Kiss
Moonstone
Party Favors
Sign on the Line
Sweet, Sweet Wine
Three Reasons to Say Yes
The Unknown Mile
Waiting for a Love Song
Whiskey and Oak Leaves

Spinsters Ink
All Bets Off

All The
Reasons
I NEED

Jaime Clevenger

BELLA
B O O K S
2019

PUBLISHER'S NOTE

Acknowledgments

Many thanks to my first-, second-, and third-pass readers. All of you shaped this story in important ways and I'm so grateful for your advice. Thank you Katie Lynch for being patient and supportive throughout. Thank you Rachael Byrne for your enthusiasm on this series. Thank you KD Williamson for your insight and for making me work a little harder. Thank you Laina Villeneuve for always being willing to read my stories. Thank you Carla for jumping in to help at the eleventh hour. Thank you Medora for another nearly painless experience (sometimes editing is almost fun because of you). And last but definitely not least, thank you Corina. For some reason, you put up with me even when I'm stuck in a fictional world with my make-believe friends. I owe you lots of kisses for all the times I stayed up late finishing just one more sentence…

PROLOGUE

Sixteen Years Ago

At the top of the landing, a long corridor stretched. Voices filtered through a few of the closed doors, but no one was in sight. Kate Owens tugged her suitcase behind her, silently counting off the room numbers.

Her therapist had insisted college would be the perfect fresh start—*new city, new friends, new beginning*—and all she had to do was pretend she hadn't spent the summer in treatment. She stopped in front of room 341 and stared at the door for a long minute. If she turned around now, her mom's "I told you so's" would go on for months. But maybe that would be better than failing all over again.

The door popped open and Kate took a step back.

A cute Asian girl smiled at her. "Were you about to come in? Obviously you were—what am I saying?" She held up a bright pink Hello Kitty sign with *Welcome* written in at least twenty different languages. "The RA said we each needed to decorate our door. I know it's dorky but I was going to put this up. What do you think?"

"I like dorky."

"Good answer. *Bienvenue, shalom*, and *aloha*." The girl grinned and turned to tape up the sign.

Kate eyed the room. Three beds, three desks, three dressers, and an assortment of suitcases crowded the space, leaving only a narrow strip of worn carpet uncovered. Nothing like home—but maybe that was a good thing.

"By the way, I'm Julia. Are you Katelyn? Or Monique?"

Before Kate could answer, she felt a hand on her elbow. Her mom had caught up. "I thought there had to be a fire with how fast you were going," Eileen said. She smiled at Julia. "Well, aren't you a peach. Julia, did you say? I'm Eileen. And this," Eileen squeezed Kate's shoulders, "is my baby, Katelyn Owens. Isn't she beautiful? Just like you. The pair of you will drive the boys crazy."

It was too late to wish her mom had waited in the car.

"My mom still calls me her baby too," Julia said, subtly winking at Kate. She turned to Eileen. "That's a lovely necklace."

"Oh, aren't you sweet," Eileen cooed.

Kate doubted Julia truly liked her mom's ostentatious diamonds, but the swift compliment had instantly won Eileen over. Julia was sharply dressed in a short black skirt and patterned maroon knit top, her black hair up in a haphazard bun with loose strands framing her face. She pulled off the look of city fashionista while still seeming comfortably relaxed. *Definitely cool.*

Kate glanced down at her own outfit. The sundress and sandals belonged at a barbeque in Sand Bluff. Not chic San Francisco. On top of that, she knew she should have styled her hair or at least left it down. She'd been too nervous that morning to do anything but pull it back in a ponytail. With her blond hair and baby face, she probably looked young enough to order a kids' meal. But even if she looked cool, she'd be the same mess on the inside.

Eileen pushed past them to walk around the room. She opened the door to the bathroom and then poked her head inside for a closer look. The upside of sharing with two roommates instead of one was that this "suite" had a private bathroom.

Judging from Eileen's frown, however, the bathroom wasn't much of a positive. She turned back to survey the bedroom again, her disapproval obvious as she took in the scratched desks and the mismatched dressers that clearly had weathered years of spilt drinks and hard use.

"Well, I guess this is what you get if you leave Texas." Eileen sniffed. "You'll be living on top of each other."

"I think it's perfect." Kate pulled her suitcase into the room, officially determined to make the best of it. She'd had to share a room at the treatment center too. That suite was posh compared to this, but at least she was used to roommates.

"I found a man just fine without bothering about college." Eileen squinted at the smudged window between the two beds. "But Katelyn wants a city slicker, I guess."

"I'm definitely not here to find a husband," Kate interrupted. "And it's just Kate. Not Katelyn."

"Well, it wouldn't be the worse thing that happened," Eileen returned.

"Kate suits you." Julia smiled. "And I'm not looking for a husband either. As weird as it sounds, I decided to go to college to learn something."

Kate grinned. "What were you thinking?"

"Right?"

Kate felt her hopes rise as Julia laughed. They were going to be friends—she was certain of it.

"Hey, roomies!"

Kate spun around at the rich alto voice. A tall, lanky, black girl with a short haircut and a disarming smile gave her a once-over. She managed, "Hi," before she felt the heat rise up her neck and settle on her cheeks. Her pale complexion could never conceal a blush, but at the moment she wanted to pull a bag over her head.

"You must be Monique," Julia said, stepping forward. "I'm Julia."

"Everyone calls me Mo." She clasped Julia's hand, her smile widening.

As Mo chatted with Julia about city traffic, Kate reminded herself to breathe. For once she wanted to be cool. She tried to concentrate on the conversation, laughing when Julia did, but found herself taking in Mo more than listening. Blue gym shorts hung low on her hips, exposing the waistband of a pair of boxers, white socks were pulled up past her calves, and a white sports bra peeked out from under the edges of an oversized yellow tank top. Her skin was a smooth dark brown and her black hair was clipped short against her head. She was beautiful. *Or maybe handsome?*

"So you're Kate?"

"What?"

"Or is it Katelyn?"

"Oh, yeah. Just Kate." She smiled and then realized Mo was waiting to shake her hand. As soon as she clasped Mo's hand, a warmth swept through her. She looked up and Mo's brown eyes caught her gaze. Her pulse thumped in her ears. It was the right moment to either say something or let go, but she didn't do either. Mo grinned, her expression half surprised and half amused.

Before Kate think of some joke to smooth over the awkwardness, Mo let go of her hand and turned back to Julia. They laughed about having an icebreaker game of Truth or Dare later and Kate felt her mother's eyes bore into her. She needed to act like nothing was wrong, but her heart was racing and a sweat had started at her armpits.

"I'm Eileen. Katelyn's mom," Eileen said, her hawkish gaze now on Mo. "You're so tall—you must be a basketball player. Are you here on a scholarship?"

The words landed like a dull thud. Kate pointedly glared, but her mom ignored the look.

"I am here on a scholarship but not for sports," Mo said. "Computer science. I'm a big math nerd."

"Computer science?" Eileen didn't hide her surprise.

"I'm crazy about numbers. And programming."

The way Mo straightened up, facing off to Eileen, and the way her voice said don't-fuck-with-me without saying it at all, made Kate want to gawk like all those tourists admiring the Golden Gate.

"I guess that's better than being crazy about boys." Eileen laughed. "When I was you girls' age, the only numbers I was thinking about were boys' phone numbers. But I hope none of you will be bringing boys up here after curfew. They were telling all the parents at orientation that they've gotten very strict about that rule."

"As long as there's no rules about bringing girls up," Mo said. Without missing a beat, she added, "Did they mention that at the parents' orientation?"

Eileen's mouth dropped straight open. Kate tried not to show her own surprise. Even without looking her direction, she knew Mo was studying her reaction.

So Mo was gay. What did it matter to her? Kate answered the question a moment later even as she argued it couldn't be true.

CHAPTER ONE

Present Day

"You're avoiding her."

"I'm not avoiding anyone," Kate said. But Julia was right. She was most definitely avoiding Mo. "How are you? How are the kids? How's Reed?"

"Everyone's good. Carly and Bryn are testing the spaghetti to see if it's done. Apparently Reed taught them to throw the noodles against the refrigerator to see if they stick, but I told them to aim for Reed instead. I just cleaned the fridge." Julia laughed. "There's a noodle stuck on Reed's glasses. I guess dinner is ready."

"I miss your little family."

"You should come over Sunday. Reed wants to have a barbeque. She seems to think that you can barbeque crab. But she thinks you can barbeque anything. Did I tell you about that broccoli incident?"

Kate smiled. "I'll see what I can do." She walked over to the window and eyed the street below. A heavy fog had settled, and in the gathering darkness, lights from the passing cars cast a pulsing glow. She'd missed the city. The day had been one of those February gems where all of San Francisco was bathed in sunshine, but the fog mirrored her mood now.

"Oh, that reminds me. The girls want to know if you're coming to Mexico."

Kate leaned against the window, feeling the chill seep through her blouse. "Tell them I haven't decided."

"Because of Mo?"

When Kate didn't answer, Julia made a clicking sound with her tongue the way she did when she was disappointed. "Kate, the trip is in six weeks. You need to decide. By the way, I told her you were back in town."

"When did you tell her that?" Kate didn't want to make a big deal about it, but the timing mattered. She pushed away from the window and walked back to her desk. If Mo had known that she was in town for the past two weeks and hadn't reached out to her... She stared at the business journal open to Mo's interview.

"I just sent her a text. Don't hate me." Julia's voice was muffled for a moment as she told someone to wash their hands.

"I wish you hadn't."

"She still thinks she's your friend. Waiting two weeks to tell her that you're back in town—"

"She is my friend," Kate interrupted. They'd once been best friends but now she wasn't certain where things stood. And it was her fault.

"Look, she was complaining about being lonely with her girlfriend gone this week. I thought you two could meet for dinner." Julia paused. "You two need to talk."

Where would they even start? Kate reached for the business magazine and flipped to the cover. Mo's face smiled up at her. "Did you know her picture's on the front of *SF Bay Business*?"

"She mentioned getting interviewed for something. Is it a good shot?" Dishes clattered in the background.

"She looks great." Nothing had changed there. Mo was wearing a black blazer with a white button-down shirt. The top two buttons were undone, revealing a triangle of smooth brown skin and enough of Mo's collarbones to make it hard not to stare. What was worse, the photographer had caught her laughing.

Kate couldn't resist tracing the tiny lines at the corner of Mo's eyes. "She topped their Forty Under Forty professionals list. I can't believe she didn't say anything—it's a big deal."

"You know Mo doesn't brag."

Add it to the list of her charms. Kate tossed the magazine on her desk. "I don't know about dinner. Maybe I could swing coffee later this week."

"You take people to dinner all the time. This time you won't even need to try and raise a million dollars before dessert. We're talking about Mo, remember?"

Raising a million dollars was easy. Dinner with Mo was much more complicated.

"Six months might have changed things. Maybe you won't even want to kiss her."

"I don't want to kiss her." Kate glanced at Mo's picture again and her chest ached with the mutinous thought of wrapping her arms around her.

"So we're still pretending you don't have a crush on her?"

"Seriously, Jules? A crush?"

"You're the one who's acting like we're back in college."

Kate sighed. When the Denver position came up at work, she'd jumped at the opportunity. It was true that she'd wanted to be involved in getting the state-of-the-art cancer treatment center built, but that was also a good excuse. She needed a break from sharing an apartment with Mo—and a break from the constant questioning of their friendship.

Unfortunately six months apart didn't help. As soon as she'd stepped off the plane in San Francisco, her first thought had been of seeing Mo again. But she'd resisted calling her. For her own sake, she didn't want to see Mo until she was ready to be friends.

She looked over at Peeves, his fawn-colored head nestled on the edge of his pink cushy bed. Lately she was careful not to say Mo's name aloud. Peeves would jump up and bark, then run in circles around the room, hoping to see her.

Her phone buzzed with a text and she held it away from her ear to read the screen. As soon as she saw Mo's name, her stomach clenched.

Mo: *You're back?! Can you meet me at Mario's tonight?*
Julia's voice came through the line at the same time. Something about Reed and the twins throwing pasta at each other. Laughing followed. Kate stared at Mo's text, feeling a rush of excitement promptly followed by a recrimination.

"Mo texted me," Kate said, holding the phone against her ear again. "She wants to meet at Mario's."

"Perfect."

Not perfect. "It's already late. I've got Peeves in the office with me today and I've still got a mountain of work to do."

"And you'll be busy tomorrow," Julia said. "And the day after. Sweetie, this isn't going to get easier. Go home and drop off Peeves. You can walk to Mario's from your apartment."

Kate's stomach rumbled in response. She'd skipped lunch in lieu of taking Peeves for a walk in the park—at least that was her excuse. In only two weeks, her clothes were getting loose again. As much as she told herself that she had control of her eating issues, stress brought back old habits.

"Mo thinks she did something to piss you off… Something to make you leave."

"I got transferred to Denver—she knew that. I left for work."

"Right. Why tell her the truth? Why talk about the elephant in the room?"

Kate exhaled. An elephant was one way to describe her attraction to Mo. "She was spending most nights at her girlfriend's house then. Talking about it wouldn't have helped."

"It may seem like a foreign concept to you, but sometimes it's good to talk about things." Julia's parenting tone had kicked in.

"Thanks for the advice, Mom."

"You're such a pain in the ass. It's a good thing I love you." Julia hollered for the kids to stop running through the kitchen. When she came back on the line, she said, "Do you want me to text her about Mario's, or are you going to put on your big girl panties and text her yourself?"

Every day that she'd resisted contacting Mo had become a sort of badge of honor. But what good had resisting done? If anything, she was only more desperate to see her.

Kate eyed the magazine again. Mo looked every bit the part of a savvy CEO of a successful startup. Funny, adventurous, sometimes nerdy, Mo had made it big. Kate had known it would happen eventually. "I'll text her."

"Good. And in case you can't hear them, the twins are yelling that they want both of their aunties to come to Cozumel."

"I can hear them." Kate couldn't help smiling. "Give your little family hugs and kisses from me." Without committing on the trip, she said a quick goodbye and hung up the line.

Kate clicked back to Mo's text. *Keep it simple*, she thought, staring at the screen.

Eight o'clock?

Mo's answer was immediate: *I'll be there!*

Kate swallowed. "Okay. We're doing this." At least they were going to Mario's and she knew what she wanted to order. Her old trainer had made her keep a diary of her meals and she'd gotten good at guessing calories. The less thinking she had to do tonight, the better.

She pulled on her coat and jingled her keys. Peeves's ears twitched but he didn't move otherwise. One of the perks of being the director of development meant she was in charge of her floor and could decide things like a pet policy. Peeves had no idea how lucky he was.

"Peeves, wake up."

Without opening his eyes, Peeves nestled his head deeper in the curve of his bed. For a Chihuahua-terrier mix, he was decidedly lazy. His bed was under her desk and unless she had meetings with a donor, he came to work with her every day. Now he was clearly hoping that she'd leave him in the office for the night.

"Come on, I don't want to be late. I've got a date with Mo."

At Mo's name, Peeves sprang up. He gave a full body shake and then trotted expectantly to the door. When Mo didn't instantly appear, he turned his big doe-like eyes up at Kate, whining softly.

"I know you miss her, but do you have to rub it in?"

Peeves's tail waved as he whined again. He raised his paw and scratched once at the door. When Kate shook her head, he danced in a circle on his hind legs. Part of her shared the sentiment and she couldn't help smiling at his antics.

"This isn't a real date," Kate reminded herself. Peeves looked up at her, cocking his head as if he didn't understand why it couldn't be. "Because she's got a girlfriend and I've got issues."

Peeves did another spin, adding a yip for emphasis.

"And I hate to break it to you, but you're not coming to dinner." She leaned down to pat his head and he tried his best winning grin. "If I brought you along, I'd only be jealous when you hopped into Mo's lap and licked her chin. There are some things humans can't get away with."

CHAPTER TWO

Mario's was open late, but it mostly catered to a lunch crowd. By eight, the place had only a handful of diners. Kate had arrived early, planning on scoping out a table and settling in before Mo got there, but there was no hope of relaxing. Her nerves were eased some when the waitress gave her a familiar smile. "Haven't seen you in here in a while. What can I get you?"

"I'm waiting for a friend."

"No problem. Can I get you a drink in the meantime?"

Kate wanted to order the house wine, but her stomach was empty. The last thing she needed was to get tipsy. "I'll take water for now."

As the waitress stepped away, Kate looked up and saw Mo in the doorway. She was holding the door for a couple who were just leaving and not looking in Kate's direction. When she turned to scan the room, their gazes met and Kate straightened up.

The business journal's photographer had gotten a good shot, but Mo Calloway was even better in real life. So tall and handsome... Kate felt light-headed taking in the sight of her.

But it wasn't simply Mo's good looks. She'd missed her. Too much.

Mo slipped off her black leather jacket and folded it over her arm. She was wearing a light gray collared shirt, which she'd paired with trim black slacks. No doubt about it—she looked like a million bucks. Kate wondered if she'd gotten dressed up for dinner. Dressed up to see her? She clenched her jaw, hoping not to give away the emotions that rippled through her.

After college, Mo's body had filled out in all the best places. She was a regular at a kickboxing gym and lifted weights, which meant she still had an athletic build. But she was less the skinny tomboy now and more the strapping woman. *Strapping? Seriously?* Did her mind have to go there?

As Mo neared the table, Kate stood up. In her heels, the height difference between them wasn't as noticeable, but she still had to look up to meet Mo's brown eyes.

"Hey, stranger." Mo smiled.

"Hey yourself." Kate smiled back. Her pulse quickened when Mo held out her arms. She stepped into the hug, begging her body not to respond. Mo radiated warmth and her embrace was as strong as ever. God, she felt good to hug. Kate quickly let go and took a step back, her heart hammering away in her chest.

"It's good to see you," Mo said, hanging her jacket over her chair. "You look great. Is that a new dress?"

Kate nodded, hoping to keep the blush off her cheeks by sheer willpower. She'd changed out of the suit she'd worn to work and, after much deliberation, decided on a silk dress she'd bought on a business trip to Tokyo.

"You look great too." *Strapping, in fact.* Kate wanted to say those words aloud, knowing Mo would laugh, but she was still unsteady from the hug. She dropped into her seat, trying to push the image of a strap-on out of her mind.

She knew Mo packed. Although Mo hadn't brought it up directly, Julia had guessed it one night when all three of them had had too much wine. Instead of denying, Mo had elaborated. It wasn't an everyday thing, she'd said, but for special occasions she had a dildo that could be bent down and worn in public with little notice. Kate had found the whole concept entirely too arousing. As much as she'd wanted to know more, she'd only hid behind her wineglass as Julia teased Mo about it not being fair that she oozed sex appeal and could pull off packing.

Mo settled into her seat. "I was going to wear my sexy dress too, but then I couldn't find my little black heels."

"Little black dress and sexy heels."

"Not the other way around?" Mo tapped her chin. "Huh. Good thing I don't have to try and be sexy."

"For you it comes natural."

Mo laughed and Kate felt the tension ease some when she joined in. Flirting was something they'd always done and she'd missed their easy banter. Plus it felt good to laugh. But their old ways had gotten her into trouble before. This time she had to be careful.

"By the way, you totally made my night. I think the neighbors may have heard me squeal when Jules texted saying you were in town. How long have you been back?"

Kate opened her mouth to answer, debating telling her the truth, when the waitress appeared. She set two water glasses down and gave Mo a wide smile.

"Should I give you a minute to look over the menu?"

"I think we're ready." Mo glanced at Kate. "Do you want to go first?"

"You go ahead." Kate hoped she sounded more relaxed than she felt. Her stomach had knotted up again. Getting through the meal was going to be a small miracle.

"I'll take the chicken artichoke panini with a side salad. Extra parmesan, please."

Kate bit her lip. That was what she'd been planning on as well—right down to the extra parmesan—but she didn't want to order the same thing now. The waitress looked her way and she quickly decided on the veggie pesto panini.

As soon as the waitress walked away, Mo said, "You always order the chicken."

"I wanted something different."

"Different can be good." Mo clinked her water glass against Kate's. "Cheers. If different isn't good, I'll share mine with you."

"You don't need to do that."

"Afraid of my germs?"

Kate rolled her eyes. "You're gonna be jealous of my pesto."

"'Want to place a bet on who gets the better panini?"

"You're a goofball."

"That's why you love me." Mo grinned. She looked around the restaurant. "I missed this place."

Kate's heart raced. Mo had no clue. "I couldn't find any place in Denver with decent paninis. Although good Thai food was even harder to find."

"At least there was some reason for you to come back."

"I had a few reasons." Kate knew she couldn't analyze every sentence or even the way Mo looked at her. This was simply dinner with a friend. But the butterflies in her stomach started chasing each other every time Mo's eyes met hers. She cleared her throat. "Guess what I found on my assistant's desk this morning?"

"A banana?"

"You and bananas." Kate laughed. "Why is that always your answer?"

"Consistency. After sixteen years, it still makes you laugh." Mo's eyes sparkled.

"For that I shouldn't tell you."

But Kate couldn't help laughing again when Mo asked, "You sure it wasn't a banana?"

"If I had a banana, I'd throw it at you right now."

"I've seen your aim. I'm not scared."

Kate pretended to be dismayed, but Mo only laughed. "Okay, now I'm curious. What was on her desk?"

"Last month's business journal. That was a great interview."

"You saw that?" Mo scrunched up her face.

"Why are you embarrassed? It's a huge accomplishment."

"I didn't know they were going to put me on the cover. You should have heard all the teasing in my office."

"They're just jealous. You should be proud. Not only are you the CEO of a successful start-up, that app you designed put your company in the big leagues. HeroToday is awesome."

"You've checked it out?"

"I donated to two different groups after the fires—because of your app. It made the whole process easy. And I loved the map that you can click on to show where you can drop off donations or where volunteers are needed."

Mo beamed. "We're working on improving that. The more local charities and groups we can connect, the faster we can help people."

"I love it. That interviewer did too. Although by the end of the article, I wasn't sure if it was the app she was gushing about or you." Kate winked.

Mo looked down at her napkin. "When I got the call about doing that interview, I almost said no."

"Why?"

"They made it sound like it was all me. I couldn't have gotten HeroToday off the ground by myself."

"A year ago you were working Internet security for someone else. Think about what you've done this past year—you deserved that top spot. You've worked hard."

"A lot of people worked hard," Mo argued.

"But it was your idea. And you did it to help people—not just to make money." When Mo sighed, she added, "Anyway, it was a good article. And you need a class in taking compliments."

"Maybe." Mo took a sip of water and shifted back in her seat. "Enough about me. How have you been?"

"Busy." Busy was true—although the first word that came to mind was "lonely."

"I know the feeling," Mo said. "But I haven't been so busy that I didn't miss you."

That was all Mo—sweet and honest. No pretenses. Kate hoped her face wouldn't betray how the words touched her. "I missed you too."

"Did you fly in this weekend? I heard a bunch of flights were cancelled with that storm in the Midwest."

"Luckily I missed that." Guilt tightened Kate's chest. "I came back two weeks ago."

"Oh, I thought..." Mo's brow furrowed.

Kate wished then that she'd called Mo from the airport like she'd wanted. "I've been slammed with this new project and haven't had time to meet up with anyone—"

"You don't need to explain," Mo interrupted. "I'm happy you made time to hang out with me tonight."

A silence stretched between them. Kate crossed her ankles and then uncrossed them a moment later. Even if they weren't as close as they once were, Mo was still her friend. She deserved the truth—or as much of it as Kate could tell her.

"I almost texted you the moment I stepped off the plane. I wanted to ask you to meet me at the dog park. Peeves missed you. But then I thought about your girlfriend…"

Kate looked at Mo's folded hands, longing to reach across the table to caress the stretch of smooth skin on the back of her hand. But a friend wouldn't do that. She looked up and met Mo's gaze.

"I did a lot of thinking in Denver. I know it's my fault we aren't as close as we used to be, but I don't want another one of your girlfriends blaming me for problems in your relationship."

"That's fair. But what happened with me and Tanya wasn't your fault. I screwed up with her all on my own."

Although Tanya had been the most outspoken, more than one of Mo's girlfriends had complained about the closeness of their friendship. And Kate couldn't in good conscience say that nothing was going on—at least on her end. For her part, Mo never crossed any lines.

"Anyway Chantal's different. She's used to doing her own thing and having her own friends. I know she'd want me to see you. And Peeves. I miss that little booger. How is my little man?"

"Ornery as ever. He got all excited when I mentioned I was meeting you and then refused to eat his dinner when I dropped him off at the apartment."

"You should have brought him here. I can get him to do anything, you know."

Kate knew Mo was right. Peeves might be her dog, but he loved Mo more. "Next time."

"So…is work the only reason you didn't tell me you were in town? I get the feeling something else is bothering you."

Mo's tone was gentle and Kate felt a fresh pang of guilt. "I'm just being weird. Like always."

Mo studied her for a minute. Finally she said, "Okay, good. I was worried that six months in Denver would make you normal."

"No chance."

Kate wanted to tell her everything then—how nothing was right in her life without her, how their old apartment smelled like patchouli and that she'd lit a whole pack of matches trying to kill the scent of the hippies they'd sublet the place to, how she'd wanted so much more than a hello hug, and how she didn't want to walk out of this restaurant alone. She was so tired of being alone. But she couldn't say any of that.

Kate unrolled her napkin and pretended to be interested in setting out her utensils. "Are you excited about Cozumel? Chantal's coming, right?"

"She can't make it. Her boss scheduled some big meeting in London that same week and he's insisting she go with him. I think she should learn how to say no, but she's trying to move up in the company. Anyway, I don't think she wanted to go to Cozumel."

"Why not?"

"I don't know… She doesn't really do sand."

"Seriously?"

Mo nodded and laughed. "She's totally high maintenance."

Kate squelched the hope that Mo and her girlfriend weren't on solid footing. Even if they broke up, Mo wasn't going to turn around and suddenly notice her.

"Well, I'm sorry she can't go." It wasn't a lie. Now her decision on the trip was suddenly more complicated. If she went, she'd have more time with Mo. But how much time could she handle when she was stuck pretending their friendship was platonic?

"She said she'll find a way to make it up to me." Mo shrugged. "Julia mentioned that you still hadn't decided if you're going. Anything I can say to convince you?"

Kate felt her cheeks get hot. There was plenty Mo could say. "It's not great timing for my work either. I've had a lot of things pile up while I was focused on the Denver project."

"I heard vacations make you more productive. Don't make me cite the source, but I'm sure it's true." Before Kate could argue that she didn't have time to be more productive, Mo continued, "I was up in Davis last weekend, and Carly and Bryn said I had to find a way to get you to say yes cause they wanted both of their aunties in Mexico. Julia told me she was planning on guilting you into it by bringing up the fact that you missed Thanksgiving and Christmas with them."

"She's such a mom." Kate needed a minute to think. Could she say yes to Cozumel and not cross any lines?

"How's your mom by the way? Eileen still complaining about how San Francisco made you bi?"

"She wasn't exactly upset that I moved to Denver. I think she hoped I'd suddenly fall for a cowboy. When I told her I was taking a break from dating men she got all upset and sent me tickets to Vegas to go see 'Thunder from Down Under' with her."

Mo chuckled. "Tell me you have pictures of that."

"I didn't go. I told her if she wanted to see a bunch of naked men dancing she should come to a Pride parade with me."

"Oh, man, can you imagine? Eileen's mind would be blown."

"I keep telling her that she'd love a drag show." Kate knew she'd never get her mom to a gay hairdresser let alone a drag show but that didn't stop her. "What good is it being gay if you can't mess with your conservative parents?"

"You're calling yourself gay now?"

"You know I hate labels."

"I love labels. I even bought myself one of those label makers for work. I label the shit out of everything." Mo winked. "You didn't exactly answer the question about Cozumel."

"You're right." And she still wasn't ready. "How's your mom?"

"I told her we were having dinner tonight and she said I had to give you a hug."

Mo had lucked out in the mom department. Not only was Shirley okay with Mo being gay, she was supportive and loving to nearly everyone who crossed her path. Early on, Kate had talked to her about her eating issues. She'd never been brave enough to talk to Mo about it and Shirley had promised not to say anything. She'd kept her word all these years.

"She also wanted me to tell you that her offer still stands for a Spades rematch," Mo added.

"She kicked my butt last time. Both of you did." Kate laughed, remembering the last game that they'd played. Having to learn the three-person variation on the usual game had been her excuse for why she'd lost miserably. "So was that hug that you gave me when you came in from your mom or from you?"

Mo seemed momentarily taken aback. She stumbled for an answer. "Both?"

"I don't know if you can count that hug as one of Shirley's hugs...they're pretty amazing. She makes you feel like you're loved all the way down to your pinky toes."

"You saying my hug was wussy in comparison?"

Kate rocked her head side to side. "A little."

Mo laughed. "For that, you get another hug before we leave."

"Maybe you should call your mom for pointers first." At least she'd be prepared for the second hug. Hopefully her body would behave.

"Don't think I haven't already sent Mom a text."

Kate wanted a picture of Mo's smile in that moment. The mischievous look was so reminiscent of old times that it was almost as if the past year hadn't happened. Maybe they could get back to where they'd been before she'd started thinking there was a chance for something more. As long as she kept her head screwed on right and didn't pay any attention to how sexy Mo was when her tongue slipped across her lips...

Mo reached for her water glass again. "Why are we drinking water when they have your favorite Cabernet here?"

Because I didn't want to need wine to face you. Kate wondered what Mo's reaction would be if she voiced her thought aloud. Not willing to find out, she said, "It's a new health fad I'm trying. Don't worry. It won't last."

Mo chuckled. "Now tell me how Denver was—really."

Kate could admit that she'd been lonely and miserable. Or she could go with a partial truth. "Exhausting. Thank God the work was rewarding."

"Most of us just want to make a difference in this world. But you actually do it."

"Look who's talking. That's what HeroToday is all about."

"I'm only a computer nerd."

Kate raised an eyebrow. "Like I said, we seriously need to work on you accepting compliments." Instead of arguing that all she did was convince rich people to part with their money so others could do the real work, she said, "People want to make a difference. Some days I feel like humanity has hope."

"There's a chance for us," Mo said, nodding.

Kate reached for her water glass, hoping Mo wouldn't see her reaction. A chance for humanity—not for the two of them sitting at a small cafe with her aching to reach across the table—was what she'd clearly meant. "I like to think so."

She thought then of all the questions she'd stopped herself from asking Mo over the past several months. Mostly she wanted to know if Mo was happy, but the question sounded ridiculous even in her own mind. Mo had that rare ability to make the best of any situation and always claimed to be happy. Besides, if she wasn't happy that didn't mean that she needed Kate.

"So are you dating anyone?"

That was one question Kate had hoped Mo wouldn't ask. "No one serious since Ethan. I mean, I've tried going on dates but…there's a learning curve when you switch from men to women. It's been a heck of a year." She took another sip of water and tried to laugh away the tension, but the water caught in her throat and she half choked. When she could breath again, she cleared her throat. "And I sound like a frog. Maybe that's the problem."

"Maybe you're kissing too many frogs."

"I don't think that's it." She coughed again and tears welled. *Dammit.* At least Mo would think her eyes were only watering. She looked up at the fan, hoping the emotion would pass quickly.

"You okay?"

"Yeah, I'm fine. Should have ordered wine."

Mo laughed.

Kate rubbed her eyes and cleared her throat again. In the few texts they'd exchanged, she'd avoided telling her about any dates mostly because there wasn't much to say. She worried now what Mo would think of her paltry dating history. "The truth is there hasn't been much kissing. I haven't let anyone get past the first coffee date."

"Want to talk about why?"

Kate met Mo's gaze, the answer nearly slipping from her lips.

"Chicken with extra parmesan?"

Mo smiled up at the waitress. "That's me."

Mo's panini smelled like heaven. Kate tried not to feel let down as the waitress set a veggie panini in front of her. Even with the pesto sauce, grilled veggies weren't as appealing as chicken layered with parmesan and artichokes. Picking up her fork, she started in on her salad, hoping Mo would forget her earlier question.

"Ty says hi, by the way," Mo said. "He texted me when I was in traffic and I told him you were back."

Kate hadn't seen Mo's brother Tyrone in over a year, but she kept up with him and his family on Facebook. She doubted that Mo knew this, however. For all of her computer savvy, she wasn't much on social media. "I miss those Sunday night dinners we used to have at his house. If I could cook like Claire…"

"I told Ty he's getting chubby. Claire's a little too good of a cook. And you should see the boys. They're so big." Mo reached for her phone. "Do you remember that time we took Michael to Fairyland? I think he was three or four. He's six now… He asked me the other day if we can go back. I couldn't believe he even remembered."

Mo held up her phone. "As for Jamal…" A plump-faced toddler grinned at the camera as his older brother gave him a hug. Neon blue frosting was smeared on both of their lips. "This was at his birthday. He turned two last week."

"I know," Kate admitted. "I sent him a little present."

Mo looked up from the screen. "You remembered his birthday?"

"It's on my calendar." Kate tried not to take offense at the surprise in Mo's voice. "I hope it was okay for me to send him something."

"Yeah, of course..." Mo's voice trailed.

"I mean, I'm his godmother. And I'm friends with Ty and Claire on Facebook. You should see some of their posts about the kids. They're hilarious." Kate stopped talking when she saw the expression on Mo's face. Was she jealous that she'd kept up contact with her brother? "Are you mad?"

"No. It's fine. Why wouldn't you be friends with them? I just feel like we've lost touch, but you're keeping up with my brother, which is a little weird."

Mo was definitely upset. Kate shifted in her seat. "I temporarily moved. I didn't drop off the face of the planet—"

"It just felt that way." Mo looked down at her plate and then added, "I didn't realize how much I'd miss you."

Mo's tone stopped Kate. It was no declaration of love. Mo had missed her, like any friend would. Still her words brought a mix of guilt and satisfaction. Kate had wanted Mo to miss her, but she felt worse acknowledging that.

"When you left, my mom asked me what I did. She likes you better than anyone I've ever dated. She and Chantal don't exactly get along."

"I'll call her and tell her you didn't do anything wrong. I went to Denver for work."

"If it was only work, why didn't you tell me when you got back two weeks ago?"

And there it was. Kate wanted to answer, but she couldn't. Holding back the truth had started that first day in college. She couldn't tell Mo what she was thinking then, and nothing had changed since.

"Whatever I did, I'm sorry."

"You didn't do anything, Mo. It was all me." Kate hoped Mo wouldn't press her to say more.

"In that case, I think you should come to Cozumel. It won't be any fun without you. And you owe me."

"I owe you?"

"Yes. After all, I had to go almost six months wondering what I did to make my best friend leave town."

Kate didn't answer. She didn't trust herself not to burst out with some stupid truth that she'd held in for way too long. What was worse—spending a week in Cozumel and still not telling Mo how she felt or missing the chance to be with her?

Mo picked up her knife and cut her sandwich in half. "We both know you wanted to order this. I'll share it if you say yes."

"To going to Cozumel? Really? You're trying to bribe me with half a sandwich?"

"I know you pretty well." Mo held the plate in front of Kate. "What do you say?"

CHAPTER THREE

By three in the morning, Kate still wasn't asleep. No amount of tossing and turning could quiet her mind, and her stomach was still reeling from the ice cream and wine. After she'd left Mario's, she'd swung by the grocery store for a pint of Ben and Jerry's and a Cabernet. She hadn't planned on finishing either, but old habits came back too easy. *Old habits...*

Kate pushed away a wave of nausea and switched on the bedside light. Resolved to at least finish the emails she'd skipped when leaving work early, she got out her laptop. Peeves grumbled from his bed in the corner of the room.

"Sorry, buddy. Can't sleep."

After a minute of staring her down, Peeves stood up, stretched, and slunk out of the bedroom, likely intent on snuggling up on the living room couch. He was as persistent about sleep as he was about treats. Kate only wished her life was as simple. As she waited for her laptop to power on, she fought back a yawn. Her morning schedule included a meeting with a CFO she'd been courting for a large gift for over two months and yet, even without sleep, she wasn't worried about that.

Instead, her mind was fixated on Mo. She was the last thing Mo needed but that didn't change how much she wanted to be back in her world. If only she could use Cozumel to prove that she could do that as a friend. Unfortunately, all through dinner her hormones had reminded her how much she'd wanted to reach across the table and touch Mo's hand. And that was only the beginning of what she wanted to do.

When they'd said goodbye, Mo had given her the promised second hug. Kate had let herself enjoy it way too much. Nothing screamed "more than a friend" than when your nipples hardened at what should have been innocent contact. But she couldn't help it. She was tired of fighting her body's reaction to Mo. What good had fighting it done?

Then again, letting her body decide things hadn't gone well either. Over a year had passed since the near-kiss that had almost ruined everything. Kate thought back to the Hawaii trip and her insecurities resurfaced along with the guilt.

At first it was perfect. Kate was engaged to Ethan then and Mo was with Tanya, but they'd gone to Hawaii without their respective partners. Julia, Kate and Mo—three friends in Hawaii for two weeks.

Then Julia met Reed. As Julia's romance flared, Kate and Mo were suddenly spending every day and night together. It was during that time that Kate realized her attraction to Mo was always going to be there no matter who she was engaged to. But she tried to ignore it.

One night she messed everything up. She was alone with Mo watching TV after a long day at the beach. It was late and the pitcher of piña coladas they'd made was empty, but Mo didn't mention going to bed. Kate's sunburn started to itch so she got out a tube of aloe and twisted around trying to reach the middle of her back.

"You look like a pretzel," Mo had said.

Without catching herself, Kate voiced her first thought out loud: "You volunteering to help?"

"I think I'll keep watching you try for a while."

"What a friend." Kate had held out the aloe and Mo reached for it, chuckling.

Maybe it was the rum or maybe it was that she was tired of guessing how Mo felt, but for whatever reason, Kate took off her shirt. She was wearing a lacy black bra and Mo's gaze immediately dropped to her cleavage. The look of desire was obvious.

Kate turned her back to Mo, her heart racing. She pulled her hair over one shoulder and reminded herself to breathe. "Right in the middle. Apparently I couldn't reach it with the sunscreen either."

"Yeah, there's a red spot."

Mo's voice sounded different. Unsteady. But Kate couldn't see her eyes. Had she imagined Mo's desire?

As soon as Mo touched her skin with the cool aloe, she moaned. The sound slipped out, but she hadn't tried to hold it in either. "That feels good."

"Straight girls are easy," Mo joked.

Kate turned then and closed the distance to Mo's lips. Before their lips met, however, Mo had shot up from the sofa.

She stood there, stock-still, with the aloe in her hand and a confused expression on her face. Kate recalled her own awkward joke about how easy it was to scare lesbians, but she knew they both understood what had happened. She had tried to kiss Mo, and no matter what she'd thought, it was clear that Mo wasn't interested.

Kate spent the rest of that trip berating herself and avoiding any alone time with Mo. Too many times Mo had complained about straight drunk girls trying to come on to her and from her perspective, Kate had done just that. She could have tried to explain then that she wasn't drunk. Or straight. Late to the party, yes, but not straight. She'd only made things worse by pretending that what she'd done, or tried to do, was nothing important.

Besides all that, Mo was with Tanya and she'd never cheat. Kate had put her in a terrible position and then tried to laugh it off. She'd never been more embarrassed.

Hawaii set off a chain of events that only partially had anything to do with the near-kiss. When they got back, Tanya broke up with Mo—accusing her of cheating with a surfer girl Mo had met—and Kate ended things with Ethan. Although she'd loved him in a way, she'd finally realized that what she felt wasn't enough. She'd never connected with him the way she connected with Mo, and no matter who she married, she needed to feel that.

She came out to her parents the same day. When her mom had asked how long she'd been attracted to women, while in the same breath swearing that it couldn't be true because she hadn't been raised that way, Kate hadn't been able to come up with an answer.

Her feelings for women had always been there, but she'd tried to fight them. Saying that she simply enjoyed close friendships with women had made sense in college. She'd been attracted to men as well. When she'd considered that she might be bisexual, she'd told herself that she didn't need another reason to be in counseling. Her list of issues was already a mile long.

She'd considered telling Mo everything then. How the attraction had always been there, but she'd fought it… But Mo could have anyone. She didn't need someone with a mountain of baggage.

Kate stared at the clock. In two hours, her alarm would go off so she could make it to the gym for a workout before her morning meeting. She reached over and turned off the alarm. There was no chance she was going to make it to the gym. It wasn't only the ice cream and the wine—one dinner with Mo and she was as sick with longing as she'd ever been.

The evening had reminded her of all the little things she'd missed—like the way Mo smelled. She had had to stop herself from leaning close more than once. And the sound of her voice. And her smile. God, her smile.

No matter what Mo's reasons had been for avoiding the kiss in Hawaii, Kate knew that there was chemistry between them. The way Mo had looked at her when they'd said goodbye at Mario's made her certain that was still true.

Kate stared at the computer screen. Instead of pulling up her work email account, she went to the resort website that Julia had mentioned. A picture of turquoise water sparkled under a sun-filled blue sky. The sandy beach was perfectly smooth, and the resort was lined on either side by dense tropical forest. She typed in the dates and waited for a list of available rooms to pop up. An image of a thatched roof bungalow with white stucco walls flashed on the screen. Clicking through the options, she found a bungalow with an ocean view and a private entry. Fortunately she had enough money to help her hormones out by picking a suite that would be far away from the others.

Without second-guessing herself, she entered her credit card number and immediately hit the confirmation button. Now all that remained was buying a plane ticket. She'd have to call Julia to get everyone else's flight information before she did that, however. She leaned back on the pillows. Mexico was probably a giant mistake. The last thing she needed was a repeat performance of Hawaii. But at least this time she knew enough to maintain physical distance from Mo. And with Julia and Reed's family going, there'd be plenty of distractions.

Peeves appeared in the doorway. He still looked sleepy and it was clear he was irritated that she was awake. He padded over to his pink bed and circled the space twice before flopping down.

"Do you think I'm an idiot for going on this trip with her?"

Peeves looked up at her and yawned. It was no ringing endorsement of her intelligence, but it wasn't exactly an argument against her decision either.

"You're probably right. I'm making this into a big deal when it's not."

Kate closed her laptop, switched off the light, and got out of bed. She walked down the hall past the living room and opened Mo's old bedroom door. Mo had cleared out most of her things when they'd sublet the apartment. She was already spending most of her time at Chantal's then anyway. All that remained was her bed, still made, and one nearly empty dresser. Kate knew that a few old T-shirts were in the top drawer because she'd checked.

For a long minute, she stood in the doorway, her gaze searching for something she hadn't seen the last time. She'd always been cautious of intruding in Mo's space and had rarely gone into her room when they'd lived together. The hippie couple had also avoided this room apparently because the scent of patchouli was missing.

Kate walked a few steps into the room, still wondering what she was doing, and then sat down on the bed. She picked up Mo's old pillow and wrapped her arms around it. The faint scent of Mo's hair product was still on the pillowcase. She breathed it in, chastising herself as she did.

They'd shared the two-bedroom apartment since moving out of the dorms. Kate had the master, and Mo, since she'd mostly slept at her various girlfriends' places over the years, had the smaller room opposite the kitchen. Months would go by when Mo never spent a day in the apartment, but there'd been nights when she was there. Kate thought of the handful of times she'd dared to knock on the bedroom door. They'd sat on the bed together and talked about their day or problems with whoever they were each dating at the time.

She pictured Mo's face, her eyes locked on hers as she'd held out the chicken panini. That was the moment Kate knew without a doubt that she was going to Mexico. She was ready to torture herself by spending a week with her even if it had to be only as friends.

Kate slipped under the comforter and settled onto the cold sheets. She shivered, waiting for her body to heat the space. As soon as she was warm enough to stretch out, she slid her hand under her pajamas. She wasn't surprised that she was already wet. That was all thanks to Mo. She didn't have to think of her for long before her body responded.

She pushed her pajamas down past her knees and shrugged off the comforter. The sensation of being exposed from the waist down in Mo's old room, on sheets that still smelled vaguely of her, aroused her even more.

When she parted her thighs, the cool air kissed her wet folds. She licked her middle finger to moisten it again and then lazily circled her clit. As she touched herself, an old fantasy came to her—Mo alone in their dorm room taking a nap and Kate, for once brave, approaching the bed.

Kate didn't have to wake Mo in the fantasy. She'd been waiting for her, knew that she wanted her. Mo watched her get close and then moved over, making room for Kate to slip under the sheet that she'd held up. Mo was naked, her gorgeous body on full display.

Kate imagined Mo reaching for her, imagined the hot kisses on her neck, as she spread her legs. She thrust her fingers inside but it was Mo that had entered her. Mo, pushing into her, taking what she wanted. Anything Mo asked, she'd do—roll onto her belly, go down on her knees… Each thought brought her orgasm closer. She squeezed her clit and climaxed with a sudden gasp. The fantasy ended the way it always did with Mo pulling her into an embrace after having her fill.

A satisfying wave washed over her and her hips went slack. She dropped her hand to cover her exposed middle and then lay perfectly still, taking in the fact that she'd just masturbated on Mo's old bed.

The sound of a door's creak made her whole body go from a wet noodle to a lightning rod. She pulled the blankets up to her chin before rolling onto her side. Eyeing the doorway, she spotted Peeves. His quizzical look made her bury her face in the pillow. At least he wouldn't tell anyone her secrets.

He wouldn't tell—but she needed to. Kate accepted this as regret replaced the brief euphoria that the orgasm had given her. Why had she gone to the grocery store for the ice cream in the first place? All the years of being good had made her think she could control her problem. Before she got on the plane to Cozumel, she needed to talk to her therapist.

CHAPTER FOUR

"I'm sorry, senorita, but there is no reservation under that name."

"You're joking, right?"

"I'm afraid not." The concierge's smile was apologetic.

Kate rubbed her temple. How was this happening? The trip had started out so well—maybe too well. She'd had no weird feelings when Mo had taken the seat next to hers on the plane and she'd almost relaxed as they'd chatted about work and Mo's family. The emergency sessions with her therapist had paid off—the dose of trazadone before lift-off probably hadn't hurt either.

Then Reed had gone down on one knee in the middle of the flight to propose to Julia and nearly everyone on board had erupted in applause. In the rush of the moment, Mo had clasped Kate's hand as she'd cheered. Everything had felt perfect and Kate had silently thanked the universe that Chantal wasn't there.

Karma must have heard. Their connecting flight got delayed, the airline lost her luggage, and now her room reservations had gone missing as well. If she'd been trying to look pathetic in front of Mo, she was doing a stellar job.

"You could bunk with me," Mo volunteered. "I've got a king-size bed. There'll be plenty of room."

"That's generous, Mo, but I made a reservation. I'm sure it's a computer glitch." Kate leveled her gaze on the concierge. "Try Katelyn instead of Kate. And the last name is Owens. O-W-E-N-S."

Although he raised his eyebrows, the concierge dutifully checked the screen again. At his headshake, Kate remembered the confirmation printout. She fished through her purse until she found it. "Here's the number."

"Ah, that will help." The concierge typed in the confirmation number, but seconds later his brow had furrowed.

"What's wrong?" Kate almost didn't want to ask.

"Your reservation was made for September 4th, not April 9th." He clicked his tongue. "In Mexico, the day goes before the month." He held up the printout and pointed to the date. "You reserved a room for seven nights beginning 4-9, not 9-4."

Kate stared at the dates, willing the numbers to change. How could she have made such a beginner's mistake? She'd been traveling internationally since she was six years old. She'd spent weeks abroad every year. But then she remembered the night she'd made the reservation. Saying she had been distracted was an understatement.

"This isn't the first time this has happened," the concierge continued. "Unfortunately, we are completely full at the moment…"

"It's fine. I'll find a room at a different resort. I'm sure there's plenty of options close by."

"It won't be as much fun if we're not all at the same resort," Mo said. "Just share with me. You're skinny and I sleep on my side. You'll probably never know I'm there."

Yeah, right.

"Besides, it'll probably only take a night or two for another room to open up." Mo looked to the concierge for confirmation.

"Unfortunately, we're fully booked until Sunday. But then I can offer you an upgrade to an oceanfront suite. That's a very nice upgrade."

"Sunday's five days from now." Although the bigger problem was the nights. It was one thing sharing a room but the same bed? There had to be another option. "You're sure there's no room with two double beds that you could switch us to? Or what about a cot?"

"No cots." He clicked his tongue apologetically. "With Easter coming up, this week is one of our most popular times."

"Yeah, I'm aware." Kate had tried to keep her tone in check, but from the way the concierge's eyebrow raised, she knew he'd felt the spark of anger she'd let slip. This was her fault, not his. She quickly read the nametag pinned to his chest and said, "I'm sorry, Luis. It's just been a long day already."

"It'll be like we're back in the dorms," Mo said.

Except in college they'd slept on opposite walls with a desk between them and Julia in the same room to stop Kate from doing something stupid. "I don't feel right sleeping in the same bed. You've got a girlfriend..."

"Chantal knows we're only friends. She'll be fine with it."

Not one of Mo's past girlfriends would have been okay with this plan. And what about her own sanity? But it wasn't like she couldn't keep her hands off Mo.

If only they'd decided on one of the big resorts finding another room wouldn't be an issue. Julia and Reed had done the planning, though, and they'd wanted a smaller, family-oriented place. They were also the ones who'd insisted on scheduling the trip over spring break when the twins were off school. At the moment their little family was probably already splashing in the pool.

"I'll buy a deck of cards and we can stay up late playing Go Fish," Mo said. "It'll be fun."

"Two keys for the room then?" Luis looked hopeful.

Mo bit her lower lip and waited. The habit was completely distracting only because whenever she did it, Kate couldn't help but wonder what Mo's lips would feel like against hers. Now was definitely the wrong time to be contemplating Mo's lips.

Maybe they could sleep in shifts. Or she could subtly place a line of pillows down the middle of the bed and hope Mo would wear pajamas. Fortunately there was plenty of room for two in a king-size bed.

"Mo, I don't know about this. Your girlfriend—"

"Will understand," Mo finished. "And you'd do the same for me."

If she kept fighting, Mo would guess the reason she was uncomfortable. "Okay, but I'm paying." Kate slid her credit card across the counter.

Mo handed Luis her credit card as well. "We'll split the charges."

"You're going to have to let me make this up to you."

"And you're going to have to relax," Mo returned. She grinned, "We're on vacation."

Relaxing wasn't on the menu if she was sharing Mo's bed. Kate sighed. "Thank you."

"You're welcome. We're going to have so much fun."

Fun. Well, that wasn't the first word to come to mind. Kate looked away from the front desk and took in the surroundings for the first time. Past the lobby was a courtyard and beyond this a sparkling pond. A huge fountain claimed the center of the courtyard with palms and flowering bushes around the periphery. Wicker sofas were set out under a canopy and brightly colored birds darted between the canopy and the trees, their songs mingling with the fountain spray.

Kate had spent the weeks following their dinner at Mario's agonizing over this trip. Sleeping with Mo every night was certainly going to complicate her plans to rebuild their friendship.

"What are you thinking about?" Mo asked. "You look serious."

"I always look serious."

Mo chuckled. "You're right. But we're on vacation, remember?"

Kate pointed to the bulletin board behind the concierge's desk. "I wonder what the prize is for the Ping-Pong tournament."

"Ping-Pong?" The excitement in Mo's voice was endearing. "Remember those game nights we used to have in the dorms? Julia was a master. Maybe we can all sign up for the tournament. I bet Julia can convince Reed. We can play teams. Although we probably won't stand a chance against them."

Playing Ping-Pong with Mo would be innocent enough, but being on the same team was probably a bad idea. Kate scanned the other activities listed on the board. If she planned it out, she could fill her days with everything from exploring Mayan ruins to scuba diving to evening dance classes.

"Or what about salsa classes?" Mo said, her gaze on the bulletin board as well. "You're a way better dancer than I am but...I've taken a few salsa classes and I always like picking up more."

As much as she wanted to say yes, Kate knew her limits. "Salsa's at the same time as the Ping-Pong tournament."

"We could try a night of each."

When Kate didn't respond, Mo started throwing out other suggestions for their nighttime activities including karaoke. Finally she stopped Mo with: "Maybe we should find out what activities the others want to do."

As soon as the words were out of her mouth, Kate wished she could take them back. Mo's expression had gone from relaxed to confused to indecipherable. Whatever her emotion, she hid it with a chuckle that didn't reach her eyes.

"Okay, I get it. Look, I know you're not excited about this room thing. If there's a sofa, I'll take it." Mo's tone had dulled. "I'll try and give you as much space as you need."

"I didn't mean that." *Space.* Mo had picked that word deliberately. Kate thought of the night she'd told Mo about the opportunity in Denver: *"I think this will be good for me. I feel like I need some space to figure myself out."* Her words had haunted her for days. She'd seen the change in Mo that night and the distance she'd instantly put between them.

Seconds ticked by. Kate knew she needed to fix this before it went any further. She had to decide to be friends or she needed to get on a plane headed home. The first step was being honest. No games.

"Actually salsa classes sound fun. I'd love to take a class with you."

Mo held her gaze for a long moment but didn't say anything. Finally she turned back to the bulletin board. "I don't know. Now I'm thinking I'd rather beat you at Ping-Pong."

Mo's tone—back to joking—eased the tension. "How about this: one round of Ping-Pong and winner decides whether we take a salsa class together."

Mo didn't hesitate. "I'm so beating you."

"You do remember that I'm the one that's good with balls, right?"

Mo laughed and the sound filled Kate's chest. She looked up at Mo and saw the smile lines she'd missed. Mo's deep brown eyes held hers. "I've missed that smile."

"Is that all you missed?"

"Pretty much."

Mo laughed again. After a moment she said, "With Reed and Julia getting engaged, it feels right that we're all here together—you know, to celebrate."

"You hate weddings."

"Not true," Mo said. "I hate the idea of marriage. I've got nothing against a good party. You know, maybe this whole reservation mess-up is fate wanting us to spend time together. Rebuild our friendship and all that."

"We're spending a week on a tiny island. I think fate is overthinking this if we need to be in the same bed."

Mo was still chuckling when Luis cleared his throat. "Okay, senoritas. You are all set." He handed the card keys to Mo along with a resort map with their bungalow circled in red. "I hope you enjoy your stay. *Bienvenidas a Cozumel.*"

"*Gracias,*" Mo said. She turned to Kate and bounced on her toes. "Should we come up with a secret knock?"

Kate couldn't help but smile. "You're such a dork."

"Sexy dork and I know it," Mo replied. She started out of the lobby, tugging her suitcase behind her as she did an exaggerated swagger. The result was one part ridiculous and one part charming. She looked over her shoulder and said, "Come on, slow poke. The ocean's waiting."

There was no direct path from the lobby to their bungalow. Instead a maze of winding walkways led from the courtyard behind the lobby through a dense jungle. Broadleaf plants and palms grew like walls on either side and the space was filled with a buzz of insects along with noisy chirps of birds. Every ten yards or so a new path sprouted off the main one and a clump of bungalows came into view. After they crossed a bridge and another clump of bungalows, Mo stopped to scan the map.

"I think we go left here." Mo turned the map upside down and then looked at where the path split ahead. "Or maybe right. Whoever designed this place couldn't have been sober. And the mapmaker was definitely high."

"I seem to recall getting lost with you more than once. Maybe we shouldn't blame the mapmaker."

Mo's mouth dropped open. "You better be offering to help, because otherwise…"

Kate laughed. "Let me see the map."

Instead of handing it over, Mo pointed to a building on the map. "Here's the lobby." She traced one of the yellow lines. "I think we're here. What do you think, map guru?"

Kate had deliberately kept a good distance between her and Mo since they'd left the lobby. Straining to see the map from two feet away was awkward, so she moved one step closer and leaned over Mo's arm. As soon as she caught a hint of Mo's musky cologne, the impulse to take a deep breath was impossible to ignore. Her body was doing her no favors.

A mess of rectangles, wavy lines, and triangles taunted her. All she wanted to do was reach for Mo. How was she possibly going to sleep in the same bed?

"So, right or left?"

She looked up from the map and realized Mo was squinting at her.

"You okay?"

"I'm fine. Where was the lobby again?"

"Here." Mo pointed to one of the rectangles and then eyed Kate again. "Maybe you're dehydrated. We're a lot closer to the equator and the sun can really get to you."

"I'm not dehydrated." Distracted, yes. And she was already tired of her mind's refrain: *Mo has a girlfriend. She's not interested.*

"Maybe we should find some water anyway. Or maybe something with a little umbrella in it."

Something with a little umbrella would be dangerous at the moment. Kate tried to concentrate. "This place has five swimming pools. Five swimming pools but no extra bungalows."

"I really don't mind sharing. I think this is going to be fun."

Kate sighed. "I just feel like an idiot for getting the dates wrong."

"But I get to feel like I saved the day." Mo puffed up her chest, looking every bit the dashing hero.

Kate rolled her eyes. "Let's say that was my plan all along." Mo being sweet and trying to take care of her wasn't going to make this week any easier. She eyed the map again. "Okay, according to this, the spa is next to our bungalow."

"After that flight, I could use a massage."

"Me too," Kate agreed.

"You're in luck," a woman's voice behind them said. "They're running a special on couples massage."

Kate turned around. A shock of red hair and a perfect smile met her gaze. The woman was wearing a pair of army green capris and a white tank top that showed off her sculpted arms. From the wrists up, her skin was covered with a heavy coating of colorful tattoos.

"I'm Terri." She stuck out her hand. "You two are Kate and Mo, right? Julia told me all about you."

Julia had mentioned that one of Reed's doctor friends would be joining them, but she had neglected to mention that she was a hot femme. By the long look she was giving Mo, there was no question that she was gay.

Kate shook Terri's hand as she introduced herself, though she doubted that was necessary. If Julia had told Terri about them, she'd probably included the details that Mo was tall, black, athletic, and androgynous while Kate was six inches shorter, white, and, by Julia's description, a very much cis-gendered blonde.

Mo held the map out for Terri to point out the hot tubs and the spa. Terri was explaining something about the massages and Kate felt a spark of jealousy. She knew Mo wasn't looking for a date and she certainly wasn't the type to cheat, but Terri was flirting hardcore. She had half a mind to tell Terri to tone it down.

"Two-for-one's a good deal," Terri finished, interrupting Kate's thoughts. "Since I'm here alone, I thought I'd practice my pickup lines. I mean, who can pass up a BOGO?"

"For real," Mo said.

Kate forced a smile. Everyone flirted with Mo. It was a matter of course. But when she looked over at Mo, she realized that Mo was looking back at her, not Terri.

"I'm game for a couples massage," Mo said. "What do you think?"

Kate ran through a list of possible answers. No way was she signing up for a massage with Mo, but she needed an out that wouldn't raise suspicion. "I think you wouldn't have any trouble finding someone to be your better half."

Mo laughed. "Damn, that's low."

Terri looked from Mo to Kate. "You two must know each other pretty well."

"Sometimes too well," Kate agreed.

"But apparently not well enough to strip down and let someone rub massage oil on us at the same time," Mo added.

Kate knew Mo was trying to goad her. She decided to one-up her: "Are you going to dare me? I'm not scared of a little massage oil."

"If it was a dare, would you say yes?"

"I'd want to know the parameters first," Kate returned. Mo held her gaze. Every time she tried to out-tease Mo, it backfired, but this time she wanted to risk it.

"Good call," Terri said. "Like what do you win exactly? Is a happy ending involved?"

Mo held up her hand. "Okay, that might have been one step too far."

Terri winked at Kate. "Looks like we called her bluff. On that note, I'll let you two get settled. I think the plan is for us all to meet up for dinner to celebrate Julia and Reed's engagement, but I'm sure we'll run into each other again before then."

Mo watched until Terri had disappeared beyond the bend in the path. "She seems nice."

"She's friendly, that's for sure."

Mo looked sideways at her. "You don't like her? According to Reed, Terri's brilliant. A pediatric internist or something like that. She treated Carly when she was so sick. And she's into triathlons. Travels all over to compete. You two would make a good match."

"She was flirting with you—not me."

"So you're not interested?" Mo pressed.

"Unlike you, I'm not into every woman I see."

"Hmm. Your loss." Mo grinned. "So did we decide on right or left?"

Kate crumpled the map. "Let's try left. We'll either find the bungalow or we'll run into a bar."

"Perfect. After we settle in, I want to go swimming." Mo maneuvered her rolling suitcase around the curve. "I wonder when they'll find your suitcase. You pack any pajamas in that little carry-on?"

Kate stopped walking and hastily called to mind all the steps she'd gone through in her decision process for allocating items to her suitcase and the carry-on. "Dammit."

"No pj's?"

Aside from a pair of underwear and a bathing suit, she'd packed all her other clothes in the suitcase that was probably still on a runway in Dallas, where they had switched planes. "Can you loan me some?"

"I don't wear pajamas. They say you sleep better naked."

"Does that line usually work?"

Mo looked back at her. "You'd be surprised."

"With you, nothing would surprise me."

"Careful, that almost sounded like a compliment." Mo winked. "We passed a little bodega after we left the lobby. I bet they sell pajamas there. And I promise I'll at least keep my boxers on. I don't want to make you uncomfortable."

The thought of Mo lying next to her in bed in nothing but a pair of boxers didn't exactly make her uncomfortable. She sighed. It was going to be a long five days.

CHAPTER FIVE

The bungalow was clearly meant as a love nest. Aside from the fact that the bed took up almost all of the space in the room and had a headboard perfect for gripping, the print above the bed was a geometric design in dark reds, oranges, and yellows that was conspicuously suggestive of two people having sex. One look and Kate couldn't stop herself from thinking of how Mo was supposed to be here with her girlfriend. This was supposed to be their love nest. At least she didn't have a visual of Chantal. She'd deliberately avoided looking her up online.

"You sure Chantal is going to be okay with this?"

Mo popped open her suitcase. "Yeah. Totally. Which side of the bed do you want?"

"I don't care. You pick."

Mo pulled out a sports bra, looked at it for a moment, then tossed it on the bed. "You keep asking if Chantal is going to be okay, but are you okay with this?"

"Yes…but I want you to ask her."

"Okay." Mo pulled out a pair of swimming trunks. "I'll call her before I hit the beach. You coming?"

"I'm going to look for pajamas first."

"Right. Pajamas." Mo held up a T-shirt. "If you don't find anything, I can loan you a shirt."

"Thanks, but I don't think you want to see that much of my butt."

"You've got a nice butt. You could show it off more." There was a pause and then Mo said, "I don't mean that you should show it off in bed—to me. It's just a nice butt." She stammered. "But obviously it's yours, and you don't have to show it off to anyone."

Kate couldn't help smiling. Mo's comment about her butt didn't embarrass her. In fact, in a strange way it took off some of the pressure. "So I shouldn't buy sexy pajamas?"

Mo chuckled and looked down at her suitcase. "No comment."

"I like it when your nerdiness overwhelms your coolness."

"You calling me a nerd?"

"You have your moments, Math Whiz." Kate was tempted to say more, but they had to sleep together later. The lines between friendly banter and flirting had to stay clear. She picked up her purse. "Call your girlfriend."

"Right. Will do." Mo smiled. "Go find some super unsexy pajamas."

The bodega had plenty of sunscreen, T-shirts, flip-flops, and hats along with a disordered collection of brightly colored ceramic bowls and vases. There was a short rack of dresses, one of which caught Kate's eye, but unfortunately no pajamas, sexy or unsexy.

When she asked about other clothing stores, the young woman working the register gave her a confused look. She tried to get her point across in Spanish, managing to ask for a store that sold clothes to sleep in, and was directed over to a stand of pastel tank tops clearly meant as a cover-up over a bathing suit. Although the bottom hem made it to her knees, the neckline dropped low enough to be indecent and the armholes were large enough to show off a good amount of breast. Unfortunately, she didn't have much choice.

Along with the cover-up, she decided on one of the dresses as well. Until her luggage showed up, she couldn't be picky. She paid for the items and then spotted Julia outside the shop. She'd paused to admire a beaded necklace hanging in the window, and the sight of her made Kate's spirits rise.

She tapped on the glass and Julia looked up.

"There you are!"

Kate stepped out of the bodega and into Julia's hug. "Congratulations again. I loved the look on Reed's face when you said yes. You two are so perfect together I almost forgot you weren't already married."

"She's asked me so many times that it became this joke but then I realized she actually had a ring this time." Julia beamed. "I still feel like I'm floating."

"I'm happy for both of you. It really is perfect."

"Speaking of perfect—Mo told me you two are bunking together. How'd that happen?"

"Not perfect and you know it." Kate stuck out her tongue and Julia laughed. She knew Julia was only teasing her, but guilt settled on her shoulders at the suggestion that this was what she'd want. And didn't part of her want it? "I screwed up and booked the wrong dates. Mo took pity on me and is letting me sleep with her but I know it's going to be weird and awkward…"

"You two need to reconnect—this could be fate."

Kate shook her head. "I don't think it's fate. I think it was me making a dumb mistake. And now I'm worried about Mo's girlfriend. I asked Mo to call her to make sure she was okay with it. Mo insists she won't mind, but I'm not so sure."

Julia seemed to consider it for a moment. "It's not like you're some random woman she just met. You're old friends."

"And I really don't want to cause a problem for Mo."

"Chantal's not Tanya. I really think she'd be fine with it."

"What's she like?" Kate hated asking, but she couldn't help it.

Julia pursed her lips together. "Maybe the less you know, the better."

"Just tell me. Gorgeous?"

"You know Mo's type. Successful, confident, charming…"

"And gorgeous," Kate finished. What had she expected? In some ways it was easier knowing Chantal was perfect. Anyway, if Mo wasn't with Chantal, she'd be with another perfect woman. Perfect wasn't her.

Julia clicked her tongue. "Maybe you two shouldn't share a bed after all. I don't think you need to put yourself through that."

"I'll be fine."

"Okay, but if tonight doesn't go well...we can squish the kids into one of the beds and you can have the other. Or we can lay blankets on the floor and tell them they're camping."

"It's probably good to have a backup plan." Kate smiled wryly. "Anyway, at least now I have pajamas." She held up the bag from the bodega.

"I forgot all about the lost luggage! You sure you don't want to sleep naked with the woman you've had a crush on for sixteen years?"

"Very funny, Jules. Now show me your ring—I barely got a look at it earlier." And at the moment she needed a distraction.

Julia stretched out her hand. A gorgeous diamond sparkled in a platinum setting. The diamond wasn't massive like some of the engagement rings she'd seen, but it was clearly an expensive cut and the delicate ring was perfect for Julia's petite hand.

"It's lovely. Reed has good taste. Are you getting her an engagement ring too?"

"She doesn't want anything until we actually get married. And she's not exactly the diamond type. I think she'll just want a simple gold band."

"Or she could go with platinum to match yours," Kate suggested.

"We should bring you with us to the jeweler's when the time comes."

"Shopping is definitely one thing I'm qualified to do." Kate immediately began considering different styles of wedding bands that Reed might like. Reed was definitely the butch one of the pair, but Kate could imagine her wearing a diamond in the right setting. "What if you got her something little to celebrate before the actual wedding...a pair of earrings? Or a necklace?"

Julia squeezed Kate's hand. "That's what I was thinking. But she's really hard to shop for. Can you help me pick something out?"

"We can go into town later and do some shopping. I have a feeling I'll be running low on outfits soon."

"Any chance you brought a swimsuit? The ocean's perfect and I think everyone will be down there for the sunset."

"No pajamas but I brought a bikini. I don't always make the best choices."

"Or maybe your subconscious was trying to help you out. Now go put your bikini on. You have to try and relax—this is your vacation. You can't spend all of it worrying about Mo."

The water wasn't turquoise at sunset, but a silvery gold and smooth as a sheet. Kate sat on the wet sand, her feet stretched to the cool water. The sound of the gentle waves brushing the shore was as soothing as the slow turn of a rain stick. She watched the yellow orb inch lower on the horizon, picking out shades of pink and orange it left behind.

Julia and Reed stood together, arms wrapped around each other, while the twins bobbed in life jackets a few feet away. Mo swam in a circle around them.

"Aunt Kate! Over here!" Bryn waved her hand. "Aunt Mo's a shark!"

"You better watch out then." Kate laughed when Mo suddenly popped out of the water and Bryn shrieked.

"Aunt Kate, why aren't you swimming?" Carly hollered.

"I'm scared of sharks." It was a plausible excuse.

"She's a robot shark. Not a real shark," Carly called back.

At that moment, Mo broke into robot mode. In fact she looked nothing like a robot shark, but the dance she did around the girls was hilarious. Kate laughed as Carly and Bryn squealed and Mo jerked from robot position to shark mode.

"Mind if I join you?"

Kate looked up at Terri's voice. "Sure."

Terri dropped down on the sand. "You've got the best spot. Isn't that gorgeous?" She nodded to the shimmer of gold that was the edge of the sun. In a minute it would be gone.

"It's beautiful."

"I love sunsets. But I never take the time to watch them unless I'm on vacation. On my last trip here, I took a picture every night. Then I hung the photos up around my office. Instead of enjoying the sunset out my window, I look at the pictures on the wall." Terri sighed.

"We're all so busy...that's why we go on vacation."

"Good point."

"There it goes." Kate held her breath until the sun dipped below the horizon. She exhaled, her body finally relaxing. "Watching sunsets every day ought to be good for your health. Like drinking eight glasses of water."

"I'm sure it is," Terri said. "The research just needs to be done."

"We should start a study."

The pink and orange streaks gave way to shades of purple. Kate wished she'd brought her phone to snap a shot, but she doubted the colors would look as vibrant in a photo. Unconsciously, her gaze tracked back to Mo. She'd stopped doing her robot dance to watch the sunset as well and was standing in waist-deep water, her back to Kate.

"How long were you two together?"

Kate glanced at Terri. "Mo and I? Oh no. We've never dated."

"Really? Reed and Julia told me you were single, but I thought...well, it seemed like you two must have dated at some point."

"We're just friends."

"Hmm. I think I'd have trouble being *just* friends with someone like her. She's beautiful, funny..."

"FYI, she prefers handsome to beautiful." Why was she giving Terri tips?

"Well, she's that too. You really never considered dating?"

Kate hesitated for a moment too long. She knew she should simply lie, but the words wouldn't come to her lips. Terri cocked her head. "You're sure there's nothing going on between you two?"

"Definitely not. She's got a girlfriend." Kate focused on Terri, stopping herself from looking for Mo's outline again. "But even if she didn't, we've been friends since college. We know each other too well to ever date."

"Meaning you're past the point of falling for each other? Or do you already know all her issues?"

"In this case, I'm the one with all the issues." And Mo didn't know the half of it. "But I was thinking more about the first option." Kate wondered if it was true that they were past the point of romantic love. Maybe Mo was…

Reed and Julia came out of the water, each tugging a kid behind them. As the kids complained about being cold, Terri hopped up to fetch towels. Kate didn't get up to help. Moments like that were precisely when she doubted that she was parent material. If those were her kids, she would have pointed to the towel stand and told Carly and Bryn to go get them and stop with their griping.

Mo swam toward shore, and when she got out of the water, Terri brought her a towel too. When Mo smiled her thanks, Kate stood up.

Before anyone could ask where she was going, she started down the beach. The sandy strip separating the ocean from the dark green trees stretched as far as she could see. She wanted to walk until she'd cleared her mind, but long before that was likely to happen, she'd have to turn back and face the evening. Why had she agreed to sleeping with Mo?

CHAPTER SIX

The buffet table was overflowing—enchiladas, two different types of chicken, roasted potatoes, black beans, rice, prawns, fried plantains, all the fixings for tacos, and a bottomless vat of guacamole. And that was only the first of the four buffet tables. Kate felt her anxiety mounting as she considered the likely calories of each dish. Whenever it was possible, she avoided restaurants with the all-you-can-eat option, but she'd have to face this every night for the rest of the week.

After two circles around, she decided on salad and a chicken breast covered in a mysterious brown sauce that smelled like molé. The baskets of bread called out to her, but she bypassed that table as well as the desserts, not letting her mouth even consider the brownies drizzled in dark chocolate and topped with perfect little peaks of whip cream.

As soon as she sat down, Mo eyed her plate. "The chicken's good. Not too spicy, but there's a little kick." She'd gone for the two-plate option and had a spoonful of nearly everything. One of the brownies was on a napkin next to her plate.

"You must be hungry."

Mo held up her fork, a prawn skewered on the prongs. "Famished. If you get bored with your salad, I can give you some pointers on what else to eat."

"I'll let you know."

"Mind if I sit here?" Terri asked, indicating the open seat between Mo and Kate.

Kate had purposefully left the seat open, hoping one of the kids would take it, but now she regretted her decision. If Terri and Mo started flirting… "Of course."

"You go for the minimalist approach to buffets like Bryn," Reed said. She pointed to Bryn's plate and then to Kate's as she sat down opposite her.

Kate looked over at Bryn's selection. One piece of fried chicken and one potato was on her plate. "I guess so. But at least I eat my veggies."

"Think you can talk to Bryn about that?"

Kate smiled when Bryn looked her direction. "Do you know why carrots are good for your eyes?"

Bryn shook her head.

"Neither do I. But you never see a rabbit wearing glasses."

Bryn and Carly both laughed and then begged for another joke. Kate scooped up a bite of salad and said, "Okay, one more. But only if you promise to try one vegetable from the buffet tomorrow." When Bryn nodded, she said, "I used to think this one was hilarious when I was your age: Why did the waiter get embarrassed?"

"Why?" Mo asked.

Kate looked up from her salad and with Mo's eyes on her, she nearly forgot the punchline.

"Why, Aunt Kate?" Bryn asked.

Kate tried to focus on Bryn. "Because he saw the salad dressing."

Bryn's brow furrowed. Between giggles, Carly said, "The salad *dressing*, get it? *Dressing*? 'Cause the salad was naked." She'd whispered the word "naked" and then clapped her hand over her mouth.

"That was pretty good," Mo said. "I didn't know you told jokes."

"I was saving you from the agony. My dad used to tell jokes at the dinner table all the time. He had a little book."

"You're lucky," Terri said. "My dad was usually too drunk to sit down at the dinner table." She raised her glass, which Kate had noticed was filled with soda, and said, "How about a toast? To Reed and Julia, for getting engaged and bringing us all to Mexico to celebrate. You're paying for all of this, right?"

When the laughter died down, Mo raised her glass and said, "One more toast." She looked over at Julia and Reed. "I thought having Julia and Kate in my life was enough trouble for me, but then Reed and these crazy kids came along. I seriously don't know how I got on before without all of you guys. I must have been a disaster."

Mo made a silly face at Carly, who was sticking out her tongue. "Terri, full disclosure, when you join this family you are officially weird."

"Oh, good." Terri looked over at Carly and stuck out her tongue. Everyone laughed.

"To the families we make along the way," Mo finished.

As they all clinked glasses, Kate felt Mo's gaze on her. "That was perfect."

"I can be even more cheesy if I put my mind to it," Mo said.

"Lord help us," Terri murmured.

"Hey, I heard that." Mo wagged her finger. "I know you've been Reed's friend for about a hundred years, but you've only been part of my family for a few hours. I don't think you get to make sarcastic comments yet."

Kate raised her glass to clink Terri's. "I'm glad you're here. I often need backup with Mo."

Terri winked. "We can take her together."

"Uh-uh," Mo said. "You two are definitely not allowed to team up against me."

"Actually, I think that's a good plan," Julia said. "But only because I know you can handle two women at a time, Mo."

"We've all heard the stories," Kate added.

Mo opened and closed her mouth, clearly flustered, as everyone else, save the kids, laughed. She looked between Kate and Terri then and said, "All right. Game on."

The rest of the meal was filled with banter between Terri and Mo. Kate only had to add in a few words of encouragement to get them going and every time she said anything, she seemed to make both of them laugh. If she didn't know better, she'd swear they were both vying for her. She tried not to think of what it might mean on either account and decided instead to enjoy their playful teasing.

It wasn't until everyone started handing off their plates to the servers, clearly signaling that dinner was over, that she remembered where she was sleeping. As much as she wanted to collapse in bed, travel-weary with the delays and the unsuccessful search for her luggage, she wasn't ready to climb into bed with Mo.

Reed and Julia filed off with the kids first and then Terri stood up and stretched. "I think it's my bedtime too. Snorkeling's still the plan tomorrow, right?"

Mo rattled off the details since she'd been the one to set up the boat. "We'll meet down at the dock at nine."

"Perfect." Terri held up her hand. "See you on the boat."

When she was out of earshot, Mo said, "You seem to be warming up to Terri."

"I think I misjudged her at first."

"Does that mean you like her?" Mo raised an eyebrow.

"I like her just fine. But not like you're insinuating."

"What am I insinuating?"

"That I want to sleep with her." Kate took a sip of her drink. "Do you think she's a recovering alcoholic?"

"Maybe. Does that bother you?"

"No." It didn't. But thinking about alcoholism brought up memories of her father that she didn't want to consider.

"You sure?"

Kate nodded. She thought of her father and all the nights she'd watched him drink himself to sleep in his armchair. The urge to tell Mo the truth battled with a cop-out answer. Steering clear of alcoholics had been only one of many side effects of the summers she'd spent with Philip. But she'd never told Mo about Philip. As far as Mo knew, Gary—the one who told silly jokes at dinner and had helped move her into the college dorm room—was her dad. It seemed too late now to say that he was actually her stepdad.

"Honestly, I didn't like her at first because she was flirting with you."

Mo picked up her glass and took a sip. She was drinking sangria and seemed to be savoring it, having only half-finished the one glass. She looked down at the swirl of wine and said, "I didn't expect you to say that."

"I'm trying to get better at being honest with you."

"Should I ask why or just say thank you?"

"I figure that at this point I don't have much to lose." The words slipped out, but Kate instantly regretted them. "Can I take that back? I know you're going to ask what I mean by that and I don't want to have that conversation."

Mo studied her for a moment. "Sure… Why talk about feelings?"

Mo's tone had been playful earlier, but Kate felt the bite in her words now. She looked down at her napkin. "That wasn't what I was saying."

"I hate to break it to you, but Terri likes you—not me."

Earlier, Kate would have argued that no femme would pick her over Mo. But now she wasn't so sure. Maybe Terri was attracted to her. She didn't know how she felt about that. Not once had she been attracted to anyone as feminine as she was.

"Whatever." Mo leaned back in her chair. "I don't want to argue."

"We're not arguing." Except maybe they were. Not about Terri. This was about not admitting feelings and not being honest with each other. And it wasn't the first time this topic had flared between them. Kate thought again about the night she'd told Mo she was moving to Denver and all the things she hadn't said. Mo had asked for the truth then and she'd lied instead. What good would the truth do?

"The thing is, I have a little more experience with women than you do."

Kate gave her a tight-lipped smile. "Are we going to have a birds-and-bees sort of conversation here? 'Cause maybe I should grab a pen so I can take notes."

"Go ahead. I'll wait." Mo cracked a smile when Kate looked up to meet her eyes. "She likes you. Why not take a chance?"

Kate shook her head. "I'm not as good at dating as you are."

"Is that a compliment?"

"Actually, it is," Kate said. "You're amazing at connecting with total strangers. You can talk to anyone. I wish I had your skill."

"Are you kidding? That's half your job—you get total strangers to open their wallets and give you millions of dollars."

Kate considered this. "You're right. I do. But I'm not dating them."

"Remember my ex, Tanya?"

"How could I forget? What a piece of work... Did she ever give back your lucky Niners sweatshirt?"

"No. Thank you for hating her for me. I appreciate that." Mo continued, "She told me one time that I was good at dating because I had no intention of falling in love. It was all a game."

"Do you think she was right?" More than once Kate had thought the same thing about Mo's love life, but she never dared voiced it aloud. It wasn't that Mo didn't seem to love whoever she was dating at the moment, but she moved on without a hitch. Or so it seemed. No one had ever caught her heart.

"I didn't at the time. Now I'm not so sure. Anyway, like you said, she was a piece of work. I'm glad I got out when I did—although she was fun naked."

"That I didn't need to know."

Mo laughed. "I love how quick you blush when sex comes up. I just mention the word 'naked' and your ears are red."

"Whatever." Kate stuck out her tongue, but this time joking didn't dispel the awkwardness of the moment. The tension from earlier still hung between them and she couldn't help thinking about getting into bed with Mo later. "Was Chantal okay with us sharing a room?"

Mo reached for her drink. "I tried calling but she didn't answer."

"So she doesn't know?"

"She'll be fine with it. Don't worry."

But something about Mo's tone made Kate more worried than she was before. Nothing was going to happen—she knew that—but why was Mo suddenly acting evasive? Mo turned to look at a passing waiter carrying a tray of cocktails and then murmured something about drunk tourists. Maybe she hadn't wanted to tell Chantal? Regardless, sleeping was going to be even harder now.

"I'm beat. Want to call it a night?"

Kate shook her head. "I need to wind down. I was thinking of going for another walk on the beach."

"We're in Mexico and it's probably pitch dark down at the water. Do you think it's a good idea for you to go walking alone?"

"You sound like my mom." Mo's protective tone hit a nerve. She was fine on her own.

Mo's jaw clenched. A long minute passed with Mo only glaring at the remnants of her sangria. Finally she polished off the last sip and stood up. "I'll see you later."

Kate watched her leave, wishing she could rewind their conversation. Mo's disdain for Eileen, who never hid her homophobia and only pretended not to be racist, was deep-seated. She could have guessed how her offhanded comment would land. And now a walk did seem like a stupid idea. But until Mo had fallen asleep, going back to the room wasn't an option either.

The waiter approached and Kate absently nodded when he asked if she wanted more sangria. She felt conspicuous sitting alone at one of the few big tables, but moving to a smaller table would be strange too. She thought of sitting at the bar but that came with a risk of some stranger hitting on her. Sighing, she stared at the oversized tank against the back wall with brightly colored fish darting between clumps of coral and resolved to take her drink with her on a walk around the resort as soon as the waiter returned. Her phone buzzed and she clicked open the text. A picture of Peeves stared back at her. Her house sitter had kept the promise of sending pictures and Kate needed to see Peeves's face now more than ever—even if the shot was of him peeing.

"Do you want to play Ping-Pong?"

Kate looked up at Mo.

"I thought you might want to brush up before the tournament."

Whatever her reason for coming back, Kate was certain that a game of Ping-Pong wasn't it. "You think I'm the one who needs to brush up on my game?"

"Maybe I need to do the brushing up." She sat down on the chair next to Kate. "Actually I came back because I don't want to fight with you. And I don't even know why we were fighting."

"I don't want to fight either." Kate wanted to wrap her arms around Mo. Instead she held up her phone. The picture of Peeves peeing on a tire was still on the screen. "Look what my house sitter sent me."

The car attached to the tire was a fancy BMW and the message below the picture said: *Have you ever noticed how he always pees on the nicest cars on the street?*

Mo read the text and chuckled. "That is totally true. Peeves is a car snob."

The waiter returned with a glass of sangria and Kate waited until he'd left to turn to Mo. "Thank you for coming back. You're nothing like my mom and I'm sorry I said that."

"Don't think I'm letting you off the hook on this Ping-Pong just cause you said sorry. Not with you acting all cocky about it."

Kate stood up. "After I beat you, you're going to wish you didn't say that."

Mo led the way to the Ping-Pong tables, two of which were set up under an overhang off to the side of the main lobby. The space was open to the evening breeze on two sides but protected from the rain. Mo picked out a ball and tossed it to Kate. "Now you're going to have to prove your skill."

Kate waved one of the paddles in the air. "Oh, I know I'm good."

"I bet I have more practice with paddles."

Kate opened and closed her mouth, saw the twitch of a smile on Mo's lips and then couldn't hold back her own laugh. "All right, you. Prepare to get your butt whipped."

"You may have to talk to my girlfriend about that."

"You're incorrigible." Kate tossed the ball up. She swung the paddle, whacking the ball over the net.

"I can be. But I don't get too many complaints." Mo returned the serve, grinning.

Kate ignored Mo long enough to score a point, which wasn't hard since Mo began bouncing back and forth on her toes as soon as a popular Spanish pop song came on the speakers at the corners of the overhang. They played until Kate had scored ten points to Mo's three and Mo tossed her paddle on the table.

"You're supposed to play until eleven points, you know."

"I'm forfeiting. I can't think with this music." She pointed to the speakers that had started to play an old Christina Aguilera song.

"You don't have to think in Ping-Pong. It's pretty much the point. The ball comes at you and you whack it." Kate paused. "But I get it. You don't want to lose to me."

Mo let out a mock gasp and Kate laughed. Not only was she having fun with Mo, she wasn't thinking of kissing her at all. It was working.

"This was a warm-up game. How do you know I'm not one of those pool-shark types who reel you in with an easy win before they ask if you want to play for money?"

"Because we both know you're not that good with balls. Remember?"

Mo chuckled. "Just wait until that tournament." She rolled her shoulders and then rocked her head side to side as if she was getting ready for that match. Then she crouched low, did a fake backhand strike, and followed with a cheer and a celebratory dance as if she'd scored the winning point.

"Wait, did we say winner decides on the salsa classes? Don't count on getting out of that," Kate said.

Mo came around to Kate's side of the table, still dancing and cheering for herself in the way that kids do when they think no one's looking after they've netted a basketball. She stopped a few feet away from Kate and then met her eyes, still grinning. "Who says I want to get out of salsa classes?" She reached for the second paddle that Kate had set on the table and bumped Kate's hip playfully with the side of her thigh. "I plan on impressing you. You oughta see these hips move."

The Ping-Pong ball rolled away once Mo had moved the paddle and Kate caught it before it fell off the table. She held it up when Mo tried to snatch it from her hand. "I've seen your hips move. It's your feet I'm worried about."

"Ouch!" Mo feigned a wounded look for a moment and then snatched the ball out of Kate's hand as soon as she let down her guard. "For your information, I've gotten a lot better since college. You haven't been to a dance club with me. I got some moves."

The sensation of Mo's hand brushing her wrist left Kate breathless and unsteady. She played off her reaction by spinning on her heel. "Whatever. We'll see who has the moves."

Mo caught up to her before she'd gone far. She swung her arm around Kate's shoulders and said, "That was fun. Thanks."

A warmth filled Kate's chest. She wanted to blame the floating sensation on the sangria but she knew better. Daring herself to go for it, she turned to smile at Mo. Mo gave her a quick wink in return, then pulled her arm off Kate's shoulders, and shot several paces forward. She turned around, facing Kate, and said, "I'm going to beat you to the bungalow. I want the shower first."

Kate chose the longest path back to the bungalow, skirting by the pools and then the ocean, now a blue so deep it was almost black with a sliver of moonlight glinting on the surface. She pictured Mo doing her celebration dance and couldn't hold back a smile. It wasn't fair that she liked everything about Mo.

Mo was slipping out of the shower when she got back. She had a T-shirt and a pair of shorts on and a toothbrush in her mouth. "All yours," she said, indicating the shower.

"You brought pajamas?"

"Not exactly. But it's no problemo," Mo said, in an accent made worse by a mouthful of toothpaste.

By the time Kate had showered and changed into the long tank top she'd bought that afternoon, Mo was in bed with the lights off. Kate flipped off the bathroom light and then brushed her teeth in the dark, happy to not have to stare at her reflection. She tiptoed over to the bed and eyed the outline Mo made under the sheet. Mo had given her the side closest to the bathroom.

Kate carefully slipped under the sheet. There was a good space between Mo's side and hers, but she couldn't relax. When Mo shifted, Kate froze. She waited for Mo to say something, wondering if she'd brush against her, and then realized Mo had only turned on her side away from her. She let out a slow breath, trying to relax.

"Tonight was nice," Mo said softly. "Sleep tight."

Mo's words seemed to come from far away. Kate murmured a response and her own voice sounded thin and uneven. Their evening had been nice and she needed to leave it at that. She closed her eyes, hoping sleep would come soon.

CHAPTER SEVEN

If she let herself think about it, Kate knew she'd fallen for Mo the moment she'd met her. And every day after that Mo had given her an excuse to fall harder. Yesterday was no exception. Kate let her mind wander to their fight after dinner. It was always the same scenario. She'd make some mistake, think she'd ruined everything, and then Mo would swoop in and fix it.

Kate rolled onto her side. She stared at Mo, wondering at the ache in her chest. If it wasn't love, she didn't know what it was. But maybe it wasn't wrong to feel that sort of love for a friend? Her body answered with a sudden urge to reach out and caress Mo's cheek. What she felt went deeper than friendship, and there was no point arguing that it wasn't a problem. It was a big one.

She didn't turn away from Mo even though she knew she should. Mo's brown skin was gorgeous in the soft morning light. Kate let her gaze travel over every bit of her that the covers didn't conceal. The sleeve of her T-shirt was pushed up to her shoulder, exposing well-developed arm muscles. Past this, Kate followed the line of Mo's neck up to her jawbone. From her smooth cheeks to the curl of her eyelashes, there was nothing about Mo's face that wasn't perfect.

Kate stopped at Mo's lips. She felt a tingling sensation on her own lips as she imagined kissing her. Despite all the energy she'd spent resisting, her attraction to Mo was like a hunger pang. Ignoring it didn't make it go away. Which was exactly why she should have said no to this trip. Emphatically no.

The first wisps of daylight widened between the cracks in the blinds and Kate reluctantly climbed out of bed. As quietly as she could, she slipped to the bathroom to pee, then sat on the toilet worrying about sunscreen and which bathing suit to wear snorkeling. Then her brain kicked into gear—her luggage was still missing.

Sighing, she reached for the still damp bikini hanging on a hook by the shower. After she'd slipped into the suit, she caught her reflection in the mirror. Her usually flat belly pooched outward betraying the fact that she'd drunk too much last night. She stuck out her tongue and then turned to critique her profile.

On one hand, she knew she was pretty. People had given her compliments her entire life on the shade of her blue eyes… on her long blond hair…even on her little nose and perfect skin. But the compliments that haunted her were about her slim figure.

It was easy to explain that she stayed in shape with spin classes and daily runs. She didn't talk about the eating issues. When she was a teen, it was anorexia and later bulimia. Then she fell to the regimen of counting every gram of fat and too many hours working out. Years of counseling later, she still couldn't look a donut in the face without feeling nauseous. A light knock made her jump.

"You gonna be in there long? I have to pee."

Kate wrapped a towel around herself and then hurried to wash her hands. "All yours," she said, stepping carefully around Mo.

"Thanks." Mo shuffled past. "You sleep okay?"

"Actually, yeah. What about you?"

"Took me forever to fall asleep." Mo closed the bathroom door. "I think it was jet lag."

Or was Mo uncomfortable sharing her bed? Kate thought of how she'd memorized Mo's body that morning and felt a wave of guilt. "I'll ask at the front desk to see if any rooms open up today. I'm sure you'd sleep better alone."

"It's not you," Mo said, her voice muffled through the bathroom door. "My brain just wouldn't turn off."

"I know that feeling." But was there more to the picture? She traded the towel for the dress she'd bought yesterday as she considered pushing Mo for more of an explanation.

Mo opened the bathroom door. "That looks nice."

"Thanks." Kate looked down at the dress. At least her belly was covered. "If my luggage doesn't get here soon, I'll be wearing a new outfit every day."

"There are worse problems to have." Mo rubbed her eyes. "This is going to sound weird but... Do you think it's a problem that I'm happy Chantal's not here?"

Hearing Chantal's name threw her. Stalling, Kate opened her toiletries bag and found her hairbrush. "I guess that depends." She turned back to the mirror as she started to work out the tangles. "Are you happy because you needed some alone time?"

Mo folded her arms and let out a long breath. "Lately it doesn't seem like we ever have any fun. I was lying in bed last night thinking about playing Ping-Pong. I forgot it's supposed to be easy having fun."

"You forgot? Says the woman who goes to the grocery store and convinces the manager to blast Beyoncé over the loudspeakers so everyone can dance while they pick out apples. You're pretty much the definition of fun."

"That was a one-time thing."

Kate held her hairbrush in the air and sang, "'Cause if you like it, then you shoulda put a ring on it."

Mo laughed. "That store manager totally got into it."

"He had some moves." Kate recalled how the manager had shimmied through the produce section with his hands in the air and how the other customers had wiggled their hips. But when Mo had started to dance Kate forgot about everyone else.

Mo picked up her toothpaste and started singing the first few lines of the Beyoncé song. When Kate joined in, Mo turned to her and smiled. They made it through the chorus without missing too many of the words and when they stopped singing, Mo's gaze was still on her. "We sound pretty good."

"You sound surprised. We used to kill it on karaoke nights back in the dorms."

"Now that was fun."

"Face it—you are fun. Maybe you need to take Chantal out for karaoke."

Mo's smile faded. "She's not into that sort of thing."

"What about Ping-Pong?"

"She doesn't do games. She gives me a hard time for playing on my Xbox."

"Ping-Pong's not a computer game." Kate hesitated. Talking about Chantal felt off-limits, but Mo had opened the door. Clearly she wanted to talk. And best friends talked about the people they were dating. It shouldn't be weird. "What does she like?"

"She likes to go out and be seen. Her idea of a perfect evening is dinner at an exclusive restaurant and then drinks after with her friends. Or going to see some play or concert that's impossible to get tickets to... But there's always a million people we have to meet up with. We can't just go see a movie. We have to have a plan for the whole night. Seriously, she makes an agenda.

"She convinced me to go to a ballet last month. I just wanted to stay home. Work's been so busy. But she heard some famous actress was going to be there—Zoe somebody. Then we had to go to this after-party and everyone was talking about the ballet..."

"That doesn't sound awful."

Mo groaned. "I fell asleep."

"At the party?"

"No—during the ballet."

"You didn't!"

"Terrible, right?" Mo's look wasn't guilty however. "I couldn't help it. That music would put anyone to sleep."

"Next time she wants to go to the ballet, give her my number. I'll be a better date."

"As much as I love the idea of you stealing my girlfriend, I'm not giving you her number."

"You're the one who's not having fun with her," Kate teased.

Mo's shoulders dropped. "I don't think she's having fun either."

"Well, you're not responsible for making her happy, but maybe she'll be happier if you're happy." Helping Mo with girl troubles was not at the top of the list of things she wanted to do, but she didn't like seeing her down and all the hours of counseling she'd been through ought to be put to good use for someone at least. "The thing is, you're not the best at saying what you need. Maybe she has no idea you don't want to go out. You are the life of the party, you know."

"My mom said the same thing. Did you two talk?"

Kate gave her a sympathetic smile. "No, but you should listen to your mom. Maybe you can go out with her friends one night and then do something chill with just the two of you the next. I can tell her how bad you are at Ping-Pong. She might like winning."

"Whatever. I'll redeem myself in the rematch." Mo chuckled as Kate raised an eyebrow. She turned back to the sink and rinsed her toothbrush. "We have to be down at the dock in an hour, right?"

"Yeah and we should probably hurry if we want to grab breakfast."

"I think I'll skip breakfast. I want to make a quick call to Chantal. I was going to call before we went to bed last night, but then I realized I'd be waking her up. London's six hours ahead."

"I know it's a little after-the-fact, but can you still mention we're rooming together?"

"I'm telling you—she won't have a problem with it."

Mo's answer wasn't exactly a yes. Again Kate got the feeling that Mo didn't want to tell Chantal about the sleeping arrangements. She stopped herself from asking Mo why. Probably she was reading too much into it.

"Want me to grab you anything at the buffet?"

Mo rubbed her belly. "Maybe a pastry?"

"You got it." Kate stopped at the door and looked back at Mo. "Tell Chantal that you wish she were here—and that you're thinking of her. Sometimes when things aren't going well that's when you really need to hear that your someone misses you."

Mo held her gaze. "Thanks for the advice. I'll see you on the boat."

"I'm not convinced chili powder belongs on everything," Kate said pushing a watermelon slice to the side and snagging the last grape on the plate.

"But have you tried it?"

Terri had filled a platter of fruit and asked to Kate to help her with it when she'd sat down next to her. They'd polished off most of the grapes and berries, but Kate had avoided all the fruit coated in chili powder, including the pineapple, watermelon, and mango.

"It seems wrong." Kate shook her head.

"A lot of things seem wrong until you taste them."

Kate laughed at the obvious sexual innuendo. She had to admit that Terri was easy company and a nice distraction. Breakfast was nearly over and she'd hardly thought of Mo or the fact that she was busy talking to her girlfriend.

Terri picked out one of the mango chunks heavily doused in red. She popped the bite in her mouth and moaned her approval. "Oh, that's good. The lime brings out the sweetness of the mango and then that little burn on your tongue from the chili… Mmm. Perfection."

"It can't be that good."

"Oh, but it can." Terri speared another bite of mango and held it out. "Try it. You might never go back."

Kate debated for a moment and then reached for the fork. The sweet tangy flavor hit her tongue. "Okay, I thought the moaning was a bit much, but…that's delicious."

"Now you gotta try the pineapple."

Kate selected a pineapple chunk with an even heavier coating of chili powder. She savored the taste, smiling as Terri waited expectantly.

"Well?"

"Honestly, I think I prefer the mango this time and I'm a pineapple lover at heart so that's hard to admit. But you're right—there's something about the combination of flavors with that lime."

"I'm glad I won you over with the mango. You can have the last bite." She pushed the plate toward Kate and glanced at her watch. "We should head out soon. Where's Mo?"

"Calling her girlfriend." Kate hoped her voice sounded even. She hadn't intended on having breakfast with anyone. In fact she'd planned on sitting by herself and moping. Thanks to Terri, she hadn't moped at all.

She stood up when Terri did and only then remembered she'd promised to grab a pastry for Mo. "I have to grab something real quick."

"No problem. I should check my messages before we head out anyway. I'll wait for you."

Kate headed to the table filled with pastries while Terri checked her phone. Being with Terri could be good for her, she thought, staring at a basket overfilled with an assortment of pastries. All she needed to do was stop thinking about Mo. "Easier said than done," she mumbled, reaching for one of Mo's favorites—a sugar-dusted twist.

"This is our first dive site," the captain said, cutting the engine. "We'll be here for about an hour." As one of the two other crewmembers handed out masks and flippers he went on to detail some of the fish that they'd see. "Miguel will jump in with you. If you have any problems, wave an arm and he'll swim over or I'll circle around in the boat and get you out. Any questions?" He waited a moment, scanning the group and then said, "Okay, let's see some fish!"

Everyone started putting on their gear, but Kate felt a wave of nausea as soon as she stood up. The ride had been fairly smooth, but the constant rocking now that they'd dropped anchor made the coffee she'd downed seem like a bad idea. Or maybe it was last night's sangria. She looked up at the perfect blue sky, exhaling, and then down at the water. It was clear enough to see several feet down and she could make out coral and brightly colored flashes well below the water's surface.

"You okay?" Mo asked.

"My stomach's a little off."

"Mine too," Mo admitted. "I think I ate those pastries you gave me a little too fast. I'm hoping it's better in the water."

"You ate all three of them in about two seconds." Kate had worried that she'd brought too many, but then Mo had polished them all off before they'd even left the dock.

"I eat fast when I'm stressed."

"Was Chantal upset?"

"Not exactly." Mo sighed. "I probably shouldn't have called her. Let's just say I'm happy to spend the next hour watching fish."

"That bad, huh?"

"Sometimes I have no idea what women are thinking."

"We can be a pain in the ass. I'm not convinced we're worth all the trouble."

"I tell myself that every time I go through a breakup," Mo grumbled. "Then I turn around and ask someone else out. I don't seem to learn."

Mo had been quiet for most of the boat ride, and Kate had wondered if she was feeling sick or if her thoughts were on Chantal. Now she had to push away the guilty thought that she was glad it was girl trouble.

"You two ready for this?" Terri asked, approaching with a wide smile.

"I don't know. All that talk about sharks and I'm not so sure I want to get wet." Mo eyed the water, pretending to be nervous.

"I loved the expression on Bryn's face when you told her how the shark almost went for your camera during your last trip here," Kate said.

"I may have gotten a little carried away with that story."

"But you stopped both of them from trying to launch themselves over the boat rails." Bryn hadn't moved from her seat after Terri recounted her tiger shark encounter and Carly had seemed to hang on every word, eyeing the water as if Jaws was circling their boat. Terri clearly had a gift with kids, but Kate had enjoyed the story as well. "I know that oceanography lesson that followed was geared for the kids, but I'm ready to sign up for your class. I didn't know any of that stuff you were saying about the coral reefs. It's really interesting."

Terri smiled at the compliment. "When I was a kid I wanted to be an oceanographer. I read every book on the subject that I could get my hands on. Actually, I wanted to be a dolphin trainer, but an oceanographer sounded more professional."

"No way! I wanted to be a dolphin."

Although it was true that she'd spent years of her childhood pretending to be a dolphin, Kate immediately wished she hadn't admitted it aloud when Mo murmured, "Match made in heaven."

"The captain said it was pretty common to see dolphins in this area. Maybe we'll get lucky." Terri turned to Mo and added, "Dolphin and dolphin trainer—you're thinking it's probably someone's fetish, right?"

Mo laughed. "For real."

Kate felt the blush hit her cheeks. "For the record, it's not mine."

"It's not mine either, but now I am going to get my hopes up about seeing a dolphin," Terri said. "As long as we don't see sharks."

She adjusted the straps on her mask and then hooked on her snorkel. "If I do get taken out by a shark, don't try and save my sorry ass. I should have learned my lesson last time and stayed out of the ocean."

Kate stopped herself from saying that it wasn't a sorry ass at all. In fact, in the black and white striped bikini bottoms she was wearing, her ass was a particularly nice one.

"I'll throw you a floaty as I swim the other direction," Mo promised.

"Gee, thanks." Terri held up her middle finger as Mo laughed. She climbed down the ladder to the jump platform and then looked back over her shoulder. "They say they can smell fear, Mo."

"Oh, I'm not scared," Mo said. "I know I can outswim Kate."

Kate put her hands on her hips as she turned to Mo. "Who says I'm going to swim anywhere near you?"

Terri's green eyes caught the sunlight as she laughed. She turned back to the water and then swung her arms, warming up for a dive.

Kate admired the toned muscles on Terri's back and legs. She did have a nice butt, but she was in great shape everywhere else as well. And although it was clear she worked out, there was also a softness about her that defied the assortment of colorful tattoos on her arms and back.

She'd never been attracted to anyone as feminine, but there was something about Terri that she was drawn to. She also had to admit that it made sense to date her. Terri was everything Kate had always said she wanted—smart, funny, confident. With her being a doctor, she was probably used to being in charge and fixing problems, but she also seemed to be able to let things go and relax. She might even be able to handle dating someone with major issues.

As soon as Terri dove into the water, Kate turned to Mo. "Are you going to be jealous if I go on a date with her?"

"Can I tease you about dolphin trainer fantasies?"

Kate sighed. "Well, that answers my question."

"I was joking."

"How about don't joke this one time." Kate tried to catch Mo's eye, but she was focused on the water where Terri was swimming.

"I won't be jealous. I still feel bad about how I acted when you were with Ethan." Mo turned and met Kate's gaze. "I'm actually excited that you're interested in Terri. What changed overnight?"

Kate considered the question. She looked over at Reed and Julia. They'd been busy slathering reef-safe sunscreen on the twins, but now they'd turned to each other, clasped hands, and kissed. "Is it crazy to want that?"

"Love?" Mo shrugged. "A little crazy."

"After Ethan I got it in my head that I wasn't long-term relationship material, but the truth is, I'm not fling material either. I know I've got way too many issues to even be dating, but I can't keep stopping myself from trying."

"Everyone's got issues. Doesn't mean we don't deserve love."

Before Kate could think of how to respond, Bryn's voice pierced the calm: "I'm not putting that on!" She pushed away the mask Reed was trying to hand to her and folded her arms. "I'm not even getting in the water."

"Okay, you don't need to scream. I'm standing right here." Reed sighed and turned to Julia. "You go ahead. Maybe we can switch off after a bit."

Kate looked between Bryn and Carly, noticing their downturned faces. "What's wrong? You two don't want to snorkel?"

"They're worried about sharks." Julia held up her hands like it was a lost cause.

Terri's tiger shark tale had backfired. "Why don't both of you go?" Kate walked over and picked up the mask. She stared through it, making a fish face at Bryn until a smile finally cracked. "I want to stay on the boat for a bit anyway. I'm waiting for my stomach to stop flip-flopping."

"Is your stomach really flip-flopping?" Bryn asked. "Can I feel it?"

"Her stomach isn't really moving," Carly argued. She looked at Kate. "Is it?"

"One time I felt a baby move in someone's stomach. It was kicking." Bryn's eyes got big. "I don't want to have a baby in my stomach. Ever."

"Babies grow in your uterus, not your stomach." Without missing a beat, Reed turned to Kate. "Are you sure about watching them?"

"Yeah, it's no problem."

Carly poked Kate's side to get her attention. "I don't want a baby inside me either."

"Not even a cute little baby?"

Carly shook her head adamantly. "I'm going to adopt."

"Good idea."

"I could stay on the boat too," Mo said. "My stomach's not feeling great either."

"If you stay, Aunt Mo, who is going to look for sharks?" Bryn asked.

"You're sending Mo to look for the sharks?"

Bryn nodded at Kate. "She's tougher than you. And tougher than my moms."

"Well, no one's going to argue with that. She's so tough she'll probably scare all the sharks out of the cove."

Mo put her hands on her hips like a superhero. "With my eyes closed."

Kate smiled. "Then you can tell us when it's safe to get in the water."

"I don't think she should keep her eyes closed," Carly said, clearly concerned about the plan.

"Okay, one eye open." Mo tapped her temple. "And you all are my lookouts for shark fins."

Once the others dove into the water, Carly and Bryn claimed their lookout spots. They scanned the crystal blue water for fins and shouted every time a fish darted past, no matter how tiny.

"They're so fast," Bryn said. "I wish I could swim that fast."

"It's even more cool being in the water with them." Kate looked for Terri and then spotted Mo swimming next to her. Mo pulled the snorkel out of her mouth and said something to Terri, who immediately laughed.

Mo was only being herself. Friendly and outgoing. But Kate felt a pang of jealousy. If Terri was interested in Mo, was she really interested in her? She looked away when Carly tugged on her shirt.

"Did you know sharks lose teeth every time they bite something?"

"I wonder if it hurts," Kate said, trying to focus on Carly instead of wondering what Mo and Terri were chatting about.

Bryn's brow furrowed. "My friend Riley lost these two tooth," she jabbed her front baby teeth and then, with a finger still in her mouth, continued, "and she said it didn't hurt at all."

"Terri said sharks grow new teeth as soon as they lose them," Carly added.

"So sharks are basically as dangerous as little kids?"

Bryn did a perfect eye-roll. "Kids don't bite, Aunt Kate."

"Let's hope not. I'm only in charge of you two until someone takes a bite out of me. Then I'll take my chances with the sharks."

Kate backed away, pretending to be scared. Bryn hopped off the bench and lunged, her arms wide like shark jaws. Carly followed making chomping sounds. Laughing, Kate scooted to the back of the boat and then when she couldn't go any further, pointed to the water where Reed and Julia bobbed.

"Mama! Mommy!" Bryn hollered.

"They can't hear us," Carly said.

But Julia waved and then glanced at Kate, checking for a signal. Kate held up her thumb. She was managing, although how long that would remain the case was in question. Julia dipped her head under the water and the twins both complained.

"We could join them," Kate suggested.

"Too many sharks," Bryn said.

"The moms would protect us," Carly said. "And Aunt Mo."

The moms. It was surprising to think that only a year and a half had passed since Hawaii. Julia had seamlessly joined Reed's family and now, even apparently from the twins' perspective, was as much a mother to them as Reed. Kate knew it hadn't always been easy, but from the outside looking in, their lives seemed perfect. Julia and Reed had the whole package.

As much as she wanted Julia to be happy, some part of her still envied that it all had worked out for her. Julia, who'd never wanted to get married or have kids in the first place, had all of it. As she watched, Reed and Julia made a circle around a shallow spot where the water was more turquoise than blue.

Suddenly Mo came into view. She had separated from the other snorkelers and was swimming a fair bit away from the boat. "Is she too far out?" Kate asked, pointing to Mo as the captain came over to the rail.

He pursed his lips, eyeing where Mo was swimming before shaking his head. "She's a good swimmer."

Kate looked at the sign next to where the captain was standing. Under a drawing of a camera flying overboard were the words: *Only you know the value of what you brought on the boat.*

The Spanish translation was below the English. She stared at the words, remembering the hours of telenovelas she'd watched with Mo. If anyone ever made a lesbian-themed telenovela with her and Mo, right about now Chantal would be showing up at the resort to surprise Mo. She'd go to Mo's room to wait for her and find Kate's things. Once she'd come to the conclusion that Mo and Kate were sleeping together, she'd devise some plan to catch them in the act. Of course there had to be an attempted murder and someone would be pregnant... In the end, Kate would tearfully admit she was an heiress with a messed up past and no hope of ever having someone like Mo. She sighed. She didn't need fiction to help with that part of the plot.

"Are you worried about Mo?" Carly asked.

Carly was the perceptive one, Julia had said, but Kate wondered how much a five-year-old could guess. "She's pretty far away from the boat. What do you think?"

Carly shrugged. "She's a grown-up."

"I think we should go save her," Bryn said. Without waiting for agreement, she went over to the pile of flippers and snorkel masks that Reed had set out in case anyone changed their mind.

Carly joined her sister at the snorkel gear and in no time at all both kids were staring up at her through the snorkel masks.

"Okay, last one in is the rotten egg," Kate said, tugging on her flippers.

Carly shook her head. "That's not even possible, Aunt Kate."

But Bryn passed Carly to get to the dive platform. "I don't want to be a rotten egg."

As Bryn teetered on the edge of the dive platform, clearly trying to decide how to get in the water, Kate had a sudden moment of panic that she wouldn't be able to handle both kids. Fortunately Reed appeared, swimming up to the back of the boat at the same moment that Bryn cannonballed into the water. Carly hopped in afterward, splashing Reed.

When Reed had recovered, she hollered up to Kate: "I got them from here. You should go check out the cave." She pointed to a darker blue area close to the rocks. "There's more fish than you can count."

Julia swam up to Reed's side. "It's amazing, Kate. You have to check it out."

Kate waited until the twins had bobbed a good distance away from the boat, one mom with each kid, and then hopped into the water. The cool water was a perfect contrast to her sun-warmed skin. She shivered at first contact, but within a few strokes, the temperature was perfect. Mo and Terri were still swimming together and she was tempted to swim over to them, but she decided to take Reed's advice instead and swam toward the cave she'd pointed out.

This was her break from thinking, she reminded herself, taking her first look under the water. The scene was straight out of a crowded aquarium. A huge school of yellow-striped fish darted past bright pink and orange coral followed by a fat silver fish that slalomed within arms reach. She treaded water long enough for an intrepid angelfish to curiously approach her and then flit away a moment later.

Following a curving shelf of coral covered with all sorts of plants and teeming with fish of every color, she found the cave Reed had mentioned and slowed down to enjoy the rocking motion of the waves. She gave a start when she spotted a stingray sweeping the sandy bottom below her. The ray was well out of reach, but as she decided to turn and start back to the boat she spotted another one only a few feet from the reef. As soon as she took one stroke, something touched her arm. She darted forward several lengths, her pulse racing. When she looked back, she saw Mo.

"I swear I wasn't trying to scare you." Mo's expression was apologetic. "You okay?"

Kate pulled her snorkel out of her mouth and pushed her mask up on her forehead. "I thought you were another stingray."

"Aren't all these rays amazing? And did you see that big reef shark?"

"Seriously?"

"It was about this long." Mo held her hands about two feet apart. "Even the kids thought it was cute."

"I'd prefer a nice little sea turtle."

"How 'bout a dolphin?" Mo pointed behind Kate.

"Don't joke. You know how I feel about dolphins." As incredulous as she was, she had to look. Past the bow of the boat she spotted a shape that was undeniably a dolphin leaping out of the water.

"Oh! It's coming our way!" Without thinking, she reached for Mo. The feeling of Mo's skin under her fingertips sent a jolt through her. She pulled her hand back but not before brushing it over Mo's shoulder and down her back as she awkwardly regained her balance in the water.

"There's a whole pod," Mo said. "Can you see them?"

A half dozen silver silhouettes crested over the waves like dancers leaping in perfect synchrony. Kate tried to focus on the dolphins, but her mind was stuck on the fact that she'd inadvertently stroked Mo's back. The move had been all reflex, for better or worse.

"Terri spotted them," Mo added.

"Thanks for coming to tell me. Where's Terri?" Kate realized then that she'd lost track of the others.

"Back in the boat. Carly and Bryn had enough swimming and she volunteered to let Reed and Julia have some more time together. I told the kids she was scared of seeing that little shark's mama." Mo chuckled. "You know, Terri was asking all about you."

"You told her I'm amazing, right?" Kate joked.

"Of course. I had to tell her the truth."

Kate expected Mo to joke as well, but her tone was completely serious. She tried to focus on the dolphins. Each time one leapt out of the waves, the sunlight turned the spray of water coming off its skin to shimmering silver.

"I know I used to tease you for being obsessed with dolphins, but they are beautiful," Mo said.

Kate's hand still tingled with the memory of touching Mo's back. "I think I deserved a little teasing. You had to put up with all my dolphin posters."

"So are you going to ask her out?"

"I haven't ever asked anyone out," Kate admitted. Could she really go on a date with Terri when accidentally touching Mo made every part of her body come alive?

"She'll say yes, trust me, so at least you don't have to worry about that." Mo paused. "And I know I already said this, but I really am sorry about how I acted when you were with Ethan. I won't be that friend again."

Mo hadn't made any secret of the fact that she didn't like Ethan. But it was Mo's jealousy that made Kate think she was interested. Unfortunately, that wasn't true. "I think it's normal for friends to be jealous of boyfriends or girlfriends. Who doesn't want more one-on-one time with their best friend?"

"It was more than that," Mo said.

"What do you mean?" Kate waited, but Mo only scanned the waves as if she were looking for more dolphins. "Want to tell me?"

"Not really. Can we forget I said it?"

"I probably owe you a few of those. I'm usually the one avoiding the conversation."

Mo looked over at her. Her smile was close-lipped. "I probably shouldn't give you such a hard time about that either."

The captain's whistle stopped Mo from saying more. It was the signal to come back to the boat. Mo looked from the boat to Kate. "Wanna race?"

"You'll win."

Mo winked. "Only if I decide not to let you win."

Kate pushed Mo's shoulder, dunking her, and then quickly pulled her own mask into place and started for the boat. She heard laughter behind her but didn't look back. By the time she reached the ladder, she was out of breath and only a stroke ahead of Mo. But she'd won.

"I can't believe it. Kate Owens cheated," Mo said, pulling off her mask.

"I didn't cheat. You never said dunking wasn't allowed." Kate cocked her head. "But if you can't handle a little dunking..."

"Oh, I can handle it." Mo splashed Kate as she reached for one of the higher ladder rungs. "Besides we were racing back to the boat and no one's in the boat yet." She laughed as Kate tried to pull her back into the water.

"That was some swimming," Terri said, smiling down at them.

Kate let go of her hold on Mo. "Thanks. Want to tell Mo that I won fair and square?"

Mo scrambled up the ladder still wearing her flippers. She landed on her butt on the platform and held up her hands. "Who's on the boat?"

Laughing, Terri tossed Mo a towel and then turned to stretch a hand out to Kate. "I'll take your flippers. It makes the climb easier."

"Thanks." Kate smiled. "Unlike some people, I'd rather not look like a goofball."

"Are you calling me a goofball?" Mo asked, her voice full of mocked disbelief.

"She doesn't have to," Terri said, winking at Mo.

"Oh, burn." Kate laughed.

Kate handed over her flippers as Terri joked with Mo about her swimming technique. Kate knew Mo could have easily beat her if she'd been trying, even after being dunked at the start. She'd let her win.

After toweling off, Kate followed Terri up the steps and then took a seat. She noticed Mo's look when Terri sat down next to her. Whether or not Mo was going to be jealous if she asked Terri out was still up for debate.

Kate turned to Terri. "Mo said you were the one who spotted the dolphins. Thanks for sending her over to tell me."

"I didn't want you to miss them. Dolphins always seem a little magical out there playing in the waves."

"I love them."

"Me too. And I have a feeling that we have more than dolphins in common." Terri cocked her head to the side. "That might be one of the worst pick-up lines I've ever used."

Kate laughed. "Believe it or not, I've heard worse."

Miguel bustled around handing out towels and bottles of water as the captain turned on the engine. Terri leaned close to point out a blur in the distance. "That's another pod, I think."

More dolphins emerged from the water and everyone on board seemed to spot them at the same moment. As the boat zipped over the waves, the oohing and ahhing got louder with the dolphins coming close to play in the boat's break. When the captain veered to the right, the pod fell back.

Kate kept her eyes on them until the sunlight was too bright. She turned to look the other direction and caught Mo staring at her. Her expression was difficult to read. At first Kate thought she was upset, her full lips a tight straight line and her eyes concealed behind a pair of sunglasses, but then she raised her hand in a slow wave and leaned back in her seat. Maybe she was only tired from the swim.

"How do you feel about tacos?"

Kate looked over at Terri. "I like them. That also might be the strangest way I think I've ever been asked out—if you're asking me out."

"I am—if you say yes. Otherwise it was just a random question."

Kate laughed.

"There's this fabulous little restaurant on the beach that I found the last time I was here. Their tacos are unbelievable. Want to go for lunch?"

Kate ignored the nagging thought that a date with Terri wouldn't change her feelings about Mo. It was past time to move on. "I'd love to."

CHAPTER EIGHT

"You're really going out for tacos?"

Kate flopped onto the bed. "Yes, Mo, tacos. Why is it so crazy that Terri asked me to go out for tacos?"

"Well, you know…tacos."

"Seriously? How old are you?"

"I'm just saying that I think it's funny that she wants to eat tacos with you."

"We're in Mexico on a tiny island. It's not like there are a lot of options for food. Anyway, I like tacos."

"Who doesn't like tacos?" Mo mumbled. "I bet Terri likes them even more."

"I like women, Mo. Clearly you don't believe me or you've got some issue with that, but—"

"I don't have any issues," Mo argued.

"That makes one of us." Kate rolled onto her belly and faced Mo. "And this is you not being jealous?"

"I'm not jealous."

"Next you'll tell me it's just that you like tacos too."

"I do like tacos."

When they'd parted from the rest of the group at the dock, Mo had started in with questions about Terri's proposed date. That she felt better with Mo on the defensive was something Kate's therapist would have "wanted to unpack," but she wasn't interested in analyzing her feelings at the moment.

Mo had showered and only had a towel on. Her brown skin contrasted with the white towel that barely concealed her breasts in a way that made Kate's mouth go dry. She thought of how often she stopped herself from telling Mo how good-looking she was. Mo had a big enough ego that she recognized her own sexiness. But with her standing two feet away from the bed, shoulders squared and hands on her hips as if she was openly challenging someone to pull off her towel, Kate was tempted to say the words aloud.

What would happen if she were honest with Mo about her attraction? Kate tossed the idea before the words had a chance to slip out. She sat up and reached for the bottle of water on her nightstand.

"She couldn't stop looking at you on the boat ride," Mo said.

"Yesterday you were trying to convince me that she liked me. Now you're upset she was looking at me?"

"I'm not upset." Mo went over to her suitcase and pulled out a pair of shorts. "So you don't mind she was ogling your breasts?"

"Ogling? Careful, Mo. That sounded a little jealous."

Mo unfolded the shorts. "You're right. Sorry. I hope you have fun eating tacos together."

"Marginally better."

Mo sighed. "I'm still upset about the conversation I had with Chantal this morning. I don't mean to take it out on you."

"What'd she say?"

"It was more what she didn't say."

Kate waited for Mo to go on, but she only turned sideways and tugged her shorts on underneath the towel. Mo dropped the towel as she pulled a sports bra on over her head.

Kate loved the curve Mo's breasts made and how the dark nipples pointed up as if arguing with gravity. She'd always felt intimidated by Mo's body, by how perfect every part of her seemed, and by the effortless strength she possessed. Like some Amazon warrior. Of course, according to myth if she'd been born an Amazon, at least one of her breasts would have been a goner. "That would be a shame," Kate said. She realized she'd said the thought aloud when Mo turned to look at her.

"What would?"

For a second, Kate considered telling her. There was a good chance Mo would have laughed. "Sorry, I was thinking aloud. What are you going to do this afternoon?"

"I think I'll take a nap," Mo said. "Then brush up on my Ping-Pong game."

"You still planning on a rematch?"

"Better believe it. I went too easy on you last night."

"Oh, really? Well, I can't wait to see you really try."

Mo posed with a fake paddle held high, her eyes narrowed as she pretended to concentrate. Even joking around, she was still damn sexy. And, Kate reminded herself, in twenty minutes, she needed to meet Terri for lunch. She needed to stop thinking about Mo.

The tacos were either the best she'd ever had or she had been starving. She finished the first two and, wiping the remnants of salsa from her lips with her finger, looked up to Terri's smile.

"That's how I felt when I first tasted these. It was like I couldn't get it into my mouth fast enough and I didn't care if anyone saw me licking my fingers."

Kate laughed and Terri clapped her hand over her mouth when she realized what she'd said. "That sounded a lot dirtier than I meant it to be."

"It's okay. I'm usually the one saying something like that with no clue why everyone's laughing," Kate said. "You have to watch out around Mo and Julia. They pick up on every double meaning."

Terri reached for her soda. She'd eaten one of the chicken tacos on her plate but was going slower than Kate. This was a date for her, Kate reminded herself. She was supposed to be on a date as well, obviously, but it didn't feel like one. She was too relaxed. And, she realized in that moment, her attraction to

Terri wasn't enough to make her feel self-conscious. She wasn't certain if that was a problem or not. Maybe being relaxed was a good thing.

"How many times have you been here?"

"To Cozumel?" Terri paused, looking up at the sky. "Four times. The first two trips were with my ex-wife. But last summer I came here alone and then Reed and Julia invited me and I couldn't say no."

"Ex-wife?"

Terri sighed. "Yeah. She didn't like tacos. Clearly our relationship was destined to fail."

Terri and Kate both laughed, and the nearest patrons, an older white couple with bad sunburns, eyed them suspiciously. The woman scowled and whispered something to the man.

Terri ignored it, reaching for her next taco. Kate considered telling the woman to mind her own business but knew she'd only make a big deal out of nothing. The problem was, the scowling reminded her of a different meal. She looked down at her plate.

Her mind spun back to Mo's nineteenth birthday. She'd wanted to treat her to something special and knowing how Mo loved ribs, she decided to take her to a place in the suburbs that advertised authentic Texas barbeque. As soon as they'd walked in, every head in the place turned. They sat down at a table and the whole restaurant got quiet. A dozen straight, white, cowboy boot-wearing assholes scowled at them. She'd asked Mo if she wanted to leave, ashamed that she hadn't thought of how Mo would be treated and embarrassed that in some ways, this crowd was her people. Mo only sat a little taller in her seat, smiled, and reached for the menu. "Don't worry about them. We're here for the ribs." Kate had wanted to reach across the table and squeeze Mo's hand then, but she'd been too scared. She still regretted sitting there not doing a damn thing.

"You okay?"

Kate eyed the one remaining taco and forced a smile. "I'm debating if I have room for one more. The problem is, once you start eating, you can't stop halfway."

"Some people say you really shouldn't stop eating until you've finished what you've started."

"I've heard that." Kate returned the flirty tone, but her conscience tugged at her. She needed to be honest with Terri. Aside from the fact that she was still thinking of Mo, there were other issues that might make Terri wish she'd never agreed to tacos. "I've never actually gone down on a woman."

Terri stopped mid-bite. Kate hadn't planned out her sentence, and she almost laughed at the words that had slipped out. It was one part nerves and one part letting go of old hang-ups. She pushed herself to go on: "I'm a little worried that I'll do it wrong when I have a chance."

Terri set her taco down and wiped her hands off on the napkin. She met Kate's gaze. "I don't think you're supposed to be perfect the first time."

"To be clear, I've had plenty of oral sex. Just not with women." She'd never had sex with a woman despite how many times she'd imagined it. But why was she telling Terri? She was so used to holding back when sex talk happened that she couldn't believe she was opening up now. She rationalized that it was because she didn't want to lead Terri on or have her expecting anything she couldn't deliver. But was it simply that she wanted to get it all off her chest? The only time she'd ever talked about sex with anyone besides her therapist was with Mo and Julia. With them, she got tongue-tied and rarely said what she was thinking. She felt how they judged her, and she wasn't brave enough to bluff her way through a lack of experience.

"I like how honest you are. Where'd you come from?"

"Sand Bluff, Texas. I'm not usually this honest. You bring it out in me."

"I've heard Texans are straight shooters."

"In every sense of the word." Kate sighed. "I'm trying to be less straight. It's been a long, hard process." She laughed, but the truth in her statement only made her feel like more of an imposter.

"So you haven't had a girlfriend yet?"

"I've gone on some dates. And I kissed a girl." Kate scrunched up her face, hearing how naive that sentence sounded. "I mean,

I know I want more than kissing. It just hasn't happened yet. Mostly I've dated guys. Not long after I started college, there was this girl on the track team...we kissed in the locker room. I wasn't really into her, but I wanted to feel what it was like. I kind of needed to test it out. Does that make sense? I've never told anyone that before."

"Makes complete sense." Terri looked over at the older sunburned couple and then back at Kate. "I have an ex-husband as well as an ex-wife. Turns out I'm really good at marrying people and pretty terrible at everything else. But I understand not being sure of what you want. And needing some time to figure it out.

"Before I met my ex-wife," she continued, "I thought I was straight. Then I realized how wrong I was about that. But it was confusing because I still was attracted to my husband." Terri paused. "Sometimes you connect with certain people and it's impossible to say why, but your whole view of yourself changes in that moment."

Kate thought of Mo again. It wasn't impossible to say why she connected with her. But sometimes she wished that connection wasn't so strong. "Thanks for telling me that you've been with men. I know a lot of people won't date someone who's bi. It's nice not to worry about that."

"This morning on the boat Mo mentioned something about you being bi. She said it in a way that...well...made me think you didn't get a whole lot of support from her."

For the first time since they'd sat down. Kate felt self-conscious. Terri was waiting for her to say something. She picked up her napkin and then set it down again. Terri reached across the table, palm upturned.

Kate felt tears press at her eyes, but she clenched her teeth to stop then. She reached across the table and clasped Terri's hand. There was no bolt of electricity, but holding hands felt good. "I don't need Mo's support on this. I got it."

"Just so you know, I like you exactly the way you are. In my book, bi people are perfect."

"There's a chance you're biased," Kate said.

"Pun intended?" Terri grinned.

CHAPTER NINE

Kate expected Mo to be testy when she got back from the lunch date. That's how she'd always been whenever she got back from a date with Ethan. This time, she surprised her, however. She was sitting on one of the chairs in front of their bungalow and hopped up with a big smile when Kate walked up the path.

"You're back! How'd it go?"

"Fine. What happened to your Ping-Pong plans?" Kate didn't want to talk about her date with Terri—at least not with Mo. Everything had gone well, but she needed some time to rehash her feelings on it. But by the excitement in Mo's voice, she guessed she wouldn't be pressed for details anyway. Something else was clearly on her mind.

"I decided I was good enough with a paddle and didn't need the extra practice."

"I'm so beating you at that tournament."

"We'll see." Mo opened the door to the bungalow and then waited for Kate to walk in first. "So the date went well?"

"It did." Lunch had been perfect, and yet she'd felt as if she was bonding with a new friend—not on a date at all. She still wasn't certain if that was a problem.

"That's great."

Kate crossed her arms when Mo had closed the door. "You're up to something. What am I about to agree to?"

"You know me too well." Mo chuckled. "But did you know that they rent scooters at the front desk?"

"I'm not doing it."

"I haven't even asked you yet."

"But you're going to and you know how I feel about two-wheeled vehicles."

"Come on, it'll be a blast. And we're talking about scooters, not motorcycles," Mo argued. "It's basically a lawn mower engine. We aren't going to be flying down the highway on a Ducati."

"I don't know what a Ducati is, but I wouldn't say yes to that either." Kate set her purse on one of the chairs as Mo gathered up a towel she'd tossed there along with a wet bathing suit and a pair of goggles. "Mo, you've seen me on a bicycle. One little rock and I'm kissing the pavement."

"This is going to be way more fun than a bicycle."

"Fun doesn't always have to involve the risk of death. Do you know that motorcycle riders account for nearly all the organ transplant donors?"

"Scooters," Mo said, drawing out the word. "Not motorcycles. And we'll wear helmets. The guy I talked to at the pool swore this was the best way to see the island. Plus the rental fee is cheap."

"Great. So we're talking about a *cheap* death trap. That makes me feel so relieved." Kate shook her head. "I'm not doing it. I don't want to crash on a scooter in Mexico. I'd never hear the end of it from my mom."

"You can ride with me. Scooters have two seats. And we won't tell Eileen." Mo held out the brochure with a picture of a scooter perched on a slope overlooking a turquoise bay. "We can circle the island in a couple of hours and make stops wherever we want. You know we'll have fun. Please?"

"I always have fun with you. It's the broken bones I'm worried about. Remember that parasailing adventure?"

"No one broke any bones. Besides I was the one with the ice pack on my butt. And this time we won't even be leaving the ground."

Kate smiled, thinking back to the pack of ice chips Mo had sat on for the evening. "You also had a big bruise on your shoulder and you could hardly walk for two days."

"Pretty please?" Mo held up the brochure. "I really want to do this with you."

"How'd I get so lucky?" But even as she said the words, her tone filled with sarcasm, she felt her resolve crack. She took the brochure from Mo and flipped it open, briefly scanning the map of the island along with a description of points of interest. Mo's words repeated in her mind. Maybe Mo was jealous of the lunch date she'd had with Terri. Was that why she was asking her to spend the day with her tomorrow? Mo's jealousy flared up in weird ways. Or maybe Mo only wanted to go on a scooter ride around the island with her friend.

"Okay, fine. But you're driving and I'm only doing this if they have good helmets."

Mo clapped her hands together. "We're going to have so much fun! Thank you for saying yes."

Kate closed the brochure, knowing that she shouldn't be feeling a surge of excitement at the thought of spending the day alone with Mo. She should be thinking of Terri.

"Oh, I almost forgot. The front desk called while you were out. Your luggage arrived and someone left you a message."

"That'd be my mom." Eileen didn't trust cell phones. It was only one of her quirks. "At least I get my luggage."

"You don't want to have a mom chat on vacation?" Mo chuckled.

"I wouldn't mind chatting with your mom. Mine? Not so much."

Luis, the same concierge from the day before, was working the front desk, and Kate waited for him to finish helping the one guest ahead of her before approaching the desk with a cautious smile. She knew how Eileen could be on the phone, and Luis was doubtlessly not looking forward to dealing with her again either. "I'm hoping you have my luggage. Apparently it was dropped off here?"

"Ah, yes," Luis said, coming out from around his desk and leading the way to a locked door opposite the entrance.

As Luis wheeled out the suitcase, Kate felt a rush of relief. At least she would have clean underwear and all her clothes. The rest of the trip might not pan out as well, but this was some saving grace. She passed Luis a good tip, and his smile widened as he handed over the suitcase.

"And a phone message was left for me as well?"

Luis led the way back to his desk and then pulled out a slip of pink memo paper. "From your mother, I think."

"She doesn't like cell phones."

"No? My mother loves cell phones. She calls me every day. Sometimes I wish she didn't like her phone so much."

Kate handed Luis another tip and then pointed to the phone on his desk. "Would it be okay if my mom called your line? I promise it won't take long."

"Of course." Luis pushed the phone across the counter and Kate quickly read the number listed on it. She texted the number to her mom adding the international code and then waited. Her mother fell for every conspiracy that smacked of government oversight and at the moment she was convinced all cell phone conversations were being recorded. Why landlines had escaped this threat, Kate hadn't asked.

The phone rang and Luis answered, but a moment later, he smiled and handed the receiver to Kate.

"Mom?"

Eileen sighed heavily, "Thank God. You're alive. They say you can't even eat the salad there. I hope you haven't been robbed."

"It's lovely here." Kate glanced over at Luis and smiled. Everyone with an overbearing mother shared a certain understanding, but she was glad Luis couldn't hear the other end of the line. "How are you?"

"Oh, I'm fine. I had to start on a new medication for my blood pressure and now I'm constipated. They say it's hereditary so you better get yours checked."

"Good advice," Kate said, stopping short of asking if she meant her blood pressure or her butt. Eileen didn't appreciate humor. "Anything else?"

"Gary can't figure out that FitBit that you sent him. You need to give him a lesson. I'll get him on the phone."

"Now isn't the best time, Mom. I'm using the resort's phone..." Kate leaned against the counter and gave Luis an apologetic look. "Is there anything else? I don't want to hold up the line."

"Stick to bottled water. I had a friend who came back from Mexico with diarrhea for a month. And I hope you aren't making international calls on your cell phone. You never know who's listening."

When Eileen hung up, Kate pushed the phone back across the counter to Luis. "Thank you."

"Of course. Everything okay?" Luis asked.

Kate nodded. She reached for her purse to give him another tip, but he held up his hand.

"I understand how it is with mothers," Luis said.

Kate took her time wheeling the suitcase back to the room. Between the birds chattering in the trees and the flowers everywhere, her frustration with her mom dissipated and her thoughts turned to Terri. She knew she should have felt a spark. Without that, she wondered if she should have told Terri straightaway that it wasn't going to work. And yet she liked Terri, so maybe it was okay to not shut anything down yet. She didn't think about Mo until she turned down the path to the bungalow.

Mo was standing by the window. Her back was to Kate, but it was obvious that she was on her cell phone. If Mo was talking to her girlfriend, it would be awkward to walk in and hear any of the conversation. Then again, Kate didn't want to stand there waiting and have Mo think she was watching her.

Finally she decided to go in and act as casual as she could. Mo turned to look at her as soon as she opened the door. Kate held up a hand in a little wave and then pulled her suitcase into the room. As soon as she'd opened her suitcase, Mo stepped outside with her phone. The way Mo switched her phone from one ear to the other, avoiding Kate's eyes, suggested that her girlfriend was indeed on the other end of the line.

Several minutes later, Mo came back into the room. Kate was still putting away her clothes, but she stopped in the middle of hanging up one of her dresses to glance at Mo when she heard her deep sigh.

After tossing her cell phone on the dresser, Mo sank down on the bed.

"Everything okay?"

"Not really." Mo rolled onto her side. "The good news is that Chantal's happy."

"What's the bad news?"

"I'm ninety percent sure she's in love with her boss. That's who she's in London with at the moment. I've never heard her this happy."

"Mo, I know how you get. But maybe you shouldn't jump to conclusions this time. She's on a work trip. Chances are there's nothing going on." Focusing on the dress she was holding, Kate finished looping the spaghetti straps over the hanger and then hung it on the rack before going back to the suitcase to fish out a wrinkled blouse. She didn't know why she was standing up for Chantal. When she looked over at Mo, she was surprised to see a pillow over her face.

"How happy are we talking about?"

Mo pushed the pillow up enough to say, "Real happy."

Kate closed the suitcase and sat down on the edge of the bed. "Do you know much about her boss?"

"Only that she's attracted to him."

"She told you that?"

Mo nodded and the pillow moved up and down with her head.

"Okay, that's weird. Why would she tell you that?"

"She asked if I'd ever be up for a threesome." Mo tossed the pillow aside. "She's totally sleeping with him, isn't she?"

"You don't know that for sure." Although Kate had to agree that the optics weren't good.

"Fuck. I don't know what to do."

"Well, you could just ask her."

"Straight up?" Mo shook her head. "So…'Hey, babe, how's London? And another thing…are you sleeping with your boss?'"

"Well, worst-case scenario, the answer's yes and you find out that she's not the right woman for you. You tell her that you need someone who's loyal and move on."

"What's the best-case scenario?"

"Best-case scenario is that you're wrong about this hunch and she's only on a business trip. But if that's the case…she'll be upset that you asked. Cheating's a big deal, and you accusing her will probably be an issue going forward. Plus she'll probably feel like you're overly controlling."

"Because I want to know if she's sleeping with her boss? I give up," Mo said. "No matter what, I'm screwed."

"Not if you don't ask. But then you have to decide if you trust her. She told you that she's attracted to him, but that doesn't mean she'll act on her feelings. Plenty of people have attractions they never act on."

"I don't think I can handle not knowing." Mo leaned across the bed and reached for a bottle of water. After she'd had a drink, her jaw muscles clenched. She shifted back against the headboard. Her high cheekbones and sharp jawline were something out of a superhero comic book. More than once, Kate had imagined tracing that jawline with her fingertip. If Chantal was sleeping with her boss, she was making a big mistake.

"Remember McKenzie?" Mo looked over at Kate, and when she didn't nod, Mo said, "I dated her for a while at the end of our freshman year." Mo crunched the plastic bottle and then let go, watching the shape slowly returning. "She was the first person who cheated on me. When you met her you told me that she wasn't good for me. I should have listened."

Kate remembered McKenzie then. But she hadn't known about the cheating. Mo had never mentioned that. Mo had invited McKenzie to a party that their dorm floor had hosted. There was no doubt Mo was smitten, but Kate had picked up on McKenzie's wandering eye right away. Although her hands were all over Mo, it was clear she was looking for her next play even then.

"After her, all these insecurities I didn't even know I had came up. I didn't want to have a serious relationship with anyone. I didn't feel like I was enough."

"You're more than enough." Kate went over to the bed. Being close wouldn't help dial down the longing to wrap her arms around Mo, but she didn't want the distance between them either. Mo shifted over to make room for her.

"So you don't think I should ask Chantal if she's cheating on me?"

"You have to do what feels right. But if you do ask, we're going to have to work on that verbiage."

"I could send her a text. You could help me write it."

Kate shook her head. "Ask her over the phone. And only if it's going to drive you crazy not knowing."

"I hate being this person," Mo said. "Why do I get so jealous? If Chantal and I break up, can you make me take a long break from dating?"

Kate patted Mo's knee. It was the safest place she could touch, but even that contact sent a flare up to her brain. Mo dropped her head on her shoulder and murmured, "Thanks for being here."

Kate fought the urge to snuggle closer. She squeezed her hands into fists and reminded herself of her resolve. *Friends.* In that moment, she understood how Chantal could have been tempted to act on her attraction to her boss. It was hell denying your body the one thing it wanted most.

"You know what we should do tonight?" Mo asked. "Try out that dance class. No one can be depressed dancing to salsa music."

"I don't think that's been scientifically proven," Kate said. But she couldn't hold back a smile. "And as I recall, you need to beat me at Ping-Pong first."

"Oh, right. That." Mo grumbled. "I was hoping you'd forget."

Kate pointed to her chest. "Me? Forget?"

"You're like an elephant. You still remember what I was wearing the day we met."

"You bet I do. Yellow tank top, blue gym shorts, and red boxers." They'd had this conversation before and Kate had managed then to make it seem like it was no big deal that she remembered what Mo was wearing that day. Now she added, "Julia was wearing that black skirt she loved with a maroon top."

"There might be something wrong with you," Mo said.

"Oh, there's a lot wrong with me," Kate returned. "But when it comes to clothes, I remember everything."

"Too bad there's no good use for that skill."

Kate stuck out her tongue, and Mo continued, "I still think it's hilarious that you remember the color of my boxers."

"If you wear shorts that low, I'm going to notice your underwear. Besides you were the first girl I'd ever see in boxers."

"You saying I made an impression?" Mo's voice held more than a hint of her old flirtatious tone.

"Something like that." Kate hoped Mo wouldn't read anything into the way her own voice sounded then. They'd joked plenty of times before about this, but now, with Mo's arm against hers, she felt like her eighteen-year-old self on shaky ground.

"Please, can we go dancing?"

"Well, we both know I'd kick your butt in Ping-Pong anyway." Kate rocked her head side to side, considering. Dancing didn't seem like a good idea, but she wanted to say yes anyway. Then she remembered Terri and the tentative plans they'd made to meet up after dinner. "I did sort of suggest that I'd hang out with Terri tonight."

Mo's face dropped. "Oh right. Terri." She tried to recover with a quick smile, but Kate recognized the mask she'd put on. "We can do another night..."

"Or we could all take the salsa class together." Kate knew that with Mo there it would be harder to focus on Terri, but she didn't want to leave Mo out.

"I don't want to step in on your date."

"Or are you worried that I'm gonna show you up in that salsa class in front of Terri?" Kate teased.

"No chance. I've got the moves, remember?"

"Then let's all take the class together."

Mo hesitated. "Let me think about it. I've got a lot on my mind with Chantal."

After their talk, Mo sent a few texts to Chantal and then turned on the television. She kept picking up her phone and staring at the screen, but Kate could tell there'd been no response. For her own sanity, Kate didn't ask what Mo had said or asked in those texts. She didn't need to wade any deeper into their relationship, and she got a sense that Mo was done opening up on the subject anyway. When she announced that she was thinking of going down to the beach to read, Mo only turned off the TV and mumbled that she was going to take a nap.

Kate had packed more than one paperback, guessing that she might need to fill some time alone, but she'd only brought romances. She regretted that decision now as she sorted through her options. It was ridiculous to feel intimidated by imaginary characters that had more experience with love than she did, and yet even the covers made her feel a little insecure. Falling in love was mostly dumb luck, but the rest of it... She eyed Mo stretched out on the bed. As much as she didn't want to admit it, she wanted her own happily ever after. Finally she picked the book that seemed to promise the most angst.

As she started out of the room, she stole one last glance at Mo. It was clear from her breathing that she wasn't sleeping, and Kate debated asking her if she wanted to talk more. She could stay if that was what Mo needed, but what comfort could she give her when she wanted Chantal?

A heaviness pressed down on her shoulders as she closed the door. She'd escaped the gloom all day, but she was fooling herself if she'd thought it was gone for good. Resisting a swell of self-pity, she took the fastest route to the beach, bypassing the pools and opting for the access path behind the bungalows. She jogged the length of the path and only slowed when she could see the water.

With a deep breath, she let the salty air fill her chest, then slipped off her sandals and wiggled her toes in the sand. The turquoise water gently lapped the copper-colored shoreline and she took her time taking in the view. After she'd had her fill of the endless blue vista, she headed down the beach, passing dozens of lounge chairs and skirting around laughing kids and couples walking slowly, hand in hand. She picked out an empty hammock strung up between palm trees at the edge of the resort's property and aimed for this. The spot looked more quiet than lonely and although there were a handful of other hammocks sprinkled around, she wanted the one furthest away.

Once she'd settled in, she opened the book she'd brought. Her thoughts roamed between the pages and the water. It wasn't until she realized that the lounge chairs around her were steadily filling with people coming to watch the sunset that she closed the book.

"Hey."

Kate looked over her shoulder and noticed Mo leaning against one of the palm trees. She wondered how long Mo had been there and then if she'd been only watching the sunset or waiting to talk to her. The sad smile on Mo's lips stopped her from a joke about her ninja skills. "Did you hear from Chantal?"

"No...I didn't really expect she'd respond. And with the time difference, she's asleep by now." Mo paused. "I passed Julia on my way down here. She said the kids are hungry. They're all getting ready to go to dinner."

"I could eat," Kate said, her stomach rumbling in response.

Mo looked down the length of the beach, past where the rocks delineated the end of the resort property and the jungle encroached on the sand. "I think I'll go for a walk. I'm not feeling very sociable."

"Want company?" Kate asked, hoping Mo meant that she wasn't up for the big group as opposed to one-on-one time. She could understand wanting a break from the noise and banter of the busy restaurant and their crowded table.

"I think I need to be alone. I've got a lot on my mind. Anyway, you should hang out with Terri."

"Do you still want to take that dance class tonight?"

"Maybe…I could probably use the distraction." Mo forced a smile. "I'll text you later."

Kate watched her leave, wondering if Mo would change her mind and hating the bitter taste in her mouth at the thought that she was the distraction Mo was talking about. She knew that wasn't what she had meant to suggest and yet her thoughts were clearly focused on Chantal.

Mo continued down the beach, heading for the distant rocks. Kate wanted to follow her, but the fact that Mo didn't want her company pushed away all the excuses her brain was making. The longer she stayed in the hammock watching Mo's outline get smaller and smaller, the worse she felt. She eyed the model on the cover of her book. "Do you have to look so happy?" A plastic smile shone back at her.

Everyone accepted the story that Mo wanted a sunset walk on the beach and was planning on eating alone later. It was so obviously not a Mo move that Kate was surprised Julia didn't ask why she was covering for her. But the twins were being a challenge, clearly overtired and complaining about the food while begging for soda, and Reed seemed tense. Terri tried entertaining everyone with a story about a fishing misadventure. The tactic worked for a while, but as soon as the story was over the kids were fighting again.

"Thanks for trying," Reed said, a note of exhaustion in her voice.

"I think we might have overdone it today." Julia glanced at Reed. "Maybe a case of too much vacation?"

"Snorkeling and then swimming in the pool for hours…" Reed nodded. "We all need an early bedtime. Myself included."

Carly and Bryn erupted with arguments of why they weren't tired. Julia quieted them down with a reminder about plans to watch a movie before bed and Reed added that only would apply if they left without a fuss about dessert. As tiring as the kids were, Kate couldn't help but notice how well Julia and Reed parented together. They backed each other up seamlessly and were still smiling at the end of their long day. When they all stood to leave, Reed reached for Julia's hand and kissed it.

After they'd gone, Terri settled back in her chair and said, "Those two have got something amazing—I'm almost jealous."

"Almost?"

"I've realized that I'm not programmed for long-term relationships. After you fail twice, you start to think the system is clearly flawed." She grinned. "Can't be me."

"Definitely not." Kate smiled back.

"Don't get me wrong, if it happened, I wouldn't fight it. But I'm not convinced that marriage is a good idea. The hard part is kids." She hesitated. "I always thought that I'd have a family by now."

"Long-term is part of the deal there."

"Right. But a few days with Reed's kids and I'm exhausted."

"I totally agree. The twins do have their moments of being awesome, but all day every day?" Kate thought back to the boat ride that morning and then the joy on Carly and Bryn's face as they spotted fish after fish. "I don't think I'm ready."

"That's what I keep saying. But I turn forty next year. Fate's deciding this one for me."

"Women have kids at forty—and older. Or you could meet someone who already has kids like Julia did."

"True. And kids aren't a deal breaker for me. In some ways, I worry that I'll regret not having them down the road. But then I think I'd rather enjoy other people's kids and skip bedtimes and temper tantrums."

"I think I want kids," Kate said. "Someday."

That was something relatively new. Ethan hadn't wanted kids, and she'd gotten used to the idea of a life without that hassle. After they'd broken up, she'd realized that she was free to think of having kids again. She knew now on some level she'd feel like she'd missed out if she was never a mom.

Since Reed had come along and with her the twins, she'd watched Julia transform into a mom. It wasn't easy and at times she thought that Julia might miss some things—like quiet evenings—but she'd never seemed happier.

"In a perfect world, how many kids would you have?" Terri asked.

"Two, I guess. I was an only kid, and I always wished I had a little brother or sister."

"I had one of each. As a kid, I would have told you that you weren't missing out on much." Terri smiled. "But I love my brother and sister now. And I can understand wishing for what you don't have. My parents got divorced when I was five. Whenever I'd see a kid in the back seat of a car back then, I'd look to see if they had two parents. That's what I wished for."

"My parents got divorced too, but then my mom remarried… It was for the best. My biological dad's an asshole." Kate felt a pinch of guilt at admitting that much aloud. She never talked about Philip. To anyone who asked, she'd always referred to Gary as her dad.

"Sorry if I brought up a bad subject."

Kate felt a weight settle on her as she tried to smile. "It's fine. We don't really have a relationship at this point. To be honest, I don't even know if he's still alive. Gary—my stepdad—is enough of a father. Two is more than I need." She wished that she could casually mention her biological father and feel nothing in response. Instead, years of therapy later, shame mixed with anger all over again.

When the waiter came by their table, she decided on another drink. Terri launched into a story about the first time she'd watched the twins for Reed, and Kate tried to focus on that. Fortunately, the diaper-changing incident that she described, with Terri having to call her own mom for help, was priceless.

The kid conversation turned to work, and Kate realized that by all standards, Terri was a catch. Not only was she a successful doctor, she was confident, attractive, and she had a sense of humor. Kate pushed away the thought that there had to be a spark as well. She liked her, was comfortable with her, and maybe Terri was exactly what she needed. At least she could finally cross off her list having been with a woman—though of course that wasn't enough reason to date her.

When she'd been in Denver, she'd taken to frequenting online dating sites. Most of the time, she weeded out potential dates with one conversation, and she needed at least a half dozen reasons for why they were compatible before she'd agree to an in-person date. Not once had she felt the urge to go out with someone who was clearly only interested in a hookup, and although Terri didn't seem like the type for that, she'd admitted she wasn't looking for long-term. But maybe short-term was what Kate needed.

She thought of Mo and glanced at her phone. Seeing the blank screen, Kate felt her spirits drop. But maybe not having Mo around was a good thing. "Any chance you'd want to take a dance class? There's this salsa class I was thinking of trying."

"I love dancing. I'm not that great at it, but as long as you don't mind a partner who sometimes misses the beat…"

"I don't mind at all."

When they left the restaurant, Kate expected Terri to reach for her hand but she didn't. In some ways, she was glad. She knew she'd overanalyze how Terri's hand felt in hers and only second-guess everything. They passed the quiet courtyard and then the tennis courts and the rec room with the empty Ping-Pong tables. One look and thoughts of the previous evening sprang up. When things were good between her and Mo, no one else could make her as happy. But no one else could make her feel as miserable either.

The dance club was on the second floor above the exercise room. With the ocean breeze wafting in the open windows, the temperature was perfect. Kate took a moment to get her bearings in the darkened space. Club music was playing, but no one had started dancing yet. A handful of couples sat around the bar, and a few more stood at the edge of the dance floor looking expectantly nervous.

Unable to stop herself, she scanned the space for Mo. But she knew that if Mo had decided to show up, she wouldn't be lurking in any corner. If she was there, she'd be front and center.

"Thanks for suggesting this," Terri said. "It's more fun going with someone than showing up to a dance class alone."

"Do you take classes often?"

"Not enough to be any good. I've taken some two-step classes and a hip-hop course. No salsa classes, but for a while I dated a woman who loved to go out to salsa clubs... My favorite is Zumba."

"Zumba?"

"Don't knock it 'til you try it," Terri returned. "What about you? Am I about to get shown up by a salsa master?"

"Definitely not. I've taken a handful of salsa classes, but most of my dance experience is ballet."

"Ballet, huh?" Terri tilted her head like she was reassessing Kate. "That makes sense."

"How's that?"

"You carry yourself like a dancer. And you've got a gorgeous body."

Kate repressed the urge to argue that she didn't. Instead, she said, "I haven't danced since college."

"Well, something stuck. Do you miss it?"

Before Kate could change the conversation, the music abruptly stopped and a young Latina woman addressed the room. Although she spoke mostly in Spanish, she used enough hand motions and interspersed English words to get everyone onto the dance floor. Kate glanced at the door again. After another scan of the bar and all the tables, it hit her: Mo wasn't coming.

When the instructor turned on the salsa music and looked around the room, her gaze settled on Kate. She motioned Kate forward and then positioned her hands and encouraged everyone to take a similar stance. Once she had everyone in position around the room, she quickly went through the basic steps. Then the instructor took Kate's hand. "Now we dance."

After only a few turns around the room, Kate felt a buzz in her body that she hadn't felt for years. It had been too long since she'd taken a dance class and longer still since she'd let herself truly relax while dancing. When the instructor let go of her, turning to address the other students and encouraging everyone to find a partner, Terri stepped up. Kate resisted scanning the room again for Mo.

"You looked like a pro out there. I hope I don't step on your toes."

Kate took Terri's hand. "Don't worry. I'm having too much fun to care."

Kate wasn't used to leading, but Terri needed to follow. There were several missteps and laughing, but they managed to get into a rhythm before long. Exactly what she'd been expecting, she wasn't sure, but she was surprised by how comfortable she felt dancing with Terri. There was nothing weird about holding her hand. Then again, everything about Terri was easy. Kate wondered again if it was wrong to not feel any excitement at her touch. But she was enjoying herself and Terri seemed to be as well. Maybe that was enough.

When the instructor stopped the music to give more feedback, Terri let go of Kate's hand. "It's fun dancing with you—you're really good."

"Thanks. You're doing great too."

"I think I have to credit my Zumba teacher for the fact that I haven't fallen on my face yet. But I am getting thirsty. Want something to drink?"

Kate glanced at the bar. She hadn't been thinking of Mo, but when she spotted her standing near one of the tables at the edge of the dance floor, a drink in her hand, all other thoughts slipped out of her mind. Mo's gaze held hers.

Terri repeated her question and Kate had to focus to answer. "Yeah, sure...whatever you're having."

"Water?"

"That's perfect."

As soon as Terri headed to the bar, Mo approached. "You two looked good out there."

"You say that like it's a problem."

"I'm trying not to be jealous." Mo's smile was tight-lipped. "Sorry. I shouldn't say that."

Kate felt a rush of emotions. "It's okay to admit it. You know I get jealous when someone gets to spend time with you and I don't."

"This is probably something more," Mo said, taking a sip of the beer she was holding. "But that doesn't change the fact that you and Terri looked good out there."

"She was making me look good," Terri said, suddenly standing next to Kate. "Water?"

"Thanks." Kate opened the bottle and took a sip. She briefly met Mo's gaze, her cheeks hot with a blush. Mo had pushed her off balance. *Probably something more...* Did Mo have to throw that line out into the universe now?

Kate knew she had to ignore the comment for the moment. She turned to Terri. "You up for more dancing?"

"My legs are complaining about the fact that I went for a long run this afternoon. Why don't you and Mo dance this next one?" Terri reached for Kate's water bottle. The music had started again. "I'll stake out a table for us."

Before Kate could argue with the plan, Terri had stepped away. Mo looked from her beer bottle to Terri and then finally to Kate. "You don't have to dance with me."

"I want to dance with you," Kate returned evenly. "I've been waiting to see these moves you say you've got."

"I think maybe I talked my moves up too much. You're the dancer."

"Look what you got yourself into." Kate grinned. "Who's leading?"

Mo cocked her head. "Are you really asking me that?"

"Only because I wanted that response."

Mo laughed. She took one last sip of her beer and then set it on the nearest table. When she turned to hold out her hand, Kate's breath caught.

All their joking was over. Kate clasped Mo's hand, her heart racing and her mind blank. Did she even remember how to dance? Mo's fingers intertwined with hers and she led the way onto the dance floor. The room swirled and her knees felt weak.

Breathe. You know how to dance.

She looked up and Mo smiled. In college they'd danced at parties, but it always with a group of friends and never at any point had she held Mo's hand or dared to dance close to her body. Everything about this was completely different.

Mo reached for Kate's other hand. "I hope I don't screw this up."

Kate stopped herself from echoing the same words. Sounding more sure than she felt, she said, "You know I'll tease you about it for the rest of your life if you do."

"Oh, trust me, I know."

The moment they started dancing, Kate relaxed. This one thing she could do. She stopped thinking, letting the music and Mo's hands direct her. She didn't try to concentrate on adding any special moves to impress Mo. All she wanted to do was follow her lead.

Every time she stepped close to Mo, the scent of her teased her senses. A surge went through her when Mo brushed against her backside, and when she felt her breath against her neck, she nearly turned to kiss her. At one point Mo wrapped her arms around her and Kate couldn't help but lean in. She loved the strength in Mo's body and the way they fit together. She didn't want the song to ever end.

But it was only dancing, Kate reminded herself, and Mo was showing off her moves to prove a point. Still, the way she held her hand, sending her into a spin and then stepping back and waiting for her to close the distance back to her, left Kate breathless. Mo's touch turned on every nerve in her body and she couldn't do a damn thing to stop that.

When Mo slowed her steps, Kate was aware that the music had stopped and the instructor was talking. But Mo didn't let go of her hand. If she'd only wanted to show off, if the dance itself meant nothing, she would have let go—wouldn't she? The instructor turned the music on again and the other dancers began moving around them.

"Everything okay?"

"Yeah...all good." *Too good.* Kate pulled her hand back, the desire she'd felt as they'd danced burned inside her. She wanted more. But she had no business dancing another song with Mo.

She looked at the table where Terri had been sitting. Their drinks were still there, but an older couple had taken up the space. "I should find Terri."

"She's over there." Mo pointed across the room. "She didn't get much of a break."

A handsome Mexican man had Terri on the dance floor. Or she had him. It was hard to say who was enjoying the dance more.

"He's a good dancer," Mo added.

"They look great together."

"You're not jealous?"

Kate shook her head. "She can dance with whoever she likes. And if she's with him, I won't feel guilty dancing another song with you."

Mo seemed about to say something in response, but then she took Kate's hand and they were in motion again. After that, Mo's eyes never seemed to leave hers and all Kate could think of was how good it felt to be close to her. Dancing gave her the excuse she needed. Once the music ended, she'd have to keep a careful distance, but until then, she didn't want to. She wanted Mo's arms wrapped around her, wanted Mo pulling her close. When Mo's gaze traveled up and down her body, there was no doubt she liked what she saw. Even if Mo wouldn't say she was attracted to her aloud, Kate could see how she looked at her. Mo wanted her, at least here, in this moment.

Several more songs passed before Kate remembered Terri. She spotted her on the dance floor still but with a new partner, an older woman who had announced at the start of the dance class that salsa dancing was all the rage in the small town in Canada from which she hailed. Terri had her laughing about something as they danced, and Kate decided to stop worrying. Terri could clearly take care of herself.

"Do you want to dance with someone else?" Mo asked.

"No—aside from the instructor, you're the best dancer here."

"I like that answer."

"What about you?" Kate asked. "You wouldn't have any trouble finding another partner. They're short on leads…"

"I'm only here tonight because of you."

They started dancing again and Mo's words ran through her mind. She already knew how Mo felt, didn't she? It wasn't Mo's fault that they weren't together. She knew that now more than ever. It was her fault, her issues, that stopped her from pressing her lips against Mo's.

For once she wanted to believe that her past didn't exist, that her old issues hadn't followed her. For one night, she wanted to push away all the reasons why they couldn't be together. She looked into Mo's eyes, saw the desire she knew would be there, and let go of the last bit of her inhibitions.

On the next step, Mo pulled her close and Kate lingered in her arms instead of spinning away. She let her hand caress Mo's lower back and the rest of the room disappeared. She didn't need to pretend to look anywhere else.

Mo stopped dancing and their eyes met. Kate fought to control her breathing. Had she gone too far with the caress? A moment later Mo let go of her hand. The music had changed to a pop song.

"That was fun. Did I pass?"

"Not bad for a club dancer." Kate hoped the light tone would cover how she really felt.

"Not bad? That's all I get? For real?"

"If I say you were the best partner I've ever had you'll never let up." But Kate felt some freedom admitting it aloud.

"Say it anyway."

The challenge in Mo's eyes seared. Kate wanted to step forward and kiss her so desperately it was hard to think of anything else. It took every ounce of control to hold her gaze as she said, "Dancing with you was incredible. Happy?"

"How about mind-blowing?"

"Don't push it." Kate smiled as Mo laughed.

She forced herself to look away from Mo and spotted Terri coming their way. Instinctively, she took a step away from Mo. With the one move, the distance between them felt insurmountable again.

"You two were amazing out there," Terri said, smiling first at Kate and then at Mo. "I think you need to sign up for one of those dance competitions."

Mo looked over at Kate with a sheepish grin. "I'll go get our drinks."

As soon as she went to get the drinks from the table, Terri turned to Kate and said, "Okay. Wow. Serious chemistry. How is it that you two haven't slept together all these years?"

Before Kate could answer, Mo came back. She handed Terri and Kate each their bottled water and then held up her phone. "I'm gonna be outside for a minute. I have to make a call."

Kate felt reality kick her in the stomach. Mo must have heard back from Chantal. She tried not to let her emotions show as she turned to Terri. "You looked great out there. How'd you like the class?"

"It was fun," Terri said.

Kate could hear the hesitation in her voice and she knew that by dancing with Mo, even if Terri had suggested it, she'd disrupted whatever bond they'd started to form. She wasn't sure what to do to fix it. Or if she should even try. It wasn't fair using someone else to get over Mo. She doubted it would work anyway.

Terri finished the last bit of her water and held up the empty bottle. "I think I'm ready for a Coke. I need some sugar. Want anything?"

"Coke sounds perfect."

Terri followed Kate to the bar. As they waited, Kate wondered what Mo was saying to Chantal. She knew it wasn't her business, but she wanted to call Chantal herself to tell her she was making a mistake if she picked anyone over Mo.

"I hope I didn't overstep when I said you and Mo had chemistry."

"No, it's fine. I just don't know what to say."

"Don't worry. I'm not asking you for an explanation. Some things you can't fight."

The bliss she'd felt dancing was gone now, replaced with a familiar ache as well as a new pinch of guilt. She'd let down Terri and she still had no claim to Mo.

"Do you know who she's calling?" Terri asked.

"Her girlfriend…She's in London on a work trip and things aren't going that great between them."

Terri clasped her hand and gave it a gentle squeeze. "I'm not one to tell people what to do, but I think you should tell her how you feel. Even if she's got a girlfriend. When you dance with her, it's obvious there's something going on between you— at least to everyone else in the room." She let go of Kate's hand as the bartender came over.

As Terri ordered, Kate wondered if she should argue again that nothing was going on. But she doubted Terri would believe her. She eyed the doorway Mo had disappeared through, hoping she'd reappear. That would only make things more awkward between her and Terri, however.

After they'd gotten their drinks, they settled in at one of the tables facing the dance floor. A server brought over a bowl of chips and salsa and Terri murmured a few words of appreciation in Spanish before digging in. Kate settled back in her chair and took a big sip of the Coke. She usually ordered diet, but one taste and she decided the sugar splurge was worth it.

"You and Mo stole the show tonight. Even the instructor was watching you two."

"She was?"

Terri laughed. "You two were in your own little world."

"That's how I get when I dance. It's the one time when I can really let go." Kate hesitated. "But I feel like I should apologize. I wasn't the best date tonight. We only danced a few songs together."

"Relax. I was the one who told you to dance with her." Terri clinked her bottle of Coke against Kate's. "And it was fun to watch you two. Besides, I had a good time dancing with Tomas and Gwen."

"You make friends wherever you go, don't you?"

"I love getting to know new people. And I love flirting."

"You're good at it. I mean, it feels authentic—it's almost as if you really like people," Kate smiled.

"Almost." Terri winked. She leaned back in her seat. "I kept hoping I was reading the signals wrong with you and Mo, but I also knew that I wasn't. The way Mo looks at you... You're more to her than a friend."

Before tonight, she would have argued that Terri was wrong. But now she'd felt Mo's hands pulling her close, seen the way Mo's eyes had traveled up and down her body...

"The thing is, we're really close friends so it's confusing and I think people read more into it than is actually there, most of the time."

"When you dance together, it's not confusing."

"Maybe what we have is different than most friendships but..." Kate stopped herself from saying Mo didn't want more. "For the record, I was telling the truth. We've never hooked up."

"I believe you. Though, in my opinion, that's worse. If you two were old lovers, there'd be history but I'd know that you tried that path and it didn't work. As it is... I don't want to get involved with someone if they're not really available. I've been down that road before."

"I understand—and I don't blame you. This is probably going to come out wrong, but I really like you and I think you'd be good for me. I wish we'd met when I was already over Mo. I can't tell you how much I've been trying to get there. I'm sorry I'm not yet."

"Don't apologize. I'm the one who asked you out even though it didn't take a mind reader to see there was more than a friendship between you two. You're pretty much exactly my type. Attractive, smart, and unavailable."

"Is there a chance we could be friends instead?"

"I'd like that. I could use a friend. Probably what I need more than a girlfriend, actually." Terri smiled wryly. "Less drama."

Kate smiled back. "I've never felt more relaxed with someone I just met. You're really genuine—there's no pretenses."

"If only there was a way to add recommendations to dating profiles."

"Oh, I could add a lot more than genuine." Kate wondered if she was making a mistake. If Mo wasn't part of the picture, she'd be kissing Terri tonight. Why was she still holding out for something that wasn't going to happen?

"I tried online dating for a while—after my therapist made me promise to do something to show that I thought I was someone worth dating."

"How'd it go?"

Kate scrunched up her face. "I bet you can guess."

"I know it works for some people. I keep wondering what their secret is…"

"Desperation?"

Terri laughed again. "I've done my share of therapy as well. At least I can say that I've worked on my emotional growth, which I'm pretty certain leads most people to a single life."

"You may be on to something. My therapist keeps saying 'love yourself and let go of the people in life who don't love you back.' Then I'm surprised when I'm living alone."

"Do we have the same therapist?" Terri chuckled. "I know you aren't looking for advice but…Mo loves you back."

"Now we're getting into complicated territory."

"My favorite type of territory," Terri quipped. "So why haven't you and Mo dated?"

"She's never asked. And I've never been brave enough." Kate felt her throat tighten. No way was she going to start crying now. She swallowed back the emotion, and said, "I've tried to let her know I'm interested. I mean, not directly, but she was pretty clear about her answer. She only wants to be friends."

"Hmm." Terri pursed her lips. She looked over at the dance floor, giving Kate enough time to try and master her emotions. "I get the feeling that Mo thinks that you don't want her."

"Really?"

Terri nodded. "I think you have to be direct."

But Mo knew how she felt, Kate argued silently. She thought of the near kiss in Hawaii and shook her head. "It's a moot point. Mo has a girlfriend."

"What would happen if you told her how you feel anyway?"

"It'd push her away," Kate said. She was convinced of that much.

"I think you need to give her the chance to make up her own mind—instead of deciding this for her. Tell her how you feel even if you think it's too late. If you don't, you'll regret it." Terri paused. "You'll probably think I'm crazy, but I love astrology. I'm thinking you're a July baby. Cancer?"

"How'd you guess? July 10th."

Terri slapped the table, clearly proud of herself. "I should get a second job."

"Aren't you a doctor? Like an internist or something? And you're into astrology?"

"Well, yes." Terri picked up a chip and dipped it in the salsa. "And most of my friends think it's silly, but humans have been studying the stars for longer than we've been practicing medicine. There's a chance that we've learned something, right?" She crunched on the chip and then reached for another. "We accept that how the moon and the stars align affect us. Why do we have to be so sure that it stops there?"

Kate shrugged. "Because there's no proof?"

"As much as I like the scientific method, I'm willing to accept that some things can't be proven—or disproven—by science. Don't take this the wrong way, but all of my Cancer friends are loyal to a fault. I think it might be a low self-esteem thing most of the time. And they all pretty much suck at dating, but they crave love more than anyone."

"There's a right way to take that?"

Terri laughed. "Being loyal is an amazing quality. And needing stability isn't a bad thing…but you can get caught in a rut that way and convince yourself that you shouldn't take risks."

"Sometimes I take risks."

"In love?"

Kate shook her head.

Terri continued, "You want someone who's gonna love you in spite of your faults, right? But you're pretty sure those faults make you unlovable." She waited for Kate's nod. "The thing is, you'd love someone, no matter what their faults. And you could commit to them forever. That makes you pretty amazing."

Kate didn't say that Terri had read her perfectly. "I don't think that makes me amazing. More like a hopeless romantic."

"That too. I love Cancer people. You know Reed's a Cancer. Took her forever to find someone strong enough to hold her, but Julia's perfect and there's no way Reed's letting her go."

Kate thought of Reed proposing to Julia in front of everyone on the plane. Reed was a heck of a lot braver than she'd ever be. "What's your sign?"

"If only that was a pick-up line," Terri said, adding a wink. She pointed to one of the tattoos above her elbow—a pair of green fish swimming in opposite directions. "Pisces. We're trouble. We can read people like an open book but never let anyone know what we're thinking. Overly sensitive, moody, judgmental, cold. My exes both gave me a long list of things to work on. Oh, and apparently I can't make up my mind. You dodged a bullet."

"Actually I found someone that has all the makings of a perfect friend," Kate said. "I've got most of those same faults. I only wish I knew what people were thinking."

"People? Or one person in particular?"

Kate smiled wearily.

"When you first met Mo, was it an instant attraction? Or were you only thinking of boys back then? She said that you've known each other since college."

Kate thought back to that first day. "I knew I was attracted to her. I'd never met anyone like her. But the only thing I really remember was this tense feeling in my stomach like Mo was going to be a huge problem for me."

"When's her birthday?"

"March 30th."

"Aries? Oh, no wonder! Yeah, you were screwed from the start. My ex was an Aries. They think they know everything, don't they? The hard part is, most of the time they're right. But they're so much fun to be with—spontaneous, daring... And they make friends wherever they go. But an Aries and a Cancer? Those stars aren't exactly aligned."

"How bad is it?"

"As bad as an Aries and a Pisces. It's another fire and water combination. Opposites attract, and good luck making it work in the long run. I know how appealing Aries can be. They're the heroes we all wouldn't mind being rescued by."

"That's Mo."

"I may be the last one you should listen to on this, but with an Aries you need to be direct. They can't guess what you're thinking. And they want someone who is head over heels for them. They're not going to wait around while you decide—even if they really want you. If they think that you don't want them, they're gone. For as brave as they seem, they're insecure too."

Kate's heart sunk. Maybe it was all bogus astrology, but it felt too close to the truth. "What if I'm too late?"

Terri considered her with a look of sympathy. "You might be. And then you're going to have to find a way to let her go."

Kate glanced at the door, wondering how long Mo would be gone. Maybe she wasn't coming back. She wished she could overhear her conversation with Chantal and then felt guilty for that thought.

"As soon as you leave to go find Mo, I'm going to ask that Canadian woman I was dancing with earlier for another round."

"You think I should go look for Mo?"

"That's what you're thinking about, right?" Terri smiled. "You're an open book."

"I don't know what to say to her."

"Start with the truth," Terri said. "Tell her how you feel."

"Ever consider being a therapist?"

"I think I'll keep my day job. My therapist always looks exhausted."

"So does mine." Kate laughed. "I'm sorry you got tangled up in being my counselor after you asked me out."

"I made a new friend." Terri smiled. "No regrets."

As soon as Terri settled in at the Canadian's table, Kate decided to go find Mo. She headed out of the club, practicing what she'd say to Mo in her head. *I know you're with Chantal but you're always with someone..."*

She jogged down the stairs and bumped straight into Mo as she turned the corner. Mo had been leaning against the building, but she'd quickly reached out a hand to catch her mid-stumble.

"Sorry. This was a dumb place to stop. Are you okay?"

"I'm fine. I'm the one who should be saying sorry. I ran straight into you. Are *you* okay?"

Mo nodded but Kate noticed her eyes were red. There were no tears on her cheeks, but it was obvious she'd been crying.

"Sorry I was gone so long. I got distracted." She jutted her chin upward and Kate followed her gaze to the star-filled sky. It was a gorgeous clear night and a thousand stars shone above them. "You don't see stars like that in San Francisco. Reminds me of the skies we saw in Hawaii."

Hawaii. Kate thought of the night she'd tried kissing Mo. The pain of that mistake hadn't ever really gone away. Mo had a girlfriend then, just like now—she didn't want to make the same mistake twice.

"Did you talk to Chantal?"

Mo shook her head. She looked down at her phone. "I was going to call her but then I got to thinking..."

Kate wished that Mo was thinking about the dancing instead of Chantal, but she had no business wanting that. Mo was in a relationship, even if it was rocky.

"Do you want to go for a walk? We could talk about it." When Mo didn't answer, Kate pushed on. "We can pretend we are out here looking at stars, but we both know this is about Chantal. You look like you've been crying. It's okay to admit you're hurting, Mo."

"I'm fine."

"You know that you can drop the tough butch act with me, right? You don't need to pretend you're fine when clearly you're not." Kate saw Mo's jaw clench and knew she'd said the wrong thing. "All I'm saying is that I won't judge if you cry. How many times have you seen me cry?"

"I don't feel like crying. Everything's just complicated and I'm tired of thinking." Mo sighed. "Why aren't you with Terri?"

"It's complicated," Kate returned.

"A walk sounds like a good idea. Beach?"

Kate nodded. She couldn't bring herself to ask what Mo meant by complicated. As much as she wanted this to be about her, if it wasn't she didn't want to know. Terri's words echoed in her mind. But she couldn't simply tell Mo that she wanted to be with her.

With every step the dance music got quieter and the ocean swells became more distinct. They passed one of the swimming pools, still dotted with swimmers lounging on the steps or floating on rafts with drinks in hand, and then crossed in front of the pool bar busy with patrons chatting in voices made overloud from alcohol. When they reached the end of the path, they both stopped to slip off their shoes.

The sand was cool against Kate's feet and she shivered with the breeze. She stole a look over at Mo, wishing she would say something first, and then noticed her furrowed brow. Mo was clearly in her own head and Kate knew a heart-to-heart conversation wouldn't be happening. "Story of my life," she said.

"What's that?" Mo looked over at her.

"Nothing. I was thinking out loud…" Kate's heart beat fast as she decided to go for the truth, even as her mind threw out all the reasons why that was a bad idea. "I said: story of my life."

"I thought that's what I heard. What's the story of your life?"

"I make excuses. Give myself an easy way out so I don't have to do the hard thing I know I need to do…and then I regret it later."

Mo kept her gaze on the water, but she slowed her pace the further they went. "I do that too. It's usually with conversations. Like you don't want to tell someone something that you know you need to tell them but then you regret it when they give you a pass."

She stopped to look up at the sky and then looked back at Kate. She held her gaze for too long. That, Kate wanted to say, was what had started her in this whole mess in the first place. From the beginning, Mo had a way of looking at her as if she could see right into her soul. And Kate had felt safe with her looking.

She trusted Mo more than anyone else. But there was something Mo was clearly holding back from her now. Well, she was holding something back as well. She couldn't exactly call Mo out.

Kate realized she was holding her breath when Mo turned and started walking again. The sound of the water's soft hiss as the waves lapped the shore seemed louder than her thoughts, and she tried to focus on that instead of all the questions spinning round.

Mo glanced over at her. "What's the conversation you don't want to have with me?"

"I want to have the conversation," Kate said. "But if I do... it changes everything."

"Sometimes change is a good thing."

If only Mo would simply guess what she wanted to say—or tell her that she wasn't alone in her feelings. With the way Mo had danced with her, it wasn't possible that she could feel nothing. They kept walking and when Mo didn't try to start any conversation, Kate began to doubt her hopes.

During the day, the resort employees set up lounge chairs in front of the water, but at night it was only a stretch of smooth dark sand. When they reached the hammock where Kate had spent the afternoon, Mo veered over to it. She pressed her weight on it, testing it with her hands and then turned and sat down, letting the hammock swing her feet off the sand.

Kate watched the hammock for a moment, gathering her courage. "I liked dancing with you tonight. Sometimes I wish that what I feel when I'm with you..." Her voice trailed. Could she really go through with this? If she followed Terri's advice, she could ruin everything. But if she didn't say anything... She lost her courage as soon as Mo met her gaze. Scrambling for a way to finish she said, "I wish life was all salsa dancing."

"No one's depressed when they're salsa dancing," Mo said, echoing her words from earlier that day.

"And there's no what-ifs. All you can think about is the music and your next step."

Mo nudged her toe into the sand, swinging the hammock again. "You were having such a good time with Terri when I got there I wasn't sure if I should stay."

"I'm glad you stayed."

"Terri's right. You're an amazing dancer. It's like you're a different person out there—you let go."

She did feel different when she danced. She was sure of herself and confident in her body. Unfortunately that feeling didn't last.

"So what went wrong?"

"What do you mean?" Kate stalled.

"You spent most of the dance class with me and then you left Terri at the club. I thought things were going well after your taco date."

"Terri's sweet. I like her a lot." Did Mo want the truth? Was she ready to admit it? "But I don't think I'm in the right space to date her. Probably I should just stick to dancing."

"Maybe I should too. All the fun without the drama." Mo's tone was light, but Kate wondered what she was covering up. "You should sign up for a competition like Terri said. You're really good..."

"We could do it together. You've gotten a lot better than when you used to stomp on my feet in those dorm dances."

"I've had a lot of practice," Mo said. "And some people stomp back—in heels. You gotta be quick."

Kate smiled at Mo's attempt to lighten the mood. She tried not to think about all the women Mo had wooed in those practice sessions. Anyone who danced with Mo would fall for her.

"I need to ask you a favor," Kate said. She surprised herself by voicing her thoughts aloud and felt unsure she wanted to go on as soon as Mo's gaze met hers.

"You know I'd do anything for you. Do we need to move a dead body?"

Kate shook her head. "You're terrible, Mo." But even as they joked, goose bumps prickled her skin. Mo probably didn't mean anything grand by her statement. It was only the simple truth. Mo would do anything for her. But there was a limit to what she could ask.

"I know everything with Chantal is getting to you. If I were in your shoes, it'd be getting to me too." Kate took a deep breath. "I hope for your sake that she isn't sleeping with her boss. Really I do. And if she's been loyal to you and she makes you happy then that's what I want for you."

"But?"

"But mostly I wish..." The words stalled. She couldn't finish the sentence aloud. In her mind, she'd said it more than once: *I wish you could be happy with me and that I could be enough.* And if her past had been different, would they be together? "I need you to tell me if this is one-sided."

"What do you mean?" Mo's eyes were still on her, but her phone was ringing. The sound slowly broke through Kate's other thoughts, and she realized it was probably Chantal. She felt sick, wishing she hadn't said anything.

"You can answer that."

"Hold on. I'll turn it off." Mo reached into her pocket for her phone, took one look at the screen, and then stopped.

"It's Chantal, isn't it?"

"Yeah, but she can wait." The phone rang again and still she didn't answer, but she didn't send the call to voice mail either.

"Answer it. It's gotta be the middle of the night in London. It might be an emergency."

"She gets up early to workout," Mo said. "She probably just read my texts. I think it's close to six a.m. It's almost midnight here. What do you mean by 'one-sided'?"

The phone rang again.

"We can talk later." What was she thinking anyway? That she'd tell Mo that she'd had a thing for her all these years and then Mo would make some wild declaration of her love? Mo was still technically with Chantal. Besides that, she'd had sixteen years to tell her she was madly in love with her and it hadn't happened. No, she'd only make a fool of herself if she said anything more. "You don't want her call going to voice mail. You two need to talk. I'll see you back at the room."

Before Mo could answer, Kate turned and headed back the way they'd come. She walked twice as fast, hardly seeing the sand in front of her feet, let alone the water, and berating herself for opening her mouth. Tears streamed down her cheeks. As soon as she reached the cement path, she broke into a run.

It was at least an hour before Kate heard the click of the door. She didn't move, watching Mo enter in the shadowy light. The bathroom door opened and closed and then the light went on. Kate stared at the strip of light at the bottom of the door, listening to Mo brush her teeth and then the sound of the toilet flushing. The strip of light disappeared, and Kate closed her eyes. She held her breath as Mo climbed into bed, hoping the mattress wouldn't give away her racing heartbeat.

"You're still up?" Mo asked softly.

"I was waiting for you to get back," Kate admitted. "Everything okay with you and Chantal?"

"I don't know. I didn't ask her if she was sleeping with her boss. When I texted her, I just said that I missed her. She'd gone to bed early and was calling back to talk...but she knew it was late so we decided to finish the conversation tomorrow."

"Maybe she just went to London for work. Maybe you're reading too much into all of this."

"Maybe." Mo sighed. After a moment, she touched Kate's arm with a light fingertip. "What about you and me?"

"What do you mean?"

"Are we okay? I know we weren't done talking..."

"It's fine. We can talk later." Kate didn't dare roll over. She clutched the sheet, wishing she'd fallen asleep already. Seconds ticked by and Mo's hand slid off Kate's arm, taking the warmth with it.

"Good night," Mo said.

The sound of Mo rolling over made her stomach clench. Who was she kidding? She'd missed her chance long ago.

CHAPTER TEN

Kate woke in the early morning light. She changed into her running shorts and a jog bra and then quietly slipped out of the room. Mo was still softly snoring, but Kate didn't chance a look at her. Her head was still a mess from last night.

The sky was streaked with pink and the distant sun was only an orange glow at the edge of the horizon. She started down the path, taking slow lunging steps to stretch her muscles. As soon as she reached the sand, she spotted Reed and raised her hand.

"You're up early. Going for a run?" Reed was in running shorts as well.

Kate nodded. "Looks like you're a morning person too."

"Yep. Julia and the kids are still sound asleep. All that swimming tuckered them out."

"I don't remember Julia being much of a morning person anyway."

"Not so much. Is Mo?"

"If morning starts after nine, yes."

Reed laughed, but Kate suddenly couldn't manage even a smile. She clenched her jaw, hoping the tears would hold off.

She was being ridiculous—she couldn't break down simply talking about Mo.

"Can I run with you?"

Reed touched the watch on her wrist, setting a timer. "I'd love the company."

As long as a conversation about Mo wasn't part of it, Kate wanted the company too. She'd spent too long last night feeling sorry for herself that she was alone—she had friends. "How far do you usually run?"

"I was thinking of going for five."

Five was more than Kate usually ran, but there was nothing like a hard run to shake a bad mood. "Let's do it."

Reed started off, heading northward and keeping to the dark, hard-packed sand. The tide was out and aside from the seashells that dotted the beach, the terrain was perfect.

After about a mile, they cleared the manicured resort properties and the island took on a wilder look. The sandy path narrowed and thickly vined trees encroached. Kate thought about the night Mo had stopped her from walking on the beach alone and the game of Ping-Pong that followed. She pushed forward, wanting to outrace her thoughts.

Reed stayed at her side but after a few minutes started to slow. "You're working on a six-minute mile. My knees can't keep up, but go for it if you can."

"My shoulder's burning," Kate admitted, slowing her pace to match Reed's stride. "I just needed to get some stuff out of my head."

"I get it." Reed touched her watch again. "Three miles to go."

By the time she got back to the resort, Kate was too tired to think. She eyed the water, wishing she could dive in. Her back and arms were coated in sweat and she didn't want to show up at Mo's bungalow stinking and red as a lobster. Of course she also had other reasons for avoiding Mo.

Reed noticed her looking at the water. She nodded toward it. "If I'm lucky, that's where I'll be spending the rest of today."

"What's the other option?"

"Julia wants to go into town to do some sightseeing, but the kids want to spend the day in the pool. They love that slide and the swinging bridge."

Kate thought of her plans. Today was the day she and Mo were supposed to explore the island on a scooter, but she wasn't sure she was up for that anymore. Getting out of it, however, would require an explanation that she didn't want to give. And the truth was, she was still looking forward to being alone with her even though the circumstances might be strained.

"But first I need breakfast," Reed said. "That's the real reason I'm a morning person. I'm thinking waffles."

"I love waffles." While that was true, she couldn't remember the last time she'd actually eaten one. Waffles were on the list of foods that triggered her—she remembered too many times when she'd eaten a whole box of Eggos only to take care of it later. But maybe after a hard run she could manage a few bites. "See you at the buffet table."

Mo wasn't in bed by the time Kate returned from the run. The sheets were tousled and Kate knew neither of them had slept well—Mo because she was thinking of Chantal and Kate because she was thinking of Mo.

Grateful for a moment alone, she showered and changed into a clean pair of capris and a tank top. After she'd combed her hair, she decided on a little makeup to bolster her confidence but then changed her mind before she had the eyeliner out. What was the point?

With her stomach begging for breakfast, she turned away from the mirror and searched for her phone and the room key. She'd missed a few texts from Mo: *Meet me in the lobby at ten for scooter ride.* And then: *Chantal is calling at nine. I may finally ask her.*

Good luck, Kate texted. *See you at ten.*

Depending on what Chantal said, Mo would need a friend more than anything else today. Kate resolved to focus on that. Her stomach growled again, and she tossed the phone into her purse along with a bottle of water, sunscreen, and her wallet. At the last minute, she went back to the bathroom and found her eyeliner. She added lip gloss and contemplated her motives. Regardless of how last night had ended, it didn't hurt to look good.

"Where's your waffle?" Reed pointed to Kate's plate.

She'd skipped the waffles after all and went for plain yogurt and granola along with a plate of mango and berries. "I decided to go for something light. I'm not sure how my stomach is going to be on a scooter with Mo driving." It was a good excuse anyway.

"Mo will take it easy with you," Julia said. "Where is she?"

"She wanted to call her girlfriend." Kate hoped she sounded nonchalant. "Where's Terri?"

"She likes sleeping in," Carly said.

"One time she slept in until noon," Bryn added. "She can do that because she doesn't have kids."

"Is that what she told you?" Reed asked.

Carly and Bryn nodded in unison. Carly added, "And she eats dessert for breakfast because she's a grown-up."

Kate felt a moment of envy imagining Terri still soundly sleeping. If only she could actually relax on this vacation. Sleeping in wasn't something she'd ever been good at, but it definitely wasn't happening with Mo lying next to her.

"Aunt Mo has dessert whenever she wants," Bryn said. "When I'm a grown-up, I'm gonna be like her."

"And eat dessert all the time?" Reed guessed.

"And I'm gonna work on computers so I can eat candy at work," Bryn added. "Mo says she can eat M&Ms all day—they have bowls all over the place."

"Hey, Aunt Kate," Carly said. "Knock-knock."

Kate was definitely not in the mood for a joke, but she forced a smile.

"Now you're in for it," Julia said. "Carly and Bryn were on my phone this morning. They've memorized about ten knock-knock jokes just for you."

"Lucky me," Kate said. But when she looked back at Carly, her smile was genuine. Probably she needed this distraction more than Carly knew. "Who's there?"

Despite Carly and Bryn's attempts, the jokes didn't hold her attention for long. Her thoughts kept returning to the looming scooter ride. Why had she said yes? Every time she considered wrapping her arms around Mo and speeding down the highway, she felt an uncomfortable mix of excitement and guilt.

"Make sure Mo wears her helmet," Julia said.

Everyone was standing up, the breakfast plates cleared. "You know I will."

"And try to relax." Julia patted Kate's shoulder. "You're allowed to have fun, you know. Even if she has a girlfriend."

Before Kate could respond, the kids scooted past arguing loudly about the best way to go down a tunnel slide.

"I better catch them before they wake up the entire resort." Julia waved over her shoulder.

Reed scanned the table and then ducked her head under it, clearly checking to make sure her group hadn't left anything behind. She snagged a toy troll from under Carly's chair and then paused in front of Kate. "Mo was telling me all about her plan yesterday. I know she's excited about spending the day with you. Don't worry. Whatever you were thinking about on this morning's run, it'll work out. I know it."

Kate wondered what Julia had told Reed. Or maybe Reed had guessed. At one point, she'd been better at hiding her feelings toward Mo. Now she couldn't seem to hold anything in, but she had to spend the rest of the day doing exactly that.

After Reed left, Kate made a sweep past the breakfast pastries and picked out Mo's favorite—a frosted cinnamon roll. If she'd skipped breakfast, the conversation with Chantal must not have gone well. Maybe sugar would help.

The lobby was nearly empty and Kate glanced over at the concierge's desk. Luis wasn't there. She sighed. She'd planned on asking if any rooms had unexpectedly come available. Managing three more nights before the promised oceanfront suite wasn't going to be a picnic.

As soon as she walked outside, the valet approached.

"Oh, no car." She wished she felt brave enough to use her Spanish. It was one thing understanding the actors in her favorite telenovelas and another actually talking to someone. "I'm waiting for someone," she added.

Kate took out her phone to check the time and noticed she'd missed several messages from Mo in the last half hour.

Mo's first text: *Not sure I'm up for a scooter ride today.*

Then: *Found out that I can cancel the rental. Unless I hear from you, I think we should try a different day.*

Mo's last text had been sent twenty minutes later: *Cancelled the scooter. I can't today.*

"Can't what?" Kate said aloud. She didn't want to text Mo back—she wanted to talk in person—but she typed a reply anyway: *Just got this. Sorry I didn't respond earlier.*

Her finger hovered over the screen as she debated saying more. Had Mo broken up with Chantal? As much as she wanted to ask, she felt the pain of knowing that Mo had asked for time alone—not her company. She sighed and tossed the cinnamon roll in the trash can by the valet.

"What a gorgeous day!" Julia said, suddenly stepping out of the lobby. "You and Mo are going to have so much fun on a scooter ride. Where is she?"

Kate felt tears press at her eyes. She quickly rubbed them away. "I thought you were spending the day at the pool. Change of plans?"

"Reed convinced me to take a quick trip downtown to do some shopping. I think she knew I was ready for a break from that kid pool."

Kate tried smiling back, but she could tell from the change in Julia's expression that the attempt fell flat. "Want some company?"

"What about the scooter ride?"

She let out the breath she'd been holding. Some of the tension went with it, but the impulse to cry was still there. "Mo cancelled."

"Mo never cancels on anything," Julia said. "Is she sick?"

"No…it's her girlfriend. She didn't tell me what happened exactly, but she wants some time alone."

"That's not like Mo. We should go find her."

Kate shook her head. "I don't think she wants that."

Julia studied her for a long moment and then the next thing Kate knew, she was pulling her into a hug. Kate melted into Julia's embrace. She squeezed her eyes, keeping the tears for later.

A car pulled up to the curb and Kate straightened up. She cleared her throat. "I don't know why I'm standing here trying not to cry. I'm not even the one having relationship issues."

"You can tell yourself that," Julia said. "But I know the truth."

Kate didn't argue. Julia was her rock. Always steady, always there. But Julia didn't need her dissolving into a blubbering mess in the middle of her vacation. "So, can I crash your shopping trip?"

The taxi dropped them off in a plaza not far from the ferry building. Most of the shops there likely had sprung up to cater to passengers from cruise liners, but the narrow streets winding away from the central plaza had a more authentic small-town Mexican feel.

Kate followed Julia around like a puppy dog for the first hour, happy that she didn't have to make any decisions about where they were going. They wandered into a half dozen jewelry shops before Julia found a necklace that caught her eye. Reed, she insisted, wouldn't like anything flashy. The piece she picked was a turquoise pedant on a silver chain. Kate couldn't see what set this one apart from the others. The windows of all the jewelry shops they'd passed were filled with turquoise and silver in every shape and design.

"Can you see the waterfall?" Julia asked, holding the teardrop pendant up for Kate's inspection.

"Oh, that's really pretty," Kate said, struck as much by the stone's simple beauty as by the fact that she'd missed the copper-colored threads coursing through the center. The threads clearly formed a waterfall design in the blue-green background. "It's perfect for her."

"I think so too," Julia said. "But she's terrible to shop for. She's always saying that she doesn't need anything and I never know if I'm getting her something she'll even like. Meanwhile she can walk into any store and find something I'd love."

Kate squeezed Julia's shoulder. "You're easy. That's why we all love you."

Julia sighed. "Do you really think she'd like it?"

"I know she would. Besides, the twins' birthdays are in December, right?"

Julia nodded.

"Then turquoise is their birthstone."

That sealed the deal. Julia picked out a sleek silver chain to go along with the pendant and then went to haggle with the shop's owner over the price. Kate knew that Julia would buy that particular pendant at any price, but for her the negotiating was part of the fun. Kate's gaze roved over the pendants and earrings. She wasn't looking for a new piece of jewelry for herself although her mother's birthday was coming up.

"See anything you like?"

Kate had stopped in front of a gold necklace. An intricate gold key formed a link in the center of the chain and her thoughts went right to Mo. She swallowed and looked over at Julia. "I was thinking of picking up something for my mom."

Julia bit her lip, examining the necklace that Kate had clearly been eyeing. "I don't think this is your mom's type. She's a little more...flamboyant." Julia pointed to a bracelet that was in a case above the table. Dark blue sapphire squares were interspersed with princess cut diamonds on a white gold bracelet.

"You're right. My mom would love that." Kate could even picture the dress Eileen would wear to go with the bracelet.

"Want me to get you a good price?"

The glint in Julia's eye made it impossible to say no. "Go for it. If it's close to a thousand I'll take it."

Negotiations took longer this time, and the shopkeeper insisted on bringing out his calculator to show Julia the price she was asking converted from dollars to pesos. After five minutes, Kate had pointed to the necklace with the key and announced that she'd pay full price for that if she got a deal on the bracelet. The shopkeeper's face lit up at the offer and Julia sighed in defeat.

They left the shop with the jewelry securely tucked away in Kate's purse and then wandered through a few more stores before deciding to stop for sodas. Julia kept giving Kate sideways glances and it was clear a question was coming, but she didn't say anything until they were sitting on one of the benches facing the pavilion enjoying their orange Fantas.

"Your mom is going to love that bracelet," Julia said, motioning to Kate's purse. "But now you're going to have to tell me why you bought that little necklace."

A cool breeze came up off the water. If not for that and the shade from the trees lining the square, the day would have been a scorcher. The cool drink still hit the spot. Kate took another sip as she stared at the trimmed lawn.

"Remember how Mo used to wear our dorm key on a string around her neck?"

"I'd forgotten about that." Julia smiled.

"Do you remember that night Mo got us to go out after curfew so we could see the stars over the Golden Gate?"

Julia nodded. "'Cause it was finally a clear night. She was right—it was beautiful."

"I've thought about that night too many times."

"Why too many times?"

Kate wondered how to answer. "There's no point regretting what you didn't do."

Julia's eyebrow raised, but she only turned back to her drink and took a long sip. After a moment she said, "It was always so cold and foggy, but that night was perfect."

"And none of us had jackets. Or pockets."

"That's right! That's why she'd put the key in her shoe. And then she thought she'd lost the key and neither of us had brought ours." Julia laughed. "What a mess that was."

That was also the night that Kate had nearly told Mo she liked her. Julia had gone to bang on the residence assistant's window. No one had brought a phone and they were stuck outside two hours after curfew. As soon as Julia had gone, Mo started to apologize about losing the key and messing everything up. She'd been worried about getting them in trouble since the whole escapade was her idea. But then Kate admitted that it was one of the best nights of her life and she didn't care what happened next. Before she could say more, Julia came around the corner, complaining about the RA, and a second later the main door to the dorms swung open.

"And then when we all went to bed Mo found the key where she'd hidden it in her shoe," Julia added.

From then on, Mo had kept the key on a little string on her neck. Kate loved to see the flash of bronze against Mo's skin and for the rest of their freshman year, the key was a reminder of that night.

"True story: I thought you two were going to kiss when I left to find that RA. Mo kept looking at you like...like she couldn't look at you enough. I was always jealous of how you two connected." Julia set her hand on Kate's knee. "What happened after you and Ethan broke up? I thought for sure you two would finally hook up."

"I thought so too. We were hanging out all the time and I kept thinking she was going to turn to me and say something. But I think she was still reeling from Tanya and I kept doubting that she was really interested—and doubting that I'd be enough for her if we actually dated." Kate paused. "Then next thing I knew she was with Chantal." It still stung that Mo had said nothing about Chantal until she'd mentioned spending the night at her house. "I should have told her how I felt, but I guess I was hoping she'd say something first."

"She didn't know if you really wanted her."

Kate thought of what Terri had said the night before. How could Mo possibly not know? "At this point it doesn't matter. The truth is, I have too many issues. It wouldn't have worked."

Julia reached over and clasped Kate's hand. "If you keep hiding behind that excuse, you're going to lose her. You need to tell Mo what your issues are and let her decide."

Kate fought the urge to pull her hand back. Julia was trying to help. She knew that. She wished she could have a normal conversation, wished she could tell Julia honestly why she was a disaster and why Mo would never want her if she knew everything, but she couldn't.

"You keep waiting for her to say something. But she's waiting for you. Until you open up to her, you're not moving past friendship."

"Mo's not waiting for me—she's been serially dating since college. And what am I supposed to do? Wait until she breaks up with Chantal and then ask her out on a date? We can't start from zero like a normal relationship."

"Why not? Maybe you need to."

"You don't understand. Even if Mo and I had just met, my issues would still be a problem. I'm not what Mo needs."

"Maybe your issues aren't as bad as you think," Julia said. After a long minute she looked over at Kate's purse. "I think the necklace is perfect. She's going to love it."

Kate felt a fresh wave of guilt. Why had she even bought the necklace? She was kidding herself if the answer was anything to do with friendship.

"Something happened that shouldn't have been a big deal." She felt a lump in her throat but pushed on. "It shouldn't have affected me the way it did anyway… And it led to all these other things that I should have been able to stop, but I couldn't. I've tried to get past it and be normal, but I couldn't. I can't."

Julia squeezed Kate's hand. "Whatever happened, you know I won't judge."

"I know. And by now I should be able to talk about it."

"Well, I don't think it would change how Mo feels about you," Julia said. "But not telling her…"

Kate's phone buzzed with a text. She didn't look over at her phone, but she knew it was Mo. Earlier, she would have jumped to check the text.

"That's probably Mo," Julia said. "She can't handle too much alone time."

Kate reached for her purse and fished out the phone. She read Mo's text: *Sorry about this morning. Didn't really sleep and knew I wouldn't be safe on the road. Broke up with Chantal.*

Did that mean that Chantal had slept with her boss? Mo was going to be a mess if that was the case.

"Is she okay?"

Kate held the phone out for Julia to read the message. After a moment, Julia clicked her tongue. "I can't say I'm surprised. Mo was with her almost long enough for it to be serious."

Mo used to joke that she was allergic to anniversaries. "She was worried that Chantal was cheating on her, but I think that was only part of it. It's like she picks women who she knows will be short-term."

"Hmm. Any ideas why that might be?" Julia asked, her voice tinged with sarcasm.

"What do you mean?"

"She's been holding out for you for the past sixteen years." Julia stood up. "Come on. She's gonna need some cheering up."

Part of her hoped that Julia was right and an equal part wanted to argue that she couldn't be blamed for sixteen years of failed relationships. "I don't think Mo's relationship issues are my fault. And not that it matters now, but I don't think she ever told Chantal we were sharing a bed."

"She told her. I know because after she got off the phone with Chantal, Mo called me. She felt guilty telling Chantal that rooming with you was no big deal when clearly it was."

Kate looked down at her phone. "I wish I hadn't put her in that position."

"Mo put herself in that position. She asked you to share her bed." Julia paused. "Look, Mo's not perfect. And the choices she makes aren't your fault. That she can't get over you is also not your fault. But that you haven't told her why you won't date her even though you're clearly in love with her..."

Was she to blame? She thought of Mo lying next to her in bed last night and of the ache in her chest when Mo had turned away. Her body had barely resisted the urge to comfort her then. And what had Mo felt?

Kate tried not to overthink her response to Mo's text even with Julia's words ringing in her ears. *I'm sorry about Chantal. Want to meet for lunch to talk?*

Julia looked over Kate's arm and read the text she'd sent. "If she's not ready to really talk—about you and her—give her a few days. But then you have to tell her how you feel. She thinks she already tried with you and Mo's too proud to ask twice."

"She never asked. There was one time…but it was only a joke." Kate thought back to the night she'd considered breaking up with Ethan. Mo had promised then that if Kate needed a backup plan, she was planning on being a spinster and wouldn't mind a roommate. It was silly and certainly no proposal, and yet Mo's words had given her the courage she'd needed to call off the wedding. She considered now everything that Mo had said that night and wondered if any of it was meant as more than a joke.

"I know that you don't want to, but you need to open up. Mo has spent her whole life taking risks. She's an out black lesbian. She's tough, but it's not like it's easy being in those shoes. For this she needs you to take the risk."

"If I say anything now, I'll be a rebound."

"What are the rest of your excuses?" Julia said, a hard edge suddenly in her voice. "Seriously, Kate. What else have you got? No matter what you tell yourself, there's no chance you'll be a rebound. If I told you that you are the center of Mo's world, how would that make you feel?"

Kate didn't answer. Was it true?

"I love you, but I love Mo too. I don't want this to keep going the way it's been with you two crushing each other's hearts by not saying anything. I've gotta look out for both of my best friends here. And honestly right now I'm on Mo's side with this. It's your move."

Kate swallowed as she met Julia's gaze. "What if you're wrong and she's not interested?"

"What if?" Julia's challenge hung in the air between them.

CHAPTER ELEVEN

The twins were still at the pool when they got back. Reed was on a lounge chair facing the pool with a book in her lap and Julia went right to her after waving to the girls. She leaned over Reed's book and kissed her. "Have you seen Mo?"

"Last I saw her, she was headed to the beach." Reed glanced at her watch. "I think that was about an hour ago. She seemed pretty down. Is everything okay?"

"She broke up with Chantal," Julia said.

"Well, that explains it. Who ended things?"

Kate was wondering the same thing. This time it mattered who broke up with whom. If any of it was because of her advice she'd feel terrible.

"If I had to bet, Mo ended it," Julia said. "But I don't want to ask. From the start, she's been more closed off about Chantal than she's been about past girlfriends."

Kate thought of how Mo had opened up to her about Chantal. Why had she done that if she hadn't talked to Julia about her?

"Aunt Kate, look at me!" Carly hollered. She didn't wait to make sure she had an audience, taking off head first down the slide. When she crashed into Bryn, who was waiting at the bottom, Kate expected a scream or at least an argument between the kids. But Bryn only splashed back and laughed.

"They've been at this for an hour," Reed said.

"Aunt Kate, watch me this time," Bryn called.

"It's like watching the cooking channel," Reed said. "They keep you entertained and you forget how long you've been sitting."

"Why don't you two take a break?" Kate suggested. "I'll watch them for a bit."

"Really?" Julia glanced from Reed to Kate.

"Don't take forever, but yes." Kate kicked off her sandals and sat down. "Go for it, Bryn."

Mo would have to pass the pool on her way back from the ocean. If she wanted to talk, Kate would be waiting. Although what she was going to say to Mo was still up for debate.

"You sure?" Julia asked.

"Yes. Go on, lovebirds."

Reed ran her hand through her already tousled hair. "I think I could use a shower."

"Me too," Julia agreed.

"Okay, I don't need to hear about your plans. Just go." Kate shooed them away as she settled back in the lounge chair. She'd decided to wear her bikini under her clothes when she'd picked her outfit for the scooter ride, and she slipped off the extra layer as Reed and Julia headed off for their alone time.

Kate didn't enjoy the lounge chair for long. Carly convinced her to try the slide and soon she was laughing and splashing in the pool. When Reed reappeared, calling to the kids to say it was time for a break, Kate realized she could have missed Mo passing by the pool. She hopped out and grabbed a towel.

"What time is it?"

"Almost two. We're going to that Coconut Cabana that Terri was talking about for snacks," Reed said. "Want to join us?"

"No…I want to wait for Mo." Kate checked her phone. No missed calls or texts.

"I figured."

From the note of understanding in Reed's voice, Kate knew that Julia had told Reed about her troubles with Mo. "Anyway, if Mo doesn't text me, I've got a book to finish." Kate leaned down to wrap a towel around a shivering Carly. Her brain needed a break from obsessing about what she wanted to say to Mo. "And one of those hammocks on the beach has my name on it."

"Which one?" Carly asked. "Can I see it?"

"Did you use a sharpie?" Bryn wondered. "I want a hammock with my name on it."

"She didn't mean that literally," Reed said. "Aunt Kate wouldn't write on a hammock."

"Someone else could have," Bryn argued. "Like Aunt Mo."

Carly, who was still shivering despite the towel, said, "One time Aunt Mo drew a heart with your name on it, Aunt Kate. It was in the middle of our sidewalk for a long time."

"But she didn't use a sharpie. It was chalk. And then one day it rained and all of our drawings washed away." Bryn scowled. "And we'd worked so hard on that rainbow unicorn."

"A rainbow unicorn sounds like a tricky thing to draw," Kate said, trying not to think about Mo's drawing. Clearly she'd only been goofing around with the kids. A chalk heart didn't necessarily mean anything.

"That was my idea," Bryn said, puffing up her chest.

"I added the rainbows," Carly argued. "It didn't look good until I colored in the rainbows."

"Yes, it did," Bryn shot back.

"Okay, you two. Time to get some food before the real fighting starts." Reed smiled at Kate. "A hammock and a book sound perfect. I can almost remember those days…"

Reed led Carly and Bryn away from the pool, intervening as they bickered and pushed each other. It wasn't long before one of them yelled and the other started crying. Reed crouched down, said something, and scooped up both kids. Kate eyed the path down to the beach. As much as she wanted to check on Mo, she didn't want to chase her down.

When Kate got back to the room, laying down on the bed sounded decidedly better than a long walk back to the hammock. There was clear evidence that the housecleaner had been through the room, but the bed sheets were askew and the room still had a vague scent of Mo's cologne.

Kate set her bag down and smoothed the sheet. She kicked off her sandals and stretched out on top of the covers, promising herself that she'd only rest for a moment. The indent on Mo's pillow caught her eyes and she felt the pang of longing sharper than ever. Neither of them was getting much sleep, she knew. Maybe it'd be best if she stayed with Julia and Reed tonight. Mo could probably use her own space. But the thought of not sleeping in the same bed made her ache all over again.

She thought of telling Mo everything and wondered at the repercussions. She was tired of keeping secrets, but she didn't think admitting everything would mean Mo would want to date her. The opposite was more likely.

After a long minute, she reached over and caressed the indent in the pillow. She picked it up and hugged it tight to her chest, recalling the night she'd touched herself in Mo's old room. All the things she'd never tell Mo...

She closed her eyes, picturing Mo looking back at her as they'd danced together. *Friends only. As if.* She'd melted at the feel of Mo's hand in hers and the longing to feel Mo's lips had been impossible to ignore. That hour on the dance floor had been a blur—the best kind of blur. Had she been fooling anyone?

Kate woke twenty minutes later to the sound of her cell phone buzzing. She rubbed her eyes and picked up the phone. A picture of Peeves filled the screen. He was snoozing in his pink bed with sunlight streaming in through the kitchen window. This time her house sitter hadn't sent a message, but the picture was enough.

The lock clicked and Kate looked up as Mo entered. She stopped in the doorway. "Shoot. I forgot to knock."

"Don't worry. I'm only looking at a picture of Peeves." Kate held up her phone.

Mo glanced at the picture. "You could buy him a blue bed."

"He likes pink," Kate insisted. "I took him to the store and that's the bed he picked."

"If I bought him a blue bed, I bet he'd sleep in it."

Kate set the phone on the nightstand. "Well, yes, but only because it came from you and he loves you more than me."

Mo smiled, but Kate could see the effort it took. She watched Mo go over to the closet and slip off her flip-flops before hanging out a towel.

"How was the beach?"

"Nice." Mo sighed. "I swam until I couldn't swim anymore."

"I'm sorry about Chantal." Kate paused, wondering if Mo would say something. She had one hand on the closet door, but she hadn't made a move to close it. "Was she sleeping with her boss?"

Mo looked over her shoulder. "I don't know. I never asked."

"She broke up with you?"

Mo shook her head. "I told her that it wasn't working for me. She said that she knew it was coming."

From the note of exhaustion in Mo's voice, Kate knew better than to press for more details. Mo went to the bathroom and shut the door. Kate leaned back on the pillows, listening to the sound of the shower. She thought of what Julia had said and wondered again if telling Mo everything was really worth the risk. On the other hand, what did she have to lose?

The bathroom door opened and Mo came out, wrapped in a towel. She went back to the closet, and Kate averted her gaze as Mo dressed.

"Have you eaten lunch?"

"Not exactly. I had a candy bar for breakfast and then some chips…"

"Can I get you some real food? The lunch buffet is still open. I was thinking of getting a salad."

"I don't want a salad," Mo said. "I don't know what I want."

"I could get you a plate with a little bit of everything."

"The beauty of buffets… Perfect for those of us who can't even commit to our food," Mo added, sighing heavily. "Nothing too healthy, okay?"

"You got it." Kate got out of bed and started for the door. "Comfort food coming up."

"Hold on," Mo said.

Kate stopped, looking back at her. Mo didn't move from her spot by the closet, and the expression on her face made Kate's heart ache. But this was how Mo got after every breakup.

"Can I have a hug?"

Mo shouldn't have had to ask. Kate looked into her eyes, the deep brown ringed with red. As soon as she'd walked in the door, Kate should have given her a hug. She crossed the room, stopping a foot away from Mo, and opened her arms. Mo stepped into the embrace. She bent her head, resting it on Kate's shoulder, and exhaled.

Kate tried to block out the warmth that spread through her as Mo relaxed against her. She held her tight, wishing she could simply be the friend she needed. When the desire to kiss Mo's cheek pushed to the front of her brain, Kate loosened her hold.

"I feel like crap." Mo stepped back, breaking the embrace, and went over to the bed. She sank onto the mattress with a heavy sigh. "You know with every other girlfriend, I could come up with some excuse for ending things, but this time…the truth was I didn't love her. I don't even know if anything was going on with her boss. I'm so messed up."

"You're not messed up, Mo," Kate said gently. "You're just really good at asking people out and not that great at making it work when things get tough."

Mo squinted at her. "Are you saying I need to be more picky or more stubborn?"

"Both might help." She gave Mo a wink. "But now maybe you need some time without a girlfriend—figure out what you really want."

"Have you and my mom been talking again? She told me the same thing."

"Speaking as one messed-up person to another, sometimes you need to listen to the people who love you. Every once in a while they know what's good for you."

"Now you really sound like my mom." Mo leaned back in the bed and kicked up her feet. "One of these days you're going to have to tell me why you think you're so messed up." She settled in on the pillows and closed her eyes.

Kate took one last look at Mo before slipping out of the room. Was wanting to kiss her a good enough reason to gamble what they had? No. Mo needed a friend. Not another lover.

The buffet line was busier than Kate had expected and by the time she got back, Mo was sitting in bed playing solitaire. Generally that was a bad sign—she'd played solitaire every night for a month after her father had died, and following most of her bad breakups, the cards came out again. With other card games, she'd laugh and joke, but solitaire was a somber thing.

"Hungry?"

Mo held up an ace and smiled. "Is that pizza?"

Kate nodded, pleased to see Mo's smile widen. "I raided the kids' section of the buffet." She handed over the first of two plates. "Pepperoni pizza, cheesy bread, chicken fingers, and—wait for it—a slice of chocolate mousse pie for dessert. As ordered, nothing healthy. I also got you a Coke."

"You're the best. Can I eat the pie first?"

"Sometimes I don't think you've changed from the day I met you." Kate handed over the second plate, smiling as Mo licked her lips.

"So you're saying I'm still as handsome as ever?"

Kate decided to take a chance and say exactly what she was thinking. "I think you're more handsome now. But don't tell your eighteen-year-old self. She'll get jealous."

"Careful, I'll think you're flirting. At the moment I'm feeling a little impressionable."

"You? Impressionable? That would be a first."

Mo chuckled. She patted the bed. "Sit down with me. This is a lot of food. I'm gonna be here for a while."

Kate sat down, careful to leave plenty of space. "You missed breakfast and swam. I bet you can make short work of that."

Mo tried a bite of the mousse. She closed her eyes and moaned. "Mmm…"

"That good?"

Mo held up her fork with a bite of mousse pie balanced on it. "Don't think about calories—I know you—just close your eyes and enjoy it." She leaned across the space between them.

Kate wasn't the type who cut out sugar and forgot about it. She thought about dessert all the time no matter how many months she went without it, and her mouth watered now at the sight of the chunk of chocolate topped with whipped cream. She opened her mouth, and Mo gently placed the fork on her tongue. As she closed her lips, the rich chocolate filled her senses.

Mo pulled back the fork. "What do you think?"

"Not bad." In fact it was better than most orgasms she'd had, but she wasn't about to say that to Mo. She licked her lips, catching a bit of chocolate she'd missed.

Mo leaned close again and brushed her finger over the top edge of Kate's lip. "You missed a little whip cream."

Without thinking, Kate caught Mo's hand before she'd pulled it all the way back. She licked the bit of whipped cream off her fingertip, watching as Mo opened and closed her mouth. Mo swallowed hard but didn't pull back her hand.

Kate felt her heart racing in her chest. She always thought there'd be a necessary buildup, a conversation that would happen before they crossed any lines, but she'd blurred everything now and the way Mo was looking at her, hardly breathing, she didn't want to stop. It was now or never. She leaned across the space between them and pressed against Mo's lips.

Time stopped then. At first all she thought of was how perfect Mo's lips felt against hers. There was no challenging pushback in Mo's kiss, only a soft acceptance. Just when she started to worry that the gentleness in Mo's touch might mean her advance wasn't desired, she felt Mo's hand caress the side of her neck. She dared herself to deepen the kiss and Mo followed her lead.

One kiss moved to the next until she reached out to touch Mo's chest. She only thought of feeling more of her, her hand slipping under the T-shirt to touch the warm skin there, but she knew the instant Mo's hand encircled her wrist that she'd gone too far. Mo broke off the kiss and let go of Kate's wrist as quickly as she'd grasped it.

Kate sat still for a moment, dizzy with the rush of what she'd done. She looked down at the bed where they were sitting, the plates of food pushed to the side along with the blankets and the pillows all askew. Her cheeks burned with a blush.

"I'm sorry," she said, quickly getting off the bed and then standing awkwardly at the side. She wondered if she should come up with some excuse or offer to leave. The kiss had been some kind of reflex. Could she say it was only that? Or an accident?

Mo eyed the slice of pie and then pressed her finger to her lips. "It's funny how you can be waiting for something for so long and then it still surprises you… I always thought we'd have some long talk before that happened."

"Me too," Kate admitted. At least Mo wasn't saying that she wished she hadn't kissed her. "I wasn't planning on it. It just happened. I kind of stopped thinking."

Mo nodded slowly. Kate wanted her to say that it didn't matter if they hadn't talked about it first. The kiss had been perfect. That much had to be true for Mo too.

"I meant it when I said I was feeling a little impressionable." Mo pushed the plates to the side and pulled her knees up to her chest. She met Kate's gaze. "In Hawaii, I thought you were drunk, but you're sober now. Don't get me wrong. I wanted you to kiss me. I've been wanting that kiss for a long time. But I think it's a mistake."

"Why is it a mistake?" Kate's voice wavered. Nothing about the kiss had felt like a mistake.

"I don't want to mess around with you. Our friendship is too important."

"You mess around with everyone else. If you don't want me that way, tell me."

Mo's jaw clenched. "You haven't been in a relationship with a woman before. What if you find out this isn't what you expected? First relationships often don't last…and then when it's over what happens to our friendship? And I just broke up with Chantal. I'm not saying that I don't want this, but I think we need to talk before—"

"Not saying that you don't isn't the same as saying that you do," Kate interrupted. The more Mo backpedalled the worse she felt. But she trusted Mo's kiss more than her words. "Dammit. I wish that had been a terrible kiss."

"There's a lot more to this than kissing."

"I'm not dumb, Mo. I know there's more." How was it that Mo, the one who jumped with both feet into every relationship she'd ever had, was suddenly overanalyzing a kiss? Kate knew she'd gone too fast. But she wasn't ready to talk about it when Mo was clearly pushing her back. "Just tell me if you don't want me."

Mo met her gaze. She didn't move to kiss her again like Kate hoped. A long minute passed, and then Mo broke their look to glance over at the pie.

"I can't say that."

"Then why did you stop me?"

Mo was quiet for a long minute. When Kate had nearly given up waiting, she said, "Your memory of that first day in the dorms is better than mine. But there are things that I do remember.

"You were wearing a sundress and your toenails were painted—you were all done up like you were going to a party even though we were all moving boxes." Mo paused. "I'm pretty sure my jaw hit the ground when I first saw you. And then you looked at me. Hands down, you were the most beautiful woman who had ever checked me out."

"I had such a crush on you," Kate admitted quietly.

"But you never said anything. I guess I always knew but… Do you remember that Truth or Dare game we played that first night? You said you'd never been in love. I wanted to be your first." Mo sighed. "But it was pretty clear then that you weren't ready. I told myself I'd wait for you. Then it was fifteen years later and you still hadn't made up your mind about dating me. And I know what you're thinking. It wasn't like I wasn't hooking up with every other woman who looked my way. I know. But part of me was always waiting for the real thing. For that one day when you'd realize what we had. God, that sounds so cheesy when I say it aloud. But it's true.

"When you broke up with Ethan and told your parents you were bi, I thought…well, I thought you'd tell me then. I thought you were in love with me and that was why you broke up with him. We went out to get that cake after your breakup and I just knew you were going to say something. But you didn't. Weeks passed and we were hanging out every night. In some ways it was perfect. But I started to think there was something wrong with me."

"I was waiting for you to ask," Kate said. "I thought you needed time after Tanya. Then I turned around and you were dating Chantal."

"When Chantal asked me out, I thought about saying no. I wasn't looking for a new girlfriend. But I was so tired of waiting for you to decide. Part of me hoped you'd be jealous. And I know how messed up that sounds."

"I was jealous."

"But you moved to Denver instead. You said you needed space to figure things out. That's when it hit me. I couldn't wait forever. If you didn't know for sure if you wanted me or not after all those years, I needed to move on."

Kate felt a swell of regret. Mo was right. She'd taken years to decide she wanted her. Yes, she'd been attracted right from the start, but she'd been scared of admitting it then. She'd had her reasons. And yet maybe those reasons didn't matter anymore. Maybe a relationship could work despite everything. Her lips still tingled with Mo's kiss. If there was a way… "It took me a little longer than most. But I know what I want now."

"Do you?" Mo's tone was cynical.

"Yes." Kate felt an uncertainty rise up inside her. Mo was holding her at arm's length in a way she'd never done. Maybe the kiss had only been lust on Mo's end.

"I know what I want. What do you want? One minute you tell me that you've been waiting all these years and then the next you say that you aren't interested because you moved on. Which is it? And how can you kiss me like that if you've moved on?"

Mo shook her head. "If we mess up our friendship—"

"Too late. I already went there. I already messed everything up." Kate waited for Mo to argue that she hadn't, but they both knew the truth. One kiss had changed everything. Their friendship would never be the same.

The silence stretched. Kate felt the tears on her cheeks, but she quickly wiped them away. Mo's gaze was on the window, her thoughts concealed.

"I kept hoping that you'd ask me out," Kate said. "I didn't want to be the one to make the first move in case you didn't really like me that way. And I know this sounds like I'm in high school, but it's the truth—I never felt like I was cool enough for you. You're always the one asking women out. I figured if you wanted me, you'd ask."

"I never wanted you to turn me down. There was never a time when I was sure that you would say yes. You were always holding back. And you have all these things you won't talk about."

"Well, when I finally stopped holding back it didn't go so well. Do you blame me?" Kate didn't want to fight. When she'd imagined telling Mo that she loved her, it hadn't been anything like this. She took a deep breath. "Look, I know I screwed up. I took too long telling you that I had feelings for you. And you know what really sucks about all of this? That was the best kiss I've ever had. Probably the best kiss I'll ever have." *And it was followed by the worst conversation.*

When Mo didn't say anything in response, Kate said, "I need to go."

"Don't leave. We're not done talking."

"I can't keep talking about it. I shouldn't have kissed you. Let's just leave it at that." All the talking in the world wouldn't change how Mo felt.

CHAPTER TWELVE

"You need to go back and talk to her."

"It won't help." Kate wanted to wallow in self-pity alone. Her tears had left her exhausted, and all she wanted to do was curl up in the sun and fall asleep.

"You kissed her. Before that ever should have happened, you two needed to have a long conversation. Dating your best friend is a big deal."

"Can we please not do this? I know I screwed up."

Julia sighed. "I don't want to make you feel worse, but I think you can fix this if you go back and talk to her."

"Go back? So she can tell me again that I'm too late?" Kate shook her head. "No way." She looked out at the water. Julia had found her sitting on the dock and had sent the kids off with Reed. As much as she'd tried to convince her that she wanted to be alone, Julia was having none of it.

"You both hurt each other's feelings. But that doesn't mean this is the end. For the record, I think Mo screwed up too. She should have asked you out freshman year."

It was way too late for debating that. Mo's words haunted her thoughts—she hadn't asked her out in college because she wasn't certain Kate's answer would have been yes. Was Mo wrong about that? As much as Kate wanted to believe that she would have gone for it then, the reality was that she'd been in college on her parents' dime and despite everything that had happened, back then she was still worrying about disappointing them. And she was scared of opening up to Mo. Some things hadn't changed apparently.

"You know what really sucks? I'm stuck on an island sharing a damn room with her. Where the hell am I supposed to go? I can't even get in my car and drive somewhere." Kate searched for her phone and then realized her purse, along with her phone, was back in the room. "Dammit. Can I borrow your phone? I want to find somewhere else to stay."

Julia set her hand over her phone. "You're staying with us. The girls have two beds in their room. They can sleep together in one and you can have the other."

Kate dropped her head. "I'm too tired to argue."

"You know I'll win anyway."

"True. I also happen to not have a wallet or a phone at the moment so I can't do a damn thing about it."

Julia smiled. "You could just say thank you."

"Reed won't mind?"

"No. And the girls will be in heaven having an auntie with them."

"Not their favorite auntie."

Julia wrapped an arm around Kate. "Sweetie, I know it seems impossible right now, but I think you two still have a chance."

"At being friends? There's no way I'll be able to be around her without thinking of kissing her."

"I'm not saying friends." Julia squinted at the line of beach behind them. Reed and the kids were building sand castles. She held up her hand and then smiled as all three waved.

"You're lucky. Reed's amazing. So are the girls. And you totally deserve all of them."

"I'm lucky," Julia agreed. She turned back and studied Kate for a moment. "Mo told me something I promised I wouldn't tell you, but… After you and Ethan broke up, she wanted to ask you on a date. She had it all planned. But Mo's not as confident as she likes everyone to think. And asking you out was a big deal. You'd come out to your parents, but you'd never been with a woman. And what if it wasn't what you'd expected? There was something else, though. She told me that if after knowing you for all those years, you still didn't trust her—"

"Of course I trust her."

Julia looked down at the water, seeming to choose her words before going on. "She doesn't think you do. And the truth is, I don't think you do either. You have all these things that you won't talk about—to either of us. When you said that your father told jokes at the dinner table, I swear Mo nearly fell off her chair. We talked about it afterwards. That was the first time you've said anything about your childhood. And I get that you and your mom don't get along, but it's more than that. There's been so many times when you just stop talking. We'll get on some subject and then out of the blue…you put up a wall. Or you change the conversation."

"Everyone has things they don't want to talk about. Besides you've met my parents. It's not like anyone wants to hear about them."

"I'm not only talking about your parents. And I'm not trying to make you feel bad about this. I can hear you're getting defensive."

Kate stopped herself from arguing that she wasn't. Of course she was. Julia had no idea why, but that wasn't her fault.

"The thing is, Mo feels like you don't trust her enough to talk about issues that come up. Or about your past. That's a big problem for her. If you two got in a relationship and you still had all these walls, all these things that you wouldn't talk about…" Julia shook her head. "You'll do what you want but until you open up to her, I know she's holding back. And I don't blame her."

"She's not holding back, she's done," Kate said, aware her voice was rising. "And right now, I'm feeling done too. Apparently I can't do anything right. Maybe I can at least move on."

Julia set her hand on Kate's. "Mo would say you do plenty of things right. She loves you, no matter what she said. Give this time. You kissed her. She kissed you back. It's not the end of the world."

It only felt that way. Kate closed her eyes, turning her face up to the sun. She wanted to disappear or at least reverse everything that had happened that afternoon. Even if she told Mo everything, all of her secrets, that wouldn't give them a reset. She'd only drag Mo into the mess that was her head.

"Do you want to go shopping?" Julia asked, suddenly standing.

"Are you kidding?"

"There's this market I discovered near where Reed and I had lunch yesterday—right along the ocean. We don't have to buy anything."

"Have you met me? I don't go anywhere without buying something." Kate sighed. In fact, shopping sounded better than spending the rest of the day feeling sorry for herself. "I don't have my purse."

"Give me your key. I'll go get it."

"I don't have my key." She'd stormed out without thinking about even that. "Can I just go back to your bungalow and watch TV? I want to curl up in bed and not move for the rest of the night. God, what was I thinking? I can't believe I kissed her."

Julia clicked her tongue. "We'll make a deal. You get one night to feel sorry for yourself, then tomorrow morning I'm dragging you out shopping. After that we figure out what to do with you and Mo."

"I'm not going to be able to watch her screw around with some other woman. I'm not going to be able to pretend I'm okay." Tears threatened again and she had to look up at the sky to stop them. It was a perfect cloudless day. Paradise. "Dammit. I messed everything up."

"Maybe. But if you want her, you could still fix it."

True to her word, Julia let Kate sack out in front of the television that afternoon and then the kids kept her from thinking too much that evening by convincing her to color with them. She passed a restless night in a narrow bed in Carly and Bryn's room while they took turns cuddling with her despite the numerous times she carried each one back to the other bed.

Hours of rehashing her conversation with Mo kept her awake, and then Julia's words left her riled and anxious. She kept returning to the question of telling Mo about her past. Maybe airing her dirty laundry would help Mo understand why she'd held back all these years, but she didn't see how it would make anyone suddenly fall for her.

The next day, Reed joined her on a morning run and then Julia insisted on the promised shopping trip. By that afternoon, Kate was exhausted, but the twins begged her to take them swimming and Julia agreed for her.

Julia seemed to think that if Kate wasn't left to her own devices, she wouldn't think about Mo. Unfortunately, it didn't work that way. Her thoughts orbited around Mo despite the distractions. Still the better part of the day slipped by without any sight of her.

"Are you going to dinner with us?" Julia asked.

The twins were sprawled in front of the television, winding down from hours playing in the sun, and Kate had been officially relieved of her babysitting responsibilities. "I'm not really hungry."

"You'll have to face her eventually."

"I know."

"And you might as well be drinking when that happens."

Kate looked over at Julia. "You're probably right."

"Anyway, it's not going to get easier if you push this off another day. Why don't you wear that new dress you bought this morning? Everyone feels better when they look sexy."

Kate sighed. "Yeah, why work on self-confidence when you can put on a sexy dress and pretend?"

Julia laughed. "You must be feeling better. I missed your sarcasm."

"Sorry I've been moping all day. I know that's no fun to be around."

"I don't think the others noticed. You do a good job of pretending."

Kate looked down at her hands. She'd been in the process of picking up the wet towels scattered about the room but now wanted to simply dump them on the floor again. Was she doing herself any favors fooling everyone? "I've been thinking about what you said…about opening up to her about my issues."

"What do you have to lose, right?"

"Jules, you ought to be a motivational speaker."

"I'm considering it as a side gig. And while we are on the subject of things you don't want to talk about, are you still taking those antidepressants?"

"Yes. And since you're being nosey, I already called my therapist and made an appointment for when we get back. I got this," Kate said, more sure than she felt.

"One more thing." Julia took the towel from Kate and tossed it on the ground. "Don't worry about a little mess. Turns out, it's healthy. That's what Reed says and she's a doctor." She spread her arms. "Come here."

Kate let Julia hold her for a long moment. She knew that if she asked Julia would let her skip dinner after all. Despite her New York exterior, Julia was a softy at heart. But Kate also knew that she wanted Julia, Reed, and even the kids, with her when she faced Mo. She needed all of their support.

"How do you think Mo's doing?"

Julia stepped out of the hug and held Kate at arm's length. "Terri was going to convince her to go scuba diving. Both of them are certified."

"Awesome." Not awesome at all. Kate made a pouty face and Julia laughed. "Does it make me an asshole if I wish this was at least affecting her?"

"You're not an asshole, but jealousy won't help either."

"Terri would be perfect for Mo." Kate had seen the attraction from the start and now that she knew Terri better, there was no denying Mo would be well taken care of.

"Well, that wasn't jealousy exactly. A little self-defeatist…"

"I'm pathetic."

"At the moment, yes." Julia gave her an understanding smile. "Mo texted me a bunch today—checking in on you. I know she feels bad. But I only told her what you were doing, not how you were doing."

"Thanks." Kate wondered how she was going to stomach eating tonight if she did join the others for dinner. "Did she seem okay last night at dinner?"

"Well, she was joking with the twins about salad dressing. I know she was thinking of you, but she was putting on a good act. That's Mo."

Kate thought of the jokes she'd told at dinner the first night—Gary's jokes. She'd kept so many secrets from Mo. She could have at least told her that Gary was her stepfather. But all her secrets were so carefully balanced that her whole world had become a house of cards. And yet after only a few days, she'd told Terri more than Mo knew. Maybe it was simply that all along she'd wanted Mo to believe her façade.

What didn't she know about Mo? It was true what Julia said—Mo put on a good act even when she was hurting. It was only those rare moments when Kate would catch her playing solitaire or staring out a window with a somber expression that she thought of what lay beneath the surface of the happy-go-lucky Mo Calloway. She'd let herself hope that someday Mo would let her know her better, but now she couldn't think of that.

"So are you coming to dinner?"

"I could use a glass of wine. And you're probably right—it won't get any easier."

"We'll leave at seven and catch a taxi to the ferry," Terri said. "The ferry takes us to the mainland. From there, we meet up with a tour guide and take a van to Tulum."

As Terri detailed the private tour of Tulum that she'd planned for the group, Kate dared a quick glance at Mo. She was sitting on the other side of the table from her and although she'd been quiet for most of the meal, it wasn't clear if she was sad or tired. If she'd spent the day scuba diving, she was probably exhausted.

"After the tour guide takes us through the ruins, we'll have a few hours to ourselves to look around," Terri continued. "Meals aren't included, but we can get a sack lunch from the resort…"

Terri had their entire day accounted for, which would have been fine except it meant that there was no chance of avoiding Mo unless Kate missed the whole trip. As much as Kate had been looking forward to seeing Tulum, now she was debating if faking a food-borne illness would be enough to get her out of it.

Mo had yet to look her way, and despite the fact that Kate had purposefully chosen the seat between Carly and Bryn, even the twins' antics weren't enough to distract her. Kate pictured the sidewalk in front of Reed's house, imagined Mo drawing a heart with her name, and then promptly wished she'd never heard that story. If Mo had moved on, maybe that sidewalk drawing had happened before she'd made that decision.

Kate picked at the whitefish fillet whose name she couldn't pronounce. Next to the fish was a mountain of nachos complete with beans, seasoned beef, sliced habaneros, and queso that Carly had insisted on putting on her plate. She was hungry, but she couldn't seem to swallow the bites that went in her mouth without a lot of effort.

"Do you think we'll be able to swim? I pulled up some pictures of Tulum online and it looks like there's a beach that you can walk to," Mo said.

Mo's voice pulled Kate out of her own thoughts. She looked up without thinking, but Mo's face was turned to Terri. *Thankfully.* Kate had already asked Julia about sleeping in the twins' room again tonight. She couldn't imagine sleeping in Mo's bed again.

"The ruins are on the cliffs above the water and from what I can tell, there's a staircase that goes down to the beach. It looks like it's easy to get down there."

"Perfect."

Kate looked down at her nachos. She picked up a chip, the edges crisp and the middle gooey with melted cheese, and then set it down again. She'd only regret the calories later. She took a sip of wine and tried to pay attention to Bryn's story about stubbing her toe on a rock.

After Bryn's story, Terri brought up the idea of going to the resort's evening entertainment—a live game show complete with a mariachi band and a couple of acrobats. Mo seemed interested, and soon the two of them were handing their plates to the servers and standing up.

When they'd gone, Kate felt a mix of relief and let down. She hadn't expected Mo to say anything to her, but she'd figured she'd at least look in her direction. As the twins launched into an argument for why they should be allowed to stay up late and go to the game show, Kate turned to Julia. "I'm going to grab a change of clothes for tomorrow."

"Sure, sweetie. We'll be home soon… No chance these kids are staying up late tonight."

The lights were off at Mo's bungalow, which was a good sign. Not trusting fate, however, Kate knocked. When there was no answer, she let herself into the room. Julia had collected a few of her things yesterday so she hadn't had to face Mo. Thankfully in addition to some clothes and her purse, Julia had snagged her room key as well. Now with Mo at the game show, Kate could slip in and grab another outfit.

She didn't bother switching on the lights. The drapes were pulled open and the window was cracked to let in the evening breeze. In the porch light glow, she could see the bed, neatly made, and that Mo had tidied up some of the clutter around the room.

She went to the bathroom and gathered up her remaining toiletries along with a bathing suit she'd hung to dry. The closet was as she'd left it, not surprising since Mo hadn't hung up any of her clothes, and it didn't take long to pick out an outfit for Tulum—shorts and another tank top since Terri had promised that the weather would be hot.

She stuffed everything into an oversized purse she'd brought especially for the beach as the game show announcer's voice filtered into the room. The Spanish words blared from a loudspeaker somewhere on the resort property, distorted and unclear but still loud. She wondered if she'd understand him if she were closer to the stage. Her Spanish needed work. But of course that wasn't why she'd opted out of the evening's entertainment. She thought of Terri and Mo hanging out together and reminded herself that she didn't want to waste energy on jealousy. Besides, she liked Terri and at the moment, she didn't want to be around Mo. Going to Tulum with everyone wasn't going to be easy. She swung her bag on her shoulder and stepped outside.

"What the…!"

Mo had clearly been reaching for the door handle when it swung open and Kate wished now that she'd turned on the lights to give her some warning. "Sorry. I had to grab a few things."

"No problem—you just startled me." Mo stepped back from the doorway. "When Julia stopped by yesterday she wasn't sure what you'd want."

"Yeah. Anyway…Good night." Kate started past her, wondering if it would ever not be awkward between them.

"Could I walk with you?"

"I'm going back to Julia and Reed's."

"I don't really care where we go. I mean, if you don't want to be around me, I'll let you go but—" Mo exhaled and started again, "I spent a lot of time thinking about everything that happened yesterday. And…well…I'm sorry about how I reacted."

"Okay."

"Okay? That's it?"

"It was my fault, Mo. You don't need to say sorry at all." Kate moved past Mo and stepped off the porch. She turned down the path, hoping Mo wouldn't follow. She didn't want to listen to another explanation of how Mo didn't love her because she'd said everything too late and she couldn't handle Mo trying to be a friend now. Maybe Mo was only trying to salvage things to make tomorrow manageable, but she'd rather muck through the tour without a big discussion beforehand.

Kate heard footsteps and knew Mo was behind her. She considered telling her to leave her alone, but she didn't need to make things worse. In a few steps, Mo had caught up and was walking alongside her.

"I know you don't want to talk but..." Mo's voice trailed. "Could you slow down for a minute?"

"You're right. I don't want to talk." To get to Julia and Reed's bungalow, they had to walk past the club where they'd salsa danced and the Ping-Pong room. How she'd fooled herself the night they'd danced together, thinking that Mo wanted her... Nothing had gone right on this trip. She should have gotten back on the plane as soon as she'd found out about her reservation error.

"I need you to at least hear me out. I don't think I'll be able to get through tomorrow if we don't talk. Please?"

Kate looked over and saw the pained expression on Mo's face. With a pinch of guilt, she realized she wasn't the only one hurting. Yes, Mo lashing out yesterday had made things worse, but they'd both made mistakes. "Let's go inside." She veered toward the Ping-Pong room.

When they stepped into the space, a motion sensor blinked on the lights. Kate crossed her arms and turned to face Mo.

"Is it too late to ask about that rematch?" Mo tried to joke, but it was clear even she was having trouble pretending. She picked up a paddle and spun it in her hand. "Look, yesterday—"

Kate cut her off. "Yeah. How about yesterday? That was fun, right?"

Mo opened and closed her mouth. The sarcasm had landed like a slap and Kate regretted it instantly. She shook her head. "I'm sorry." Mo was right—somehow they needed to reach an agreement on how they were going to move forward. This wasn't only about getting through tomorrow. It was every day after that.

"S'okay. After yesterday, I deserve it." Mo set down the paddle. "You said when you kissed me you stopped thinking. I did too."

"I don't think we need to rehash what happened. I'm sorry I kissed you. I won't do it again." Kate wondered if Mo would see through her words. She didn't regret that kiss. The only thing she was sorry about was that she couldn't kiss her again. Maybe someday she'd fall in love and have another kiss that compared. Fall in love *again*, she immediately added. Mo would always be her first. Kate exhaled. "I don't know how we're going to do it, but I think we need to pretend it never happened."

"It feels weird to not talk about it, but if that's what you want..."

"Thanks." Kate cleared her throat. Mo was right—it was weird—but this wasn't the first time they'd pretended. "How was your day?"

"I played a lot of solitaire."

Post-breakup solitaire. Maybe Mo was more attached to Chantal than she'd let on. "How was scuba diving with Terri?"

"Didn't go."

Kate wondered how she could be simultaneously happy that Mo hadn't spent the day with Terri and unhappy that Chantal had claimed enough of her heart that she would spend an entire day of her vacation lamenting the breakup.

"Today's my dad's birthday," Mo said. "He would have turned sixty."

When Kate looked over at Mo, she realized her eyes were moist. That was why she'd looked exhausted at dinner. She'd clearly been crying. Why hadn't she realized it earlier? "Oh, Mo. I'm sorry."

"He's been gone for a while now, you know, but I felt like talking to him today. Fuck cancer."

Without thinking of whether it was a good idea or not, Kate went over to her. She wrapped her arms around Mo's shoulders and then pulled her close. Mo dropped her chin on Kate's shoulder, sighing softly.

"Thanks for the hug."

As much as she'd hoped it wouldn't happen, as much as this needed to be only a friendly hug, the feel of Mo's body sent heat flooding through her. There was no way around it. She still longed for Mo. When her arousal was too much, she took a step back, pushing away the "if onlys" that popped up despite everything.

"You've had a hell of a week."

"My mom said the same thing," Mo said. She leaned back against the Ping-Pong table.

"Did you tell your mom I tried to kiss you?" Kate knew Mo told her mom everything, but did that include this?

"You did kiss me," Mo clarified. "And no. I started to tell her about our conversation, but I knew she was going to tell me I screwed up and I didn't want to hear it."

Kate wondered if that meant Mo thought she had screwed up or only that she didn't want to hear her mom say it. "We both screwed up. So much for a vacation in paradise."

"Reality followed us." Mo picked up the Ping-Pong ball and tossed it to Kate. "I thought we weren't talking about the kiss."

Kate caught the ball. "I don't want to play."

"Me neither." Mo's gaze settled on Kate. "Sometimes I wish you could actually talk about things. And listen to what someone's saying. Instead of walking out when it gets hard."

"Yeah, well, I've got issues. Anyway, you told me I was too late." Kate fought to keep her tone light, choosing her words carefully. "Would you stay around after that?"

When Mo didn't respond, Kate tossed the ball back. Mo didn't try catching it, and the ball hit the cement floor. Kate watched it until it rolled under one of the patio chairs opposite the Ping-Pong table. She wanted to tell Mo that was how all of this made her feel, like no one would ever want to catch her, but it sounded ridiculous and overly dramatic even to her own ears.

"I'm not the only one with issues. You've got a few." She could give Mo a list of ways she'd sabotaged past relationships by not taking care of her own needs, of how she undercut herself over and over, and of how she didn't see her own value.

"Everyone has issues," Mo said. "But some of us actually work on them. I know it seems crazy…"

"I've been working on my issues for years." Kate wanted to tell Mo to leave her alone and work on herself, but she held back the words. She started to turn away, thinking she should have gone straight to Reed and Julia's place instead of here, then stopped and said, "I don't owe you an explanation. And after yesterday…Honestly I don't feel like opening up and having a heart-to-heart."

"You're right. You don't owe me anything. Have a good night."

Kate met Mo's gaze. Neither of them moved, though clearly Mo was giving her an exit. Her anger was stilled by the tears that were welling in Mo's eyes. Before they fell, Mo wiped them away and cleared her throat.

"You can probably guess how much I don't want to cry in front of you," Mo said. She seemed to be waiting for Kate to either say something or leave. When Kate did neither, Mo took a deep breath and let it out slowly. "I know I screwed up yesterday. But I think we can agree we both have made mistakes—starting that first year in the dorms."

Kate wanted to argue that it wasn't her fault that she hadn't been ready to date Mo in college. Her relationships then had been superficial at best and there was no way she would have been able to let Mo close. Back then she'd gone on dates as much to try and feel normal as to keep anyone from asking why she wasn't. Of course Mo didn't know about that. She thought of Julia's words. It was true that she'd held back, that she'd kept secrets, and yet she still didn't see how owning up to all of it would change anything now.

But what did she have to lose? When Kate realized the answer was nothing, she went over to one of the chairs opposite the Ping-Pong table and sat down. "I don't want to leave."

"That's not always the same thing as wanting to stay."

"What do you want to ask me, Mo? I'll answer anything. You probably won't want to hear it, but maybe that's not for me to decide."

"I don't want to force you to open up."

"You're not forcing me to do anything," Kate said. This was her decision. "What do you want to know?"

"Whatever you want to tell me." Mo's words were clipped, as if she doubted this conversation would lead anywhere.

Kate stopped the sarcastic quip that formed on her lips. She didn't want to fight anymore. "You're right," she started. "You said you always felt like I was holding back. I was."

"Why?"

As much as she knew that now was the time, she still didn't want to tell the whole story. If only she could leave some parts out. Kate closed her eyes and said, "I never wanted to tell you what my 'issues' were because I knew you wouldn't look at me the same after." She opened her eyes and briefly met Mo's gaze. "And I loved the way you looked at me. You made me feel like the sexiest person in the room."

"You usually are."

Kate didn't let Mo's admission stall her. "You know how you don't like to be alone?" She waited for Mo's nod. They both knew that was the reason she went from one relationship to the next. "Well, I don't like to let anyone close."

"Maybe we should go see a therapist together. That'd be fun."

"I've been in therapy since I was thirteen," Kate said. "You're going to need to catch up."

"Since you were thirteen? Like regularly?"

"Every month. It used to be weekly, but I've improved." Kate held up her hands, forcing a big smile. "Can't you tell?"

"Actually, I can. In college you were this quiet girl who didn't want anyone to notice her. But now you've got this confidence. You walk into a room and everyone looks your way. Especially when you're working. Remember that gala you dragged me to? All those moneybags couldn't wait to write you a check."

"It was for a good cause." And she knew how to handle rich bastards. That was one thing she'd learned early.

"It was about more than the cause. Those people couldn't wait to give you their money. They know you're going to make things happen—and make a difference. You've got your shit together more than anyone else I know." Mo paused. "And it's not only that you're good at your job. You don't let anyone else tell you how to lead your life. You know what you want. That's why it never made sense to me when you'd say you had issues."

"Well, you learn a few things about yourself in almost twenty years of counseling. Like what you want in life. But that doesn't mean you're brave enough to go for it." Kate looked at Mo and her body took that precise moment to remind her of exactly how good Mo's lips had felt on hers. She pushed away the thought that she would never kiss her again and said, "You knew I saw a therapist. You've teased me about it before."

"I didn't know it was a regular thing. I shouldn't have teased you. And I knew you took antidepressants, but I never thought you really needed them. You never acted like you were depressed."

"Turns out they work."

Mo nodded. "Growing up I always thought people who went to therapy must be really messed up—or they had too much time on their hands. You know in the black community it's almost taboo. But now I know how much it can help. People need to talk to someone... Why'd you start going? Because of the eating thing?"

"That's the short answer," Kate said. Mo had lived with her long enough to guess that truth and she wasn't surprised. In some ways, it was a relief to have it out in the open. But she was glad Mo hadn't named it. Anorexia. Bulimia. Orthorexia. She hated all the names. Even the new ones.

"What happened?"

"I stopped eating." It was simple, when she put it that way, but of course there was more to the story. "It didn't happen right away. First I stopped eating certain things that weren't good for me anyway. Potato salad. Hot dogs. Chips. Before long I was only eating salad. If I ate anything else, I'd take care of it."

Kate expected Mo to say something. When she didn't, Kate almost asked if she'd heard what she'd said. But she knew she'd heard and she pushed herself to go on.

"After a month of inpatient treatment, I agreed to weekly meetings. Talking to my therapist helped more than the medication so I quit the meds, but then things got bad again. Worse, actually. I took a bunch of my mom's sleeping pills and ended up back in the hospital. One therapist told me I'd never be able to stop going to therapy. Or stop the meds. I thought I could control it. Like everything else."

"How bad did it get?"

"I don't want to tell you how much I weighed. It was bad. I couldn't look in a mirror. Have you ever tried putting eyeliner on without a mirror?"

Mo didn't laugh at the joke. "Do you know what triggered it? I'm probably asking the wrong question..."

"I've been in therapy for years. That question's easy." Except it wasn't. She hesitated, searching for the words. "My dad." It was only part of the answer, and she knew Mo wouldn't let her stop with that.

"Gary?" Mo seemed genuinely surprised.

"Gary's my stepdad." Here came the truth. There was no going back once she'd said what came next. She'd always worried that one question would lead to another. She hadn't lied and she didn't want to. But she'd certainly avoided the truth.

"My biological father lives in Amsterdam. He was working in Houston when he met my mom—he's big in finance and most of his work then was with oil execs." The basic details were easy. "My parents got divorced when I was three. He went back to Amsterdam and my mom started seeing Gary. It wasn't long before we moved to Sand Bluff, where Gary was from. I don't remember much about life in Houston and nothing about the time when my mom and my dad actually lived together… Probably that's for the best. My mom said they fought all the time."

"That's hard."

"Not if you don't remember it. Starting when I was six, my mom sent me to Amsterdam every summer to stay with my dad. I don't think it was his choice to have me there. She said that she needed a break from me."

Mo reached out her hand, but Kate shook her head. They were only a few feet apart, but she didn't want any contact. She had to get everything out first. Then she needed to see how Mo looked at her after.

Mo dropped her hand. "What's your dad's name?"

"Philip. His last name's Eriksen. Technically he's Philip William Eriksen. The third."

"Sounds like a king."

"He's got enough money to be one." Kate wondered if Mo knew what she was doing. It was the same thing one of her first therapists had done. Ask the easy questions first. She knew the routine, but she wondered if with Mo it was intentional or simply her intuition. "Gary legally adopted me so I got his name. Owens."

"Philip...did he do something to you?"

That tone was all Mo. Ready to go slay a dragon. She thought of Terri calling Mo a hero, but Kate knew it was too late for someone to save her. "It wasn't so much what he did as what he didn't."

She considered skipping to the punchline like she'd done with some of her past therapists, but she knew Mo would need the whole story. She owed her that. "Philip's an alcoholic. That's why my mom left him. But for the most part, he manages his drinking. Or at least he used to...I haven't seen him since I was thirteen.

"He inherited two houses—one in the city and another on a lake. The lake house is where we'd go most of the time. It was this huge place with a big deck overlooking the lake. There was a rope swing on one of the trees that went out over the water. My dad pretty much ignored me, but it wasn't an awful place to spend the summer.

"He liked to entertain his friends from work. No kids—just a bunch of old guys. There was this one time..." Kate's voice echoed in her head as if someone else had taken over telling the story. "I'd gone down to the lake after dinner. I didn't like to hang around the house when his friends were over, and I didn't understand much of the conversation anyway—they spoke Dutch except when they talked to me.

"After the sun set, the wind came up and I got cold. I'd forgotten a towel so I went back to the house dripping wet. I was shivering by the time I got to the back porch. There were still a handful of guys sitting around drinking and smoking cigars. One of them stood up and came over to hug me, saying he'd warm me up. I tried pushing him away. But his hand went up and down my chest and then right there with my dad looking on like it was nothing, he slid his hand under my bathing suit."

"Shit."

"I got away from him and ran into the house, but I could hear him laughing...and my dad saying nothing."

"God, that's awful."

"It shouldn't have been a big deal." And if it had ended there, maybe she could have put the memory in a little box and forgotten about it. "He followed me up to my room. Probably made some excuse about going to the bathroom or something. My dad didn't stop him."

Kate tried to ignore Mo's look of concern. She couldn't handle worrying about her reaction now. "I got him to leave before he'd done much more than feel me up." She stopped, swallowing back the taste of bile. "After that night, he kept finding excuses to come around the house.

"When my dad wasn't paying attention, he'd corner me. He was always giving me these compliments—about how I was this perfect woman. I didn't want to touch him, but I couldn't get away." She felt a wave of nausea at the memory of what he'd made her do. "I was only thirteen and he was this big guy... I told my dad that I didn't want him coming around anymore, but he brushed it off. Said the guy liked me and he was just being friendly."

She'd cried over all of it too many times. Now her eyes were dry as if there was nothing left. "The thing is, I know a lot of girls go through much worse. But the hardest part was that no one thought it was a big deal."

"It was a big deal," Mo started.

"He didn't rape me, you know, so what was I crying about? I called my mom and asked if I could come home early."

Instantly she was back in Philip's house again. She stood in the kitchen, the phone cradled to her ear, her whole body shaking as she begged her mom to hear what she wasn't saying. Philip had started drinking early that day and she knew his friends were coming over that night.

"She told me that we couldn't change the tickets," Kate said, wanting to finish so the nausea would subside. "I tried to tell her what was going on, but I couldn't make myself tell her everything. I told her about the towel thing and she said men were like that. She told me that I should have brought a towel down to the lake."

"God, I'm sorry. You must have been so scared. How could your mom not let you come home?"

Kate didn't have any answers. She knew Mo was trying to wrap her mind around the mess the same way she'd done so many times. What had her parents been thinking? Maybe they simply hadn't understood. Or maybe they hadn't cared.

"The next summer I refused to go to Amsterdam and my mom was all put out. Gary and she always planned these big trips when I was gone. From then on I stayed home when they went on their summer vacation. That was my punishment for not being compliant."

"I knew there was a reason why I hated your mom. Now I hate your dad too. And that mofo who touched you. If I could go back in time and beat up his ass—"

Kate interrupted: "You'd think that something that happened one summer when you're thirteen wouldn't mess you up for the rest of your life."

"You were sexually assaulted." Mo's anger was clear. "That was bad enough."

"It took me years to figure out that the problem wasn't what happened—it was what *didn't* happen. No one stood up for me. No one protected me. I was on my own."

"I wish I'd known you then."

"No, you definitely don't. Things got really bad after that summer. It wasn't until I ended up in the hospital that I stopped to think about what could have happened." Kate closed her eyes, pushing away the memory of waking up with an IV line in her arm and her mother's lecture that followed. "I went to this place where everyone was on antidepressants and they force-fed you. After a month of that supposedly I was better with the eating thing. I came home and started taking my mom's pain meds. Gary's too. They had a stockpile, but when that ran out I found ways to get my own… That landed me in rehab."

"You were in high school when all this happened?"

Kate nodded.

"All I did in high school was play video games."

"Well, I was an overachiever." Kate gave Mo a wry smile. "One of my therapists told me I needed to get out of Sand Bluff. I'd always wanted to see the Golden Gate Bridge—random, I know—so I decided to apply to SF State. But I didn't figure anything would change. I was wrong. My life started over when I met you and Julia."

"You've always had that thing against pain meds. I never thought about why."

"I've always had a thing against food too."

Mo smiled sadly. "True." She reached out her hand again, but Kate still didn't move to clasp it. Sighing, she set her hand back on the Ping-Pong table. "You went through hell. Thank God you survived."

Kate wanted to argue that God didn't have anything to do with it. Her body simply wouldn't give up. But she respected Mo for her faith and held back those words. What did she know anyway? Maybe she should be thanking God.

"Anyway. Now you know." Kate didn't want to look at Mo. She didn't want to see the judgment in her eyes, if it was there, or the pity, which she knew would be. "I should have told you sooner, but I didn't want this to change the way you acted with me. I didn't want to be messed up. You should have taken one look at me and asked for a transfer to a different room."

"If I'd known all this then, there's no way I would have asked for a transfer."

Kate trusted Mo, but she knew if she'd told her everything then, it would have changed the dynamic between them. There was a good chance they still would have become friends. But would Mo have been attracted to her? Did it matter now?

"I kept hoping I'd be normal some day. That I'd get over my issues…" And that Mo would want her anyway. Kate wondered why she'd held onto that hope for all these years. Now she simply felt ashamed for all the times she'd flirted. There was no arguing that she'd wanted Mo's attention. But she wanted more than that. And if Mo had known the truth…

"I told your mom about the eating thing. And that I'd gone to rehab. I never told her why and she didn't ask. She just hugged me and said that if I ever got in a bad place again to show up at her doorstep."

"My mom's the best."

"She is. You lucked out." Kate paused. "I'm sorry I led you on."

"You didn't lead me on."

"Yeah, I did. I knew we'd never be together, but I wanted you to like me anyway."

"Why couldn't we have been together?"

"Were you not listening to any of that? I'm way too fucked up." Kate shook her head. "You deserve someone better than me, Mo."

"That's the first time I've heard you say the F word. And you're wrong."

Minutes passed. Kate thought of leaving but standing up seemed like too much effort. She felt hollowed out. There was nothing left to say and nothing left to risk. The Ping-Pong table creaked and after another minute, Kate felt Mo's hand touch her shoulder. She didn't try to hug her or say anything useless like it would get better with time or that she understood. She just stood there. Kate dropped her head so her ear was resting on the back of Mo's hand.

"I wish I deserved you," Mo said quietly. "You have no idea how much I wish that. And you are definitely not fucked up."

For several minutes neither of them said anything. Kate didn't want to move, didn't want to end the connection she felt with Mo, the warmth of her hand and the feel of her standing so close. But she had to get over wanting what she couldn't have. She stood up and Mo's hand fell off her shoulder.

"I should go…"

Mo looked out at the dark path and then back at Kate. "Don't go to Julia's tonight. Come back to my place."

Now she offers. Kate stopped herself from saying those flippant words aloud. She knew Mo wasn't offering anything more than comfort. But she couldn't handle being wrapped in her arms tonight. "You don't need to worry about me. I'll be fine."

"I know you'll be fine. But I'm asking you to stay with me anyway."

"As a friend." Kate shook her head. "I don't know why I just said that. After everything I told you, obviously you're asking as a friend."

"Last night I said things I wish I could take back. But I'm glad I messed up. Otherwise I don't think you would have told me everything tonight and I'm really glad you did."

"That makes one of us." Kate felt the press of tears in her eyes. Telling Mo everything had exhausted her reserves. "I can't go back to your place tonight. I'll see you tomorrow."

She started out of the Ping-Pong room without waiting for Mo to say good night. Before she'd gone far, she heard Mo behind her. She looked over her shoulder and Mo's steps slowed.

"I don't want to let you go," Mo said.

"I'll be fine."

"I know you will. But I won't."

Kate hadn't noticed how fast she was walking, but now she realized they were nearly to Julia's bungalow. She turned around and faced Mo. "What would make it easier for you to walk away?"

"Nothing would make it easier. I don't want to walk away." Mo's eyes searched Kate's. "I couldn't sleep last night. I kept thinking about how good your lips felt on mine. I didn't want to stop you. But I didn't want to lose you as a friend. And now I really don't."

"I can't go back to being friends with you, Mo," Kate said, her voice cracking. "Maybe you can pretend nothing's going on between us, but I can't. Every time you kiss someone else I'm going to wish it was me. After what you heard tonight I know you aren't interested, but I can't help how I feel."

"Tonight only made me love you more." Mo took a step closer to Kate but didn't move to touch her. "But I never wanted to risk our friendship by dating. We have too much going to chance it, you know. And if this were sixteen years ago this all would be a lot easier, but—"

"Would it be easier?" Kate shook her head. "Whatever. We can say it's that I'm too late. For future reference, don't tell someone you love them and then follow it with 'but.' It only makes it hurt more." It wasn't the first time that Mo had told her that she loved her. Mo was generous with her love. But Kate couldn't hear the words now.

Kate turned and walked away. She swiped the tears off her face, more angry than ever that she couldn't control that one small thing. They'd both screwed up. Again.

When she reached Reed and Julia's porch, Kate looked over her shoulder and saw Mo a few steps behind her. Kate thought of ignoring her and going inside without another word. Julia had given her a key, so she didn't need to knock. But she turned to face Mo. "What? Did you come up with another way to tell me I missed my chance with you?"

Mo stepped forward and kissed her. There was no question on her lips, no hesitation. There was no wondering if this was something Mo was going to regret. She knew exactly what she was doing, and Kate didn't stop her body from responding. It felt too good. Too right. She let her lips part, allowing Mo to deepen the kiss, and the thought crossed her mind that yesterday had only been testing the waters. This was Mo showing her exactly what she was capable of.

Kate stepped back, breaking off the kiss. "Dammit, Mo." She shook her head. "Why'd you do that?"

Mo looked taken aback by the question. She stammered for an apology.

"I don't want you to say sorry," Kate said, stopping her. "This isn't a game. You can't tell me that you don't want me and then kiss me like that."

"I never said I didn't want you. I want you so much I can't think of anything else."

"You're the smartest person I know. If you want me so much, Math Whiz, I need you to start thinking." When Mo didn't respond, Kate continued, "But if you were only trying to prove that you're a good kisser, you made your point."

"I'm not trying to prove anything. Maybe I shouldn't have said that I loved you, but it's the truth. And you didn't let me finish earlier. What I was going to say was that if this were sixteen years ago it would be a lot easier to ask you out on a date. Now I know exactly how much I'm risking. But I want to ask you out anyway."

Kate didn't know what to say. "You have terrible timing, you know that? Now if I say yes I don't know if you only asked me because you don't want to lose our friendship or if you really want a relationship. Or maybe you only feel sorry for me. That I really don't need."

"You have no idea how many times I've wanted to ask you out," Mo said. "But it never seemed like the right time. I kept coming up with excuses for why you'd turn me down. First it was because you only dated guys. Then it was because we were too different. Then it was because we were too close. Then it was because we'd been friends for too long. It was always too big a risk. But I know now that I can't keep making excuses for why it wouldn't work when the truth is I'm just scared of losing you. Nothing you told me tonight changes how I feel about you."

Kate considered Mo's words. "I still don't know if you want to date me or if you don't want to lose me as your friend."

"I'm in love with you." Mo's eyes never faltered from Kate's. "I won't try to kiss you again if you don't want that yet—or if I need to prove something to you first—but I want to be with you. And not only as a friend."

Wasn't that all she needed to hear? Doubt held her back. Kate knew that Mo's concerns, even if she called them excuses, weren't unfounded. Maybe differences that had never been a problem before would be an issue when they tried to date. What would happen when things got hard for all the reasons Mo had brought up? Would Mo feel like she'd been pushed into the relationship and regret it?

"I need to know that you'd be strong enough to walk away from our friendship if I'm not really the one you want."

"You've always been the one I want." After a long moment where Mo was clearly waiting for Kate, she sighed and said, "What if we start over? Go out on a date like normal people."

"Normal people?"

Mo smiled. "We could pretend."

Kate couldn't help thinking that Mo would change her mind after she had time to think about everything she'd told her. She definitely wasn't normal and there was no use pretending otherwise.

"Will you go out with me, Kate Owens?"

"I don't know what the right thing is anymore. I can't think."

"Well, I'm pretty smart. I could help you out." Mo tapped her temple. "The right thing is saying yes."

"You're a pain in the ass."

"Is that a yes?"

Kate wanted to say yes. The word was waiting to slip out. "Ask me tomorrow."

"I'll ask you the day after that too," Mo promised. "Until you say no."

"Good night, Mo."

She turned to go up the steps to the bungalow. When she reached the door, she looked back. Mo was waiting for her.

"I don't think I'm gonna sleep tonight." Mo's smile held a tinge of sadness.

Kate wasn't certain she would either.

CHAPTER THIRTEEN

Carly and Bryn were up at the crack of dawn and bouncing on her bed. "Wake up, Aunt Kate. We're going on a field trip today!"

Kate covered her head with her pillow as she silently begged for another hour of sleep. This was her punishment for not trying to sleep as soon as she'd left Mo last night. Last night... The memory of all that had been said came rushing back to her. And Mo's kiss.

Kate took a deep breath. What hung in the balance would be settled today. And everything was out in the open now at least. Not only had she told Mo, Julia and Reed knew as well. They'd been waiting up for her and when she'd walked in, Julia's face, a wreck of worries, had made her realize she couldn't keep the secret from her. The kids were already asleep and Reed had offered to leave to give them privacy, but Kate had asked her to stay. Once she'd broken the seal, she didn't want to keep anything inside anymore.

She'd expected pointed hard questions from Julia and got a few. Reed, on the other hand, had only given her a hug and said that she knew Mo loved her no matter what. They were still family, she'd said. Reed's words repeated in her mind now. She'd given Kate enough comfort to sleep and that was more of a gift than she'd probably realized. But now that morning had arrived, Kate wondered what her answer to Mo's question should be. Admitting that they both wanted the same thing didn't mean that they should go for it.

Her mattress bounced, jostling her out of her thoughts, as Bryn wrestled her onto her back, laughing. Carly tugged at her pillow and soon Kate was blinking away the morning light.

Carly's look was triumphant. "She's awake!"

"Am not," Kate argued, pulling the pillow back into place as she reached for the sheet. Did she really want to have kids?

Bryn got ahold of the corner of the pillow and pulled with all her weight. Kate didn't stand a chance. But she kept her eyes squeezed closed.

"She probably needs tickles," Bryn said.

"No tickles this early in the morning," Kate said, waving a finger in the air. "I'm not getting out of bed until the first number on that clock is a six." She didn't know if either could tell time, but she wagered that it couldn't possibly be six yet. Her head ached too much. "By the way, I found the candy wrappers."

Both kids went silent. Bryn's voice quavered as she said, "What wrappers?"

"Jolly Ranchers. Skittles. And Chocolate Kisses. Someone hid them under this pillow." She'd heard the crinkling as she'd adjusted the pillow last night and then been amazed at the stash. Where they'd gotten all that candy was the first question... "I think you two should fess up 'cause if it comes from me, you know you're going to be in bigger trouble."

Bryn grumbled about not ever getting enough candy and then Carly meekly said, "I'll go tell the moms."

"How about we wait to tell them about the candy until that first number is a six? It might go over better if we let them sleep. Today might go over better if we all go back to sleep..."

"Look, it's already a six," Bryn said, pushing Kate's eyelids open. "Tickle time?"

The next hour was a flurry of activity. Kate volunteered to help get the kids ready so that Reed and Julia could relax for another half hour. But getting two kids dressed, their teeth brushed, and their hair combed proved no easy task. Particularly since they argued over who would go first for everything. Even who would go pee first was a five-minute debate.

When both kids were ready to leave, Kate realized she still hadn't showered herself. Julia only laughed when Kate asked how she possibly got everything done in the morning and was still on time to work. Mo was distracting her as well. She could hardly process one thought without stopping to wonder how the rest of the day would go. More than ever, she longed to see her. Adrenaline had her on a nervous high and she knew she wouldn't relax until she saw her again.

Breakfast was a hurried affair. The twins were thrilled at the prospect of being able to skip the healthy options in favor of the easy-to-grab-and-go assortment of pastries. Kate looked around for Mo until Julia noticed and said, "Mo and Terri had breakfast early. They sent me a text. They're in charge of getting us a taxi."

As soon as they stepped out of the lobby, Terri hailed them. "We got a van that can take all seven of us."

"Perfect," Julia said.

Reed winked as she looked over at Kate. "Just when you thought you were going to have a break from our craziness."

"She likes our craziness," Bryn argued, slipping her hand in Kate's.

"It does keep me from thinking about my own craziness," Kate admitted.

Carly caught Kate's other hand. "Aunt Kate, you're not crazy."

She squeezed Carly's hand and said, "Thanks, sweetie." No way could a five-year-old know that a silly remark could tug at her heart, but she appreciated the caring look Carly gave her anyway.

"But you can be weird sometimes. In a good way," Carly added.

Mo came around the side of the van then. "Who's weird?"

"Aunt Kate," Bryn said. "But she's not as weird as you."

Mo met Kate's eyes. "Hey."

"Hey." Kate's heart jumped up to her throat, and there was no way she could have managed more words. Fortunately Carly took that moment to launch herself into Mo's arms.

"No one's as weird as Aunt Mo!" Carly cheered. "That's why we love you."

"Is that why?" Mo spun Carly around as Bryn hollered to be next.

Once she'd given both kids a whirl, she pointed to the van and they grudgingly climbed in, chattering about wanting more spins later. Mo stepped back from the open door and turned to Kate.

"How are you?"

"I'm okay," Kate answered truthfully. She felt lighter and more clear-headed than she had in months, actually. "You?"

"I've never been this nervous waiting to find out if someone's going to say yes to a date." Mo's voice was quiet enough that no one else could hear. The twins were bickering in the van and Terri was chatting with the driver while Reed and Julia were going through their backpacks once more to make sure they hadn't forgotten anything.

"Hmm. That's tough."

Mo chuckled. "Did you sleep okay?"

Before Kate could answer, Carly whined, "Are you getting in, Aunt Kate? You have to sit between Bryn and me or we'll fight the whole way."

"For real," Mo said. "Good luck. I'm going to sit up front and try to get some advice on the local scene from our driver." When Kate cocked her head, Mo added, "In case someone says yes to a date."

Surprisingly, the driver was a woman. All of the other taxi drivers they'd seen had been guys, but it wasn't until she answered a few of Mo's questions that Kate realized she was also probably a lesbian. She had a short haircut and wore little makeup, which seemed unusual compared to other Mexican women her age, but when Mo asked about her family and she admitted she was single with no kids, a flag went up. Kate wondered how it was that Mo managed to find lesbians wherever she went. It was as if she had a beacon that they homed in on from miles away.

Kate tried to eavesdrop on the conversation in the front seat, but given the distraction of Bryn's questions about Tulum—she wanted to know if Mayans still lived in the ruins and then everything else about Mayans including what they ate for breakfast—she missed a lot. It didn't help that Mo was trying to ask everything in Spanish. When Kate caught snippets about the local scene and recommended restaurants, she felt a rush of nerves. Mo was planning a real date.

The ride to the ferry building didn't take long, and soon Mo was paying the driver with a generous tip as everyone else piled out. As they waited in line for tickets, Mo came to stand next to Kate.

"How is it that you find them everywhere?" Kate wondered. "Or is it that they find you?"

"Are we talking about the driver?" Mo acted surprised. At Kate's raised eyebrow, she added, "I swear I don't even have to try. They just come to me. All I have to do is show up."

"Everyone knows Mo's irresistible," Julia said. Clearly she'd overheard their conversation. She stepped back from the ticket counter, letting Reed buy the tickets while she kept an eye on the kids. "But I think what you meant to say, Mo, was that you show up and they come."

Mo half coughed, half laughed, and Terri reached over to pat her on the back. "It's not a bad reputation to have," Terri said, chuckling. "But you were laying it on pretty thick back there. I'm surprised she didn't hand you her number."

"Maybe Mo's losing some of her *mo*jo," Julia said.

Mo laughed. "Jules, that's low."

"Julia knows you can take it," Kate said.

"That's the rumor anyway." Mo grinned back at her.

"Hmm. So it's only a rumor?" Kate returned.

Mo's eyebrows raised, but for once she didn't have a response.

Julia looked over at them with a curious expression. "Today's going to be interesting."

"I hope so." Mo held Kate's gaze.

Kate knew the others were looking at her as well, but she couldn't look away from Mo.

Once they'd settled onto the ferry, Kate pulled out the little travel book she'd brought about the Mayan Riviera and flipped through the pages until she found the section about Tulum. Terri had taken the seat next to her, with Reed and Julia in the row ahead of them and Mo across the way with Carly and Bryn.

Kate tried to concentrate on the book, but she couldn't help stealing glances Mo's direction. When Mo looked up and met her gaze, the memory of their kiss returned to her lips. She could almost feel Mo pressing against her.

Terri leaned over and pointed to the picture of an iguana perched on a cliff overlooking the turquoise ocean below. Behind the lizard was a wall of rock from one of the preserved ruins. "Wouldn't mind that view. Can you imagine what that place must have looked like when the city was in its heyday? Now the iguanas run everything. I watched a whole documentary on Tulum... I hope we get a good tour guide."

"Me too." But Kate had a feeling she wouldn't absorb much of what the guide told them. Across the way, Bryn and Carly were excitedly bouncing between their seats and Mo's lap. She overheard Mo trying to convince them to sit quietly, but they were giggling too much.

Terri nodded in Mo's direction. "Props to her. I'm just not a kid person before ten in the morning."

"Try six a.m. They woke me up asking if I wanted to be tickled."

Terri looked surprised. "What happened to you and Mo bunking together?"

"Sometimes you just can't pretend there's nothing going on."

"But you two seem better today. There's less tension. I wondered what was going on last night. She left the game show before it even started. Did you two have a friend argument or something more?"

"It wasn't exactly an argument." Kate hesitated. "We talked, and some of it was hard but...things are better."

"Good. After watching the two of you dance together, I still think you two need to take a chance on being more than friends."

"What about how the stars aren't aligned for us and all that?"

Terri shrugged. "Astrology's probably a load of crap."

"You have the Pisces symbol tattooed on your arm."

"I've always liked fish. And there's something appealing about the symbolism of being able to change your mind. You know, the fish are going in two different directions." Terri glanced over at Mo again. The twins were momentarily in their seats, but only because Mo was showing them a magic trick with a handful of pesos. "I think she might need some reinforcements over there. Maybe the twins would like to hear about Tulum."

Kate doubted that ancient history would interest kindergartners but they did love to be read to, and a story was a surefire way to get them to sit still. She gathered her things and looked over at Terri. "I still think you'd make a good counselor."

"I'll consider it if I need a second job." Terri smiled. "Good luck."

It wasn't until after the tour that the group split up. Terri wanted to wander around and take more pictures, the twins were harping for a picnic, and Mo had looked longingly down at the ocean. Kate made a quick decision and parted from the others, saying she wanted to dip her feet in the water. She made her way down the narrow wooden staircase that led from the ruins to the water, hoping Mo would follow.

The water was a cool relief. Kate wiggled her toes in the sand, letting the waves crest at her calves. After hours in the hot sun hiking from one crumbling stone building to another, she was tempted to strip down and dive in, but she hadn't brought a suit.

"Going in?" Mo asked, coming up behind her.

"I wish. I didn't think to bring a towel. Or a bathing suit."

"Me neither." Mo peeled off her shirt and tossed it on the beach well out of range of the surf, then turned to face the ocean and dove head first into the next wave.

Kate watched her for a moment but before Mo could catch her staring, she made her way out of the water. She found a spot shaded some by the overarching cliffs, and settled in on the sand with the book she'd brought about the ruins. All the "what ifs" her mind was churning out kept her from seeing the words on the page, but she pretended to read anyway. Every few words, she looked out at the water and each time, her gaze lit on Mo.

The tour had gone better than she'd expected. Terri had hit it off with the guide, and the woman gave them more than their money's worth, but all the details on Mayan civilization blurred each time Mo had stepped close to Kate.

Kate looked up again, telling herself she was only making sure Mo was okay. A swell pushed Mo off her feet but she recovered quickly and then swam for a bit. After a while, she veered toward the shore and stood up again. She scanned the beach until her gaze settled on Kate. Instead of pretending that she was interested in the book, Kate raised her hand. Mo waved back, her expression serious.

Kate wondered at Mo's thoughts. But if there was one way that she and Mo were alike, it was that they had never been able to read each other. Maybe they'd both spent too long hiding their emotions. Now they were too good at doing so. She watched Mo battle the shore break until she'd gotten her bearings on the beach.

"Anything in that book about the Mayan concept of age?" Mo asked, shaking off water droplets. "I keep thinking about what the tour guide said—about how Mayans didn't consider your age important."

"Only what year you were born." Kate squinted up at her. "That struck you too, huh? And all that stuff about standing on the shoulders of your ancestors... Unfortunately, there's nothing in here about that. I wonder if the tour guide was making it up. They probably ad-lib some of it to keep the tourists happy."

Mo sat down gingerly, as if the sand was too hot. "Why make it up? Probably it's not in the book because it isn't an easy concept for tourists to grasp—that what you do in life isn't as important as what already happened before you even were born. We like to think about our potential. What we can do in this life. We don't like to think anything's preordained."

"True…" Kate tried to focus on the page and not how close Mo was sitting. "All that stuff about their calendar and the way they charted the planets is amazing."

"And you call me a math whiz," Mo said, grinning at the nickname that had stuck since college. "But the virgin sacrifice and the bloodletting is a little much."

Kate scrunched up her nose. "Along with burying your dead under the house."

Mo looked behind them at the limestone cliffs. One of the largest of the ruins, El Castile perched at the edge and the rock wall was as formidable from this vantage point as it was ancient. "Have you ever been to a ghost town and felt like people were watching you? You know, like the spirits were peeking out of the windows?"

"I get that feeling here too," Kate agreed.

"You can almost imagine some Mayan king plotting his return with every sunset," Mo said.

"Good thing neither of us are virgins."

"No kidding." Mo looked over at her and grinned.

Kate felt a rush as Mo's eyes held hers and knew she had to change the subject. "Do you think Terri's latched onto another tour or is still making friends with the dearly departed?" She'd stopped to read every placard and even took notes. Mo had teased her about this until Kate had made a quip about how the spirit world might be listening. If anyone was in touch with the supernatural realm, it was Terri. Mo had agreed, saying that Terri had an eerie intuition and leaving Kate to wonder again what Terri and Mo had talked about last night.

"I'd bet on the spirit world. Should we head back soon and find everyone?"

"Probably." Kate closed the book but didn't stand. "Do you think about your ancestors much?"

"And how I'm standing on their shoulders? All the time." Mo picked up a handful of sand and let it sift through her fingers. "Probably some of them would be disappointed."

"None of them should be. You're amazing. Kind, brilliant, funny..."

Mo picked up another handful of sand. "I don't know if they'd see that."

"Everyone sees it, Mo." Kate debated finishing her thought. Finally she said it: "Sometimes I wish I didn't."

"How should I take that?" Mo studied her for a moment, waiting for her answer. When she didn't say anything, Mo turned to look out at the water. "I talked to Chantal last night. She called after we'd talked."

"How is she?" Kate tried to keep her voice even. If Mo wanted to go back to Chantal she wasn't certain she could stop her.

"She wanted another chance. She doesn't think either of us gave it a good try."

"What did you tell her?"

"That she was probably right." Mo paused. "I told her I'd been in love with someone else for a long time and shouldn't have dated a lot of the women I'd dated. And that I was sorry."

"How'd that go over?" Kate tried to slow the rush of emotions. In one breath, Mo had told her what she'd always hoped but someone else was hurt because of it.

"Oh, you know, pretty well." Mo's tone was joking, but from the look in her eyes it was a cover. She clearly felt bad. "Chantal had a guilty conscience too. She slept with her boss that night we broke up. Apparently it was the first time..."

"You called it."

"Sometimes you want to be wrong. I guess it didn't go well since she texted me afterward. And I saw she changed her status online to single so she's back to looking." She sighed. "Why is love so complicated?"

"You haven't dated me yet. Just wait."

"That almost sounds like you're thinking of going on a date with me." Mo straightened up. "Are you?"

"I don't know. Now that Chantal is single... I do love the ballet. And getting dressed up. Is she on Instagram?"

"Don't you dare!" Mo playfully pushed her shoulder. "You wouldn't, right?"

The idea of dating any of Mo's exes was ridiculous, but at least they were back to teasing each other. She couldn't help smiling when Mo raised her eyebrows, and she laughed when Mo asked again, "You wouldn't, right?"

Holding up her hand, she said, "I do solemnly swear not to date any of my best friend's exes. Unless..."

Mo cocked her head. "What?"

"You know I'd have a hard time saying no to good orchestra tickets."

"Is that all it takes?"

"You'd be surprised." Kate winked. "I guess we should go find the others."

Mo nodded, but she didn't get up. After a long minute of staring at the water, she looked back at Kate and said, "Hey, I got a question for you."

Butterflies suddenly filled Kate's stomach.

"What are you doing tonight? I don't have orchestra tickets, but I'd really like to take you out to dinner. There's this place that has salsa dancing..."

Kate drew a heart on the sand and put MC in the center of it. How long had she been waiting for Mo Calloway to ask her out? "Salsa dancing doesn't sound bad."

"Or we could do something else." Mo ran through a list of other options that she'd thought of, including dinner on the beach.

Kate interrupted with, "Is dinner in bed an option? Or we could skip dinner altogether."

"Wait, is that yes to a date?"

"Yes."

Mo's smile stretched across her face. She got up off the sand and then held out her hand. "Dinner first. This time I want to do everything right. You know, until one of us screws up."

Kate let Mo help her up, but once she was standing, she didn't let go of her hand. "Don't screw this up. You've already got my heart in your hands."

Mo looked down at their entwined fingers and then at Kate. "I could say the same to you."

Mo gave her hand a squeeze and the rush that went through her felt entirely too good. To stop herself from saying something she'd regret later, because it was way too soon to be thinking of forever, she looked up at the cloudless sky. But she couldn't help thinking of forever. The endless blue seemed to dare her to say the words. She looked back at Mo, her heart thumping hard.

"You scared?" Mo asked.

"No."

"Oh, okay, good. Um, me neither."

Kate loved Mo's sheepish smile. She wanted to smile back without any worries about what came next, but one last doubt nagged at her. "I should tell you something, though."

"Uh-oh."

"You know how I have all these issues…" Kate paused and Mo's expression looked truly worried. She pressed on. "Well, some of that applies to sex. It's not that I'm not into it or anything—I love it actually. But I like to be in charge."

"Are you secretly a dominatrix?"

Kate laughed. "How'd you guess?" She winked and Mo's smile flashed. "Just kidding. You didn't get that lucky."

"You're wrong. I got real lucky."

But Kate knew she was the lucky one. For the first time, she was going into a relationship holding nothing back. She'd put all of her crappy cards on the table and Mo had picked each one up.

She stood on her tiptoes and met Mo's lips. The sound of the crashing waves overshadowed the bits of conversation from the others on the beach and the feeling of Mo leaning into the kiss made the moment perfect. *God, don't let me screw this up.*

When they broke off the kiss, Kate reached down to gather her bag and the book she'd brought. She wondered when she should tell Julia. She couldn't wait long. As they started up the steep, uneven stairs, Kate wondered what a date with Mo would be like. In some ways, she'd already been on hundreds of dates with her. But everything was going to be different now.

Near the top, Kate lost her footing on a rickety board and reached for the railing. Mo's hand caught her first. When Kate clasped her hand, Mo held fast. Her grip didn't loosen when they spotted the others. *Now this is real*, Kate thought, seeing Julia's eyes zoom right to their locked hands and realizing that no part of her wanted Mo to let go.

CHAPTER FOURTEEN

Julia, Reed, and the kids had made plans to spend the afternoon at the beach, and Terri announced that she'd be sleeping in one of the hammocks until dinnertime, but Mo hadn't mentioned any agenda.

Kate loved how close Mo stood when they were waiting for the ferry and she loved how she settled in comfortably in the seat next to her on the ride back to the island. Although they hadn't discussed it, she was certain Mo was planning on spending the afternoon with her, and she loved how easy it all felt. In some ways, it wasn't that different than how they used to get on. Kate realized it probably wouldn't feel different until they were alone together again. All bets were off then.

As soon as they entered the lobby, Luis, the concierge waved to Kate. He held up a key, smiling as he did, and Kate instantly knew a room had become available. She looked over at Mo, wondering what she should do. Mo had scarcely ended things with Chantal, and after everything Kate had told her yesterday she had to have her doubts about taking things too fast.

But Kate knew that with the way her heart raced every time Mo clasped her hand, her need for Mo wouldn't be contained for long. She was certain she couldn't share the same bed with her and keep her hands, or her lips, to herself.

She approached Luis, smiling as he relayed the news that the oceanfront suite was now available. Mo hadn't gone on with the others, and she waited now in one of the chairs facing the fountain as Kate signed the paperwork for the new room.

"I'm sorry again that I wasn't able to accommodate you earlier this week. I hope it wasn't too much of an inconvenience to share with your friend."

"Everything worked out," Kate assured him. "But I'm looking forward to an ocean view."

"You won't be disappointed," Luis promised. "This one is my favorite."

Once Luis had finished, Kate went over to where Mo was sitting. She held up the room keys. "We got upgraded."

"We? You sure you want me there?" Mo stood up. "I'm totally fine in the other bungalow. For real."

Kate heard the doubt in Mo's voice. What she wanted more than anything was to wrap her arms around Mo with no clothes between them, but she wondered what Mo would think if she told her that outright. Maybe it was too soon. "I get it if you want your own space."

"I don't want my own space."

Kate could see the indecision still on Mo's face. "But?"

"I don't want to rush this."

"Sixteen years doesn't feel like we're rushing," Kate said.

"What if you change your mind?"

"It took me sixteen years to make up my mind. Can you imagine how long it takes me to change it? You know how stubborn I am."

Mo's face cracked with a grin, and Kate knew she'd said the right thing. They could wait, but there was no chance that her feelings were going to change.

"But if we are talking about you…" Kate's voice trailed. "I know you just broke up with Chantal. If you want to wait, tell me. But if you're worried about me, don't be. I may suck at relationships but—"

"But you don't suck at sex?" Mo's grin widened. "So I've heard. Although sometimes sucking isn't a horrible thing."

Kate felt her cheeks flush. She lowered her voice and said, "All I was trying to say earlier is that I don't have issues with sex as long as I'm, well, you know..."

"In a leather outfit with a whip? By the way, I love it when you whisper." Before Kate could stammer a rebuttal, Mo snagged the room keys from her hand. "I also love getting a room upgrade."

Kate followed Mo out of the lobby. Every step felt charged. When Mo stopped to let an elderly Mexican couple cross in front of them, Kate felt a rush of nerves. Mo was coming to her bungalow for one reason—and Kate had been the one to push for it. What if she wasn't ready after all? As much as she wanted it, there was a good chance her anxiety would get in the way.

Mo bumped against her hip. "Sorry." She didn't hide her smile.

"You're not sorry," Kate said. She bumped her hip against Mo. "Neither am I."

"By the way, I liked kissing you on the beach today. How'd you feel about all the people staring at us?"

"I didn't notice," Kate admitted. "But I don't blame them for staring. You're hot."

"Actually I think it was you they were looking at. You're the one who's hot."

"Do you know how much I want you to kiss me right now?" Kate kept her voice low despite the fact that she doubted the elderly couple would care.

As soon as the pair had crossed to the other path, Mo turned around. She was inches away from Kate's lips, and the nearness of her body took all the air from the space. "I have some idea." She turned and started walking again.

"Dammit," Kate said once she'd got her breath back. "That was low."

"Was it?" Mo looked over her shoulder and winked. "I think I get to pay you back some for all the times you've asked me to give you a back massage over the years."

"I gave you plenty of back massages in return."

"Yeah. And trust me—that was just as hard."

"What was hard?"

"My nipples," Mo returned.

Kate laughed. "Good to know." She thought of all the so-called innocent massages they'd shared over the years. Was any of it innocent?

"Are we almost there?"

"Getting antsy?"

Mo chuckled. "I like foreplay as much as the next person."

"Oh, is that what this is?"

Mo stopped walking and turned to Kate. Before she realized what was happening, Mo's lips pressed against hers. The kiss took her breath away. Teasing was over. She didn't want Mo to pull away, and she didn't care who saw them in the middle of the path. Her body was begging Mo not to let up. When Mo did break off the kiss, her lips felt as if they were missing something.

"I really like kissing you," Mo said.

Thank God. Hopefully sex would go as well. She worried she'd talked it up too much. Aside from the fact that she'd never been with a woman before, there was the problem of her body arbitrarily deciding to freeze up during sex. More than once she'd had to stop and apologize. As long as she was calling the shots, she could usually get through it and she hoped Mo would understand.

As they neared the beach, Kate pointed to three bungalows off by themselves between a clump of trees. "I think that one closest to the water is ours."

"That'll do," Mo said, heading down the narrow path.

A flight of stairs led up to the elevated front porch. Mo paused on the first step. "You sure you're ready for company?"

"I'm positive."

As Mo went to unlock the door, Kate slipped her hands around Mo's waist. Mo had the key card against the scanner, but her other hand stalled as soon as Kate touched her hips. Kate shifted, closing the space between their bodies. The key card slipped out of Mo's grasp.

Kate leaned down to pick up the key before Mo could. As she stood up, she let her hand brush along the inside of Mo's leg until she reached her knees. She handed off the key and then encircled Mo's waist again. "Do-over?"

"I think I'd have less trouble if my vision wasn't blurred," Mo said, holding the key up to the scanner once more. She waited for the green light to flash.

As soon as the light flashed, Kate slid her hand under Mo's shirt to touch her midsection. Mo missed turning the handle with the light and the keycard slipped out of her hand. She banged her head against the door and laughed.

"Let me know if you need help."

"I think your help might be part of the problem." Mo leaned down to pick up the card and then turned around to hold it out to Kate. "Your turn."

Kate stepped forward, held the key up, and before Mo had a chance to slip her hands around her, opened the door. She grinned back at Mo. "Gotta be quick."

Mo clicked her tongue. "Some things are different with women. It's not about being fast."

"Oh, really? I may need a lesson," Kate returned playfully. She knew Mo was teasing, and she told herself she could handle it. "First time, you know…"

"Something tells me that this isn't going to feel like a first time. When I kiss you, it feels like I've been kissing you my whole life."

Kate squinted at Mo. "Okay, that's either weird or mushy. I don't think I'm ready for you to be mushy."

Mo grinned. "Check out that view." She pointed to the sliding glass doors on the far side of the room.

Flowers were set in a vase on the table by the door and wine was cooling in ice on one of the nightstands. The bed was similar to the one in Mo's bungalow, but instead of facing a small window with a view of trees, this bed faced sliding glass doors that opened to a separate balcony. Beyond the balcony was the ocean with only a handful of trees and the beach between.

Mo stepped past the entryway and walked around the room. "I could get used to this place." She opened the sliding glass doors and stepped outside. The scent of the ocean came in with the breeze.

Kate put down the bag she'd brought to Tulum, wondering if they should have stopped at Mo's bungalow first to pick up a change of clothes. She'd been too distracted earlier to think of anything but how much she wanted to get to their room. "I'm going to pee."

The bathroom was nearly as big as the bedroom with a Jacuzzi tub as well as a walk-in shower for two that had a bench and dual heads. She sat down on the toilet and wondered if Mo would want a shower first. First. Before what came next. Her chest tightened. What would happen if things didn't go well?

She flushed the toilet and rinsed off her hands, her gaze still on the shower. It wasn't as if she'd never showered with someone before. And yet she knew this time would be different. It wasn't only because Mo was a woman. In some ways, that was the least of the differences. This time she'd be with someone who she'd been in love with for years.

"Everything okay?"

"You should come check out this bathroom," Kate said, wiping off her hands on one of the plush towels. Even the towels were a decided upgrade from the last place.

Mo stepped into the bathroom and looked around. "Damn. I'm ready to move in. How much do you think the monthly rent is on a place like this?"

"I bet we could afford it."

Mo cocked her head, studying Kate. "What are you thinking?"

"Why do you ask?" At that precise moment, she'd been contemplating Mo's body, but she wasn't going to admit that. The idea of being naked with Mo was both intensely appealing and slightly terrifying. Maybe a shower would be the best way to get the awkward part over with.

"Because you have this look on your face..." Mo chuckled. "But I have a feeling you aren't going to tell me, are you?"

"I'm debating."

"Hmm. Don't debate too long." Mo stepped past Kate and headed back to the bedroom. "You should come check out the view from the balcony."

Kate followed her as far as the bed. She watched Mo step out onto the balcony and then turn around.

"You sure you're okay?"

Kate nodded. "I was thinking about asking you to shower with me."

"What about our date?"

"Is there a rule that we have to go to dinner?" Kate hoped Mo's answer was no. "I don't know if I can handle waiting much longer."

"We've been waiting for sixteen years. I bet you could resist until after dessert."

"What if I don't want to?" Kate kicked off her sandals and then pulled her tank top off over her head, knowing Mo's eyes were on her. The thrill of knowing that Mo was watching her undress didn't come with any wave of anxiety. Whatever happened, she knew Mo would let her take the lead. Hopefully that would be enough.

Mo didn't come closer, and somehow that gave Kate the courage she needed. She unhooked her bra and then rubbed the line under her breast from the wire without looking up to see if Mo was still watching. After she had her shorts off, she stood for a moment in her underwear, eyeing Mo.

"You coming or not?"

Without waiting for Mo's answer, Kate turned and went to the bathroom. She kept the door open as she waited for the hot water. Any moment she expected Mo to come in. As she slipped off her underwear, she felt a heady rush at the thought that when Mo did see her, she wouldn't try to cover up. She stepped into the line of water, letting the day's sweat rinse off her skin.

"I could get used to this view too." Mo leaned against the doorway, her eyes not leaving Kate's. Kate felt that Mo wasn't letting herself really look at her yet and she understood. They'd resisted crossing lines for so long that it wasn't a simple matter of stepping across them now. She only hoped Mo would figure it out soon.

"You don't have to shower with me if you're feeling old-fashioned. We can do dinner first." Kate turned her face into the water. She closed her eyes as the stream pelted her forehead and cheeks. When she glanced over her shoulder, Mo was taking off her clothes. She had her back to Kate. Her shorts were off and her sports bra hung from one of the towel hooks. Kate looked away before Mo turned around. The truth was, Mo wasn't the only one who was going to have trouble crossing those lines.

The shower door opened, and Kate busied herself pouring shampoo into her hand. She rubbed her hands through her hair, foaming the shampoo, as she heard the sound of the second showerhead turning on. Mo stood naked next to her, but she stopped herself from looking. She closed her eyes and let the water rinse away the suds.

When she opened her eyes, she glanced in Mo's direction. She'd stepped into the water, rinsing her face and head, then turned to let the water skid off her back and down her legs. The water droplets glistened and Kate reached out to catch one as it flowed from Mo's shoulder blade down to her hip. Mo froze at the touch and Kate could sense that she held her breath. Slowly, she let her hand slip down Mo's hip, and rivulets of water covered the place where her finger had been. She turned away and let the spray hit her face.

"Do you know how many times I've stopped myself from saying that you're beautiful?" Kate said.

"How many?" Mo asked.

"At least once a day for as long as I've known you. I'll let you do the math."

"I got you beat. I stop myself at least a dozen times every day." Mo reached for Kate's hand and brought it up to her lips, kissing the knuckles and then spreading her fingers. Shivers went through Kate as Mo kissed her palm. When she let go, Mo turned off the water and stepped out of the shower.

Kate stayed in the shower, watching as Mo toweled off. If she'd been with a man, she was certain they would have had at least made out. Given all her issues, she'd rarely let anyone inside, but she'd learned enough other ways to satisfy their desire. And she'd been sure of that desire. She'd thought she'd known Mo's interest, but with her quick exit, now she doubted herself.

Was it possible that Mo wasn't ready? Or that she didn't want a sexual relationship? Kate hoped both answers were no. Remembering the way the muscles in Mo's arms clenched as if she'd barely kept herself from reaching for her earlier, Kate was certain she hadn't misread her. Either Mo was being cautious for Kate's sake or she was doing it for her own. Kate turned off the water and reached for a towel. After she dried off, she combed out her hair, staring at her reflection instead of looking into the bedroom to see what Mo was up to.

When she came out of the bathroom, Mo was stretched out on the bed. She was wearing the board shorts she'd been in earlier but hadn't bothered with her sports bra or a shirt. Julia had joked more than once about Mo's perfect breasts. The few times Kate had seen Mo without a shirt, she'd pretended not to look. Now as she lounged back, Kate openly stared. Julia was right. Mo's breasts were perfect, round and full, and although she'd never thought much about breasts or nipples—her own were two small pink-tipped mounds with little to write home about—she couldn't deny the allure.

"I was hoping you'd still be naked."

"This is pretty close." Mo turned on her side. "I didn't know if you'd changed your mind. Suddenly things felt a little different."

"I didn't change my mind." Kate knew that Mo was saying there was no pressure, but it was there anyway. "It's possible I'm nervous."

"I was worried it was only me," Mo admitted.

Why hadn't she seen it before? Mo always pulled back when she was nervous.

Kate sat down on the bed. The towel was still wrapped around her, and she adjusted it to make sure it didn't fall. "Is it really okay with you if I'm in charge? I know you've got more experience and I'm guessing you're usually the one calling the shots."

"Usually." Mo held out her hand, palm upturned. "But nothing about this is usual."

Kate clasped her hand. "Is that a good thing or a bad thing?"

"Definitely a good thing. But it also means there's more pressure."

"Something tells me you can handle the pressure," Kate returned. "Considering some of the women you've dated…"

"I've been with plenty of women. But this time I'm with someone I really like."

"I won't tell all those other women."

"That did sound bad, didn't it?" Mo hmmed. "Most of the time, sex is a fling and then I get to liking the person afterward. This is totally different."

"Yeah, this time you might not like the person afterward."

"I doubt that. I already know she's whip-smart. And hot. Really hot. Plus she knows I'm a nerd and she still likes me." Mo chuckled when Kate gave her a side-eye. "I've had this thing for her for so long—so long that I can't remember what I fantasized about before I met her."

Kate laughed. "You've fantasized about me?"

"Are you saying you haven't fantasized about me?"

The heat of a blush raced up her neck. "Can I plead the Fifth?"

"No."

Kate grabbed one of the pillows and tossed it at Mo. She laughed when Mo dodged it. "For your information," she said, reaching for another pillow, "there was a time when you were the only one I fantasized about."

"What happened?"

"I watched *Wonder Woman*." Kate couldn't believe she was admitting her fantasy out loud. "You know that island with all those warrior women?"

"Wait, Wonder Woman?"

"It wasn't so much her as all those other women."

"Like an orgy?" Mo asked, her eyebrows raised.

"Something like that." Kate tossed the second pillow, and Mo ducked easily again, grinning. "Watch out. My aim might get better."

"I'll consider myself warned," Mo said, holding a pillow up as a shield. "So before you got into orgies…what were you fantasizing about when you thought of me?"

"Oh, no. That's all you get."

"Why stop now?" Mo peeked around the pillow.

The urge to push past the pillow and kiss Mo was hard to resist. "Never in a million years did I think that I'd admit any of my fantasies to you."

"Because you were worried that I'd think it was weird that you were into orgies with comic book characters? Why would you think that?"

Laughing, Kate climbed across the bed on her knees. She pushed the pillow down. Mo was still chuckling. "Alright, smarty pants, you can tease, but it's not that weird. I even read an article about it. Plenty of women have fantasies about group sex."

"With Wonder Woman?"

"And all those hot warrior women."

Before Mo could say more, Kate closed the distance between them. The kiss was playful at first, but it turned into more as soon as Mo let go of the pillow. Mo's lips parted and Kate deepened the kiss, moving closer still. Her towel slipped down her chest, but she didn't try to pull it back up, and when she leaned against Mo, the sensation of her nipples brushing Mo's sent a rush through her.

The question of how far she was ready to go nudged its way into her mind with every kiss. She'd thought she'd stop at kissing, but she couldn't seem to make her body pull away, and when she reached out to caress Mo's breast, her low groan only made Kate want to touch her everywhere else too.

One kiss followed another. She'd never desired anyone as much and every part she touched only made her want more. Soon she was pushing down Mo's shorts. Her pulse quickened when Mo helped, shimmying out of the board shorts between kisses.

Mo's hands stayed on the mattress, and Kate knew that she wouldn't touch her until there was some signal that she was ready for that. With Mo, there was no danger that this would go to a place where she wasn't comfortable. Mo wouldn't push. She was safe to do what she wanted.

Her towel was completely undone now, and when she leaned down to meet Mo's lips again, skin met skin. She didn't hold back a moan of satisfaction, and Mo's responding kiss sent a wave right to her center.

Reaching for Mo's hand, she placed it on her breast and watched Mo's lips part. As much as she wanted to give herself to Mo without holding back, she hoped Mo would understand that it couldn't happen yet—if it ever did. She only hoped Mo would be satisfied with what she could give her.

Distracted some by Mo plying her nipple, Kate took Mo's other hand and kissed each fingertip. No doubt about it, Mo knew what she was doing. A tingling pulse had already started at her clit. But she knew a few things too, she reminded herself. Even if she'd never been with a woman, she knew how to give pleasure. Opening her lips, she sucked Mo's middle finger into her mouth. Mo shuddered and Kate licked her palm before slowly pulling back her head. As Mo's finger slipped out of her lips, the look of pure desire on her face eclipsed every other thought.

When she'd fantasized about Mo, she'd always imagined her on top, even though she knew that wasn't how they'd probably have sex if it ever happened. She'd never let anyone be on top of her, in fact. But she wanted Mo that way. "Someday," she breathed the word out loud and Mo met her gaze.

"Someday?"

"Someday I want you on top of me."

"That could happen sooner rather than later."

Kate looked down at her and drew a line over her lips. Mo's tongue lashed out too late, and she only smiled at the miss, holding her gaze as Kate outlined her jaw. Of all of the things she'd wanted to touch, Mo's face was something that had been forever seemingly off-limits. Now Mo held still as she traced every line. "You know how I said I really liked sex?"

"As long as you're in control. Trust me, I was paying attention. I'm pretty sure you also admitted to being a sex goddess. Do you have a leather outfit that you wear when you do the dominatrix thing? 'Cause I could be into that. And as for toys…"

"I'm trying to be serious here." Kate rolled her eyes when Mo pretended to crack a whip, but she couldn't help smiling. She wasn't ready to have sex with toys, that was for sure, although the thought wasn't awful. "I need to know if you're really okay not being in charge."

"I was ready to wait another sixteen years to have sex with you. I can handle you being in control for a while."

For a while. That was the answer, she knew. Kate nodded, trying to ignore the tightness that had stolen into her chest. She stopped the "what ifs" before they made it to her lips. "Someday I'll ask you to take over."

"Something to look forward to… But did I mention that I'm okay with you using restraints?"

Kate laughed. The last little part of her that had been hanging back now willingly stepped forward. She'd held most of her body up so only their breasts had touched, but now she lowered herself over the length of Mo. When her center pressed against Mo's, she pushed down with her hips, savoring the feel of short hair against her skin.

"God, you feel good," Mo murmured.

Mo's voice only turned her on more. Stroking her hand along the length of Mo's leg, she drew more sounds of approval. When she moved to the inside of Mo's thigh, her body begged her not to stop. But she hesitated. Would Mo want to take this slow?

As if in answer, Mo pushed her hips up. Kate slipped one finger inside. She wasn't sure what she'd been expecting, but feeling Mo's body clench around her and the sensation of being inside was better than anything she'd imagined.

"Mmm…You got more than one finger?"

Mo let her hips drop back to the mattress, but Kate followed her. She slipped in another finger and Mo's responding purr lit up her own body. It didn't simply feel good. She'd never felt anything like it. Touching her own body had never given her a high like this. She pulled out and circled Mo's clit, knowing well how to give pleasure to that, and watched Mo's lips part in a silent gasp. Mo was right. It didn't feel like this was the first time. Somehow she already knew what Mo wanted.

As Kate slid her fingers inside again, Mo thrust her hips up and moaned. Kate thought then of when they'd danced together, Mo's hips pressing in rhythm against hers. She'd felt intoxicated by Mo's body then, but this...this was infinitely better. She matched Mo's rhythm with her hand, hardly believing that it was possible every time Mo's hips jutted up, asking for her to push deeper. Mo's jaw was clenched, and she knew when her breathing changed that her orgasm was coming. Kate wanted to keep going, to watch her come, but there was one thing she wanted before that happened. She'd thought of it, wondered what it would be like, and she hoped Mo wouldn't stop her.

Leaning down, she breathed in Mo's scent before slipping her tongue over her clit. When she heard Mo's sharp intake of breath and felt her body tighten around her, she didn't want to straighten up again. She shifted between Mo's legs, her fingers still working but now adding her tongue every few strokes. Mo combed through her hair as she moaned.

Kate didn't let up and the sounds of Mo's desire grew louder. Their bungalow was off by itself, but she wished everyone could hear. She was doing this to Mo—bringing these sounds to her lips. If she could, she'd keep Mo in bed for the rest of the night finding every new way to please her.

Finally when she couldn't wait any longer for the climax, wanting it almost more than she thought Mo wanted it, she sucked Mo's clit between her lips. Mo's thighs tightened around her, and the hand that had been combing her hair clenched in a fist. Kate let her lips go slack for a only moment. Then she took Mo's clit into her lips again.

Mo cried out when the orgasm rushed through her. She held Kate tight against her and then pulled her up to meet her lips. They savored one long kiss before Mo seemed to melt.

Kate placed light kisses from Mo's neck down to her toes as Mo lay perfectly still, clearly enjoying the afterglow.

"Come back here..." Mo tugged Kate up to her lips for another kiss and then wrapped her arms around her. The strength in her hold felt almost possessive. Kate didn't want to admit how much she liked it.

"Where have you been my whole life?" Mo said, chuckling as if she couldn't believe what had just happened anymore than Kate could.

"Right here," Kate said, snuggling against her chest.

"Remind me again how long I have to wait till you let me touch you like that?"

"Someday," Kate promised. She brushed her lips over Mo's collarbone. "You knew I wouldn't be ready, didn't you? That's why you didn't try anything in the shower."

Mo gave her a gentle squeeze. "I know a thing or two about the mysterious Kate Owens," she said simply. "But I have to admit…I wasn't expecting you'd be that good with your tongue."

Kate laughed, pushing up off of Mo's chest. "Why not?" Her groin was still on Mo's and when Mo shifted, her hair tickled the inside of Kate's thighs.

"Well, I guess it's partly because you've been with guys and I figured—"

Kate crossed her arms. "You're going to have to get over this thing you have against bisexual women, starting about now."

"I am, huh? Well, when you put it that way…" Mo pushed her hips up a half-inch. If Kate hadn't been sitting on her, the movement would have been imperceptible. As it was the slight shift was exactly enough to send a tremor to Kate's clit.

Kate squeezed her legs. "Mmm. I hope I don't take too long deciding I'm ready for you to be on top."

Mo clenched her jaw. "You and me both. You have no idea how hard it is holding back."

"You have more willpower than anyone else I know. You'll survive." Kate smiled and leaned down to plant another kiss on Mo's lips. "But trust me," she whispered, "I can't wait for the day when you are having your way with me."

"Way to make me even harder," Mo whined. "I do have limits, you know."

"Get ready to test them." Kate shifted off Mo, grinning as she did. Everything was different this time. There were no secrets. She didn't have to explain why she needed to be in control and instead of the tense arguments she'd had with guys she'd been with, they were already joking about sex. "I'm taking another shower. You can join me again if you want."

"I'd love to, but I don't know if I can handle it. I'm not sure you realize how sexy you are soaking wet."

"I'm not saying you can't touch me at all. I want your hands on me. And I promise I'll show you where the line is." If she ever let anyone cross those lines, she knew it'd be Mo.

CHAPTER FIFTEEN

"You rented us a scooter?"

Kate smiled. "Don't act so surprised. I can be spontaneous."

"I know but...what'd you call them? A two-wheeled deathtrap?" Mo shook her head. "I figured you must have thrown a party when I cancelled last time."

"I wanted to spend the day with you. But we get a redo on that whole day."

Mo looked over at the clock on the nightstand. There was something she clearly wasn't saying and Kate felt a moment of uncertainty. She should have asked if she had other plans. Maybe spending all day together wasn't what she wanted.

"I should have asked before I made the reservations. If you want to do something else..."

Mo scratched her head. "Here's the deal. I kind of made reservations for us too. We have a couples massage scheduled at three. But that would mean we were spending all day together and I'm not sure if you'd want that."

"Considering that I debated trying to convince you to spend all day in bed... Yes. I want to spend all day with you. For a minute there, I thought you were going to say that you'd rather do something alone. I was about to be crushed."

"After last night you really think that?"

"Insecurities die hard. I'd love to do both. A massage sounds amazing."

Mo got up off the bed and wrapped her arms around Kate. "I don't want to do anything that would crush you. And I'd love to spend all day together. And the next day. And the day after that."

"Can you be naked for most of that time?"

"Who needs clothes?" Mo grinned. "Wait, when do we fly back?"

"Tuesday." And that was going to come entirely too soon. "Although I can remote in for work."

"Good idea. How much do you think it'd be if we extended our reservations for the rest of the month?"

"Room service is going to add up," Kate said, playing along. It was nice to imagine spending a month with Mo in this bungalow. They'd called in room service last night and had their dinner date on the balcony. Naked. Then they'd called room service again this morning. Other than going out on the balcony, they hadn't left the room and they'd used the resort's bathrobes in lieu of clothes. But somehow they'd both managed to make reservations without the other knowing. Kate hadn't thought beyond plans for that day, but now she wondered what would happen when they went back home.

"Other than missing Peeves, I have no reason to be anywhere else."

"I forgot about Peeves!" Mo shook her head. "We'll have to go get him."

"When does Chantal get back from London?"

"Friday." Mo sighed. "I've got some time to figure out where I'm moving."

"You don't want to move back in with me?"

"I do," Mo said, kissing Kate's forehead. "But I've made the mistake of moving too fast before. I don't want to make any mistakes this time. I want us to date for a while before we start living together."

"This is not a typical relationship. We've already lived together."

"We lived together as friends—and this is Day Two of something totally different. Day One was amazing, and so far Day Two sounds like it is going to be even better. I'm not going to risk messing up something this good because of housing logistics."

Kate knew Mo was right, but she wanted to argue for her to move back in anyway. It wasn't only that she was lonely without her in the house—she felt safe with her and the thought of sleeping every night in her arms was too good to pass up. Last night's sleep was the best she'd remembered in years. She decided now wasn't the time to convince Mo, however. "We'll talk about this more later."

Mo raised her eyebrows. "Oh, is that right?" She laughed. "I like how you think you're calling the shots on everything."

"Get used to it."

Mo kissed her lips, drawing away her breath and then slid her hands under Kate's robe to settle on her hips. She'd held her that same way in the shower that morning and Kate had nearly melted. "Mmm. You can call the shots now."

"Can't fool me. I know you're not that easy," Mo said, kissing her again. "But I like a challenge."

"You're in charge on the scooter. I'm going to close my eyes and just hold on."

"Too bad we have to get dressed for that."

"Speaking of which—get your sexy self dressed before I decide I need to have my hands all over your body again." Kate felt a surge at her clit. She hadn't had her fill of Mo, and it was hard standing close without touching her.

"That's an option? 'Cause this scooter thing can totally wait…"

As it turned out, they landed back in bed one more time before they made it out the door. It was only when the front desk called, asking if they still wanted the scooter that they got dressed. They stopped by the old bungalow to change out of the clothes from Tulum and then went to the lobby. Luis smiled as they approached the desk. If he noticed Kate's hand in Mo's, that didn't change his friendly tone.

"My friend Jorge has the scooter out front for you," Luis said. "And I made sure he brought two helmets."

"Perfect," Kate paid the scooter rental and gave Luis a tip.

"You have a message from your mother as well. She called last night."

Kate let go of Mo's hand to reach for the note that Luis held out. She turned to Mo. "Can you check out the scooter while I call my mom? Hopefully it won't take long."

Mo seemed happy to be off the hook at waiting through the call and headed out the front entrance as Kate found her cell phone. She texted her mom, knowing that she'd call the resort number instead of texting back.

After waiting nearly ten minutes for a call, she looked over at Luis and shrugged. "Maybe I'll pick up a calling card and try reaching her when we're out."

Luis gave directions for the closest gas station with phone cards and a pay phone and then added, "I hope you and your girlfriend enjoy the scooter."

Kate smiled, but she tensed at Luis's words. Last night they'd officially crossed the line from friends to girlfriends. She didn't want to change anything about what had happened, but there was still a lingering doubt that she'd be enough for Mo.

"Over here," Mo said. She'd been leaning against a pillar, clearly waiting on her, but she straightened up as soon as Kate stepped out of the lobby. "The scooter's parked in the shade. I took it on a quick spin to make sure it wasn't a deathtrap." Mo pointed toward a red scooter propped up on a kickstand. "Here's your helmet."

"Where's yours?" Kate asked, fitting the helmet on her head.

"I left it on the scooter. Here. Let me help." Mo stepped in front of her and adjusted the chinstrap Kate was tugging on. She got the strap into place so it wasn't riding against Kate's ears and then she slid her finger down, checking the buckle.

Luis's words were still on Kate's mind along with an uncertainty she wished she could shake. It wasn't that she didn't want to be with Mo. If she could spend every night in her arms, she knew she'd never grow tired of waking up with her. But how long before Mo got tired of dealing with her issues and wanted someone who could give her what she was used to having?

"Let's hope this is a good idea."

"I promise I'll get you back in one piece. Eileen will kill me if anything happens to you."

"That's your only reason?" Kate raised her eyebrows. "My mom?"

"That's not my only reason. I don't want to miss out on a two-for-one massage either."

Kate laughed. "Okay, let's do this. Just don't get us killed."

"Deal." Mo held up a key. "You've still got that life insurance policy, right?"

Kate pushed Mo's shoulder. "Don't even go there." Mo was her beneficiary and she knew it. As Mo spouted off a laundry list of organizations she'd donate the money to, Kate realized that no matter what happened next in their relationship, she had no intentions of changing her policy. Maybe someday she'd tell Mo that she'd gotten her wish—she was her first love. No one else came close.

Mo popped the scooter off the kickstand and then climbed on, waiting for Kate to settle in behind her. She adjusted her own helmet and then looked over her shoulder. "Okay, copilot, which way are we going?"

Kate pointed to the right. Luis had said that there was only one main road that circled the island. She'd decided that she wanted to ride for a bit before searching for a pay phone and a calling card. Her mom could wait.

Mo pushed off from the curb and suddenly the scooter was zooming forward. Kate felt a moment of unsteadiness, eyed the pavement, and then wished she hadn't. She wrapped her arms around Mo's waist and talked herself out of a moment of panic. Mo knew what she was doing. All she had to do was relax. Kate shifted closer, narrowing the space between her chest and Mo's back.

"Now this I could get used to," Mo said, grinning over her shoulder.

"Keep your eyes on the road. I'm about to pee myself back here."

Mo laughed and the sound rumbled through her chest and filled Kate's. She hugged Mo tighter and, because that was where she could reach, kissed her shoulder. As many times as she'd kissed Mo's shoulder, always playing it off as a friendly reminder of their closeness and often joking one moment after her lips made contact, this time it reminded her of all the other places Mo had let her kiss last night. She rested her chin on Mo, breathing in the familiar scent of her, and then raised her gaze to the view beyond the road.

They angled south, and as the road curved, a vista of turquoise water appeared in a break between the dense green trees. Kate's breath caught as she took in the ocean, stretched across the horizon and seemingly endless, with the sun sparkling on the cresting waves. A moment later they'd passed the spot and the jungle was all around them again.

Kate thought of suggesting to Mo that they go back to that beach later. There was a strip of sand and a deserted little cove that would be perfect for a picnic. But she didn't want to do anything but hold onto Mo now. "This is perfect," she said, unintentionally voicing her thoughts.

"Tell me if I'm going too fast."

Now that the road had straightened, Mo had increased their speed. The wind whipped Kate's face, but instead of the fear she'd felt earlier, there was only a craving for more. She pushed herself to say what she was thinking: "Can this thing go a little faster?"

Mo nodded. "Don't let go."

"No chance."

The engine revved like an overeager lawn mower and she kissed Mo's shoulder again. For the first time, she wasn't worrying if Mo would guess her feelings. Whatever happened next, at least everything was in the open now. She was done hiding.

For most of the ride along the southern tip of the island, the view was of the ocean and Kate couldn't get her fill of it. They passed sandy beach after sandy beach, interspersed with sheets of pockmarked rock jetting out into the ocean and patches of bright vegetation that lay like a smooth carpet between the road and the water. She let Mo decide when they would stop.

They pulled off once simply to sit and listen to the waves crashing on a bit of rocky coastline. Their next stop was at a roadside bar perched on a cliff. The bar boasted half-naked servers and more incredible views of the ocean, but Kate couldn't seem to look anywhere but at Mo. After a drink and a shared order of nachos, they got back on the scooter and started northward. The surf, when they had a view of it, was higher on this side, and the wind blew white tips over the deep blue.

Few cars passed and there were only enough buildings for it to be a surprise when they came across one. Between the dense jungle growth and the more wild feel to the ocean, it seemed they'd gone to an entirely different place, but the island was small and before long, the road was turning westward. Two lanes opened to four as they approached a town.

"Want to stop and walk around a bit?" Mo asked. She had to raise her voice to be heard over the wind.

Kate nodded, thinking that she still needed to phone her mom as well. She didn't look forward to calling her, but there was no use avoiding it. Eileen had been known to send out search parties if she didn't return a message.

Mo pulled off the main road and slowed as they entered a residential area. As they followed the signs toward the central plaza of the town, the roads got busier with cars, pedestrians, and scooters zipping in and out of the lanes. When they stopped at an intersection, another scooter carrying an entire family pulled up beside them. In addition to a young mom cradling a baby in her arms, a man was driving the scooter and a toddler stood on the footboards. Kate smiled and waved, but the kid only crinkled his eyes at her. As soon as the light changed and the family's scooter pulled forward, the toddler looked over his shoulder, gave her a wide smile and waved.

"That's adorable," Kate said. "It's a good thing all kids aren't that cute. I'd have ten of them by now."

Mo glanced back at her. "I think we should talk about that."

"I don't really want ten kids. I was joking."

"But you want kids, right?"

"I think so...why?" The tension that had all but vanished resettled in her neck and shoulders. Mo's tone was serious. After being with Chantal, had she changed her mind about having kids? She eased up her hold on Mo and shifted on the seat. Now that she had gotten used to riding the scooter, she really didn't need to hold Mo for balance.

"So, what's your kid plan?" Mo asked.

"What's yours?" Kate returned.

"I asked first."

Kate exhaled. She wasn't certain if they were even dating yet by Mo's standards. Did they have to talk about kids already? Mo had turned left and they were cruising slowly down a one-lane road with brightly painted two-story villas on either side of them.

"I feel like kids are something we have some time to think about."

"So you don't have a plan?" Mo pressed.

"I guess I don't. Ethan didn't want kids so I imagined my life without them and that was fine. But then...when we broke up I started thinking about having a kid someday. That's all."

Did Mo really expect her to have this all figured out? Yes, she'd thought about having kids. She'd even thought about how it would work with Mo. And more than once she'd planned a conversation in her head about sperm donors. She spotted a convenience store on the corner of the street and pointed to it. "Can we stop here? I want a bottle of water and I need to make a call."

Mo parked the scooter and then waited for Kate to slide off before dismounting. When she tugged off her helmet, her short hair was as perfect as ever. Her expression was hard to read, but Kate knew that something was bothering her.

"Do you have a kid plan?" Kate pulled off her own helmet, hoping that the low ponytail she'd pulled her hair back in earlier was faring well enough.

Mo pulled the keys from the ignition. "This isn't really about kids. I'm just wondering if you have a plan for any of this. Have you thought about what it's really like to be in a relationship like this?"

"Like this? Like with someone I've been friends with—and had a crush on—for sixteen years? News flash: Yes, I've thought about it. I've daydreamed about our life together about a million times."

Mo clenched her jaw. "Reality isn't always so easy."

"Where is this even coming from? You were the one who didn't want to move back into our apartment too soon. Now you're upset that I haven't thought about kids?"

"I'm not upset."

"Bullshit."

"Whatever. Let's just drop it." Mo placed the kickstand and got off the scooter. "I want to get some water. I'm thirsty."

Kate couldn't handle calling her mom then. She didn't even look at the phone cards, deciding to wait until they got back to the resort. One battle at a time…

Mo bought two bottles of water and a pack of Peanut M&Ms and then looked over at her. "Did you want to make that call?"

Kate shook her head. Mo opened the bottle of water as they stepped outside. She held the bottle out for Kate to take and then said, "I want to have kids with you. Does that freak you out?"

"No," Kate said, entirely sure of her answer. She took a long sip of the water, her eyes not leaving Mo's.

"That's a start." Mo opened the pack of M&Ms and held one in her palm for Kate. "I've always thought we'd be awesome co-parents."

"If we're together, we'd be parents like anyone else. Not co-parents." Kate held out her hand for another M&M. After she'd crunched that, she added, "And if it's okay with you, I'd ask your brother to be the sperm donor. I mean, if I'm the one carrying the kid. I guess I figured I'd be the one, but if you want to as well…"

"I knew you'd already have thought about this."

Kate stepped in front of Mo. God, she loved how Mo looked with that cocky smile lighting up her face. "You know me pretty well, huh?"

"I'm getting there. You probably still have a few secrets."

"No secrets." She set one hand on Mo's hip. "Only a few plans." They were standing in the shade under the green and white striped overhang out front of the store and although she knew the store owner was probably watching them, no one else was in sight. She leaned close and Mo met her lips. The kiss felt like a promise of more to come, and Kate ran her tongue over her lips as she pulled away. She wanted more.

"I love that you'd want to ask Tyrone to be the donor. How long have you been thinking about that?"

"About having kids with you or having your brother's sperm inside me?" Kate pretended to count on her fingers. She stopped and looked up at Mo's smile. "A long-ass time."

Mo chuckled. "I'm going to try not to think about the fact that my brother's sperm is gonna be inside you. But I know he'll say yes. And it's perfect."

"He's not as handsome as you…but I want as close to you as I can get."

Mo smiled again. "Can we say we've seen enough of this island now?"

"You want to head back for that massage?" Kate guessed.

"That too. But mostly I was thinking of everything we did last night and how I'd really like a repeat." Mo stepped close and the kiss she paid in return left Kate weak-kneed. She pulled away, glancing behind them at the store window.

The store owner had likely gotten more of a show than either Kate or Mo wanted, but it took all of Kate's resolve not to beg for another kiss. She exhaled and pulled her phone out of her purse, already planning what she wanted to do with Mo when they got back. After their massage, she didn't plan on leaving the bungalow. "Let me figure out the fastest way home."

CHAPTER SIXTEEN

"Your mother called again," Luis said. "She said it was urgent."

Kate handed the key for the scooter to Luis, forcing a smile. The last thing she wanted to do at the moment was talk to Eileen. Mo was waiting for her by the fountain, thinking that this stop at the lobby was only to return the scooter keys. Her back was to Kate as she watched the birds flitting between the trees and the water. Kate looked from Mo to Luis and then pulled out her phone. "Would you mind if I have her call back now?"

"No problem." Luis waited as Kate typed the text. "Did you enjoy the scooter?"

Kate hit the send button. "I loved it. Cozumel is a beautiful island."

Just then, the phone on Luis's desk rang. He picked it up and then looked over at Kate as he spoke into the receiver: "Yes, of course. One moment please, señora."

"Let me guess. My mom?"

Luis held his hand over the phone and said, "I think our moms should call each other. Then we could relax."

"I'll suggest it." Kate took the phone from Luis, hoping whatever urgent thing Eileen had to say wouldn't take long. More than ever, she was looking forward to that couples massage.

"Hey, Mom. How are you?"

"Oh, I'm fine." She let out an exaggerated sigh. "It's your father."

"What's wrong with Gary?"

"Philip. I debated calling you, but I knew telling you was the right thing."

Kate listened as her mom relayed the news. *Breathe*, Kate thought. She took a deep breath like her first therapist had taught her and slowly exhaled. Her hand was shaking the phone against her ear so she switched hands and turned away from Luis's questioning gaze. "Wait, his liver's failing?"

"That's what his secretary said. I'm not surprised with the way he always drank. They've moved him to some kind of hospice facility, but he wants to die at home..." Eileen's voice trailed. "I know how you feel about him, but he's asking to see you."

"I haven't seen him since I was thirteen. He hasn't called once." Kate squeezed her hand on the receiver, trying to stop the shaking. "Mom, he did nothing to stop that bastard. The guy was his friend. They're probably still friends."

"Don't shoot the messenger." Eileen huffed. "I only told his secretary that I would let you know. For heaven's sake, don't you think I'd rather not tell you?"

"Well, I wish you hadn't. What does he expect? Me to jump on a plane and go see him in Amsterdam?"

"It's your decision, Katelyn." Eileen paused. It was clear from her tone that she hadn't expected Kate to agree. This was all a formality. "You always do whatever you want no matter what anyone else tells you anyway. I don't expect you to start listening to me now."

Kate ignored the jab. Eileen viewed independence as a flaw and couldn't see how she had encouraged it. "Is that all you needed to tell me, Mom?"

"Well, I didn't think you'd want to hear about the new lawyer Gary hired. He's very handsome, Kate. And single. Of course you'd have to come back to Sand Bluff to meet him and I know how you feel about that."

"You're right. I don't want to hear about the lawyer." Kate rubbed her forehead. A headache was coming on. "I have to think. I'm not sure what I'm going to do."

As Eileen ran through a list of reasons why not to go to Amsterdam, none of which included her father's asshole friend, Kate pictured Philip in his house by the lake on that last morning. They hadn't hugged. She'd shuddered when he stepped close so he didn't try. He'd walked her down to a waiting taxi and then said something about how she should send him a note so he knew what to buy her for Christmas. That was all she remembered. She never sent any note.

Now she wondered if Philip deserved all the anger she'd directed at him. He wasn't the one who had touched her and part of her felt some pity for him now, dying alone with only the people he paid to be at his side. But he'd done nothing to stop his friend from coming back. Those last few weeks at the lake had been a sort of hell. Could she go back and face it all again?

"Mom, I need to get off the phone. I'll text you when I decide what I'm going to do." Without waiting for the perfunctory "I love yous," Kate handed the phone back to Luis.

"Is everything okay?" Luis looked clearly concerned.

"Not really. Thanks for letting me use the phone." Kate reached for her purse, but then Mo stepped forward and handed Luis a tip. Kate wondered when she'd walked over and how much she'd heard.

"That was Eileen?"

Kate nodded. "I can't talk about it." She felt the tears pushing at her eyes.

"Okay… Let's go back to our room."

Kate hardly saw the path. She followed Mo, grateful that she hadn't tried to hold hands or make any contact and then feeling guilty that she was so ready to reject contact if it was offered. She wanted to be alone to process everything that Eileen had said. It wasn't that she couldn't tell Mo, but a weight had suddenly dropped on her and she knew the brief bit of happiness that had been the past twenty-four hours was over. This mess certainly wouldn't help their new relationship—if she dared to even call it that.

Each time she considered the question of going to Amsterdam, her answer was that she owed Philip nothing. She could call him on the phone when she got home to hear whatever it was he needed to say. A dying man deserved to be heard out, but she didn't need to offer more. He probably had no clue how he'd damaged her and yet...that didn't change the fact that he'd stood by and said nothing. The person who was supposed to protect her hadn't cared. And then he'd forgotten about her.

Kate realized where they were only when Mo had stopped to unlock the door of their bungalow. Mo held open the door, eyeing her with obvious concern, but Kate only murmured that she wanted a shower. She stripped in the bathroom and then numbly stepped into the water.

"Whatever it is," Mo said, leaning against the bathroom door, "I'm here for you. I won't make you tell me, but it's possible you'll feel better if you say what's going on. I can tell that Eileen said something that just pulled the rug out from under you."

Kate didn't look back at Mo. "I have to go to Amsterdam."

"When?"

"Right away." Now that the decision was made, she knew she needed to get it over with as soon as possible. "Tomorrow or the day after. As soon as I can get a flight."

"I'll get online and find us tickets."

Us? Mo was volunteering to go with her? Eileen hadn't even made that offer. But Eileen was clueless. Kate shook her head. She wasn't going to subject Mo to whatever breakdown she had in Amsterdam. This was something she needed to do alone.

"Why are you shaking your head? I'm not letting you go back to Amsterdam alone."

"Philip's dying. He's asked to see me. All I'm going to do is hear him out and come home." Kate was formulating her plan as she spoke. "I only need to go for a few days." A long weekend, nothing more.

"And I'm coming with you."

The sureness in Mo's voice made Kate question for a moment if she was right in wanting to leave her out of this. But then she thought of all those days after she'd come home from Amsterdam. How she'd fallen asleep with a bottle of her mother's sleeping pills clutched to her chest, knowing there was a way out of her misery when she was ready for it, and then how she'd starved herself, hoping her body would simply slip away while no one was looking.

"I'm going alone." Kate turned away from Mo and let the water pelt her face. Mo didn't argue, but Kate knew by the way that she closed the door without another word that she was upset.

The longer Kate stayed in the shower, the worse she felt. Clearly the day had started out too perfectly. Waking naked with Mo's arms around her, still on a high from everything that had happened in the hours before sleep, must have been a moment stolen from someone else's reality. That wasn't her life. *Or if it was, the day was bound to end up like this.*

A stabbing cramp started up in her stomach and Kate turned off the water. She stepped out of the shower and the pain got worse. Doubled over, she stared at the tile floor while her drips made a puddle at her feet. The toilet was only a few feet away and the thought of vomiting gripped her. It had been years since she'd needed to do that to ease the pain, but the impulse was still as strong as ever. And yet she knew the cramp wouldn't go away. Vomiting lessened it for only a while. As soon as she ate again, it would be back, along with all the awful thoughts that made her think of wanting to end it forever.

It shouldn't be like this anymore, she argued. Years had passed and she'd had enough time to do whatever healing should have been done. She wasn't a scared, powerless thirteen-year-old. And hadn't she been happy only hours ago? Truly happy?

Kate straightened up as she tasted bile. She wouldn't give her body that satisfaction. The easy way out had always been a lie. Reaching for a towel, she dried her eyes, hating the tears that wet her cheeks. She went over to the toilet and slammed the lid down.

Going back to Amsterdam was going to dig up everything she'd buried. On one hand, she wanted to prove to herself that she could survive it. And on the other hand, she wanted to reject the plan simply because the word "Amsterdam" brought back a tide of panic. She didn't think that Philip would give her an apology or say anything that might right all the past wrongs. But if she went to see him one last time at least she wouldn't feel as if she'd owed him anything. There was no way, however, that she was putting Mo through any of it.

Mo was sitting cross-legged on the bed eyeing her phone screen. She looked up as Kate came out of the bathroom. "We leave tomorrow at nine. There's a layover in Atlanta and then we take a red-eye from there to Amsterdam."

"What are you talking about?"

"I bought our tickets," Mo said.

"You did what? I told you I wanted to go alone." Kate felt the anger spring out of nowhere, but Mo only stared back at her. "You don't understand. I don't want you to come."

"I'm not letting you do this alone."

"Mo, you have no idea what this is going to be like—"

"You're right. I don't. And I can't understand everything you've been through. Probably I never will. And this won't make anything right, but I can't stand to let you go alone."

"Mo—"

"Please let me come."

Mo's voice was more gentle than Kate deserved. It stopped Kate from screaming back at her despite the urge. Why did she think she could buy tickets without asking her first? She'd clearly gone against her wishes.

"What's going on between us, Mo, whatever it is, just started. We've been together one night. One night. You might not even like me in a week."

"Bullshit," Mo said quietly. "We've been together sixteen years. With a lot of ups and downs. And if you think back on it all, I've always been there for you. Whenever you needed me. I never once walked away when things got hard." Mo's voice softened. "And finally when I feel like I wasn't crazy waiting for you all those years… I'm not giving up now."

Kate shook her head. "This is my mess, Mo. I'll go to Amsterdam and then we can figure everything out when I get back."

"No. *We'll* go to Amsterdam. I'm not saying that you need me. I'm asking you to let me come. Forget about everything that happened yesterday—none of that matters."

"Forget about it?" Was Mo serious? There was no way Kate could forget anything about yesterday. No other day had come close to being as good. But now the fantasy she'd created in her head of being with Mo was seeing the light of day. God, what was she thinking? Why had she kissed Mo in the first place?

"I'm saying that you were my best friend before that and you'll be my best friend after. Even if yesterday hadn't happened, I'd still want to go with you." Mo stopped. "If you can't let me in…"

"I don't know that I can let anyone in, Mo." Tears were pushing at her eyes. "Maybe we should go back to being just friends."

"Is that really what you want?"

When Kate didn't answer, Mo tossed her phone face down on the bed sheets and pulled her knees up to her chest. She sat there, staring out the window and at the ocean line beyond their balcony. It was the same gorgeous view as the day before and yet everything had changed. Kate wanted to go back in time. They'd stay on that scooter and ride around the island until they found a place to stop for dinner. Then they'd come home late and Luis would have already left for the night. Not knowing any better, they would have slipped back to their bungalow.

Mo looked over and met Kate's gaze. "Do you think being friends would hurt less?"

Kate didn't answer, and the longer Mo held her gaze, the more the ache in her chest seemed to press out all the air from her lungs. She knew Mo didn't deserve getting pulled into her disaster, but she also knew that they couldn't go back to being friends. It was all or nothing. She crossed the room and came over to Mo's side of the bed. When she held out her hand, Mo clasped it.

"This was not how I wanted today to go."

"Me neither." Mo chuckled, but a tear streaked down her cheek. She looked up at Kate with a wry smile. "But we're having so much fun, why stop?"

"Only you could be joking right now." Kate gently swiped Mo's tear with her thumb. It was impossibly hard stopping the "I love you" that formed on her lips. She eyed the bed, thinking of everything they'd done last night. "Is this how it usually goes when you start sleeping with women? One amazing night and then all of your life problems come to a head the day after?"

"Pretty much. The good news is almost everyone gets through that first day. Then you get another amazing night."

"Almost everyone? What do you think our chances are?"

Mo cleared her throat. "Right now I'd give us fifty-fifty."

"I want to change those odds. I like you so damn much, Mo. I don't know how I'll get by if…" She shook her head. "I know what you're thinking. I shouldn't say things like that."

"That wasn't what I was thinking."

Mo pulled her close and met her lips. Their first kiss had been like a step across a tightrope three stories from the ground. Last night's kiss had blurred her vision and left her throat dry for more. But this kiss…this was coming home to someone's waiting arms. Mo's lips felt right in a way nothing else could. When Kate drew back, she knew her heart was going to break if dating didn't work.

"I'm sorry I'm not up for that couples massage. I'm sorry for a lot of things, actually."

"You sorry for kissing me?" Mo asked.

"No. I think I could die not sorry for that."

"How would you feel about laying down with me for a bit? I totally get it if you aren't in the mood for being touched. I'm not suggesting that."

Kate undid the towel tied at her chest. Mo's gaze went right to her breasts, and Kate couldn't help but smile at the soft whimper she made. "Scoot over."

Mo shifted to the middle of the bed and then pushed down the sheets. As Kate settled in, Mo pulled off her shirt and then took off her shorts. She was wearing red boxers underneath the shorts and as soon as she lay down, Kate reached out to trace the waistband.

"I didn't vomit. I thought about it…" Kate paused. "That probably sounds disgusting. God, I'm such a mess."

Mo tilted Kate's chin upward so their gaze met. "I can handle your mess. I don't like you any less when you tell me these things. I like you more 'cause you're letting me in. Let me come to Amsterdam."

Kate nodded. She didn't trust her voice to say more and was glad when Mo kissed her instead. Mo's arm wrapped around her, pulling her close as one tender kiss followed another.

CHAPTER SEVENTEEN

It wasn't until they'd gotten off the plane that Mo looked down at her shorts and sandaled feet and said, "Are we going to need coats?"

"Already on it. We can get everything we need in the airport. There's two stores we need to swing by."

While Mo had slept for most of the red-eye from Atlanta to Amsterdam, Kate hadn't been able to nod off even for a moment. To keep herself from obsessing over what would happen after they landed, she'd connected to the plane's Wi-Fi and drafted a half dozen work emails before scrolling through the listings for the Schiphol airport clothing shops.

Her house sitter hadn't complained about watching Peeves for an extra few days, and she knew no one at work would miss her as long as she promised to check her email. The only ones that seemed upset about the change in plans were Julia and Reed's kids. The twins had cried through their last breakfast together and only dried their tears when Mo and Kate promised a special "Auntie Day" where they'd both spend the day with them. Aside from that promise, Kate hadn't been able to think about any future beyond the three days in Amsterdam. Fortunately no one pressed her. She guessed that Mo had explained enough to Julia and Reed, and maybe even Terri, since everyone had resisted asking any questions and only gave her long hugs when the taxi came. That was exactly what she wanted and she was thankful Mo knew.

Picking out clothes for Mo was more fun than she'd expected. Mo was clearly happy to let someone else shop for her and along with a pair of jeans and new slacks, Kate chose a few new shirts for her and a coat that would work for winters in San Francisco as well as during this trip. She sent Mo to the changing room with everything, and when Mo stepped out, the casual resort wear replaced with dashing European fashions, Kate's breath caught.

"Damn. You are so hot."

Mo looked down at her outfit. "Guess this will do?"

"It'll do." Kate went over and straightened Mo's collar. Aside from the store clerk, they had the place to themselves and when he wasn't looking, Kate brushed her lips against Mo's cheek. The look Mo gave her in return was worth it. She took a step back when the impulse to kiss her lips flared. "Too bad I don't have any excuse to buy you a new suit. I love seeing you all dressed up."

"I'll get dressed up for you anytime. As long as I don't have to wear a tie."

"I know how you feel about ties." The only conversation they'd had about ties had made her uncomfortable at the time. She'd asked why Mo didn't wear ties when she wore a suit. Mo had answered that ties were only good in the bedroom. Kate had stopped short at that and never brought it up again despite how many times her mind came back to it. One day maybe she'd feel brave enough to convince Mo to show her what she meant. "Now we need to get you some shoes."

"What about you? What are you going to wear?"

"I packed half my closet. The only thing I need to find is a jacket."

"You sure?"

Kate nodded. "Clothes aren't what I'm worried about."

Mo lightly kissed Kate's forehead. "Thank you, again, for letting me come with you."

"You bought the tickets," Kate reminded her. "What was I supposed to do? Tie you to the bed?"

Mo's eyes widened. "Please tell me that would be an option someday."

Kate laughed, feeling emboldened by the look of desire in Mo's eyes. "Go try on the rest. And I'm paying for all of this. Don't argue."

For as many times as she'd been to Amsterdam, Kate knew that she ought to have a feel for the layout of the city, but even the few landmarks she recognized seemed to be in the wrong place or somehow altered. Rationalizing that she'd rarely spent more than a few nights at Philip's apartment before they'd drive to the lake house each visit seemed a plausible explanation, and yet she knew it was more than that. She'd blocked the city from memory, willing it away as best as her thirteen-year-old self could manage. But no matter how she tried to forget it, she could recall every nook and cranny of the lake house.

The taxi dropped them off at the hotel, and when Mo asked if she wanted to lay down for a bit, Kate shook her head. Despite the lack of sleep, she wasn't tired. She was wound up too tight. Mo suggested they get some food, and Kate agreed but when they sat down at a restaurant near the hotel, she had no appetite. She'd settled on a salad and soup, mostly to keep Mo from worrying.

"So should we talk about the plan?" Mo asked, picking up a bread roll. The tone of her voice made it clear she didn't want to push. "Are you thinking of going to see him tonight?"

"Tomorrow. I sent a message to his staff."

"His staff?" Mo buttered one side of her roll. She'd ordered the soup and salad as well, which Kate only realized now she hadn't eaten much of either.

"I'm guessing that the only people who are with him now are the ones he pays." Kate paused. "Maybe I shouldn't give him such a hard time. I hardly know the guy. Probably he's changed a lot."

"People don't change that much," Mo said.

"Do you not like your soup? You can order something else."

"Actually it's good." Mo set down the roll without taking a bite. "I'm nervous."

"You're nervous? The same person who does a robot dance in front of total strangers just to make people smile?" Kate thought of Mo dancing in the ocean with the twins. That moment seemed a lifetime ago.

"I'm nervous for you."

"I'll be fine." Kate picked up her fork and stabbed a leaf of lettuce. "All I have to do is listen to him."

"You're not going to say anything about what happened then?"

Kate stared at the lettuce leaf. If possible, the salad was even less appetizing now. She set down her fork. "I'm only here because I don't want him to die and then feel like I owed him this one last thing. I don't want to owe him anything."

"Well, jeez, we could leave now. You'll never owe him anything."

"I can hear him out," Kate said, fortifying her resolve. "And I figure I might as well have something new to tell my therapist."

"What about me?" A hint of a smile tugged at Mo's lips.

"Oh, she's already heard an earful about you," Kate admitted. "I can't wait to see her face when I tell her that I finally kissed you."

"How much have you told her about me?"

"Let's put it this way: If you meet her on the street, you should probably worry."

Mo laughed, and Kate felt the first bit of lightness buoy her spirits. Since the taxi had dropped them off, the whole of Amsterdam had seemed to press down on her. She'd felt as defenseless as she had the last time she'd been in the city. A taxi had brought her from the lake house to the city, and she'd spent one night alone in a hotel room her father had paid for. She'd hardly slept that night, anxiously waiting for a plane to take her away from the nightmare. As she matched Mo's smile, she reminded herself that this time she wasn't alone.

By the time they got back to the hotel, Kate was relaxed enough to lay down. Mo offered a massage and although she had reservations about how well that would help her unwind, after five minutes she was taking off her blouse. When Mo started to rub the hotel lotion onto her back, Kate took off her bra as well. She wasn't ready for Mo to give her a front massage, but her hands were making Kate wonder what she was missing by only letting her touch her back.

At some point during the massage, she fell asleep. She woke up with Mo softly snoring next to her. The clock on the nightstand read a quarter after four, and it took a minute for her to realize that she'd slept for over twelve hours straight. Mo was fully dressed, but she'd kicked off her shoes and pulled the blankets up to cover them both and the room was pitch dark aside from the clock.

The urge to pee got her out of bed, but she slipped out of the extra soft bed as quietly as she could, hoping Mo would stay asleep. Bumping her way to the bathroom, she closed the door and flicked on the light. Compared to the bathroom in Cozumel, this place was tiny and everything about it reminded her she was in the Netherlands again. She went to the toilet and peed, staring down her reflection in the mirror above the sink.

At one point, she'd considered coming back to confront her father. An astute therapist that she'd had only for a brief time in high school had talked her out of that plan. It would have been a disaster then, but would today be any better?

A soft knock pulled her from her thoughts, and she quickly stood and flushed. "Just a minute."

Mo looked half asleep. She rubbed her face with the back of her hand and squinted at Kate. "Are we going for a run?"

"You want to go on a run this early?"

"Well, I was thinking you might want to..." Mo cleared her throat. "So is that a no? 'Cause I'd really like to pee and go back to cuddling."

"See you in bed." Kate placed a light kiss on Mo's cheek and then moved out of her way. Before she lay back down, she stripped off her pants and snuggled into the warm space Mo had left. She watched the strip of light below the narrow bathroom door, waiting on Mo.

The light switched off as Mo opened the door. She tiptoed back to bed, chuckling when she realized Kate had taken her place. "You're one of those people who is always cold in bed, aren't you?"

Kate smiled, knowing Mo couldn't see her face in the dark. "Lucky me, you sleep warm. I'm hoping you also spoon."

Mo went around to the other side of the bed and settled in behind Kate. When she realized Kate was naked, she moaned softly.

"Take off your clothes," Kate said. "I want to feel you against me."

Mo pulled away for a minute and the bed bounced as she tugged off her pants and slipped out of her shirt. When she pressed against Kate's backside again, the warmth of her body and the feel of her breasts brushing Kate's shoulder blades was almost too much. Kate had to stop herself from turning around to face her, thinking of tracing the lines of her smooth skin and finding the secret places that made Mo shudder.

"Better?" Mo asked.

Kate reached behind her and found Mo's arm. She placed Mo's hand on her hip, knowing that Mo would only have to move a few inches to find the spot that was quivering with need. She wanted to be ready to let Mo make love to her. But would she ever be ready? She shifted her butt back until she felt the short hairs at Mo's center. Mo's sharp inhale was the response she'd hoped for.

"This is almost perfect," Kate said.

"What would make it perfect?"

"If I could let you do all the things I want you to do to me."

Mo's grip tightened on her, but she didn't say anything in response. Kate closed her eyes. "I might have a total breakdown today. I really don't want you to see me that way."

"Are you worried that I can't handle it?" When Kate didn't answer, Mo continued. "I can. After today is behind us, I'm still going to like you as much as I do right now. I especially like your butt and I guarantee that won't change." Mo kissed the back of Kate's head when she laughed. "This is torture. You know that, right?"

"I know you can handle it." Kate shifted so Mo's hair brushed against her skin again. "I got you something when we were in Cozumel. It's something little… I've been too embarrassed to give it to you."

"Why?"

Kate hesitated. "I thought maybe you'd think it was cheesy."

"Go get it. I want it." Mo released her hold on Kate. "You know how much I love cheesy. Are we talking telenovela cheesy? Or is this more the level of Hallmark Christmas movies?"

"More like after-school-special cheesiness." Kate climbed out of bed. She didn't need the light to find her purse and she remembered exactly where she'd put it. Since she'd hidden it in the inside pocket along with her mother's bracelet, she hadn't taken it out. Her fingers found it and she felt a new wave of doubt. But she padded back to the bed and slipped in under the covers with the necklace in her hand.

"Give me your hand."

Kate spread Mo's fingers before letting the chain slip out of her hand onto Mo's palm.

"I can't see it. Is it a necklace?" Mo guessed. "And this part… it's a key, isn't it?"

"Do you remember the time we went to see the stars come out over the Golden Gate? I really wanted you to kiss me that night."

"I want a do-over," Mo said.

Kate shifted closer and found Mo's lips. When she pulled back, she said, "Let me get through today. Then we can talk about time travel."

CHAPTER EIGHTEEN

Whether or not Mo liked the necklace, the fact that she was wearing it gave Kate more courage than Mo probably knew. After an early call to her father's secretary that wasn't answered, Mo convinced Kate to go for a run in the hotel's small gym, which consisted of a treadmill and an exercise bike along with a small rack of weights. The run helped let off some steam, but by the time they got back to the room, there was still no message from the secretary. They showered separately in the tiny bathroom and shared a plate of deli meats and cheeses that Mo had ordered from the hotel's cafe.

When her cell phone finally rang, it was close to eleven. Kate picked up the call before the first ring had ended. "Hello?"

"Kate Owens, please."

The woman had a brusque accent, and Kate didn't recognize it as belonging to her father's secretary. "This is she. Who is this?"

"I'm Philip's nurse, Bernadette. He's asked me to ring you."

Maybe her father was too weak to call himself, but Kate couldn't help thinking that he simply didn't want to be bothered picking up the phone. "Is he up for a visit?"

"A short visit, yes. It's kind of you to come all this way, but he needs his rest." Bernadette paused. "He's been moved out of the nursing home... He wants to be at home for what time he has left."

Kate had hoped for the impersonal environment of the nursing home. She braced herself now for being in Philip's space. "Does he have the same apartment?" She struggled to remember the street name.

Bernadette rattled off the address that was familiar as soon as Kate heard it and suggested that she come in an hour when he'd have awoken from his nap. It wasn't until Kate hung up the phone that she realized she hadn't mentioned that she'd be bringing someone.

She looked over at Mo. "I think he's getting worse. He got himself moved out of the nursing home."

"Is that a good idea?"

"I'm guessing they don't let you drink at a nursing home." She remembered her father saying that he couldn't sleep without having a drink first. He'd need that crutch to face death as well.

Mo scratched her head. "So he's going to be drunk? I don't know about this... You know you shouldn't be feeling any guilt about seeing him at all."

"I know." Kate stood up. "Part of this is for me. Let's go. I want to get today over with."

As soon as the taxi pulled onto her father's street, Kate realized her hands were shaking. Everything was too familiar. How was it possible that she was back? At least they were in the city instead of the lake house. She never wanted to see the lake again. Mo reached over and took her hand.

"You okay?"

"Haven't vomited yet."

Mo squeezed her hand. She'd been distracted looking at the sights they passed and seemed surprised when the car stopped.

"Is this it?" She looked up at the house they'd parked in front of. "It's huge."

"He owns the whole place, but the house is split up into apartments. His flat's on the third floor." Kate paid the driver and got out, her legs suddenly shaky. She waited for Mo before starting up the steps. Once they reached the front door, Mo turned around. The house overlooked one of the canals and had a good view of the city.

"It's pretty here."

"At one time I would have agreed with you." Kate eyed the red call button. She didn't want to press it, but she couldn't turn back now.

"We could call him instead."

Kate shook her head. "I need to do this in person."

"Want me to press the button then?"

"Yes, please." Her stomach was doing somersaults. She wondered if it was too late to take Mo's advice and skip this visit altogether.

Mo pressed the button and then wrapped an arm around Kate's shoulders. "We got this."

Bernadette's voice answered.

When the lock clicked, Mo held open the door. "You look a little pale."

"Just catch me if I faint," Kate said, hoping her joking tone played off how terrible she felt. She stepped past Mo and then clenched her jaw as the scent of the building hit her nose. It wasn't an awful smell. It reminded her of an old library. But the familiarity of it made her legs unsteady.

"Remember you don't owe him anything," Mo was saying. "You don't have to be nice."

Kate didn't answer. She made her way through the entryway, trying not to look at her surroundings as she angled for the stairway.

Mo stopped on the second landing to catch her breath. "It must have been hell getting a sick guy up all these stairs."

"I'm sure someone carried him."

"Does he have servants and stuff?"

"I know he has a secretary and a nurse. And a bunch of lawyers…He used to have a cook and a maid. Maybe he still does…"

"Maybe you should just tell him that I'm your friend."

Kate started up the third flight of stairs. "You don't want me to introduce you as my girlfriend?" The fact was, she'd been debating this very thing off and on all morning. But not because of how her father would react. She wasn't sure how Mo would react. Were they even girlfriends by Mo's standards?

"You should say whatever you want to say but…maybe it would make it less complicated."

Kate stopped on the third landing. She turned to face Mo on the stair below her. "Nothing about what happens next is going to be uncomplicated. But you don't have to come inside. You can wait here if you want."

"It's not that. Does he know you like women?"

"He doesn't know anything about me."

Mo stepped up to the landing. "So if you introduce me as your girlfriend, you're also coming out. And I'm black. If he's anything like your mom…"

"I'm introducing you as my girlfriend unless you don't want me to. I hardly know my father. I hope he's not a racist homophobic asshole like my mom because I don't want to put you through that, but at this point I don't care what he thinks about me. You're the person I love." Kate tensed, realizing the word that had slipped out. "It means a lot to me that you were willing to come here. He can go to hell if he doesn't like you."

Mo held out her hand and Kate clasped it. Her heart was pounding in her chest. Had she said too much? Before Kate had time to obsess over whether she should have avoided the L word, the door to Philip's apartment opened.

Bernadette was almost as tall as Mo. She had long silver hair pulled back in a braid that accentuated her thin frame and gave her a look of a crane about to take flight. While she wondered at how that image had popped in her head, Kate shook hands and quickly introduced Mo.

The word "girlfriend" had little visible effect on Bernadette, but Kate felt it ripple through her chest. *Girlfriend.* Saying it aloud had a steadying effect which was strengthened by the fact that Mo didn't let go of her hand.

Bernadette showed them into the front room and then asked them to wait a moment while she went to tell Philip that they'd arrived. As soon as she stepped away, Kate took a deep breath and exhaled slowly. Mo looked over at her.

"You doing okay?"

"So far." Kate scanned the front room, crowded with expensive, uncomfortable furniture, and imagined what Mo might think of it.

"I feel like I'm in a museum," Mo said under her breath.

"Well, most of the furniture was last in a castle so you're not far off."

"Are little knights going to pop out of that dresser?" Mo chuckled.

"Maybe. That bureau was a gift from some fancy duke to one of my grandfathers. I don't think there's any knights inside, but you could check. We might need one later."

Mo grinned. Although Kate didn't know the history of any of the other furniture in the room, she recognized everything. From the red velvet settee to the high backed and uncomfortable love seat opposite it, nothing had changed since the last time she'd been in this room. Maybe her father had moved things in the other rooms, but she was certain nothing had been altered here.

"He's awake," Bernadette said, reappearing in the hallway. "I'm afraid he's not up for getting out of bed, but if you'd like to follow me…"

"Of course."

Kate had never been in her father's room before. She always had the guest room when they were in the city and since it was near the kitchen and the television, she had little excuse to explore further. As she followed Bernadette, questions swirled in her head. Was it weird that she'd never seen the inside of her father's bedroom? Or was it only more evidence that what little relationship they'd had once had been too superficial to count? It didn't seem right that someone she hardly knew had caused so much damage in her life.

Unlike the front room with its museum feel, the hallway was almost homey. Along with a curio filled with pipes and other odd trinkets, framed pictures hung along the walls. One picture caught Kate's eye. The shot had been taken at the lake house and she remembered the T-shirt she was wearing although the smile jarred her. She knew the picture had been taken that last summer. But it was before everything went wrong. For that brief moment, she was a careless thirteen-year-old enjoying a sunny day by the water.

"That's you, isn't it?" Mo said quietly.

Kate nodded. Bernadette didn't hear Mo's question, and she was already at the end of the hall waiting for them. It was hard not to wonder why her father had framed that one picture. Most of the other shots were of landscapes or people she didn't recognize.

Mo caught her hand and gave it a gentle squeeze. "You can do this."

Kate looked over at her. Her stomach was a tight knot and she didn't want to move, but she held onto Mo's hand and started walking again.

The drapes were drawn in the bedroom, and it took a moment to adjust to the dim light. As soon as she recognized her father, his feeble body propped up on pillows, the urge to leave hit Kate in the chest.

"Kate." His voice sounded strangely weak, hardly the man she remembered.

She let go of Mo's hand and stepped closer.

"I would have liked to have seen you sooner," he said. He shifted on the bed and grimaced. When he settled again, he squinted in the weak light, clearly appraising the stranger at his bedside. "You've changed... I remember a little girl."

Kate couldn't think of what to say. Was she supposed to apologize for growing up? For not staying in touch with him? "I'm sorry you're so sick."

"I'm dying. It's my own doing." He motioned to an empty bottle of vodka on his bedside table and then looked over at Bernadette. "Thank you for showing her in."

Bernadette took this as her dismissal. She turned to Mo as if she expected her to follow, but Kate immediately said, "She'll stay with me."

Bernadette gave one nod and closed the door behind her. Silence followed and Kate wished that Bernadette had stayed. With more people present, this could feel like a business meeting instead of a personal matter.

"I'd ask you to sit, but everything's a mess. The nurse insisted on setting everything up like another hospital room."

"I'm fine standing. Can I get you anything?"

"I'm well looked after." He shifted on his pillows and the pain on his face was obvious. With a nod to the vodka, he said, "They won't let me have more than a little sip until I've eaten supper."

Kate wondered how much was allotted after supper, but she stopped herself from asking. If he downed the whole bottle, what did it matter now? A wave of pity hit her. This man who she'd blamed for so many things...

"I'm sure you're wondering why I asked you here." He pointed at a stack of papers on a desk near the window. "I've already written a will and the lawyers will see to all of that, but there was something I wanted to ask you." He cleared his throat again. "If you didn't know me, how much would you ask me to donate to your cancer foundation?"

"You know what I do?"

"I'm not that much of a drunkard that I can't use a computer."

Kate tried not to let her surprise show. She'd assumed he wouldn't know anything about her life. "I research all potential donors before I approach them. I never ask without knowing how much they want to give. The truth is, I don't know you as well as I know most of the donors I ask."

"That's fair. Before you ever ask, you already know how much they want to give? How is that possible?"

"Some of it's intuition," she admitted. "But I always do my research first."

"I'll save you the trouble. I have a lot of money and I haven't managed to spend it all on vodka. How much do I want to give?"

Kate considered his question. She knew it wasn't theoretical. But did she want to ask him for anything? "We want to develop a new program to help families with kids undergoing cancer treatments link up with other families in the same situation. Part of this would be an app that would connect parents as well as guide them through the process of a new cancer diagnosis... I need a donor to seed this project." Kate hadn't pitched this to anyone other than a few people on the board and yet the pieces were falling into place even as she spoke. "Five hundred thousand would get us started."

"What would you do with five million?"

"A lot more." Kate answered smoothly. She'd had conversations like this before with men who wanted to impress her with their money. If it was for a good cause, and she knew that it was, she didn't care how much they preened. But this didn't feel like preening. Her father wasn't trying to impress anyone. He was dying and maybe only wanted to know that something good would come of it. She could give him that much.

"We also want to expand the number of apartments we have near the hospital so parents can stay close to their kids. Most of the time they spend too much money and time travelling between their home and the hospital."

"Done. Will you hand me the phone?" He pointed to a cell phone opposite the vodka bottle. "I might not remember this later..."

Kate waited as he made a call. Philip's words were few and then he passed the phone over to her. She guessed the voice on the other end was a lawyer or maybe a banker. After confirming the amount, the woman asked for a number to reach her later so they could finish the details.

"You've been keeping track of what I'm doing," Kate said, replacing the phone on the nightstand. "Why didn't you try and reach out sooner?"

"A dying man can admit he's made mistakes."

Kate wondered if she could accept this as the only apology she'd get. But maybe she didn't need any apology. If he'd offered her money straight out and not as a donation to the foundation, she would have flatly turned him down. As it was, she couldn't say no. The money would help a lot of families. But was that really the only purpose of this meeting?

Kate looked at her father again. She knew this was the last conversation they'd have and maybe she should simply say goodbye. But something held her in place. "You should have said something to him," she started. "Why didn't you?" Her hands shook so she squeezed them into fists, but there was nothing she could do about the timbre of her voice. "It happened right in front of you. You could have stopped him from coming over."

"He'd been a good friend for years..." He eyed Mo and then Kate again. "There's no point in bringing all of that up now, is there?"

Mo's jaw clenched. "Do you have any idea how much you hurt—"

Kate held up her hand, stopping Mo midsentence. Philip didn't respond. Even if he heard everything, he'd deny there was any wrongdoing on his part. In his mind, she'd overblown the matter—that's what he'd said before. He was right about one thing. There was no point in bringing it up again. "Is there anything else you wanted to tell me?"

Philip shook his head. When he closed his eyes, it was clear the meeting was over. A minute passed and then another. Kate wondered if there really was nothing left to say. The sound of snoring jolted her from her thoughts. He'd fallen asleep.

Mo held out her hand. "Let's go."

Kate clasped Mo's hand and let her lead them out into the hall. Bernadette was waiting in the front room. "He said that you wouldn't be staying."

Kate stopped herself from saying that he'd never wanted her here. The photograph in the hall gave her pause and she understood her father even less now. "How long do you think he has?"

"If he stopped drinking..." Bernadette sighed. "I don't think it will be long. A few weeks."

As they headed for the door, Kate took one last look at the front room. Now she'd think of it always as a museum—full of secret tragedies and joys. But furniture that no one sat on or touched was worth as little as anything else that had outlived a purpose.

They stepped outside and Kate took a deep breath. Mo looked over at her. "You okay?"

"I think I will be." If she could let go of all the memories and leave what happened at the lake house…

"Should I call a taxi?"

"I'd rather walk." Kate had no idea how far they were from the hotel or any memory of the drive there. All she knew was that she didn't want to think for the rest of the day. "Can you take me somewhere?"

Mo pulled out her phone and brought up a map. She looked over at Kate. "Are you cold?"

Kate realized then that she was shivering. "I think I'm just tired."

Mo slipped her phone in her back pocket and then took off her jacket. She hung it around Kate's shoulders. "We need cocoa."

"Cocoa?"

"You'd be surprised—a mug of hot cocoa fixes a lot of bad days. That's what my dad always used to say anyway."

Kate wasn't certain that any drink would work this time. "You find us cocoa and I'll give it a try."

CHAPTER NINETEEN

"I want to help you on that app," Mo said. "The one you were telling your father about. If I did it on my own, and you weren't paying someone else, you could put more of his money to those family apartments you were talking about."

"I'd want to pay you."

Mo had slept for most of the plane ride back to the States, but she was awake for the leg from Atlanta to San Francisco and clearly she'd been thinking. "So I can help you? We can fight about the money part later."

Kate smiled. "I haven't pitched the idea to the full board yet, but I'd love your help. I wouldn't feel comfortable not paying you, however. Your company designs apps. It's what you do."

"Do you know how much something like that could have helped my mom when she was going through everything with my dad? And it'd be more than a social app for connecting people... We could have a volunteer tab where folks could offer up rides or housecleaning services. Or even babysitting. Once you've been through something like that, you want to help other people who are in the middle of a crisis. Emotional support is great, but families need basic help getting through their day." Mo paused. "I looked online yesterday to see what's out there. We can do better."

"We? I don't know anything about making an app."

"You're the one with the idea."

"But I only came up with it because of your app. HeroToday made me think of all the things we could be doing better."

"Which is why we should work together on this."

"I want you to move back in with me," Kate said. She'd spent the last day in Amsterdam thinking of a way to bring up the conversation but had lost her nerve each time she tried. Mo had taken care of everything since they'd left her father's apartment. She'd held her as she cried herself to sleep that first night and now Kate didn't want to think about sleeping alone. "It's going to be hard sleeping alone tonight."

"Getting attached?" Mo tried to joke. She looked down at their interlaced hands. "I'll stay at your place tonight."

It wasn't enough, but Kate stopped herself from begging. Maybe it wasn't fair of her to ask for more of Mo. "Thank you."

Mo studied her for a moment. "I hate when I make you sad. I just don't want to rush this."

"I'm not sad," Kate lied. "And I know you're right. But I wish I were easier."

"Relationships are hard. It's not just you."

"Yeah, but when you've been with someone else and things get hard… Usually you've had sex with them more than once. Then you don't mind dealing with their crap." Kate forced a smile. "You got everything the first week."

Mo didn't laugh. "You think this week would have been easier if we were having a bunch of sex? This isn't a typical relationship for either of us. I just got out of a relationship and then everything happened with your father. Don't think that I want to take it slow because I don't want to be with you. That isn't it at all."

Kate knew Mo was right. That's what had stopped her from bringing the conversation up earlier. But the doubts hadn't gone away. "What if you get bored with what we do in bed?" She hated to ask the question, but the thought had crossed her mind more than once. She didn't want to be a disappointment, and the reality was, even if she'd had no problems pleasing a guy, she wasn't certain Mo would be satisfied for long.

"You clearly can get me off. And even if you couldn't, that's why they make vibrators."

"There's more to it than that and you know it."

Mo shifted in her seat. After a moment she said, "You're right. And every time you snuggle against me I'm ready to beg you to let me touch you. But I can handle it. I want a relationship more than I want a night of hot sex."

Kate knew Mo wasn't trying to hurt her feelings with the hot sex comment, but it crushed her anyway. "What if I want you to have both?" She broke her gaze with Mo, wishing that they weren't sitting in an airplane. Kate feel caught in the tight space.

Mo didn't say anything and the silence stretched. Finally Kate said, "I don't want to hold anything back from you. But I can't let go yet, and the truth is I don't know how long it'll take me to get there."

"I'm okay waiting."

Kate wanted to say that Mo didn't understand—that she might never get to that point with her—but she held back the words. Arguing wouldn't help. Knowing how willing Mo was to wait for her only made Kate feel more insecure about dating at all. What she asked of Mo wasn't fair.

Peeves was so ecstatic to see Mo that he peed all over the doormat, which necessitated a spot of unexpected cleaning. Between that and rummaging through a nearly empty fridge for dinner, Kate mostly kept herself from thinking of the conversation on the plane and the fact that Mo was only staying for the night.

Mo put her suitcases in her old room and Kate stopped herself from saying how the room was waiting for her to move back. She thought of the night that she'd slept in Mo's bed and the fantasy that she'd enjoyed then. In every fantasy, Mo was the one in charge. She wished her body would let that happen in reality.

It wasn't until after they'd both showered and Peeves had leapt excitedly into the center of the bed that Mo dropped any hints on if she'd changed her mind on moving back. She picked up Peeves, snuggled his head, and then said, "Sorry, little dude. You gotta sleep in your pink bed tonight. Tomorrow you can have my spot."

"I make him sleep in his pink bed every night. Otherwise he wakes me up. And you know he likes pink," Kate said, more out of the habit of defending his clear preference for pink than anything else. *Tonight.* Mo hadn't changed her mind. She would be back at Chantal's tomorrow. Kate knew that was part of the problem. Mo wasn't going back to her own place. She was going back to her ex-girlfriend, who was doubtlessly an easier lay than she'd ever be. It was crude to think of it that way, but her insecurities couldn't help but remind her of it. She wished Mo could see her perspective.

After Mo settled Peeves in his bed, carefully tucking his blanket around him, she looked over at Kate. "You put your pajamas on."

"Well, you got dressed after the shower. I thought that meant..." Kate's voice trailed.

Mo was wearing a loose tank top and a pair of shorts. When she moved, the armholes on the tank top showed the side of her breast, and Kate couldn't help noticing the curves.

"It's been a long day," Mo said. She went to the bathroom, rinsed off her hands, and got a glass of water. When she came back to the room, she walked up to Kate and kissed her forehead. "Don't get me wrong. I like sleeping naked with you." She handed the glass to Kate.

Kate took a sip. She stared at the water for a moment, feeling exhausted and on the verge of tears even though she had no reason to cry. "You don't find it frustrating? Tell me the truth."

"A little." Mo met Kate's gaze. "Especially when you rub your butt cheeks against me." Mo's smile hid whatever her real emotion was, and she shook her hips playfully.

Kate handed back the water glass. She pulled the covers down on her side of the bed and got in, trying to ignore the fact that Mo held back. Mo switched off the light and then climbed in on the other side. She settled her arm over Kate's, kissing her shoulder.

"Can you roll over?" Mo asked gently.

When Kate did, ready to argue that she wasn't up for talking, Mo kissed her lips. A soft whimper escaped Kate's throat. What Mo's lips did to her wasn't fair.

"I don't want to be fighting," Mo said.

"We're not fighting. I'm just a mess. And I don't want to be, but—"

Mo stopped her apology with another kiss. When she pulled back, she said, "I don't want to ever fight. I know you're upset and right now you feel like sex is going to fix this and maybe it would fix something but…I need you to give us some time. I'm not going anywhere."

"If I were any other woman that you've dated, we'd be having sex tonight, wouldn't we?"

Mo didn't answer.

"I'll take that as a yes." Kate pushed away from Mo. "I don't want you to have to pick between hot sex and a relationship with me. I know that you want both. You deserve both. And I know I'm not going to be enough for you."

"You're pretty smart," Mo said softly. "But you don't know everything."

Kate stopped herself from arguing. She wanted to be wrong this time—more than ever. Her eyes watered, and she turned on her back, quickly wiping the tears away. She'd told herself that she was done crying.

Mo shifted close and kissed her cheek. "It's your turn to get some sleep. You let me sleep on the plane. This time I'll stay up and watch out for monsters."

Kate closed her eyes. She didn't want to sleep. She wanted to take off her clothes and beg Mo to fuck her. If only she could say those words aloud.

CHAPTER TWENTY

Kate had been certain that she wouldn't fall asleep and yet she woke up the next morning with the groggy feeling of having slept too long. She rubbed her eyes and sat up in bed wondering what day it was. Peeves was missing from his pink bed and Mo was gone as well. The smell of coffee awakened her nose. Mo made the best coffee. She insisted on a little French press and brewed only one cup at a time. Although she'd teased Mo about how long it took her to make a cup of coffee, she'd always loved the sounds of the grinder and the amazing aroma that followed.

"Morning," Mo said, peeking into the room. "I hope I wasn't too noisy. You were sleeping so soundly."

Kate stretched and then ran her hand through her hair, guessing that it was a mess. Mo leaned against the doorway, carefully studying Kate. She was wearing one of the button-down shirts she'd gotten in the airport in Amsterdam along with the new dark blue jeans and looked as if she'd already showered. Standing there, she seemed oblivious to how good-looking she was. Sexy didn't cut it.

"What is it?" Mo cocked her head. "You've got this look on your face…"

"You're hot—that's all." Kate pushed away the thought that Mo would get plenty of looks from other women in that outfit. "Please tell me there's coffee and that amazing smell isn't a figment of my imagination."

"There's coffee. I also made you breakfast." Mo walked over to the bed. She sat down on the edge. "I'm sorry about last night. I feel like I screwed up."

"You didn't screw up. It was all me. Again." Kate wasn't ready for a heavy conversation first thing, but she could tell Mo had been thinking. Before Mo could say anything more, Kate said, "I don't have any food. How'd you make breakfast?"

"Peeves and I went shopping. Your fridge was too clean." Mo grinned. "I took your big purse that Peeves can sit in. Fortunately I didn't see anyone I knew. I stayed away from Safeway. Figured the gas station minimart was safer. And then we made a stop at that new little coffee shop across from Murdoch's. I wanted to buy some coffee beans, but Peeves growled at the barista and I got some serious looks from everyone else in the place."

"I don't know if those looks were because he was growling or because you had a dog in a purse."

"Are you saying I'm not the usual demographic that has a purse dog?"

"Something like that." Kate smiled, knowing that Mo was baiting her. "But I would have loved to have seen it anyway." It was hard to imagine Mo carrying a purse at all, let alone the big Armani bag she always used when she took Peeves to the store.

"I have to admit, it was nice not to have my wallet jammed in my pocket."

"You could carry a clutch," Kate suggested.

"A clutch? Like one of those little purses that don't even fit your phone? Yeah. Right."

"Some people think they're sexy," Kate returned. "I have a couple you could try."

Mo turned to show off her profile and then struck a pouty pose worthy of a runway model, pretending to hold a tiny purse.

She broke role and chuckled. "I'd rather have that duffle bag with Peeves inside it."

"I bet Peeves was in heaven."

Hearing his name, Peeves bolted into the room and hopped on the bed. He circled around three times, excitedly licking first Mo's hand and then Kate's before plopping down between them. Kate leaned forward and rubbed his head. "I missed you, little booger." He promptly rolled on his back to show off his belly. "Mo had to fill in as my protector."

"I need to work on my growl."

"You were perfect, actually. Maybe too perfect." Kate gave Peeves one more pet and then swung her legs off the bed and stood up. "What time is it? I feel like I slept forever."

"Almost noon. What do you mean by too perfect?"

Kate ignored the question. "Is it Friday?" She went to the bathroom and half closed the door enough to have some privacy but still to hear Mo's voice.

"Saturday." Mo paused. "Are you going to ask what our plans are for the day?"

Kate finished peeing and then went over to the sink. Her hair was tousled but didn't look nearly as bad as she'd worried it would. She rinsed with mouthwash after combing her fingers through her hair and then poked her head out of the bathroom. Mo had shifted on the bed and was stretched across it, lying on her belly and petting Peeves.

"You're not going back to Chantal's?"

"I thought maybe I'd wait 'til later. My mom wants us to come over. She wanted to plan dinner, but I told her to hold off until I talked to you... How would you feel if I tell her about us?"

Kate met Mo's gaze. "Don't you think it's a little soon?"

"Yesterday you wanted me to move in. Telling my mom is a baby step compared to that."

"Telling your mom is not a baby step. It's a big deal."

"Not compared to living together."

"We lived together before," Kate returned.

"It'd be different this time. We'd be sleeping in the same bed." Mo got up. "Look, I know you don't want me to stay at

Chantal's, but you know nothing's going to happen, right? You can trust me."

"Of course I trust you," Kate argued. "That isn't the point."

"Then why is it a problem? I'm only staying there for a few weeks until I find another place."

Mo was always loyal. Kate knew that much. She was no cheater. But Kate didn't want to imagine what would happen if Chantal tried to win Mo back. It would only be natural for Mo to start comparing them. And there were other things too.

"Is Chantal good in bed?"

"Don't go there."

"Why not? I think it's a reasonable question...I know sex is important to you. You said you'd never last in a relationship if good sex wasn't part of it. And you'd rather be with someone who lets you be in charge, right?" Kate paused. When Mo didn't answer, she said, "What's your definition of good sex?"

"I'm fine with what we've done in bed. We're taking it slow and—"

"You're not fine. You're settling." Kate shook her head. Mo's answer only made her feel worse. "I know you'd rather be with a real lesbian... Someone who knows what they're doing. And you'd probably rather be with someone who's not white."

"What are you talking about?" Mo's voice raised. "You know me better than that. I don't care what color skin you have. I can't believe you'd even say that."

"I just know you could be with someone that would be easier—in so many ways." Kate's voice cracked. "Dammit, Mo. Why are we even doing this?"

"Because I like you. And I thought you liked me." Mo cussed under her breath. She looked at the door as if wondering if she should leave, but she didn't move except to make a fist and then release it. A long minute passed, and when Mo spoke again, her tone had softened: "I never said I'd rather be with a real lesbian. And I've dated plenty of women who were white. And Black. And Asian. And Latina. Why would you even go there?"

"And all of them were probably a hell of a lot less complicated than me."

"You're right. They were," Mo shot back. It was obvious that her patience was gone. "But am I still with any of them?"

"Maybe you should be. Maybe you should be with Chantal."

"This is fucking bullshit. You're scared of being in a relationship with me? Fine. Say it."

"That's not it." Kate felt a wave of nausea. She couldn't still sweep all of this under the carpet with a few words. It was past a simple apology. But Mo had insinuated all of those things in the past. At the time, Kate had only been a friend, of course, and none of it had been directed at her. But it didn't make it less true.

"Then what are you trying to do?" Mo clenched her jaw. "I don't want to fight. And I don't know where you got all of that crap in your head, but it isn't true."

"You told me that lesbians were easier."

"When did I say that?"

"You were dating Julia's friend from work. Maddie. You'd only gone on a couple of dates…" Kate didn't want to go on, but she couldn't stop. She had to get all of it out. "When you broke it off, I asked you why. You said dating women was just a thing she wanted to try out. And that you were tired of being someone's learning curve."

Mo exhaled. "Well, I shouldn't have said that. But Maddie isn't you. And neither is Chantal. And I don't even know why we're talking about them. I'm not bringing up Ethan, am I? Or the other guys you've dated. I'm not asking if I'll be enough for you or if you're going to change your mind and go back to men."

Why had she started this argument? Couldn't she simply pretend that everything was fine? But what good would come from going back to pretending?

"Who we've dated before isn't the point," Mo continued. "I feel different when I'm with you—I can be me and you love me the way I am. You understand me in ways no one else does. I don't have to pretend anything. This time everything's different."

"Everything's different… For one, I'm a hell of a lot more complicated than the other women."

"I can handle you being complicated." Mo held Kate's gaze for a long moment. "I'm sorry if I said things to make you think I wouldn't want to be with you. But I don't care that you're white. And I don't care that you like guys too. All that matters is that you like me."

Maybe that was all she needed now, but how long would that hold? Kate fought the impulse to tell Mo that it wasn't worth it. There were so many reasons why Kate wouldn't be enough for her.

"I want you. Only you. If you don't want this, tell me. But don't make it about something else." Mo paused. "Maybe you need some time after everything in Amsterdam…"

"Maybe you're right. Maybe I do need some time," Kate said, her voice breaking. "I just think you're going to realize—"

"Realize what?" Mo interrupted. "That I want to spend the rest of my life with you? Too late. I already figured that out."

Kate looked at the bed, the sheets disheveled, and then over at Mo. "What happens when I'm not enough?"

Mo crossed the room. She stopped a foot away from Kate. "What I've had with other women I've dated could never compare to what we have. And you know I'm not the type of person to walk out. But if you keep pushing because you don't really want this…"

"I want you to be happy." Tears welled, but she clenched her teeth and kept them at bay. She wasn't enough for Mo. She knew that.

Mo stepped forward and took her hand. "I love you. If you aren't in love with me, say it."

Kate swallowed. She couldn't say it. She'd been in love with Mo since forever. But that wasn't the point. She could control everything in her life. Except this. And maybe that meant this wasn't supposed to be. She pulled her hand back and Mo's face fell.

Mo waited another minute, as if holding out hope that Kate would change her mind. Finally she said, "This week's been crazy. For both of us… Give me a call when you're ready to talk."

Peeves whined as Mo left the room. He looked up at Kate but didn't budge from the bed. Somehow he knew he couldn't follow her. Still his eyes seemed to beg Kate to do something to fix this. Kate murmured an apology to him. That was all she could do. She didn't seem to be able to move. After a long minute, the front door opened and closed.

The sound of the lock clicking into place sucked all the air from the room. Kate crumpled on the bed. Peeves ran over to her, anxiously licking her hands. She expected the tears to finally fall, but she was too empty and numb to cry.

"Your human sucks," she said. "You should go live with Mo instead."

Peeves only whined again in response.

Minutes passed and Kate couldn't convince herself to get up. She knew she needed to eat, but she didn't want food. All she wanted was Mo. The image of Mo, standing on the doorstep of her father's apartment in Amsterdam wearing the necklace she'd given her suddenly pushed into her mind. Mo hadn't taken the necklace off.

After a half hour chewing herself out and repeating her list of flaws, she reached for her phone.

"I screwed up," she said as soon as Julia answered. The tears streamed down her cheeks then.

"Mo's been texting me nonstop," Julia said.

"What'd she say?"

Julia sighed. "She's venting. You don't really want to hear everything she said. Mostly it's been a list of the ways that she screwed up, however. Not you."

"She didn't screw up anything. It was all me." Kate choked back a sob. "Shit."

"It's bad enough that you're cursing?"

Kate pulled her knees up to her chest as she sat up. She wiped away her tears. Julia and Mo always joked that hell would freeze over before Kate took up swearing. She didn't care if other people swore, but she still heard her mom's reprimand anytime a cuss slipped out. Was she still her mother's daughter? Scared to cuss? Unwilling to take risks? Needing someone to protect her even as she fiercely denied it?

"Mo probably hates me right now."

"She doesn't hate you. Why don't you just call her and tell her you're sorry?"

"I need to say that in person. Besides I can't talk to her over the phone right now."

Julia sighed again. "Why do I feel like we're back in college?"

"Do you have Chantal's address?" Kate said, suddenly getting out of bed as her plan formulated. "I don't even know her last name."

"Chantal Boyd, I think... Hold on a minute." Julia hollered for Reed. Kate could hear her asking and then a moment later, she came back on the line. "Reed says we sent her a Christmas card. She's pulling up the Excel worksheet she made with everyone's addresses. I love my sexy nerd."

"Sexy nerds are the best." Kate sniffed. She shouldn't have let Mo walk out upset. How many times did she have to screw things up?

"Tell me about it." Julia chuckled. "You really think you should show up at Chantal's without calling her first?"

"I don't think Mo would leave here and go have sex with Chantal." As the words tumbled out, Kate realized the possibility. "Do you think she would?"

"No... I just thought you might want to give her warning that you were coming."

"I can't talk to her without seeing her face." Kate slipped out of her pajamas in the bathroom and started the shower. If she was going after Mo, she didn't intend to do it with greasy hair.

"Reed found it. I'm going to text you this, okay?"

"Perfect. And, Julia, can you not tell her that you talked to me?"

"Got it. Lips are sealed. Good luck, sweetie." Julia paused. "For the record, as bad as this may seem right now...I know Mo's hoping you fix this."

"Me too."

CHAPTER TWENTY-ONE

After a quick shower, Kate changed into a clean pair of leggings and a light pink blouse that dipped low enough to be indecent if she leaned forward. The outfit hugged her curves and made her feel sexy, especially when she paired it with her favorite boots. Once she'd finished with her makeup, she worked on her hair, deciding after too much thought to pull it back instead of leaving it down. She added a pair of hoop earrings Mo had given her compliments on and went to check the finished product in the full-length mirror on the back of her bedroom door. She stared at her reflection. This time looking good wasn't enough. Mo was either going to accept her apology or not.

She passed the kitchen where Mo had set up their breakfast, ignoring how her stomach clenched at the sight of the cinnamon rolls she'd left. She pulled up directions to the address Julia had sent and tugged her jacket off the hook.

One step out the front door and she spotted Mo. She was in the stairwell, sitting on the first step with her head in her hands. When she heard the door, she looked up.

"You're wet."

"It's raining," Mo said. "Please tell me you aren't going out on a date looking that good."

"I was coming to track you down." She held up her phone. Mo's compliment bolstered her courage. This time she wasn't going to hide behind any of the old insecurities. "I convinced Julia to give me Chantal's address. I thought you'd be there."

"I thought about it. Then I went for a walk instead."

"In the rain?"

"I didn't want to go to Chantal's. I always come to you when something goes wrong." She looked Kate up and down again. "You got dressed up to come find me? In case you were trying, you look hot as hell."

"I wanted to look good when I apologized." Every part of her body begged her to go to Mo, but she held back still. Mo's hair glistened from the rain and her new jacket was drenched. Because of her. Her words. Her fears. "I'm sorry."

"Makeup and everything just to say that?" Mo's lips curved in a half smile. "That's an awful lot of work for two words."

"I got more." Kate paused, gathering courage. "I love you. I've loved you for a long time."

Mo nodded. "I know."

"But I really don't deserve you."

"You really do. But sometimes you are a pain in my ass. A sexy pain in my ass..."

"Do you want to come in? You've got to be freezing."

"Not yet." Mo scooted over to make room on the step where she was sitting and patted the spot.

Kate gave up trying to hold back. She crossed the landing and sat down on the stair, leaving a few inches between her and Mo. "You sure I'm not too much of a pain in the ass?"

"No." Mo hesitated. "Do you remember the last time we had a conversation out here? I'll give you a hint: I didn't have any pockets for a key."

Kate immediately pictured Mo in a cowboy hat. Her cowboy hat. "That was one of those nights I don't think I'll ever forget." She couldn't believe Mo was bringing it up now.

"My underwear made an impression?"

"I don't think it was that." Kate smiled. Mo was doing it again. She could make her feel better no matter how much she'd screwed up.

"God, that was embarrassing." She looked over at Kate and in a terrible Texan accent said, "Howdy, pard-ner."

Kate couldn't help laughing and the heaviness in her chest lifted the moment Mo joined in. "You looked so damn sexy in that hat."

"You should see me in chaps." Mo grinned. "When Tanya kicked me out, I figured it would be five, maybe ten minutes before she took pity on me and let me back in. She was trying to prove a point, I guess. But I had no phone, no keys…"

"And no pants. Or shirt."

"Good thing I was wearing underwear," Mo said, laughing again. "You were supposed to be staying over at Ethan's. I'd never been so glad to see you come home. I didn't know how long she was going to keep me locked out. I even thought about knocking on one of the neighbors' doors."

Kate remembered the surge she'd felt seeing Mo's bare chest, her gorgeous long legs stretching down the steps, and the black bikini underwear that showed off her toned thighs. She'd tried to suppress the feelings she'd had that night for so long. "I thought you always wore boxers."

"Sometimes I like to mix it up." Mo continued. "You walked past me, unlocked the door, took one look at Tanya, and then turned around and said, 'Why didn't you ask if you could borrow my hat?' I can't remember a damn thing you said after that." Mo started laughing again. "You just kept looking up at the hat and shaking your head even though I was locked out, basically naked, and Tanya was eating a bowl of cereal in our living room like nothing was going on. But it was the hat that really bothered you."

"Because you've always asked before you borrowed anything of mine," Kate said, unable to keep the smile from turning up her lips. The truth was, she'd had to focus on the hat because as soon as Mo stood up and walked over to the door where she'd been standing, all other thoughts left her mind.

"Tanya was so much drama." Mo shook her head. "Why did I stay with her for so long? She threw the hat at me after she pushed me out the door. Sorry your hat was part of that fight."

"I couldn't believe she would do that to someone. Actually, I can. Tanya never treated you the way she should have. That day wasn't even the worst of it."

"She kicked me out of my own apartment naked. How much worse did it get?" Mo chuckled. "I guess I should say thank you for focusing on the hat."

"It was hard to pretend I didn't notice other things."

"Oh, really? Like what?" Mo baited her.

"Like your eyes, Math Whiz."

Mo laughed again. "God, it feels good to laugh." She wiped her eyes and sighed. "You officially know all my secrets."

"Only fair. You know all of mine." Kate paused. "I love you so much that it hurts."

"You too?" Mo scooted over so that their legs were touching. "Hey…I got an idea."

"Uh-oh. I know that tone. Am I about to agree to something that requires a helmet?" Kate wanted to stroke her hand down Mo's jeans, but she kept her arms folded.

"I was thinking of an old-fashioned date. No helmets. Want to go out to dinner with me?"

Kate smiled. "I'd love to."

"That was almost too easy. And after dinner we can—"

"We can come home and you can make love to me," Kate interrupted. At Mo's raised eyebrow, she added, "Was that too forward?"

"Well, I asked you out on an old-fashioned date. I was thinking about a movie."

"I don't want old-fashioned unless that means you fuck me until I can't think."

"Actually, I think that is what old-fashioned means." Mo winked. "You know, you said 'you fuck me,' not the other way around."

"I did." Kate felt the blush rise up her neck. Mo hadn't misunderstood her, but she was still nervous about it.

"I don't want you to do something that makes you uncomfortable."

"I know you'll stop if I ask you to."

"'Do you really think this is going to work? You and me and a real relationship?" Mo asked, her voice uncharacteristically tentative. "Because I really want this, but I don't want to get my hopes up."

"Get your hopes up." Kate took Mo's hand and kissed it. She held Mo's hand against her chest. "This is going to sound cheesy but... You're the one for me, Mo. I know it. I've been in love with you for years. My heart's been trying to say that for a long time, but my messed-up head kept getting in the way."

"You know you put my hand on your breast, right? I mean, I'm guessing you wanted me to feel your heart, but your blouse is really thin and I'm pretty sure that's your nipple."

Kate laughed. She leaned forward and met Mo's lips. When she pulled back, Mo's eyes were still closed. She opened them a moment later and smiled. Kate knew it wasn't a mistake. She could look at that smile for the rest of her life.

"Can we eat breakfast now?" Mo asked.

"For the rest of the day, you're in charge." Kate leaned against Mo's shoulder. "I don't want to try and control everything anymore. I'm tired. And I keep screwing up."

"The rest of the day, huh? Does that include the evening hours?"

Kate nodded.

"For real?"

"For real. But I don't think you should wait until tonight to try and seduce me. I'm feeling ready to let you do anything."

"Anything?" Mo paused, her eyes going up and down Kate's body. "In that case, let's eat. I'm starving. I bought yogurt and granola if you wanted to be healthy, but those cinnamon rolls smell amazing."

"You know me well." Kate was hungry, but she was anxious for Mo to touch her and doubted she'd be able to eat much before than happened. "You know we could have breakfast after..."

"Breakfast is the most important meal of the day," Mo quipped. When Kate started to argue, Mo kissed her. "I promise the wait is going to be worth it."

Mo's persuasive tone only made Kate want to skip breakfast more. They kissed again when they stood up and again in the doorway. As soon as they were inside, Kate tried to angle them toward the bedroom, but Mo turned to the kitchen instead.

"I woke up this morning thinking of this." Mo picked up a cinnamon roll and took a bite before she kissed Kate again. "Why is it that the best cinnamon rolls in town are at a gas station minimart?"

Her mouth tasted so good that Kate wanted more when she pulled away. She reached for her own cinnamon roll and licked the icing. "I don't know if I can wait for you to eat that whole cinnamon roll."

"Do that again and I don't know if I'll be able to either."

"Do what?" Kate asked coyly. She slid her tongue over the top of the roll nice and slow. Mo's low groan was the perfect response. After she took a bite, savoring the sugary cinnamon, she said, "You should have kissed me a long time ago."

"You should have kissed *me* a long time ago," Mo argued. She went over to the coffee carafe and grumbled. "The coffee's probably cold."

"It'll still taste good." Kate held up her mug and Mo poured. She added cream and then sat down at the table despite her body's longing to pull Mo to the bedroom. This time she wasn't in charge, she reminded herself.

When Mo finished pouring her own mug, she sat down opposite Kate. "I love having breakfast with you. Feels like old times."

Kate took a sip of the lukewarm coffee. "Still delicious. Like someone else I know."

Mo grinned. "Who? I might be jealous."

Mo was more handsome than ever. This was not like old times. It was infinitely better. She slid her foot up Mo's calf. Because she could.

When her toe got up to Mo's knee, Mo choked on the sip of coffee she'd just taken. She set down the mug, chuckling, and said, "Why'd I say breakfast was important?"

Kate pulled her foot back and smiled, crossing her legs. Mo looked over at her and the desire in her eyes made Kate's mouth go dry. She was ready to beg.

"So how long are you going to make me wait? Are we talking after dinner with your mom?"

Mo took another bite of her cinnamon roll. "We can have dinner with my mom a different night. I want to take you to this place I read about a while ago—it's up the coast a ways but there's a view of the water and we have to get dressed up 'cause it's fancy. You know, your sort of place."

"As much as I like to get dressed up, you know you don't need to woo me. I'm already hooked."

"Too bad. I'm going to woo the pants off you anyway. I've been wanting to take you to this spot for years. It's possible I planned out our first date more than once. But in my head it was summertime and we'd go to the beach afterward. It's too cold for that this time of year."

"We've already been on more than one perfect date." Kate had a list of her favorites. "Watching the stars come out over the Golden Gate...parasailing in Hawaii...scooters in Cozumel. And that gala that I took you to—God, I had the hottest date in the place that night."

"If only I had known we were on a date...then you *really* would have had the hottest date."

"We've had a few missed opportunities." Kate loved the confidence in Mo's voice and the way she was looking at her as if she had every intention of making up for lost time. It gave her the courage to say what she'd been thinking. "There's something I've been wanting to ask you about that gala." Mo's expression turned to concern, and she quickly added, "I promise it's nothing bad. I'm just a little embarrassed to say it out loud." She swallowed, knowing that she had to be direct or she would lose her nerve. "Were you packing?"

Mo laughed. "Oh, man. No. Did you think I was?"

"I wasn't sure. I mean I thought maybe... You said that you did for special occasions and... I couldn't see anything, but I kept thinking about it." She felt her cheeks get warm. "After we got home, you went to your room and I had to go to mine. In my head, you were packing. It was hot."

Mo's mouth dropped open. "You fantasized about that?"

Kate covered her face with her hands as Mo whistled. When Kate peeked over at her, certain she was still blushing, Mo said, "Thank you for telling me. Now I know what to wear on our date."

"Would you?"

"Hell, yes." She laughed. "And don't stop yourself from asking. I think it's fucking hot."

"Well, while I'm asking, I've got one more request." Kate paused. "I want to tell your mom. Not tonight. Tonight I only want you. But soon. The sooner the better."

"And here I was hoping that you were going to tell me another secret fantasy. I mean, I already know about the orgies with Wonder Woman."

"You are not allowed to tell anyone about that. Ever."

"Too late. Julia already knows."

"You did not tell Julia! Tell me you didn't tell her."

"You said that plenty of women fantasize about orgies with superheroes. It's no big deal, right?" Mo's smile widened and Kate knew then she was only joking. She kicked her halfheartedly under the table and Mo pretended to wince, laughing as she did.

"For that, I ought to tell Julia about that time with Tanya and the cowboy hat. Between that hat and those bikini underwear...I couldn't stop staring. So damn sexy."

"How sexy?"

"Let's just say I was jealous of Tanya. It wasn't fair. She was a wench, and it was my damn hat."

Mo laughed again. "I'll make it up to you. Promise."

"These cinnamon rolls are delicious and your coffee is amazing even cold. But can we please say that we've eaten enough breakfast?"

"You're terrible at waiting." Mo licked the sugar glaze off her fingers. When she went over to the sink to rinse her hands,

Kate stood up too. She waited until Mo reached for a towel and then stepped between her and the counter.

Mo eyed her, drying her hands. "This is you not being in control?"

"I may need some practice."

A smile played on Mo's lips. "I can help you out there." She tossed the towel on the counter and stepped forward, her lips pressing against Kate's. Mo's kiss promised that this time would be different. Her tongue pushed and Kate felt her body give in as her lips parted.

When Mo pulled away, Kate opened her eyes. Mo held her gaze. "You can change your mind anytime about how this goes. Just say the word."

Kate shook her head. She didn't want to change her mind. Mo kissed her again. She caught her hand and stepped backward toward the bedroom.

"You know, I've been teasing you about waiting, but you have no idea how hard this is making me," Mo said.

Kate felt a thrill race through her. "Show me."

They managed to get to the bedroom, Mo kissing her all the way and Kate trying not to take over. She focused on Mo's lips and her hands moving over her clothes. God, she wanted those hands and lips on her bare skin.

When Mo slid her hands under Kate's shirt the room spun. Kate closed her eyes, reminding herself again that she needed to let go. She wanted this. Mo's hands moved to her breasts, fingertips tracing over her bra and sliding under the lace. There was nothing rough about her touch, but there was no denying that she was going after what she wanted. Feeling Mo's desire only turned her on more.

"Can I take off my clothes? I want to be naked."

"You look so hot all dressed up for me," Mo said, her voice husky. But her hands undid Kate's bra.

A whimper slipped out of Kate's lips when Mo caressed her nipple. Mo's hands moved down to her waist. Kate held still as she pushed her pants over her hips. She sucked in a breath.

"Even your underwear is sexy."

"Guilty pleasure," Kate admitted. "I only buy sexy underwear."

She kicked off her boots and then Mo helped her the rest of the way out of the pants. As she straightened up, Mo's hand stroked up the inside of Kate's thigh.

"Mmm," Kate murmured. Before she had time to say how much she wanted her hands in other places, Mo was helping her out of her shirt. When she took off Kate's bra, her response—a low moan—only turned Kate on more.

"I keep thinking that I'm going to wake up and this whole week will have been a dream," Mo said.

"Good dream?"

"This part is." Mo traced a fingertip down Kate's bare arm.

As much as she wanted to stand there and let Mo touch her, she felt a rush of nerves. She turned to the bed and pushed down the covers, needing to get through the next step.

Mo caught her hand. "Hold up. You okay?"

Kate nodded. She didn't want to tell Mo how nervous she suddenly felt. She wanted to be as confident receiving as she was giving.

"I don't mind going slow," Mo said, guessing her thoughts. "Only makes me want you more."

"Let's say that's my goal." She sat down on the bed facing Mo. When Mo touched her face she shivered. Her hand was hot and the room wasn't cold. It was all nerves. *Relax. Breathe.*

"You can stop me anytime," Mo said.

Kate let her knees gap. Mo's gaze went right to her center and Kate felt a pulse there as if she'd already touched her. She spread her knees further.

"Or you could do that." Mo moved between Kate's legs. "It's like you know exactly how to turn me on. And then you turn me on a little more. Do you know how much I want you?"

When Kate looked up, Mo leaned down and met her lips. Having Mo between her legs was almost too much, but the urge to push her back was overridden by wanting to pull her closer. She reached up and played with the end of Mo's belt, tugging it but not undoing the buckle. If the tables were turned, she'd already be on top of Mo. It was hard being patient, and the buildup was only making her desire more intense. If only Mo would touch her, she'd realize how wet she was making her.

As soon as she let go of the belt, Mo undid her buckle and hitched down her jeans. Her gaze never left Kate as she undressed, and when Kate leaned back on the bed, she shifted on top of her. She'd anticipated a wave of anxiety, but Mo's body felt like a warm blanket being pulled up to her chin. She breathed in, taking in her scent and willing her body to relax.

Mo's kisses started at her lips. She moved to her neck and then down her chest. Every place that Mo brushed her lips over tingled. Her tongue made a slow circle around Kate's nipple before she sucked it between her lips. Kate felt a pulse at her clit when Mo repeated the move. As soon as she'd gotten used to the rhythm, Mo shifted lower.

When Mo kissed the space below her belly button, Kate had to grip the sheets to keep herself from stopping her. She didn't want to stop her. She knew exactly how good Mo had tasted, how good it had felt to be inside her, and she wanted to let Mo have all of that. Have all of her.

She glanced down and caught Mo's eyes. She'd kissed in a pattern down to Kate's middle but hadn't touched her center yet. Now as Mo held her gaze, Kate desperately wanted to feel her there. She arched her hips up, but Mo only kissed the inside of her thigh. Then she shifted up to kiss Kate's lips again. Her leg moved between Kate's and subtly rubbed. She missed the spot Kate really needed to be touched.

"I want you," Kate managed.

"You have no idea how much that turns me on." Mo kissed her neck. "You sure this isn't a dream?"

"Maybe a really wet dream," Kate said, distracted by the sensation of Mo's leg between hers.

Mo chuckled. "You saying you're already wet?"

Kate wanted to show Mo exactly how wet she was. She tried to shift so that Mo's thigh would press against her needy clit, but Mo adeptly moved her leg.

Thwarted, Kate dropped her head back on the pillow. "Somehow I didn't see you as a tease."

"Is that a problem?"

Kate could hear exactly how much Mo was enjoying this. And the truth was, she loved how Mo was making her body beg. Whatever hesitation her mind had about letting Mo run things, it was evident her body shared none of it.

Mo pushed her hips forward, pressing her center against Kate's. The sudden contact and the feel of Mo's wetness had Kate clutching the sheets again. "Oh…"

"You like that?"

Kate nodded, licking her lips. She loved the way Mo was looking at her—like she was memorizing this moment. She reached up and brushed a fingertip over Mo's dark nipple. The tip responded to her light touch, and Mo made a low sound in her throat.

"I don't want to go slow anymore," Mo admitted. "I want you…"

"Show me."

When Mo moved between her legs, Kate closed her eyes. She tried to keep track of everything so she could recall it later—the feel of Mo's breath on the inside of her thighs, then the sensation of her fingers parting her folds, then Mo's face dropping between her legs. But as soon as Mo's tongue whipped against her clit, she knew she wouldn't remember anything else. She thought Mo would push inside with her fingers, but she didn't try. She knew what she was doing and even if practice had something to do with it, Kate wasn't complaining. The way she worked with her tongue, never slowing and changing her pattern as soon as Kate thought she knew what was going on, was some kind of magic. Kate nearly laughed. Mo would love hearing that she was magical. She knew what she doing all right.

Kate felt her orgasm coming. Her breath came in gasps and she reached for Mo, wanting to pull her close at the same time as she wanted her to stay in place doing exactly what she was doing. When the climax hit, Mo pressed inside and Kate felt her body clench, trying to pull her in deeper. She found Mo's hand, one finger inside, and raised her hips. Mo sank in and a tremor raced through Kate. She gripped Mo's wrist until her taut muscles finally relaxed and then quickly pulled Mo's finger out. When she rolled on her side, Mo followed, wrapping her arms around her while she rode out the aftershocks.

Kate wasn't certain how long they lay that way, Mo holding her as if she worried that once she let go, she wouldn't get to hold her again and Kate savoring the feeling of someone cherishing her. Time had seemed to slow for them, but she wanted it to stop altogether. This was what she'd been missing all along, Kate thought, not daring to move a muscle. She'd needed Mo more than she'd ever realized.

"I love you," she whispered.

Mo kissed her cheek but didn't loosen her hold. "I love you too."

CHAPTER TWENTY-TWO

That night they only made it out of the apartment to take Peeves for a walk. The remainder of the cinnamon rolls and the yogurt sufficed for lunch. Dinner was a package of ramen with fried eggs. Mo added hot sauce and claimed it was delicious, but Kate hardly tasted it. She ate simply because she was famished. Food wasn't what she wanted. Fortunately it wasn't hard to convince Mo to take her back to bed. Mo couldn't seem to get enough of her.

Kate had never spent an entire day having sex. The concept of making love had always seemed theoretical. Sex was an act. It had always felt satisfying in the same way scratching an itch did, but she was no more connected to the person before or after. With Mo, sex changed everything. It altered how she looked at Mo in the mid-morning light, how she felt when Mo took her hand as they said goodbye, Mo promising that she'd be back that evening, and it changed how she felt when she looked in the mirror later. As cliché as it all was, she knew Mo had made love to her. For the first time, she truly felt loved. Not simply desired, but loved.

Mo had said she wanted to go to Chantal's to pack up a few boxes of clothes, but it was clear from the way she'd barely made it out of the house that she didn't want to be apart anymore than Kate did. Kate didn't ask if having sex for hours on end was Mo's usual routine in a new relationship. None of it felt routine, but if it was, she didn't want to know. For her, it wasn't the start of a new relationship. It was the start of the only relationship she ever wanted to have. That thought made her feel ridiculous and she promised herself that she wouldn't say it aloud. But it wasn't any less true.

After Mo left, Kate went for a run, showered, and then started a load of laundry. She was too antsy to crack open her laptop or check her work emails and decided to face reality on Monday. For the rest of the day, she wanted to bask in thoughts of Mo and plan for what happened next. When her phone rang, she tried not to get her hopes up that it would be Mo. They could stand to be apart for a few hours at least.

"Hey, Julia. How are you?"

"Wow. I can hear you glowing all the way from here."

Kate laughed. "I don't think you can hear that."

"Trust me. I can hear it. Mo sounded just as lovesick. You know you never called me back yesterday. Hold on a minute," Julia said. "I've got a kitten climbing up my leg."

"A kitten?" Kate wondered if the fact that Mo sounded that way meant this time was different for her too. She could only hope…

"I convinced Reed that the girls needed a pet. We got two."

"You got two cats? Why?"

"Because they're adorable. We just brought them home from the shelter. I'll send you pictures. We have one orange and one black. They like to cuddle together—you wouldn't believe the cuteness."

Kate couldn't hold back her smile. "You once told me that cats were too much of a commitment."

"I said that?" Julia laughed. "Don't tell Reed."

Kate heard the sound of Carly and Bryn's voices in the background. "The kids must be over the moon."

"They are." Julia sighed. "You know how I also said that I never wanted to be a mom? That was dumb too."

"You're an amazing mom."

"I have my moments." Julia cleared her throat. "So…I take it yesterday went well?"

Kate wondered if admitting the truth would tempt fate. "You could say that."

"You're smiling right now, aren't you? Fricking glowing. Ugh." Julia laughed. "Okay. You two are going to have to give me a minute to get used to all of this. I mean, I knew when she went to Amsterdam with you that you two were probably hooking up, but everything was such a whirlwind when you left and then yesterday…well, yesterday I wasn't sure how far things had gone."

"They went pretty far." Kate tried for a serious expression, but her cheeks ached to smile again. "Does amazing sound too cheesy?"

"I'm happy for you. For both of you."

"I do have one question…" Kate felt the heat of a blush on her cheeks but she rushed on. "Have you ever asked someone to wear a strap-on? I know Mo has them and we kind of joked about it, but is that something I'm supposed to ask for? How long would you wait? I don't want to screw anything up."

"Just ask. And that's all I'm going to say. From here on out, I really don't want to think of my two best friends having sex. All I'm going to imagine is you guys cuddling. Mo said that she'd just had the best sex of her entire life, but I made her promise not to tell me any details. I'm holding you to the same rule."

Kate hopped up and down on her toes. She wanted to let out a cheer. Thank God Mo felt the same way. "So you aren't upset that we're, you know, doing this?"

"I've been waiting for you two to fuck for sixteen years now. All the tension's been driving me crazy." She laughed. "However. I do think we need to talk about her moving in with you. Are you really ready for that? She said that you'd suggested it and that she didn't want to sleep anywhere else. And I get that it makes sense and everything…"

"But?"

"I think she should rent a room or couch surf with us for a while. Or she could even stay with her mom. I just think it's too soon."

"It doesn't feel too soon." Kate knew rationally that it probably was too soon, and yet the fact remained that they'd lived together for nearly half of their lives.

"Have you even gone out on a date?"

"We've gone out on a hundred dates. I already know I love her. And the sex is—"

"Remember the rule," Julia interrupted. "Good cuddling. Let me pretend."

"Life-changing cuddling. How's that?"

Julia sighed. "But her moving in with you is a big step."

"I never should have gone to Denver. And I should have kissed her in college. Or I should have told her how I felt when we were in Hawaii last year. I can't tell you how many times I've stopped myself, how I've held back. Now that I know she wants me too…I don't want to let her go. And I don't want to sleep a night without her." Saying it all aloud made Kate more certain than ever.

"Yeah. She pretty much told me the same thing. So when are you two having kids?"

"Okay, now who's going too fast?"

Julia laughed. "I can't help it. You two are going to be amazing parents."

"Give us a year."

"What about kittens?" Julia shrieked. "Damn those claws hurt on the inside of your thigh. It's a good thing you're cute."

"Send me a picture."

"I will. And sweetie, whatever you and Mo decide about moving in together…I know you two are meant for each other. It's always been that way."

As soon as Kate hung up the line, a text from Mo flashed on her screen: *Can I pick you up at six? The movie starts at eight thirty.*

I can't wait, Kate texted back.

I love you.

Without hesitating, Kate typed: *I love you too.*

She stared at the texts for a long moment and then took a screenshot of the image. Sixteen years later and finally it was easy to say those words. But they weren't only words. Mo had her heart.

EPILOGUE

Six Months Later

"You sure you're up for Aunties' Night?" Reed had asked the question more than once. "Bedtime can be rough."

"Are you kidding? We're gonna have a blast," Mo said. "And it's only one night."

"What could possibly go wrong, right?" Julia laughed even as she said it. "We'll leave the girls' insurance cards on your kitchen table just in case."

"Along with the list of emergency numbers," Reed added. "And I'll have my phone on me. You can call anytime. I'll keep it on vibrate during the concert."

"We'll be fine," Kate said. "In fact, you're going to be jealous that you missed out once you hear about all of our adventures. Mo's got about two weeks worth of activities lined up for the kids."

"And after all that we're going for ice cream." Mo looked over at Kate and grinned. "You guys are gonna be missing out on a party."

Just then, Bryn flew past Kate, screaming, "Carly's it! Hide!"

Reed looked over at Julia and whispered, "So not jealous."

With Bryn's screech, Jamal toddled over to Kate and held up his arms. She leaned down to scoop him up just as Michael ran into the room. Not only were they taking care of Reed and Julia's kids, they'd wanted to include Mo's brother's kids as well for the inaugural Aunties' Night.

"Why aren't you hiding?" Michael hollered. "Carly's IT!"

"I got a plan," Mo said. "As soon as Carly shows up, I'm hiding behind Aunt Kate."

"Aunt Kate, you better run," Michael said, bolting out of the room.

"Oh, I plan on it. I'm running behind Mo. She's going to protect me." Kate bounced on her toes until Jamal giggled. "Isn't that right?" For some reason, Jamal let Kate pick him up but screamed whenever anyone else besides his parents tried. It was a personal honor and she took advantage of it by spoiling him every chance she got.

"You look pretty good with that kid in your arms," Julia said. "When's Mo getting you pregnant?"

Mo chuckled. "I'm working on it."

Suddenly Carly burst into the room with a loud, "I found all of you!"

Reed turned and picked her up. She kissed Carly's head and said, "Be good, sweetie. Mama and I are heading out. If you need us, Aunt Mo will let you use her phone." As she set Carly down, she added, "Make sure you tell all the kids to eat lots of sugar before bed so your aunties get a taste of reality."

"Got it. Sugar before bed." Carly high-fived Reed with a conspiratorial wink and then looked over at Mo and Kate and said, "Don't worry. My moms like to play the opposite game."

"That's what Carly's telling you now," Julia said. "Wait until eight o'clock when all the candy in your place mysteriously disappears." She grinned and hugged Carly. "Love you, sweetie." As she let go of her, she called out, "Bryn, wherever you are, we're leaving. We love you. Be good."

"I'll tell her when I find her," Carly promised. She dashed down the hallway toward the bedroom shouting, "Since I found you first, Aunt Mo, you're it next!"

"Happy Auntie Night," Reed said, backing up to the door.

"Quick, run," Julia said, pushing Reed's shoulder. "Before they have second thoughts!"

As soon as the door closed behind them, Mo turned to Kate. "So...I have something to tell you."

"What is it?" She was already worried by Mo's tone. What did she have up her sleeve now?

"You know how it's Auntie Night? It's also our six-month anniversary."

"No, it's not," Kate said. "We kissed on..." She stopped herself, quickly doing the math in her head. "Oh, jeez."

"Yep." Mo grinned. "And I love you."

"That's what you wanted to tell me?"

Mo nodded. She stepped forward and kissed Kate's cheek. Jamal tried to push her away, but Mo only tickled under his chin and said, "She's mine, buddy."

Kate loved it when Mo said those words. Loved when she introduced her as her girlfriend, loved when Mo caught her hand and pulled her close before they walked into a room. All of it. She loved everything about being Mo's girlfriend.

"You know, Julia's right," Mo said. "You do look good with a kid in your arms."

"You'd look good with a kid in your arms, too," Kate returned.

"If he'd ever let me hold him." Mo pretended to pout. "Good thing the other three like me. Are you sorry we're missing the concert?"

"Not even a little bit. I'm with you. Right where I want to be." Kate looked between Mo and Jamal's smiling face. Just then, a screech pierced the air and Jamal clapped his hands over his ears. "Sounds like Carly found Bryn."

Jamal wiggled in Kate's arms then, asking to be put down. She set him on his feet and he toddled down the hallway in pursuit of the older kids. He paused halfway to the bedroom and looked over his shoulder and waved.

"How is he so cute?" Kate asked, her heart leaping when Jamal smiled at her. "How is it even possible?"

"They make them cute on purpose, you know. To lure you in." Mo took that moment to step forward and wrap her arms around Kate. "That was my plan all along too."

Kate smiled. "Well, you succeeded."

"Do you really think we're going to survive this night?"

"Are you kidding? We got this." Kate found Mo's lips. Kissing her never got old. As Mo's arms tightened around her, Kate relaxed. She let her lips part and waited for Mo's tongue to slip across hers.

Mo pulled back and said, "Maybe we should call the parents and ask them to pick the kids up early. I'm suddenly thinking of several other things I'd rather do tonight."

"Several? Or just one?"

"Okay, maybe just one."

After six months, they were still flirting as much as they'd done at the beginning. And it was still a thrill every time she realized Mo would do more than tease.

"I did get you something for our anniversary. I just had it in my head that it was next week."

"You keep me around to remember numbers," Mo said. "But I think secretly you're just as good and you like to pretend you're not so you have a good excuse."

"A good excuse for what?"

"Oh, like that time you made reservations at the resort for the wrong date so you could sleep in my bed instead. Remember that?"

Kate laughed, playfully pushing Mo's shoulder. "You know that wasn't on purpose."

"Do I? I mean, I know you thought I was impossibly sexy and you were looking for any way possible to get in my—"

"Alright, Math Whiz," Kate interrupted, still laughing. "You know what happened with those reservations was an accident. And you may be the sexiest person I've ever met and I may be completely in love with you, but that doesn't mean I won't make you sleep on the sofa tonight if you keep teasing me."

"You think we're actually going to sleep tonight? We've got four kids in the house." Mo kissed her again. "And it wasn't an